AN
ABSOLUTE
BLOODY
DISASTER

AN
ABSOLUTE
BLOODY
DISASTER

BOOK 1

LINDSAY CLEMENT

NOVELITICA

To request permissions, contact the publisher at novelitica@gmail.com.

ISBN 9781737359302 (hardcover)
ISBN 9781737359319 (paperback)
ISBN 9781737359326 (ebook)

First edition, October 2021.

Edited by Rachel Doyel

Cover design by Franzi Haase | www.coverdungeon.com
Instagram: @coverdungeonrabbit

Layout by Lindsay Clement

Novelitica
3842 Tuscany Dr. Unit 8
Santa Clara, UT 84765

www.lindsayclement.com

For the Rachels:

For the one who has given this story as much love as I have.

And for my creative writing teacher in fifth grade, who told me that the bloody sink in my story was "too creepy."

If she could see me now.

AN
ABSOLUTE
BLOODY
DISASTER

PROLOGUE

SAN FRANCISCO, CALIFORNIA
SPRING 2018

A STORM IS ROLLING IN.

The girl stands in front of an easel in a pair of paint-covered overalls, a wild mess of orange curls tied on top of her head with a green bandana. Her brush moves in practiced strokes as she covers the canvas with oil paints of warm Mid Yellow, blending it into vivid Vermillion, then into the deep Ultramarine of the darkening sky.

But her usual twilight color isn't hitting the right notes tonight. It's too bright, too saturated. The sky roils above her, inky tones of Prussian Blue creeping from the east and swallowing any hope she had of seeing the stars.

A sudden snap of wind stirs the stray curls framing her face, and she sighs in defeat. San Francisco has a habit of surprising her with bad weather. She starts packing up her supplies, annoyed that her painting is still too wet to store safely in its storage bag. She'll have to carry it to the bus stop and hope for the best. With any luck, she'll make it there before the rain starts.

But she has never been one to rely on luck.

Her phone rings in her pocket and she retrieves it—her brother's freckled face smiles up from the screen.

"Hey," she says, propping the phone between her ear and

shoulder. Old leaves skitter around her feet in the growing wind, the sound almost ominous in its urgency.

"Hey, Al," he replies. "What's your status? I just ordered from Dragon Diner and it will be here in twenty minutes."

"*Yes,*" she groans, her stomach growling at the mention of their favorite Chinese restaurant. She clicks the cover onto her plastic paint palette as thunder rumbles from afar, and a chill lifts the hair on the back of her neck. "I assume there will be Five-Flavor Shrimp."

"Do you know me at all?" he scoffs. "Dad would kill us if he found out we didn't honor our sacred, completely arbitrary family tradition."

"There's a first time for everything, right?" She wipes the brushes hastily on her overalls and shoves them and her other tools into a zippered pouch.

The storm clouds have moved over the bay now, absorbing what light might have been left over from sunset. Though she has visited this park dozens of times—with its little brick pathway and time-worn sundial—something feels different tonight. Almost unfriendly, like the park is watching her. Warning her to get out.

A bright flash of lightning illuminates the sky, followed immediately by a deafening clap of thunder. She jumps. One of her painting knives slices across her skin, and she curses loudly as blood wells in her palm.

"Are you alright?" Her brother's voice is anxious. "It's looking pretty stormy out there. Do you want me to pick you up?"

"I'm fine," she mumbles, wrapping her hand in a nearby paper towel. "I'll text you when—*ah!*"

Something lands on her from behind, a pair of strong arms wrapping around her torso. She struggles against her attacker, but a hand claps over her mouth just as heat explodes at the base of her neck.

She tries to scream. She tries to run. But the arms are unyielding, the pressure in her neck blinding. She is vaguely aware of the kiss of icy raindrops as they begin to fall, biting into the skin on her cheeks, and her hands claw desperately at the demon who refuses to set her free. Her brother's voice calls out through the pain as everything goes black.

"Alison? Alison, are you there? *Alison!*"

Tonight wasn't her lucky night, after all.

1

THERE'S SO MUCH BLOOD.

Not that I'm complaining.

A human girl sits upright at the head of the dining table, her eyes wide and glassy, a soft smile tugging at her lips. Blood oozes from two puncture wounds on her neck, a striking red against the white of her skin. It drips down her chest and soaks into the collar of her floral blouse, making her look like the unsuspecting murder victim in a B-list horror movie.

"Come on, Xander," I say, sidling over to him. The scent of the girl's blood fills the room with metallic warmth, and hunger claws its way up my throat. "Just one taste."

"No." My brother sits next to the girl, his attention divided between his dinner and the phone in his hand. He can't seem to put it down these days.

"You can't bring dinner home and expect *not* to share. It's downright cruel."

Xander pockets his phone then makes a show of dragging one finger through the girl's blood. He makes eye contact with me as he licks it clean.

I glare at him. *"Rude."*

"You already have dinner plans," he says in that bored voice of his, as though he would rather be talking to anyone else.

"Yes, but there will be *rules* there."

"There are rules here, too. 'Leave no—'"

"I know," I snap. I'm talking through my fangs now—they have a bad habit of showing up when I'm hungry. And I'm hungry *a lot*. "But would it kill you to share your food every once in a while?"

"She's not just *food*, Charlotte," Xander says, his expression morphing from one of annoyance to one of distaste. "She's a human being."

"Right," I say, sinking into an empty chair with an audible *thump*. It creaks loudly, and Xander winces. "What's this one's name?"

Xander always learns a human's name before he feeds on them, a habit I've never understood. It doesn't matter to me if I know the girl's name or not. She'll taste the same either way.

I'm sure Xander would love to offer a scathing remark—maybe something about my complete lack of respect for our overpriced European furniture—but instead, he coaxes the girl's head sideways with two fingers to her chin. "Go ahead," he murmurs, capturing her glassy gaze with his. "Tell her your name."

Until now, the girl hasn't moved or spoken, thanks to Xander's Compulsion. But now she looks at Xander like he's the most beautiful person she has ever seen.

Show-off.

"Amy," she says dreamily, offering Xander a lovesick smile. "My name is Amy Wilde."

"Great," I say, laying on the sarcasm. "Now I'll always remember her. 'Amy Wilde, the meal Xander wouldn't share.'"

"I'm not obligated to share with you," Xander says.

"Of course you are." I swipe a finger through her blood and suck it clean, groaning involuntarily at the familiar coppery taste.

Delicious.

Xander snarls when I make a second attempt, swatting my hand away. "I said no, *repa*. I've already fed from her, and I don't trust you not to kill her."

"It's been two hundred years, Alexander," I say, glowering. "When will you stop using that nickname?"

"As soon as you cease being my sister, Lottie."

"And what a glorious day that will be." The chair legs screech as I push back from the table. Xander winces again.

"You know Victoria will kill you if you scratch her floor."

"Oh, it's even her *floor*, now?"

I may live in this house with my brother and his perfect fiancée, but the two of them have made it very clear: nothing inside it belongs to me. At this point, I'm not even sure if my bedroom is my own.

Xander turns to Amy—his fangs emerge, pressing on his bottom lip—then pauses, fixing me with a sidelong glare. "Don't you have somewhere to be?"

When I don't move, he shrugs, leaning to bury his teeth in Amy's throat.

I watch him for a few seconds, fuming, before stalking away, not stopping until I'm in my room on the other side of the house.

Xander and I used to share all our meals. Granted, that was before we cared about not killing people. Somewhere along the way, Xander grew a conscience and I—well, I grew an appetite. My brother has become practiced and careful when he feeds, unlike me, the two-hundred-year-old vampire girl with no self-control.

Maybe one day I'll be as disciplined as he is. But I doubt it.

◊　◊　◊

I emerge from the shower into a bathroom full of steam. The words, "I VANT TO SUCK YOUR BLOOD," are written on the fogged surface of the mirror.

"Ha ha. Very funny, Victoria," I mutter, and a bright giggle echoes from somewhere upstairs.

I use my forearm to clear the remaining condensation from the mirror and find a ghostly figure staring back at me. There was once a time I couldn't see myself in mirrors at all. Something about the silver backing, I think. Now I stand here in perfect reflected clarity, somehow both pale and dark, with green eyes too big for my face and wild, umber hair and lips that are somehow always chapped.

And of course, there are my freckles. I had always hoped I would grow out of them as I aged—that my skin would smooth and the annoying dark spots on my nose and cheeks would fade. But they remain, infuriatingly, the way they were on my nineteenth birthday in Belarus. The day I stopped aging. The day I was Turned.

Some birthday present.

A loud ping from my phone announces a new text message.

Be there in five, *collwr llygaid doe*.

I glare down at Pippa's insult.

Who are you calling a doe-eyed loser,
you bottle-blonde Welsh demon?

Ooh, good one!

She follows it up with a thumbs-up emoji.

I smirk and chuck my phone onto my bed. The last thing I want to do is be late for the biggest party of the year. It's a good thing I'm speedy.

Four minutes and forty-seven seconds later, Pippa's car horn blares outside.

"You're early!" I yell, struggling to pull on my second boot.

I bolt into the hallway and almost run into Xander, who is carrying a sketchpad and a coffee mug filled with colored pencils.

"Charlotte," he scolds, whirling out of my way, "watch where you're going. One of these days you won't be paying attention and you'll end up with a handful of pencils in your chest."

"Already happened."

Xander's eyebrows flick upward. "Come again?"

"It was sometime in the fifties, I think," I muse, plucking a green pencil from the cup and twirling it between my fingers. "You were out seducing some poor housewife, and I tripped and landed face down on a cup of your charcoal pencils. Missed my heart by a good six inches, but it hurt like hell."

"Why haven't I heard about this?"

"Because I didn't tell you. The pencils may not have killed me, but you certainly would have."

The pencil slips from my hand and Xander snatches it midair, shaking his head in exasperation. "I'm surprised you haven't killed yourself by now, Lottie. You're clumsy enough."

I shove his arm. "I'm surprised you haven't gotten yourself killed by now, Xander. You're obnoxious enough."

Pippa honks again.

"I'm *coming!*" I bark, knowing she will hear.

Her voice echoes quietly in my ears. "Hurry up, slowpoke! The Majestic is waiting!"

"How do I look?" I ask Xander, giving a little twirl. I somehow managed to tuck my flowy white shirt into a pair of extremely tight leather pants I found at the thrift store. They are at least two sizes too small, but I don't technically need to breathe. So, they're great.

Xander smirks and the collection of steel rings in his nose and ears glints in the dim hall light. "Positively offensive. An insult to vampire-kind."

"Perfect."

Pippa is waiting outside in her red convertible Corvette—a car that pushes the boundaries of being ostentatious—her platinum hair fluttering in the cool breeze. She waves enthusiastically as I head down the marble steps and onto the moonlit pavement.

"Girl, you look *hot!*" Pippa calls, shooing Nik into the backseat with Rose. Nik fixes her with a withering glare, but silently obliges. "Where did you find those pants?"

"Rose's closet," I jest, hopping over the car door to land semi-gracefully in the passenger seat.

"Hey!" Rose flicks me on the back of the head. "Just because I like fashion doesn't mean I like dressing like a prostitute from the eighties."

"That's because," Nik inserts dryly, taking a quick swig from a leather-wrapped flask, "you already went through that phase when you actually *were* a prostitute in the eighties."

Rose raises a sardonic eyebrow. "Right. *Me.* A *prostitute.* That's like saying Pippa was a nun for a period of time."

I burst into laughter, joined loudly by Pippa as she shifts the car into gear.

◊　◊　◊

Every Halloween, the pompous traitor known as Kaleb Sutton manages to throw the most ridiculous, unnecessarily lavish costume party in the state, and half the world wants in. He only gives invitations to vampires of the San Francisco "elite"—whatever the hell that means—while the humans are chosen at random by some sort of lottery system. I can only imagine how many hopeful sorority girls are disappointed every year.

The party is at the old Majestic Theater, across from which a collection of lovesick couples stares out over the water, watching the yellow lights of the Oakland Bay Bridge as they shine eerily through a blanket of chilly fog. Their dreamy gazes and dark coats are a sharp contrast to the scantily-clad party-goers standing in line, ignoring their sightseeing opportunity as they wait desperately for a last-minute opening on the airtight guest list.

As we approach the front doors of the theater, I can't help but laugh at our assortment of terrible vampire costumes. Rose is in a white cocktail dress, the color striking against the warm brown of her skin, with blood dripping from her "sliced" neck; Nik, in all his brooding glory, is wearing a beautifully-detailed—though painfully stereotypical—vampire costume that Dracula himself would envy; and Pippa looks more like a bleached-blonde Morticia Addams than a vampire, the neckline of her form-fitting black dress plunging into a deep V ending just above her belly button. I look like some kind of suave, swashbuckling vampire-pirate hybrid, complete with knee-high boots and a black silk cape. We look completely ridiculous.

The four of us walk straight to the theater's doors, garnering dirty looks from those waiting in line.

"Invitation?" The big, human bouncer folds his arms across his chest with a suspicious frown.

I roll my eyes. We have never received an invitation to Kaleb's party, but that doesn't stop us from attending. Anything to spite that backstabbing sociopath.

"Oh, we don't need an invitation," Rose sings, her voice light and haunting with its slight French lilt. She reminds me of a songbird, her petite frame and bouncing dark curls giving her an air of innocence. Though with how practiced she is at Compulsion, it might be more appropriate to compare her to a siren.

Rose steps directly in front of the bouncer, locking eyes with him. "Kaleb invited us. We're his guests of honor."

The bouncer stares at her, wide-eyed and transfixed, then blinks a few times. "Yes, of course. Kaleb's guests of honor. Right this way."

A girl in a provocative nurse costume glares at us and hisses something to the Grim Reaper standing next to her. I can't see a face under the hood, but the figure nods solemnly.

Rose smiles sweetly and we follow her through one of the many gilded doors leading inside.

The Majestic was once a beautiful theater reserved for fancy, highbrow events like symphony orchestras and operas before it went bankrupt sometime in the nineties. It has since been turned into the most amazing party venue in San Francisco. The seats have all been removed and the ground leveled to make way for a huge, polished dance floor, though the ornate stage and carved balconies remain, usually reserved for private parties, weddings, or quinceañeras.

Tonight, however, the whole theater is filled to bursting, and the five gold chandeliers on the ceiling make the room glow with a hazy sheen. The floor, balconies, and stage churn with hundreds of humans in a wide variety of costumes, their bodies filling the air with the scent of sweat and alcohol and ecstasy. At least, *most* of them are humans. I spot a few other vampires gliding in their midst—fangs glinting wickedly under shadowed eyes—but they pay us no notice.

Pippa nudges Nik and points to a particularly drunk-looking group of college girls. "Dibs."

Nik flashes her a challenging, languorous grin. "Not if I get there first."

He slips away, stalking through the crowd like a lion on the prowl, and Pippa trails after him with determination.

I glance at Rose, who has her sights set on a pair of tipsy boys leaning on the bar, a predatory smile tugging at her lips. At one time, she might have drained the two of them in a few remorseless minutes, but not anymore. Now her self-control is near perfect, her siren's call used for nothing more than a quick meal and a quicker release. Now she can focus her attention on other things, like keeping my appetite in check.

It's a good thing, too. There will be no killing tonight. Not when

Kaleb's watching. *"Nullum corpus,"* as he would say. Not that I care anymore.

"Well," Rose says, her voice carrying over the loud music, "shall we?"

◊　◊　◊

An hour or so later, I'm leaning against the wall with a bright-eyed Rose, hidden in the inky shadows of the mezzanine. I am hypnotized by the darkness, the music, the pounding of warm blood under sweat-soaked skin. I rest my head on the wall behind me, reveling in the boozy scent of human intoxication.

"This is what I imagine Heaven will be like," I say, glancing at Rose. I draw a hand across my mouth, wiping away the remnants of my last sample. She was sweet, like hot apple cider from my earliest memories, and tinged with the bright bitterness of cranberry vodka. "If we ever make it there, of course. I wish we could do this every night."

"If we did," Rose smirks, watching Pippa as she carefully lures her next victim into an alcove near the stage, "we might drain the whole city."

"And I should care about that because...?" I sound drunk. In vampire terms, I probably am.

Once upon a time, I cared about not murdering people. But becoming a vampire changed something in me: the desperation for human blood overpowered any inhibitions I had about the sacredness of life.

Needless to say, my moral compass doesn't exactly point north anymore.

Rose snags a drink from the hand of a brawny Roman centurion. He gapes at her for a few seconds before grinning, his angled eyes raking her from head to toe. For a moment, I think he might make a move, but Rose fixes him with a murderous glare that sends a chill up my spine.

"Don't touch me," she Compels through a snarl, and the centurion's eyes widen in shock before he slips away.

I look back out over the sea of squirming people. Nik has one hand on the waist of a green-haired witch, the other caressing the exposed hollow of her throat, and she visibly melts under his touch. His hips sway fluidly with hers, and I smile as he bares his fangs and sinks them into her neck. The girl sags against him, her eyes closed, her lips parted in unmistakable pleasure.

Only Nik can drain the life from someone and leave them begging for more.

"Hey, beautiful."

My head snaps sideways to stare at the Roman centurion standing a few feet from me. Strands of once-tidy black hair stick to his damp forehead, and his dark, slanted eyes meet mine from under thick lashes. I have no doubt that he has had one too many drinks tonight, made obvious by the fact that he seems a breath away from falling over.

"Can I help you?"

"I love your vampire costume." He grins drunkenly. "Very gory."

I smile down at the fresh blood staining my shirt. "Thanks."

"Do you want to dance?" He offers a hand.

I raise an eyebrow. Everything about this guy screams, *Guy Who Only Got Into College Because He Plays Football*. He is most decidedly not my type.

"Sorry, Six Pack. I'm not here to meet my soulmate." I grin, flashing my fangs, but he doesn't flinch. All part of the costume, I suppose.

"Come on, sweetheart," he croons, taking a step closer. "You're the hottest girl I've seen at this lame party. And I can't leave until you give me at least one dance."

Something in his tone raises the hair on my arms. I don't know if it's his words or the surety with which he says them, but I want nothing to do with this hammered jock. I open my mouth to shoot him a scathing response, but am interrupted by a hand clapping down hard on his shoulder.

"Dude, leave her alone." The hand belongs to another centurion with sandy blonde hair, undoubtedly a friend. His voice holds a calm command, and I get the impression that he has diffused similar situations before. "Don't be a creep."

Centurion One glares at him. "You only live once, man. And this vampire chick is super hot. I have to dance with her." He speaks as though I can't hear him. It's infuriating. Disgusting.

Centurion Two's freckled face twists into a grimace. "Jason. *Stop.*"

Centurion One—Jason—shoves his friend aside, his eyes never leaving mine. He wraps a muscled arm around my waist, sliding his hand down to the base of my back, his fingers pulling at the fabric of my shirt.

My hand is instantly at his throat, squeezing just below his jaw for maximum discomfort. Heat rushes to my face and I know that my eyes are darkening, sinking, turning me into the monster that I am. I watch with sick satisfaction as his face morphs from confidence to disjointed confusion.

"Listen here, asshole," I growl. "I said *no.*"

Both his hands clamp onto my forearm as he struggles for air, the skin of his cheeks deepening from pale gold to deep fuchsia. His pulse quickens under my fingers and my mouth begins to water. It would be so easy to take him, right here in the shadows, and drain the life out of him until the lewd smirk has been wiped from his stupid face...

"Charlotte."

Rose's warning snaps me from my trance just as Nik appears next to her, his eyes narrowed.

"That's enough," Nik says, his voice tight.

"Is it, though?" I purr. "Shouldn't he be taught a lesson?"

Without waiting for an answer, I pull Jason toward me and tear into his neck, holding him tightly as the sweet nectar of his blood coats my tongue. I feel him thrashing as Rose's arms tighten around my midsection, but I don't care. The blood renews my energy and wakes me from my drunken stupor as electricity crackles through my veins.

Anger does tend to add a bit of a kick.

Nik's fingers dig into my biceps and I'm suddenly flying backward, my fangs catching for a moment on the skin at the boy's throat. I cry out in surprise and Rose regretfully catches Jason before letting him slump to the floor.

"You shouldn't have stopped me, Nikolas," I snarl through a heaving breath, wiping the blood from my chin with the back of my wrist.

"You know our rule, Lottie," Nik murmurs, caging me against him. His cognac eyes are unreadable. *"Leave no bodies.* Not even by accident." He glances upward, anxiety darkening his expression. "And especially not here."

Pippa appears from out of nowhere, staring down at an unconscious Jason with curious, judgmental eyes. "Probably not a good idea to break Kaleb's rule when we're at *his party,*" she mumbles, and I shoot her a cold glare.

"But I didn't break it," I say. "And besides, I wouldn't care if I did. I stopped caring the moment Kaleb left New York."

Nik's mouth contorts into a crooked frown. "Well, we care, Charlotte." His voice is deep with worry. He doesn't look at me. "Rose, get her out of here. Pippa and I will take care of...*that.*" He motions to the heap of bleeding jock that is Jason.

A soft face appears to Nik's left, and I recognize him instantly as Centurion Two. His eyes are widened in horror and something akin to fascination.

"You—you just—" he stammers, searching for words he'll probably never find.

"No, it wasn't—" I start, but he has already disappeared into the crowd. *"Dammit!"*

I dart after him, ignoring the concerned voice of Nik behind me. If I let this boy get away, he could ruin everything. And worse, Xander would have my head.

As I brush past werewolves and nurses, angels and harlequins, something green glints from a balcony above, where two shadowed figures whisper together. They motion toward me and I curse internally, knowing whose icy eyes are watching. I flash him a defiant middle finger as I make my way out of the theater.

Kaleb is not going to be happy about this.

I burst through the front doors and slam directly into the Grim Reaper I saw earlier, though his nurse companion is nowhere to be seen. It seems that he still hasn't been allowed inside; he must not have an invitation. We topple to the ground in a tangled mess of black fabric, and I catch a full-lipped grimace peeking out from underneath his hood. He yells a loud, "Hey!" as I scramble away from him, but I don't look back as I tear down the sidewalk.

Centurion Two is nearly to the end of the block, half-walking, half-running toward what I assume is his car. He reminds me of a gazelle from a nature documentary, his strides bouncing and purposeful, his entire body on alert.

"Centurion Two!" I call after him. His head swivels to look at me and his eyes widen before he breaks into an impressive sprint.

Really?

I close the distance between us easily and grab his arm, swinging him around to face me. He tenses as his frightened, golden eyes meet mine, and I'm suddenly aware of Jason's blood crusting around my lips.

"Who—" He pauses, then starts again. I can hear the pulse thrumming wildly at his throat. "What on Earth was that?"

"That's an odd question."

"Well, if I saw what I thought I saw, then you're an odd person."
I blink. "Excuse me?"

He frowns at his captured arm and frantically tries to yank it away. "If I didn't know any better, I'd say you were a—"

"What, a vampire?" I sneer, squeezing his arm tighter. "It's a Halloween party, dumbass. Costumes exist."

His wary eyes find mine and there's a distant uncertainty swimming in them, more puzzlement than fear. I stare at him curiously for a few seconds, trying to unravel the emotion playing on his face. One could almost call it intrigue.

The golden boy takes advantage of my small lapse in focus and manages to wriggle free. He turns to run, but I grab him by the strap of his fake centurion armor and flip him around again, a snarl grinding in my throat.

"Listen," I snap, digging my fingernails into his tanned forearm. I feel a sudden sense of urgency; for all I know, Kaleb could be spying through a secret window to make sure I erase this poor boy's memory. A chill creeps through me as I imagine his disconcerting pale eyes boring holes into my skull.

Now that the idea is in my head, I can't seem to shake it. Someone is *definitely* watching me.

"I am nothing," I hiss at the boy, the words tumbling out in a rush. Something shifts in the corner of my vision and my eyes flicker sideways, but I see only the night-darkened street. "I am no one. Your friend is an incompetent idiot who drank way too much, and someone spilled fake blood on him. You called him a cab and now you're going home. You won't remember me or my friends. Got it?"

Centurion Two stares at me blankly for a few seconds as the Compulsion sinks in. He finally nods once, dazedly, then disappears down the sidewalk, leaving me alone in the seething shadows cast by the Majestic's shimmering marquee.

2

I SIT ON THE CURB outside the theater, my arms folded in defiance, and Rose and I watch as, one by one, bright yellow cabs pull up to taxi the drunk party-goers home. I usually love the expressions on the cabbies' faces when they see which half-dressed, sweat-covered booze hound is about to slide into their backseat. But tonight, my enjoyment is dimmed by anger: at Jason for putting his hands on me, at Kaleb for his threatening omnipresence, and at myself for being so out of control. It puts a damper on what would have otherwise been a fabulous evening.

The stream of people exiting the theater is thicker than usual, like a dam has opened and is emptying the entire building onto the sidewalk at once. I get the sinking feeling that the party is over. And that it may be my fault.

Nik's familiar footfalls sound behind me and I turn to see him crossing the wide sidewalk with a look of apprehension. Pippa trails silently.

"Charlotte—" Nik begins, but I stand abruptly, cutting him off.

"I know. I'm sorry, Nikolas."

Nik lifts my chin with gentle, cool fingers, urging me to meet his eyes. The incandescence of the theater lights makes them glow like a pair of dying embers. I have always thought that Nik belongs in movies with his long legs, broad shoulders, strong jaw, and head of thick, auburn hair. He even has an alluring scar cut through his eyebrow, an accent of imperfection on the otherwise pristine angles of his face. Any Hollywood actor would sell their soul for a face like his.

Rayna, Nik's twin sister, always said his profile belonged on a coin.

The worry in Nik's molten eyes has simmered to regret, and his eyebrows pinch together.

"No, I'm sorry, *darahi*," he says, placing a hand on my shoulder. "I shouldn't have snapped at you like that. But when Kaleb gets upset..."

He trails off, but I mentally finish the sentence: *When Kaleb gets upset, there's no telling how he'll react.* And we don't particularly want Kaleb reacting to anything.

Shame burns in my throat. Rose's jaw is clenched, and Pippa watches me with disinterest; it's nothing they haven't seen before.

"Let's just go home," I say quietly.

Nik kisses me softly on the forehead. "That sounds good to me."

◊   ◊   ◊

The ride home is long and silent. I know Nik will be fine—forgiveness is a superpower of his, with Kaleb as the glaring exception—but I can't help the guilt bubbling in my chest. Not for hurting Jason, but for making such an absolute spectacle of myself. And at Kaleb's party, of all places. It's like I have a death wish.

Pippa slams her car into park and we pile out of it in a cloud of awkward tension. The first glow of morning reflects warmly off the towering, whitewashed facade of the house; the ivy creeping up its walls stands out like a dark spiderweb.

Xander greets us at the door, dressed in black running pants and

21

a black turtleneck, his feet bare. He holds a glass of scotch in one hand and wears a considering smirk.

"I see the night was a success," he muses, taking in our bloodstained costumes. "I hope you got your fill of blatant rebellion for the year."

"You could say that," Rose mumbles.

Xander shoots her a questioning look, and she stands on her tiptoes to whisper something in his ear. He nods. "Well, Victoria will kill anyone who gets blood on the floor," he says slowly, "so the four of you might want to shower."

Pippa takes off toward my bedroom.

"Hey!" I cry, but she's gone. I can already hear the shower running. "Don't you dare touch my lavender body scrub!"

Nik and Xander exchange a tense glance—a standard greeting for them, these days—before Nik slips away and disappears downstairs to use one of the guest bathrooms. Xander squeezes Rose's hand and she smiles up at him before flitting up the grand staircase leading to the loft.

When we're alone, Xander frowns. "Rose tells me there was an incident."

Tattle-tale.

I worry at the edge of my cape, where a few dark drops of blood have painted a constellation on its ivory inner lining. "Yes. One involving a very handsy Roman centurion."

Xander's face is stoic. A beat of uncomfortable silence passes before he asks, "Did you kill him?" The words come out tightly, as though he is bracing himself for my response.

"No, I didn't *kill* him. 'Leave no bodies,' and all that."

He nods, his lips pursed. Disappointment rolls off him in waves. "I assume Kaleb saw you."

I think of the shadowed figures watching me from the balcony, the bright spot of green winking at me in the darkness like a tiny emerald flame. "Yes."

After another beat, Xander sighs. "For your sake," he says, rubbing his temple with two fingers, "I pray Kaleb will let this one go. But in the meantime, it sounds like you need a drink."

I follow him into the kitchen, where Victoria has appeared in an oversized white sweater and gray leggings. Her black hair frames a pale face with high cheekbones and a pair of shimmering, slanted eyes. Xander pecks her quickly on the lips before sidling over to the wet bar.

"Red wine, X," I call to him, and he responds with a tiny nod.

I slide onto a barstool next to Victoria and she smiles knowingly. "Rough night, huh?"

"You have no idea."

Victoria's eyes flicker to my bloodstained shirt, then back up. "It looks like you may have had a little too much fun. I hope none of you tracked blood into my house."

"*Our* house," I counter, and she smiles. "And we did have fun. Until I did something stupid, as usual."

She laughs and pats me on the shoulder. "There, there. You know you can always talk to me."

"Gross," I growl as I slap her hand away, but I find myself laughing with her.

I wasn't sure about Victoria when we met her in the 1920s. She was everything I wasn't—voluptuous, charismatic, and drop-dead gorgeous—and it was easy to be intimidated by the way she oozed confidence and magnetism. Xander, on the other hand, fell in love with her at first sight. She is Xander's other half: where he is unyielding and passionate, she is flexible and level-headed. They are perfect together. And I hate it.

"Alexander," Victoria trills, waving her manicured hand in the air, a massive engagement ring sparkling on her finger. "Pour me a glass, will you?"

Xander scowls at her, but expertly plucks another wine glass from the cabinet and fills it without looking.

"So, tell me what happened." Victoria narrows her dark eyes, regarding me with genuine interest. Her skin is perfect. Freckle-less. Porcelain.

"Well, there was a guy dressed like a Roman centurion—"

"Ooh, sexy."

"Shut up," I groan. "But yeah, he might have been a *little* sexy. That is, until I refused to dance with him and he put his hands all over me like a sex-crazed frat boy." I grimace. "So, I grabbed his face and, uh…I drank him."

Victoria shakes her head thoughtfully, taking the glass of wine that Xander waves in front of her. "And let me guess: Nik freaked out a little?"

I nod, taking my own drink from Xander and chugging half of it in one gulp.

"Because of Kaleb?"

I nod again.

"Listen, Lottie," Victoria says, taking my hand. "We all do stupid things from time to time. Don't be so hard on yourself. Plus, the guy sounds like he deserved it."

"Oh, he did," I smirk, and she laughs.

◊　◊　◊

When I finally make it downstairs after a long and arduous shower, the others have already claimed their sleeping spots for our annual post-rebellion slumber party, spreading out on the game room floor in a giant pile of pillows and blankets. Victoria has herself draped over Xander, Pippa is on her side with her back pressed into the sectional, and Rose is curled into a ball in a nest of pillows. Nik, in typical Nik fashion, is flat on his back with his hands clasped over his ribs; he would look like a corpse if it weren't for the subtle rise and fall of his chest.

I climb quietly onto the sectional and watch their shallow breathing, my mind replaying the night's events in an infinite loop. My behavior was impulsive. Reckless. It's something that wouldn't have happened if Rayna were with me. I can't help but wonder how the night would have ended if I had just let Jason go, but wondering has never gotten me anywhere.

I wonder every day what Rayna would do if she were alive.

A sharp knock at the front door cuts through the silence. It is short, quick, and its syncopated rhythm is unmistakable. I haven't heard that knock in over a century.

Nik bolts upright, followed more slowly by Xander, who gently nudges Victoria off his chest with a soft kiss to her forehead. He rises calmly but reluctantly, fixes Nik with a warning glare, and slips upstairs.

"What the hell is *he* doing here?" Pippa hisses, sitting up.

"Isn't it obvious?" I ask, glancing down at her. "I ruined his stupid party."

"You did not," Rose says, though the tightness in her voice suggests otherwise.

Victoria frowns. "Wait. Are you saying *Kaleb* is at our front door?"

"Yes," I grumble, collapsing against the pillowed back of the sectional.

"Awesome. Maybe I'll finally get to meet the bastard."

The front door creaks open upstairs and a painful moment of stillness follows. Nik shifts to sit next to me on the sectional, his eyes wary, his broad shoulders stiff. The five of us wait in palpable silence, not daring to breathe. It feels like an eternity before Xander finally clears his throat.

"Kaleb."

"Hello, Alexander." Kaleb's velvety, British voice is strained but not unfriendly. "It's been a while."

"Has it?" I can practically hear Xander's grimace.

It's been a hundred and twenty-one years, but who's counting?

There's another long pause, during which I can only assume Kaleb quietly judges the cut of Xander's sweater. "Though I would love to catch up, I'm not here for you, my friend. I'm here to see your lovely sister."

"She's *out*." Xander enunciates each word sharply.

"I'm not an idiot," Kaleb snaps. "She may as well have been screaming with how loudly she and the others were whispering downstairs. Charlotte, dear," he calls, "do come here."

Four heads snap in my direction, and I roll my eyes before jumping to my feet. If Kaleb wants to see me, I'm not going to deny him the pleasure.

"Lottie," Nik says, his eyes bright. "Let me come with you."

I raise an eyebrow. To say that Nik and Kaleb parted on harrowing terms is an understatement. "Are you sure?"

"Absolutely."

We emerge into the foyer to find Kaleb standing regally under the portico, his blazer rimmed with a halo of morning light. I squint, my eyes burning.

"Xander," I say. It sounds like a question.

Xander purses his lips but ushers Kaleb inside, closing the door behind him. I exhale in relief as the foyer plunges into comfortable darkness.

It has been a long time since I've seen Kaleb—let alone *spoken* to him—but he hasn't changed a bit in the last century. He stands tall, but not *too* tall, with coiffed walnut hair and striking, winter-blue eyes glinting with unearned confidence. A shadow of perfectly-sculpted stubble lines his jaw. His clothes are pristine, from his rose velvet blazer to his pressed black slacks. Even his shoes are polished to a bright sheen. The emerald at his throat winks menacingly from its gold setting as he regards our small group, and I resist the urge to rip it from his neck.

26

"It seems," Kaleb muses, "that you have continued to live nocturnally. You do know that you can build an immunity—"

"We know, Kaleb," Nik remarks warily, his gaze fixed somewhere near Kaleb's shoes. "Get to the point."

One of Kaleb's eyebrows flicks upward and he examines Nik curiously, as though observing an old painting for the hundredth time. "Ah, Nikolas. I do miss your forwardness."

Nik presses closer to me but says nothing more. His hand is tense where it rests on my lower back.

Xander stands near the door with his arms folded tightly against his chest; I can tell he is restraining himself, his eyes regarding Kaleb coolly. Part of me wishes he would reach out and snap Kaleb's neck. Not that it would kill him, but it would sure be fun to see.

Kaleb takes a few steps forward with his hands clasped pretentiously behind his back. "Charlotte."

"Yes, Kaleb?" I say, my voice sickly-sweet. "Why are you here?"

Stupid question. Stupid, stupid Charlotte.

Kaleb's eyes narrow, as if to say, *You know why.* "You've cleaned off all the blood, I see."

I look down at my red silk camisole. "I'm surprised you can tell."

The corner of his mouth twitches, but his eyes darken with disappointment and something that may or may not be pity. Anger flares in my chest.

"I was watching you tonight, Charlotte," he says, taking another step. I recoil as his familiar scent of crisp cologne and cigarette smoke fills my nose. "You were doing so well. Ambrosia hardly intervened. Until, of course, you went overboard with that dashing Roman centurion." He leans in and his fangs slip from his gums, glinting dangerously behind his upper lip. "You know I can't have you causing trouble at these parties of mine. I am your Alpha, after all, and outbursts like the one I witnessed reflect poorly on my leadership abilities."

"Assuming you had any to begin with," I mutter, and Xander glares at me.

Kaleb's eyes don't leave mine, but he continues as though I said nothing at all. "You were *seen,* Charlotte," he says, putting emphasis on each word. "By *humans.* I had to end the party prematurely due to your lack of discretion."

The blonde-haired centurion's face flashes in my mind, his eyes glazing over as I Compelled his memory away. "But I fixed it," I say, remembering the feeling of watchful eyes on my back. "You know that. I caught up to that boy before he made it to the next block."

Kaleb stares at me, unblinking, for a few long seconds, and I shrink under the intensity of his gaze. "You must know the centurion boy isn't the only one who saw you. There were at least ten others that I counted. We had to Compel all of the humans—and I mean *all* of them—to be safe."

I open my mouth to reply, then close it again. I hadn't considered the fact that others may have seen me. I was too caught up in my desperation to remove myself from the memory of a single golden-eyed boy.

"I have been more than lenient by allowing you all to 'sneak in' to my Halloween party every year," Kaleb says. "But if you attempt to murder my guests, I can't promise I will grant such leniency in the future. You remember our rule, don't you?"

Oh, I remember it. No one will let me forget.

Nullum corpus. Leave no bodies. The idea may have been Kaleb's, but I'm surprised how often the words fall effortlessly from the lips of both Xander and Nik.

"She didn't break the rule, Kaleb," Nik says carefully.

"Don't think I wasn't watching you as well, Nikolas."

Nik flinches, but his hand doesn't stray from my back.

Xander clears his throat. Kaleb's eyes flicker in his direction and he stills. It's a reaction I would usually associate with fear or embarrassment, though if Kaleb feels either, his expression doesn't show it. His eyes are unyielding as he stares down at me, and a chill of defiance shivers in my chest.

"You're just lucky we behave as well as we do," I snarl at him. "It's not like we have anyone to impress. If we wanted to, we could have drained half the party before you had even descended from that ivory tower of yours."

"Careful, darling," Kaleb says, halving the distance between us. He adjusts the buttons on his sleeve once, twice, three times. His tone is menacing, but the dispassionate stiffness doesn't leave his shoulders. "Remember that while you are in my city, your life is not your own. I could reduce it to ash with nothing but a word."

"Or with a match," I retort, and Kaleb's eyes harden to flint. "Besides, I don't see how you could possibly ruin my life more than you already have."

Kaleb stares at me for a few seconds, his expression unreadable, before Pippa's sharp voice cuts through the silence.

"I think it's time for you to leave," she says, emerging from the basement stairwell with Rose and Victoria close behind her. The three of them cut a trio of menacing silhouettes in the darkness.

"Hello, Philippa," Kaleb says with infuriating fondness; Pippa flinches slightly, as though the sound of her name surprises her. "Ambrosia." Rose stares at him, her eyes dark and watchful. "And—" Kaleb looks at Victoria and frowns, his head tilting to one side. "I'm sorry, I don't believe we've met."

"Victoria," she replies in a clipped tone. "And you must be Kaleb. Charmed, I'm sure."

Xander bites the insides of his cheeks.

"Well, my friends," Kaleb says, eyeing us all warily, "it has been a pleasure to see you all, but I feel I may be unwelcome."

"What was your first clue?" I mumble.

Kaleb's footsteps echo loudly in the vaulted entry as he moves toward the door. "Charlotte, darling," he says, glancing back over his shoulder, "do behave yourself. We don't want another scandal, do we?"

His words slice through the dark like a scythe. While our little gang has been involved in a number of unsavory situations, I can tell by the way Kaleb watches me—his gaze steady and direct—that he has a specific instance in mind.

And he's right. We don't want another scandal. Not like Golden Gate Park.

Kaleb stares at Nik for a long moment, then throws the door open and disappears down the front steps. A strip of sunlight passes over Pippa's face and she hisses loudly before Xander slams the door shut. We all stand in stunned silence until Victoria breaks it.

"So, that was Kaleb. What an *ass*."

I nod in agreement and stare after Kaleb, hoping I'll gain sudden x-ray vision and be able to see him through the door. Kaleb wasn't always so cold; there was a time when we all trusted him with our lives. But then Rayna happened, and our trust dissipated like morning sunlight burning fog off the bay.

3

AFTER KALEB'S UNWELCOME HOUSE CALL, I want to be anywhere but this mansion we call a house. The sharp scent of his cologne still lingers in the foyer like an intrusive memory, sparking aggressive bouts of *déjà vu* each time I walk by. It isn't an unpleasant smell—it's bright and cold and infused with something almost minty—but the negative emotions it brings to the surface are enough to drive me mad. I can practically see the starry sky and feel the heat of the flames as they flicker in Kaleb's pale blue eyes while he watches, unruffled, as our world burns to the ground.

Why Xander insisted we move to San Francisco to be under Kaleb's manicured and bloodstained thumb, I'll never understand.

"Hey, X?" I call, shaking my head to dislodge Kaleb's lingering presence. "I'm going out."

Xander appears from around the corner, a blue pencil tucked behind his ear. "You're doing *what?*"

"I'm going *out,*" I repeat, emphasizing each word slowly. "Do I really have to explain myself?"

Xander crosses the kitchen to peek through the back window where the sun is doing its best to break through a weak cloud cover. "It's the middle of the day, and the storm is still a ways off. You're not getting suicidal on me, are you?"

"No, moron," I say, snatching my jacket from a hook on the wall. "I just need to get out of the house. I'm not Nik."

The words are out before I can stop them, and Xander glares at me reproachfully. The topic as it relates to Nik is taboo in our house, forbidden by Xander after a certain sunny day in Chicago. He has yet to explain exactly what happened.

Xander narrows his eyes and I avoid them, staring instead at a stray sliver of sunlight on the floor that has managed to slip through the curtains. It highlights a few dust motes in the air, and I have the sudden urge to reach out and touch them. Anything to distract me from the painful, omnipresent discomfort that hovers between me and my brother.

"Give me a call if you feel like you're burning up," Xander says, boldly ignoring my previous statement. "I'll bring the car."

"Sure thing."

He turns and glides down the hallway, his strides long and purposeful. Something tells me he won't be sleeping for the rest of the day.

◊ ◊ ◊

One perk of being a vampire is the fact that, technically, I don't have to breathe. It's a hell of a lot more comfortable than the alternative, but a lack of oxygen isn't going to kill me. After all, I can't suffocate if I'm already dead.

Since moving to San Francisco a few decades ago, I have adopted running as a hobby; it's easy to forget my anxieties when there is salty wind in my hair and asphalt pounding under my feet. It's one of the few normal things I can do to clear my head. It's either this or drain the blood from a small town, but with the constant threat of Kaleb's watchful eyes, I usually try to avoid the latter.

A dark cover of storm clouds is rolling over the bay when I arrive at the Embarcadero—just as I hoped—though bad weather never seems to halt tourism. Ferries glide lazily across the water, packed with overweight people in sunglasses and cargo pants and fanny packs who simply *must* see the Golden Gate Bridge. Food vendors call loudly from their carts, advertising churros and fresh corn dogs, the scent of hot oil mingling sickeningly with car exhaust, concrete, and sea spray. Children scream for sweets while hordes of honeymooners buy useless souvenirs. Somewhere in the distance I hear a mother frantically searching for her child, a man being mugged, two cars screeching to a halt as they collide in a chorus of scrunching metal and shattering glass.

Humanity is a glorious mess.

I lean heavily on a railing overlooking the bay and inhale deeply, breathing in the scent of saltwater and seafood and humans and blood.

Always blood.

Rayna once told me that it would stop affecting me one day. She always insisted we spend time around humans—dancing with them, drinking with them, following them to the places where they gathered—because she just *knew* it would help me learn self-control. I'm afraid it backfired rather spectacularly, considering the fact that I never managed a single outing without sinking my fangs into at least one neck.

Sometime in the 1850s, I think she gave up on me altogether.

In a sudden San Francisco miracle, the sun peeks out from behind the threatening cloud cover and the skin on my bare face and hands instantly begins to prickle. The sun won't kill me. Not right away, anyway. It's more of a slow burn, the way the sun seeps moisture from earth: a few minutes is fine, ten minutes is agony, and by thirty minutes I'm cracking and burnt like a dry creek bed in the desert. Best to avoid that.

I shove my hands into the pockets of my jacket and turn away from the sunlight, darting across the street and into the shade of an awning at an overpriced souvenir shop. A few people around me step into the cool November sun, unzipping their coats and holding their arms out, as if doing so will somehow help them absorb more of its warmth.

I suddenly find myself craving the darkness and solitude of my bedroom. The world feels too bright today, even with the threat of an oncoming storm. When the sun fades into shadow again, I make my way down Embarcadero and toward home.

A large group of people huddled on the sidewalk grabs my attention and, against my better judgment, I push through the warm bodies to see what all the fuss is about. A spray-paint street artist with dark hair and a Real Madrid sweatshirt—one of the area's regulars—stands from his seat on a five-gallon bucket and lifts his newly-finished art piece. It depicts a starry night over the bay, the lights from the Golden Gate Bridge reflecting colorfully on the water. It's nothing I haven't seen before—street art like this is a dime a dozen—but I have to admit Real Madrid's execution is impressive.

The tourists applaud enthusiastically, impressed in a way which tells me that, unlike me, they've never seen a street artist before. Most of them begin to clear out, but a few stragglers stay behind to purchase prints that will undoubtedly get bent in suitcases on their way home.

Just behind the artist is a tall boy accepting payment from eager buyers. He has a confident air about him, all tanned skin and honey-blonde hair and a set of strong shoulders flexing under a yellow sweater. Two white earbuds hang idly from his neckline. Each customer he talks to leaves with a bright smile on their face—it feels like I'm watching the human embodiment of a sunflower in full bloom. There's something in the shape of his face, the glow of his eyes that seems familiar.

Where have I seen him before?

He notices me watching him and his expression warms.

"Hi there!" he calls, waving me over. "Is there anything I can help you with?"

The sun pierces through the clouds for a few agonizing seconds before disappearing again, but not before it highlights the threads of gold in the boy's hair. I take a few steps in his direction and recognition jolts through me: sandy hair, athletic build, golden eyes, and a smattering of freckles over his prominent cheekbones. The memory of last night resurfaces, a frightened face watching as I drained the life from his idiot friend.

Centurion Two.

"No," I say sweetly, though I suddenly feel uneasy. "I was just admiring your friend's work."

A grin spreads slowly across his face, transforming his features the way the San Francisco sun transforms the bay. Big teeth flash behind the curve of his lips. "Noah is amazing, isn't he? I would join him but, unfortunately, I'm a terrible artist."

I smile, and a bit of my anxiety subsides.

"I know how you feel," I say. "My brother is an artist and creates some *amazing* things, but the closest I've ever come to painting something worthwhile was when I dumped an entire tray of paints onto the floor of his art studio. The result rivaled Jackson Pollock."

"That's not saying much, considering the fact that any two-year-old's art could rival Jackson Pollock."

I stare at him. "You actually know who that is?"

"Of course I do. My sister was an art major at SFSU. What kind of brother would I be if I didn't know an absurd number of increasingly terrible modern artists?"

Centurion Two grins again, and his eyes crinkle slightly at the corners. His good humor is effortless. Genuine. I almost laugh, though I'm not sure why.

"This might sound weird," he says a little too forcefully, his eyes searching, "but have we met before?"

I freeze, my mind once again replaying the events of last night. I Compelled him. I told him to forget me, to forget my friends, to forget what happened to his worthless companion, Jason. No, he can't remember.

"I don't think so," I say through a thin smile.

"Are you sure?" he asks. "You look really familiar."

"Sorry, pretty boy," I scoff, "but your face isn't ringing any bells." Sarcasm is a good idea, right?

One eyebrow quirks upward. "You think I'm pretty?"

I take it back. Sarcasm was *not* a good idea.

"Well, you're not *terrible*-looking," I say, and it's not exactly a lie. He has a nice angled face, shaggy blonde hair, and full lips. But the *freckles*. I've made my stance on freckles very clear, yet here the universe is, taunting me with them.

"Thank you?"

"You're welcome."

He's frowning at me now, and I can tell his mind is trying hard to recall my face. But he won't remember; practiced Compulsion doesn't work that way. Once a memory is gone, it's gone. There's no getting it back.

"Are you sure we haven't met before?" he asks. "Do you work around here? Or maybe we've had classes together at San Francisco State. I swear I've seen your face. It seems like a hard one to forget."

"Positive," I say, embarrassment prickling through me. There's a beat, during which Centurion Two eyes a pair of honeymooners flipping through paintings. The artist—Noah—is already seated at the bucket again, spraying a new page with a layer of glossy black paint.

"Well, since we apparently *haven't* met before," Centurion Two says, "I guess I should introduce myself. I'm Tristan."

I take the hand he extends, startled by his casual confidence, and flinch slightly as I feel the soft pulse fluttering in his palm. Still, Rayna would be so proud of me. *Shaking a human's hand, are we?* she'd say. *What, no teeth this time?*

I shove hypothetical Rayna away. "Charlotte," I offer. "Charlotte Novik."

"Nice to meet you, Charlotte Novik." Tristan says my name like he's known it for years. "Now I know where I've seen you before."

My heart stutters in my chest. "You do?"

"Yeah," he says slyly. "You're the girl I met on the Embarcadero the day after Halloween."

I sigh, relieved that he didn't say something more incriminating. "I guess you're right."

It has been a long time since I've had a one-on-one conversation with a human that didn't involve Compulsion, blood-sucking, or some freaky combination of the two. I am totally out of my element here. What am I supposed to talk about? Current events? The dichotomy of good and evil? Sports?

He's a college boy. He *has* to love sports.

I'm staring at Tristan, trying to decide which sport he may have played in high school—soccer? Or maybe lacrosse, with those strong shoulders—when the sun appears again from behind the clouds, bringing a warm flush to Tristan's cheeks. The heat-and-blood combination startles me and my fangs jump to attention. I snap my mouth closed.

Part of me—the part that speaks in Xander's bored, commanding voice—is telling me to go home *now,* Charlotte. If not for the fact that I may shortly turn into what resembles a pile of desert sand, then for the fact that the last twenty-four hours haven't been great for me, and I should probably quit while I'm ahead.

As if to convince me further, the sun burns brighter through the cloud cover and I'm starting to feel the familiar—and extremely unpleasant—sensation of my tongue drying to the texture of rough sandpaper. I swallow, and I might as well be swallowing graveyard dirt. I need to get back home, and fast.

Tristan considers me for a moment with pursed lips, as if mulling over a question in his head. "I know this is a little forward, but I'm just about done here with Noah—would you like to grab a coffee with me? There's a great little café around the corner with *incredible* chocolate croissants."

My eyebrows shoot up in surprise as I try to ignore the heat scorching through me. I press my tongue to the roof of my mouth, willing my fangs back into my gums. "What?"

"Coffee," he says slowly. "Would you like to get one? With me." My expression must not be a good one, because his confidence falters slightly. "Or...not?"

I laugh once, bright and loud, then realize my mistake. Tristan frowns at me, a touch of hurt clouding his features.

"You're serious?" I ask, and the words come out dry and croaking. "I'm sorry, I didn't mean to sound...like that. But I have some really hot friends. And, when I say *hot,* I literally mean model material. I'm not usually the one getting asked on coffee dates."

"I can't imagine how any of them can be better-looking than you, but if they are, you might have to introduce me."

I feel almost offended, but catch a playful glint in his gold eyes as they shimmer in the late autumn sunlight.

"I can't do coffee," I say, feeling a surprising pang of regret as Tristan's expression falls. "Right now, anyway. I have to get home. I have...dinner plans. With my artist brother."

"Oh."

"Sorry," I say, coughing against the creeping dryness in my throat.

"No, it's okay," Tristan says. "To be honest, I would have been surprised if you actually said yes." He thinks for a moment. "This probably sounds less appealing, but some friends and I are getting together to hang out tonight. Noah will be there" —he motions to his friend— "and it'll be super casual. Will you be done with dinner by eight?" When I purse my lips, he adds, "There will be booze, if that affects your decision. Olivia keeps her wine fridge well-stocked."

I'm not sure who Olivia is, but it seems harmless enough, hanging out with a group of humans. Though I did nearly murder one of Tristan's friends last night. What's to stop me from trying again?

"You want me, a girl you just met, to come to an intimate hangout with you and your friends tonight? For all you know, I could be some psycho serial killer."

Or a vampire.

"You don't strike me as a serial killer, Charlotte." Tristan's voice resonates with an emotion I can't place. "What do you say?"

The sun is out in full force now and I'm barely listening to Tristan. Another minute and the skin on my face will start to shrivel like a piece of old leather, and it won't be pretty. I throw my hood on in an attempt to shield myself from the scalding heat, and Tristan's eyebrows pinch together.

"Are you okay?"

"I'm fine," I say brusquely, a familiar agitation burning in my chest at the concern in his voice. It's the same concern that Xander exhibits when he thinks I'm about to make a poor life decision. My fangs slide out again, and I'm suddenly too aware of the pulse throbbing incessantly under Tristan's skin. "I need to go," I say through tight lips.

"What about tonight? Eight o'clock?" Tristan asks, his tone uncertain.

"Sure, I'll come," I say, though it's more to get out of this conversation than anything. I'm already walking away, fumbling for my phone. "Pick me up at the old Pruitt mansion. Do you know where that is?"

"No," he calls after me, "but I can Google it. Why there?"

"You'll find out!"

I dart up the street before he can say anything else, elbowing my way through the throngs of people filling the shop-lined sidewalks. A few tourists dive hurriedly out of my way, glaring at me from behind tacky sunglasses, and I manage to knock over a wire rack with a sign boasting POSTCARDS, 3 FOR $1. The shop owner yells a few profanities at me as I pass by, but I'm too distracted by the metaphorical steam rising from my skin to care. I squint up at the sun, annoyed by its sudden desire to be seen, and immediately hiss as the light fries my eyes.

Idiot.

Xander picks up on the first ring. "Charlotte?"

"You were right."

"You'll have to be more specific."

"The sun is out, and I'm already swallowing sand. I need you to come get me."

There's a rustling sound followed by the jangle of car keys. "Where are you?"

I stumble to an empty street corner and sag against the windows of a sage-painted coffee shop, sliding to the ground and taking shelter behind a large hedge. The dappled shade provides a modicum of relief, though my skin still feels like it might actually be on fire.

I swivel my head until I find the telltale green street signs. "Beach and Mason," I say, each word coming out more breathless than the last. "The corner of Beach and Mason."

"I'll be there soon." Xander hangs up and I'm left alone on the sidewalk, hiding from the daylight like a wounded animal sheltering from the rain. At least my skin hasn't started to crack.

Yet.

Thunder rumbles in the eastern sky, reminding me of the approaching storm as a gust of moisture-soaked wind picks up stray pieces of trash. They scuttle through the gutter as an ominous cloud suffocates the sun and plunges the world into a blanket of damp gray.

A loud chorus of male voices catches my attention, and I watch as three twenty-something boys jaunt excitedly down the sidewalk across the street. The shortest of the group holds a phone in front of him, taking what looks like a video as they laugh at some unspoken joke.

Tourists.

"Hey, are you okay?" A curly-haired girl lowers herself into a crouch next to me. "It looks like you could use some help. I'm a nurse. Is there anything I can do?"

Poor girl. She should have kept walking.

"That's nice of you," I say, squinting up at her. I can see the pulse of blood under her skin, hear the deafening sound of her heartbeat. "There is one thing you can do."

"What's that?"

I smile, draw her toward me, and plunge my fangs into her neck.

4

"CHARLOTTE! NOT FAIR!"

The London night is surprisingly warm, even for July, and lamp lights cast dancing shadows on the nearby buildings. The smell of smoke and soot fills the air as chimneys empty themselves into the sky, creating a veil of black that chokes the yellow moon. I dash through the streets, weaving through alleys, over walls, around darkened corners. Rayna's footsteps echo behind me, fading then reappearing as she falls behind then inevitably catches up.

"You cannot blame me for your general lack of speed and stealth," I tease, lifting my skirts as I vault over a stone wall and into a small garden.

I risk a glance over my shoulder, but I do not see Rayna. I freeze, realizing I can no longer hear her footsteps, either.

"Rayna?" I call, just as something—or rather, someone—lands on my shoulders, knocking me to the ground.

Rayna and I wrestle for a few seconds, our silk skirts rustling as they pick up dust and soot from the garden, before Rayna pins me with a strong forearm against my neck.

"Get off me," I growl, but we're both grinning.

She stands and brushes the dirt from her dress, offering a hand. "When will you learn? If you are winning the race, never look back."

"You're right," I reply as she helps me to my feet. "I should not have looked back. I should have looked up."

Rayna laughs and fixes her mussed hair with expert fingers. It has been a while since the two of us have had time to ourselves, what with our brothers and Kaleb constantly hovering around us like a trio of nervous, over-protective bees. But tonight, the boys have business at the Boheme, leaving us alone to do whatever we please.

Glass shatters across the street and our heads swivel toward the sound. A pair of men leans against the wall of a crumbling tavern, bathed in warm light that leaks through one grimy window. Their postures suggest that they have been drinking. A lot.

The taller of the two spots us and his mouth stretches into a lewd grin. "Hello, ladies," he drawls. His hands are empty and shards of green glass litter the ground at his feet. "What are you doing out here alone? Do you not know this is a most deplorable part of town?" The other man snickers.

Rayna glances at me. "Care for a snack?" she asks, her mouth quirking into a familiar devil's grin.

"Always."

We cross the narrow street and approach the two men, my nose protesting as the overpowering scent of alcohol washes over me. I usually enjoy the smell of a strong whiskey, but when mixed with the stench of male body odor, it makes me want to vomit.

"Are you sure we want to bother with them?" I hiss at Rayna. "Frankly, they're disgusting. And in more ways than one."

The men straighten as we approach, their eyes uncharacteristically sharp, their posture almost predatory. It seems they may not have had as much to drink as I thought. I feel my hackles rise as Rayna tilts her head to the side.

"Lovely ladies," the shorter man says through a gap-toothed smile. One of his teeth is metallic gold. "All alone. Such lovely ladies should not be alone on such a lovely night."

Rayna grins menacingly and drops into a shallow curtsy. "We are lovely, are we not?"

The taller man reaches for her and hooks a clawed hand under the neckline of her dress. The hollows under Rayna's eyes turn immediately to a deep purple, two veinous bruises spoiling the smooth paleness of her face.

I laugh loudly, anticipating Rayna's reaction. "You, my dear man, are a fool."

He stares at me, dumbfounded, as Rayna snarls loudly and reveals her set of razor-sharp fangs. A terrified yowl escapes his lips and he yanks his arm away, but not before Rayna has a hand at his throat.

"Charlotte is right. You are a fool." Rayna jerks him toward her and buries her face in his neck. The man screams and thrashes, but he is no match for her.

"God in Heaven," gasps the shorter man as he turns to run, but I snatch him by the wrist.

"Not exactly," I purr. He looks down at me with pale terror in his black eyes. "Did you think your friend was the only one who would enjoy the pleasure of our company tonight?"

I sneer at him and a shout forms on his lips. Before it can sound, I plunge my teeth into his neck where the pulse hammers under his damp skin. I grimace for only a moment at the salty tang of his alcohol-induced sweat, but the flavor is overpowered instantly by the warm, metallic taste of fresh blood.

The man struggles in my grasp, but I only hold him tighter, one hand on his head, the other wrapped snugly around his torso. His blood is tinged with something smooth and sweet, and I recognize it belatedly as bourbon. It does wonders to diminish the taste of acrid sweat seeping from his pores.

I sink to my knees as the blood fills me, sending warmth and life to every finger, every toe. Energy crackles through me and I inhale deeply, drinking, drinking, as the man begins to sag in my arms.

A strong hand grips my hair and forces my head back, my fangs popping softly as they catch on the man's skin. Rayna looks down at me with a huge grin on her face, and I let my head fall backward. Starlight encircles her amber hair like a halo. My watchful angel.

"What is our rule?" she asks in a leading tone.

"'Nullum corpus,'" I recite, and shake her hand loose from my hair. I stand and the man slumps to the ground, unconscious and bleeding, but very much alive.

If not for Rayna, I would break our rule at every chance, though Kaleb has emphasized it since he first found me and Alexander. "Much better for self-preservation," he says. While I agree with him, it is often easier said than done.

"Good Lord, Lottie," Rayna says, staring down at the bleeding duo on the ground. "We have become positively dangerous."

"I will never understand how you manage it."

"What?" Rayna questions, linking her arm with mine. "The menacing bit? Or the 'Lord' bit?"

"The latter," I chuckle. "Speaking Heaven's name. You make it sound so easy."

"It is easy," Rayna grins. "For me, anyway." She veers down the street and away from our midnight snack, her eyes growing thoughtful as she stares out over the approaching Thames. "But you must remember, dear Lottie—anything that is easy is hard first."

"*Ja nie razumieju ciabie,*" Xander barks in Belarusian, an old habit that resurfaces when he feels any semblance of emotion. He slams the door shut behind us and I stalk off toward my bedroom. "What the *hell* were you thinking?"

45

"I was *thinking* that I was burning." And that I'd just finished a conversation with the boy who watched me drink his friend last night. "My skin was starting to feel like a piece of meat left too long on a barbecue. I needed blood, so I took it."

"Charlotte, you just killed a girl in *broad daylight!*" Xander yells, hot on my tail. "And on the *wharf,* no less. If you could have waited *two minutes...*" He sighs loudly. "You *know* I have blood bags in my car. Why didn't you wait for me?"

"It wasn't technically *on* the wharf," I snap back, ignoring his question. "It was *near* the wharf."

"Does that matter?"

"I was burning."

"You were *foolish!*"

I stomp into my room and strip off my bloodstained jacket and t-shirt. "I'm not apologizing to you, Alexander."

"I'm not the one who needs an apology," he growls. "You should be apologizing to Nik. To Pippa and Rose. They put their necks out for you constantly, and how do you repay them? By killing a girl on the wharf. Oh, and did I mention that it was in *broad daylight?* And all this after Kaleb shows up at our *house* this morning—"

"I can take care of myself!" I roar, making Xander flinch. "I never asked them for this! It's not my fault that you all seem to think I'm a time bomb that needs constant supervision."

"But you *do* need constant supervision." Xander leans against the doorframe, fuming, though his eyes remain still and watchful as a cat's. "Your selfish behavior today confirms as much."

"Maybe you should all stop trying so hard," I say coldly. "It's not like I'm good for anything, anyway."

The tension in the room subsides and a wave of concern passes over Xander's face. "Charlotte—"

"*Niama.* I don't want to hear it." My gaze drops to the floor. "Just leave me alone."

Xander frowns and slowly folds his arms over his chest. "Fine. But you better start thinking about what you're going to say to Kaleb when you see him again. I might not be there to bail you out next time."

"Screw Kaleb," I grumble. "He can go to Hell."

"No, Charlotte," Xander says, his anger calming to remorseless pity. "If you're not careful, that's where you'll be going. And it will be no one's fault but your own. You won't always have someone following you around to keep you out of trouble."

The implication hangs in the air between us, and I know that Xander is thinking of her, too.

"Rayna never policed me like this."

"Rayna is gone," Xander states matter-of-factly, the words melting the tension like a hot knife through butter, "and you were a different person then. We all were."

He turns and glides down the hall without another word. I resist the urge to throw something, and instead release an animalistic scream before collapsing to the floor.

I lie on my back and spread my arms and legs out like a starfish. Maybe if I stay here long enough, Xander will come back. Maybe he'll make a joke and we'll laugh and this will all be put behind us.

I scoff. A girl can dream.

My eyes wander through the dark. Unlike Xander's minimalistic, clean-line bedroom or Victoria's pink-and-white paradise, my room is a den of clutter and disarray. The canopy bed I insisted on buying is never made, and my desk is covered with the ghosts of old hobbies I have long-since abandoned: a pile of half-filled notebooks, a Leica camera from the 1970s, a few history textbooks with dog-eared pages, and a jumbled collection of paintbrushes and pencils. Nothing seems to hold my attention anymore—not since I hit about year one hundred.

Immortality can be monotonous.

I wait. But Xander doesn't come. I can hear him now, scribbling away in his studio the way he does when he wants to avoid a problem. Unfortunately, it's hard to avoid a problem when its bedroom is right down the hall.

When I was Turned, it wasn't this bad. Xander struggled with self-control, not me. Somewhere along the road, we traded places, making me the disaster and Xander the insufferable do-gooder with a penchant for bossing me around.

But I couldn't help it. Once I realized what it really meant to be a vampire, the whole world opened up to me. There is nothing like the tang of blood on my tongue or the power I feel when I take down someone twice my size. When I was Turned, everything changed. I became something better. *Other.* And I haven't looked back.

◊　◊　◊

The light peeking around my curtains has faded to a dim purple, the last color of twilight before the city plunges into darkness. I glance at the clock on my nightstand: 7:45 PM.

Tristan will be here in fifteen minutes.

The last thing I should be doing tonight is hanging out with a human boy and his gaggle of human friends. Who's to say I won't snap and kill them all?

But I'm curious. Tristan seems, for lack of a better word, *nice.* Nice in a way that makes me feel like I wouldn't mind talking to him again. In fact, I kind of *want* to talk to him again.

Plus, Xander will hate it. So, I'm definitely going.

I pick myself up from the floor where I've laid, unmoving, for the past few hours, and stretch out the stiffness in my arms and legs. My reflection stares back at me from my floor-length mirror and I laugh out loud when I realize I'm still in just my bra and jeans, a shadow of dried blood staining my neck and sternum.

"Maybe I should just go like this," I mumble to myself.

I spend a few minutes freshening up my tangled hair and cleaning the bloody residue from my neck, then dig through my closet until I find a fresh pair of black skinny jeans and my favorite Aerosmith t-shirt.

Aerosmith is still cool, right?

I'm zipping up my jeans when I hear a distant knock on the front door, followed by Xander's bare feet padding through the foyer. With a jolt, I realize I neglected to inform him about my evening plans. If he didn't want to murder me before, he sure as hell will now.

I throw my t-shirt over my head, grab a pair of black Converse shoes, and dash into the hallway just in time to hear Xander's voice.

"Can I help you?"

"Yeah, um...I'm looking for a girl named Charlotte." Tristan says my name with a verbal question mark.

"I'm sorry, who are you? We aren't—"

"Xander!" I bolt into the foyer and my socks slide on the polished stone, my arms flailing a few times as I struggle to keep my balance. "I forgot to tell you. This is Tristan. I'm going to hang out with him and a few of his friends tonight."

Xander's eyebrow twitches, but he quickly smooths his expression into one of calm interest. He turns to Tristan. "Forgive me, Tristan. I wasn't aware we were expecting anyone."

Tristan stands timidly in the doorway, his face illuminated by the cool porch lights, still wearing his yellow sweater from earlier with the addition of a caramel leather jacket. A white moth flutters near his face and he shoos it away. His eyes are wary, but he responds to Xander with a friendly smile. "It's not a problem."

"Tristan, this is my brother, Xander." I motion awkwardly between them. "The artist." Xander casts a withering eye on me as Tristan nods. "He can be a little bit intense sometimes. Usually when he needs a nap or when he couldn't be bothered to eat dinner."

"I thought you had dinner plans," Tristan says, an eyebrow flicking upward.

Xander stares at me expectantly, as if to say, *Explain yourself out of this one, Charlotte.* His rigid posture is reminiscent of one of the marble statues at The Louvre.

"Right," I lie. "We did. But Xander eats like a horse. Can never get enough." I slink sideways and link my arm with Xander's. "Would you excuse us for a minute, Tristan? I'll be right out."

Tristan blinks a few times before nodding, and heads back down the porch steps.

Xander detaches himself from me and pinches the bridge of his nose. "Charlotte. I know you can't be this idiotic."

I plop down onto the floor, sliding my feet into my shoes. "I met Tristan on the Embarcadero and he invited me to hang out with his friends. That's it. End of story." I yank hard on my shoelaces. "Maybe it will make me feel better about what happened at Kaleb's party."

I grimace immediately, knowing I've said too much. Xander's eyes turn murderous.

"That was the boy you nearly *killed* last night?"

"No, he's not Centurion One, if that's what you're thinking," I say, tying my second shoelace with a flourish. "He's Centurion *Two*."

"There were two of them?"

"Yes. I only drank the one, though. Tristan..." I consider lying, but know it will do no good. Xander is a Charlotte lie detector. "Tristan saw the whole thing. He's the one I had to chase down the sidewalk."

Xander mulls this over for a few seconds, his jaw working stiffly. "And I'm supposed to, what, just let you go to a party with him? After what happened today? What's to stop you from doing something incredibly stupid?"

"You don't have to *let me* do anything, Alexander," I growl. "You're not in charge of my decisions. Besides, I can handle it." I try to sound confident, but my voice falters.

Xander sees right through me. "Can you?"

It's a valid question.

"I'll be fine. Not like it matters. I'm going whether you want me to or not."

"Well, then Rose is going with you."

"What? Why?"

"Really, Lottie?" he asks dryly. "Do you have to ask?"

If I were to choose someone to come with me tonight, Rose would be last on my list. Not that I don't like her, but she and Xander have a uniquely annoying relationship. He was the only one who was able to get through to her after Kaleb brought her home in Paris, screaming and thrashing like a wild animal. She could relate to Xander, I think. Very few of us have experienced such a complete loss of control.

Rose tells Xander everything, which is why I don't trust her.

I grumble incoherently and hop to my feet, glaring ruefully at Xander. "If taking Rose will make you feel better, then fine. But I'm not going to wait around here until she shows up."

"She's already on her way," Xander confesses, rubbing the back of his neck with one hand. "I texted her because I was—I thought you'd appreciate the company."

"Oh." For all his rules and scathing comments, sometimes Xander can be thoughtful. I'm never sure how to respond when he is. Still, I wish he would have called Pippa instead. "Okay then."

As if on cue, Rose bounces up the front steps and slides through the open doorway wearing a pair of white jeans and a fuchsia sweater, her hair shining in perfect, black ringlets. She touches Xander's arm and he smiles softly down at her. "What's this about going some-where? I heard something about a centurion. This doesn't have anything to do with those boys from last night, does it?"

I walk outside, pulling her behind me. "We're going to a human party," I say nonchalantly. "All very casual. Tristan said there will be booze."

"Hold your breath," Xander murmurs from inside, and the front door closes behind us.

Rose leans toward me. "Who's Tristan?"

Tristan's grinning face appears around the edge of one of the high-cut hedges lining the street. "You're not talking about me, are you?"

"Only a little," I say, and Rose side-eyes me as she recognizes our chauffeur. "Tristan, this is Rose. She's one of my best friends. It's okay if she tags along, right?"

"Of course!" he says with a bright smile. "The more, the merrier, as far as I'm concerned. I'm sure Olivia won't mind."

Rose considers him for a few seconds before her glossed brown lips break into a grin. "I like him," she whispers, just quiet enough that Tristan doesn't hear.

Tristan opens the passenger door of his sporty black Mazda and motions us inside. "Hop in, ladies," he says. "We don't want to be late."

5

"So, YOU REALLY LIVE THERE?" Tristan asks, dumbfounded.

Despite the coolness of the leather seats in Tristan's car, I've never felt warmer. I can't remember the last time I interacted with a human I had previously Compelled, if ever. They usually disappear, never to be seen again. It feels wrong somehow, like I'm hiding the truth from an amnesiac whose condition was caused by me hitting them over the head with a two-by-four.

I nod. "You better believe it."

"Awesome," he mumbles, turning down a narrow street lit by dim orange street lamps. "And I thought *my* parents had money. How do yours afford it? Are they both surgeons or something?"

I catch Rose's eye in the rear-view mirror and she smirks.

"It's technically Xander's house," I say, and Tristan raises a skeptical eyebrow. "He just lets me live there if I promise to keep the wild parties to a minimum and do the laundry from time to time."

Tristan scoffs. "No way. What kind of twenty-two-year-old has that kind of money?"

"Xander is twenty-four, actually. He's older than he looks." An understatement, considering he was born in 1800. "And he just happens to know a lot about the stock market." At least, I assume that's still where he gets his money. I haven't asked in a while.

I can't tell Tristan the truth about the mansion: that we Compelled a very nice, very stupid real estate agent to give us the house for free when we moved from Chicago at the turn of the century. We could technically pay for it, but choose instead to spend our money on other things, like plane tickets and fancy booze and luxury cars we—in standard, Hollywood vampire fashion—never drive. My BMW hasn't seen any action in *months*.

Tristan shakes his head. "I feel like you're lying to me, but I'm going to let it slide because I *really* want a tour."

Xander would hate that, so I reply with, "That can be arranged."

The car comes to a slow stop in front of a classic San Francisco walk-up with a blue-and-white facade. We all pile out onto the moon-lit sidewalk and a blonde girl appears in the doorway, the hemline of her soft blue sweater barely reaching the waistline of her jeans.

"It's about time!" she calls, lifting a glass in our direction, then turns to yell over her shoulder. "Hey guys, Tristan's here!"

There's a small chorus of *woo*s from inside as we approach, and the girl greets Tristan with a too-familiar hug. She regards me and Rose with her nose in the air, a pair of tiny silver starfish gleaming from her ears. "And you are?"

"Olivia," Tristan warns, "be nice. This is Charlotte—you know, the girl I told you about?—and her friend Rose. They're going to chill with us tonight. Cool?"

"Sure, whatever. Come on in," she says, though it seems like she would rather jump into a snake pit than let us into her house. Her eyes rake us sharply before she twirls around and sashays inside.

"Wow," I murmur. "She's friendly."

"Don't mind her," Tristan says dismissively. "She gets like this every time I bring a girl over. She's had a crush on me since the second grade" —he leans in like he's sharing a juicy bit of gossip— "but you didn't hear it from me."

Tristan's eyes glow like amber in the dim warmth of the porch light, sparkling with mischief and excitement and *life*. I regard the smooth length of muscle stretching down his neck to the hollow between his collarbones. Underneath his skin, a pulse: alive and warm and beckoning.

There's a pause, and Tristan runs a hand through his hair. "Come on," he says finally, stepping through the doorway with an apprehensive smile. "We better get inside before the booze is gone."

I move to follow him but Rose catches my arm.

"What was that?" she whispers, concern edging her voice.

"What was what?"

"*That*. You were staring at Tristan's neck for, like, ten seconds. Are you sure you can handle this?"

Was it really that long? "Yeah, I'll be fine," I say. "And if I'm not, that's why you're here."

"I'm not here to clean up your messes, Lottie," Rose counters sharply. "I'm not your maid."

She bites through the last word, her lip curling. I swallow the unease flaring in my chest.

"I never said you were, Rose. Relax."

She doesn't. Her mouth curves into a soft smile, but a stray bit of annoyance glints in her eyes. "Well, Tristan probably thinks you're a total freak now, so we won't need to worry about him falling in love with you or anything."

Something small and sharp shoots through me. It must be nerves. We're about to walk into a human party, after all. "Let's go inside. We don't want anyone getting suspicious."

Olivia's house is a California surfer girl's paradise, from the driftwood dining table to the pale aqua paint to the bubblegum pink surfboard hanging over the fireplace. A giant macrame net on one wall boasts a collection of Polaroids and is strung with hundreds of tiny white lights, while a Himalayan salt lamp casts a warm pink glow over the room.

A small group of humans is scattered across the chenille-upholstered furniture, a smattering of crackers, cheese, and various fruits and sweets carefully arranged on the glass coffee table between them. Everyone looks up as we enter.

Tristan greets us each with a glass of peach schnapps. "A drink for the newcomers?"

"Thanks," I manage as my nose fills with the scent of alcohol-tinged blood. This is a lot of warm bodies for such a small living room. I take a long sip of the schnapps, focusing on the syrupy flavor as it burns down my throat.

"Everyone," Tristan announces, "this is Charlotte Novik and her friend, Rose...?"

"Montclaire," Rose offers.

"Rose Montclaire. We just met, so try to make me look good, alright?"

The others look at him, then at each other, and immediately burst into laughter.

"As long as you don't open your mouth, T, I think you'll be fine," says a brawny boy with gleaming black hair and angled eyes. I almost choke on my drink as I recognize Jason, AKA Centurion One, grinning up at us from a lounge chair.

The cocky boy I almost killed last night is sitting here, six feet away from me, sipping bourbon from a martini glass.

"You can ignore Jason," Tristan sighs. "He's a few french fries short of a Happy Meal, if you know what I mean."

"Hey," Jason challenges, "don't go insulting me in front of the hot girls."

"It's not an insult if it's true."

"I'll drink to that," he says, downing the rest of his drink.

For some reason, knowing that Jason also annoys Tristan makes me feel a little bit better about almost killing him.

"So, that's Jason," Tristan quips, reclaiming the conversation. "You met Olivia" —she stares at me acidly— "and this is Noah, and Bree."

I recognize Noah as Tristan's street-artist friend, looking trim and tan in a fitted blue t-shirt. Bree—a girl with deep tawny skin and a head of shining, dark hair—gives us a little wave, a collection of cowrie-shell bracelets clacking on her wrist.

"Have a seat," Tristan insists. "We don't bite."

Rose and I exchange a knowing glance—the kind reserved for best friends and inside jokes—and take seats on the sofa next to Noah.

"Welcome to the party," he says warmly, smoothing back his thick, ebony hair as he collects a handful of almonds from the coffee table.

"Thanks," I reply quietly, smiling back at him. "I saw you down on the Embarcadero today. My brother is an artist too, so I know good art when I see it."

"Oh," he says, blinking in surprise. "That's nice of you to say. Tristan said you were there, but I'm sorry, I didn't notice you. Too many adoring fans, I guess." He winks.

"So, Tristan," Olivia says loudly, unwittingly interrupting our conversation. She pops a grape into her mouth. "We were just talking about our schedules for next semester. Have you decided which classes you're taking?"

Tristan sinks into the lounge chair next to Jason, kicking a foot onto the opposite knee. "No, not yet." Olivia and Bree glance quickly at each other, but Tristan doesn't seem to notice. "I'm still trying to decide on a major. Well, besides 'Undeclared.'"

Noah frowns. "What happened to Psychology? I thought we had all our classes planned out."

"I don't know," Tristan replies, not meeting Noah's gaze. "It's just not for me, I guess."

Noah's eyes flick toward Olivia. Concern flashes between

them before Noah sinks back into the couch. I feel like I'm missing something.

"Just do what I'm doing, man," Jason offers cheerfully, regarding the others for a few seconds before turning to Tristan. "General Studies. Easiest major on the planet."

"Yeah, but what are you going to do with a degree like that?" Bree asks, tucking her legs under her. The question sounds more rhetorical than genuine.

Jason scoffs. "Who cares? I won't need a degree if I get drafted by the NFL."

The humans collectively groan. They've obviously had this discussion before.

Tristan looks at me, his eyes inviting and curious. "Are you in school, Charlotte?"

I choke back a laugh. "No school for me. I'm not exactly the ambitious type."

"Then what do you do?" Olivia asks. "You need a degree for just about anything these days, unless it's babysitting. Or prostitution."

"Olivia!" Bree gasps, then turns to me. "Please excuse her complete lack of manners."

I open my mouth to reply, but Rose captures the blonde girl's attention with sharp eyes. "You were just joking, right Olivia?" Her tone is forceful. Compelling.

Olivia stares at her for a moment, then blinks dazedly. "Yes. Yes, I was joking."

Rose's Compulsion skills are scary. It's one thing to Compel a human at point-blank range; it's another thing entirely to Compel someone from across the room. It's usually more of a production: getting the human's attention, focusing your energy, maintaining eye contact, the whole shebang. But Rose has it down to an art. She could whisper across a throne room and make the king bow to *her*.

"She may not be going to school," Rose says, steering the

conversation in a more comfortable direction, "but Charlotte is brilliant. She speaks more languages than a mockingbird."

"Really?" Bree asks, leaning forward in her chair. "Which ones?"

Being an immortal has its perks, one of which being unlimited time to learn new skills. We moved around so often during our time in Europe that I had to learn a new language every decade or so. I might be better with languages than Xander, a fact that I remind him of every chance I get.

"Well," I muse, suddenly eager to show off for this little group of humans, "English, obviously. Belarusian, Czech, French, Welsh, Italian, Russian...how many is that? I can stumble through Latin pretty well, and know a good amount of conversational Mandarin."

"*¿Qué pasa con el español?*" Noah asks, watching me with poorly-hidden excitement.

"*Un poco,*" I reply, and he grins.

"I can swear in Spanish," Tristan says. "Does that count?"

Olivia rolls her eyes at him. "We can *all* swear in Spanish, Tristan. Spend two minutes with Noah Romero and you'll know every curse in the book."

Noah throws an almond at her.

"I don't buy it," Jason chimes in. "Say something in Bel—Belriz—the 'B' one."

"Belarusian?" I think for a moment—it's been a while since I've spoken much in my native language; Xander and I are basically American at this point—but finally come up with a nice little zinger. "*Vy huscie jak alkahoĺ i škadavannie.*"

You taste like alcohol and regret.

Rose chokes on her drink.

"What did you say?" Jason asks, looking offended.

"Oh, nothing important," I say, and Rose grins.

"Say something else!" Bree exclaims, clapping her hands together. "How about French? I've always wanted to go to France."

I turn to Rose, enjoying for a moment the simple joy of intellectual superiority. *"Quoi dire?"* I ask. *What should we say?*

"Tu pourrais dire à Jason que ses chaussures sont déliées," Rose replies in her perfect, native French. I glance at Jason's feet—his shoes *are* untied.

We both erupt into laughter, the humans watching in bewilderment.

"I don't think I like this game," Jason grumbles, and Tristan laughs at him.

"You're the one who asked for a demonstration," he points out. "Don't be surprised when they make fun of you for not tying your shoes."

A stunned silence follows Tristan's words and I stare at him, his eyes meeting mine with a warm spark of mischief.

"You speak French?" Olivia asks after recovering from her initial shock. "Did I know this?" She leans toward Bree. "Did we know this?"

"My sister studied abroad in France, remember?" Tristan says. "She practically forced me to learn so we could tell stupid jokes without our nosy friends eavesdropping."

An uncomfortable lull follows as the humans—minus Tristan—exchange wary glances. Anxiety pulses from Noah, his posture stiffening, his heartbeat quickening.

I swallow hard.

Olivia suddenly jumps to her feet, almost knocking a pair of wine glasses from the coffee table. "I forgot to slice the apples!" she says a little too loudly. "Be right back." She scuttles to the kitchen, leaving the rest of us to marinate in the awkward silence.

"So," Noah almost yells, sliding to the edge of his seat, "did you guys hear what happened near the wharf today?" The humans all shake their heads. "I was packing up my painting supplies, and all of a sudden there were, like, ten police cars tearing up the street, sirens blaring." Noah's voice is serious but it carries an undercurrent of excitement, making his blue eyes flash. "Apparently, someone found a girl dead on the sidewalk by that little coffee shop on Beach."

Oh damn.

Rose puts a firm hand on my knee.

"Ew, are you serious?" Bree asks through a grimace. "That's so creepy."

"It gets better!" Noah's excitement is baffling. I shift a little closer to Rose, feeling exposed. "Her neck was broken and she had bruises on her arm. Oh, and get this: I talked to a tourist who saw the whole thing. He said she was *completely drained of blood*. But I bet you won't hear that on the news." He leans backward with a confident grin, blissfully unaware of the horrified looks on the others' faces.

Jason leans forward. "So, what? You think she was killed by a vampire or something?"

Noah shrugs. "Maybe."

"Don't be stupid, Jason," Bree says. "Vampires aren't real." She turns to me and Rose. "You'll have to excuse Noah and his incredible nerdiness. He loves this kind of stuff."

"They could be real!" Jason retorts, pouring more bourbon into his martini glass. "There's no proof that they *aren't*. What do you think, ladies?" He eyes me and Rose expectantly.

The universe is really having fun with me today.

I glance nervously at Rose. "Vampires are fake, obviously."

Jason rolls his eyes. "Typical smart girls, ruining all my fun." I sneer at the backhanded compliment. He looks at Tristan. "You're being awfully quiet over there, T. What do you think: vampire or psycho killer?"

I'm startled by the pained expression on Tristan's face. It may just be the light, but he seems paler somehow. Distant. I try to ignore my nagging anxiety at the memory of last night, Tristan's eyes wide with terror, his frantic struggle as he tried to escape me.

Tristan blinks quickly, a mask of confidence sliding over his features. I stare at him, but there is nothing off-kilter about him now. Maybe I was imagining it.

"Psycho killer," he says, his posture relaxing as he winks at me. "Obviously."

"Ha!" Bree exclaims as Jason and Noah groan. "Tristan agrees with the girls. We win."

"Way to betray your own gender, Tristan," Noah grumbles, and Jason nods in solemn agreement.

A loud curse from the kitchen shocks us into silence.

"Olivia? Are you okay?" Bree calls.

Rose and I are frozen, my gaze fixed on the floor as Rose's hand tightens on my leg. We don't need Olivia to tell us what happened. We know.

The scent of blood fills the room and I immediately hold my breath, but it's too late. My fangs stab through my gums like a pair of spring-loaded daggers, piercing the edge of my tongue, and heat blooms behind my diaphragm. It creeps up my spine, filling my chest before spreading up my neck and into my cheeks.

Rose's teeth snap together loudly. She may have more control than I do, but there's only so much she can do when she's surprised. I risk a glance at her and notice the tightness of her mouth, the dark veins blooming in the whites of her eyes.

Coming here was an awful idea.

"Yeah, I'm fine," Olivia responds from the kitchen, cursing again. "New knife. I sliced my thumb, but I'll live."

I am suddenly aware of every heartbeat, of the quickened pulses in wrists, in chests, in necks. The sound is deafening, the metallic scent of blood intoxicating. Rose wraps her arm around my waist, her fingers digging into my ribs.

"Lottie," she hisses, a warning in her voice.

"Charlotte, are you okay?" Tristan asks, and my eyes snap up to meet his. He watches me with an intense concern that makes me feel self-conscious, and I am grateful for the dim lighting. I hide my face—the darkness of my eyes—with a rigid hand.

"Yeah," I lie. "Just a little squeamish, is all."

Tristan moves to stand. "Let me get you some water—"

"No, I'm okay. I just—I need some air."

Without another word, I leap from the couch and hurry out the front door, careful not to run *too* fast. The cool night air immediately douses the heat burning under my skin. I take a deep, shuddering breath to clear my senses as I stumble down the porch steps and onto the empty sidewalk.

It was only a matter of time before one of the humans bled. They're so fragile. So *alive*. So easily damaged.

As much as I hate to admit it, Xander was right. I can't handle this.

Movement flickers in the corner of my eye. The night is quiet, silver moonlight shining pitifully through a thin layer of clouds and casting haunting shadows between the surrounding buildings. I peer into the darkness at either end of the street, crouching in anticipation of who—or what—might be waiting.

Cold blue eyes hover in my subconscious, accompanied by the ghostly memory of cigarette smoke and sharp cologne, and I wonder again if I'm being watched.

After a few tense moments, a screech cuts through the air and a mangy cat leaps from an alleyway, bolting past me and into the street.

I exhale. "Stupid cat."

I take a few more deep breaths to ensure the blood-tinged heat has left my eyes, then turn back toward the house, nearly running into a dark shape that has materialized behind me. The figure towers over me, the hood of his black, zip-up hoodie shadowing his face. An unnerving smile spreads to the corners of his crooked jaw, and he leans over me with the coiled anticipation of a rattlesnake.

Acting on pure instinct, I swing a fist toward him. He catches it easily, squeezing my hand and twisting it sharply to the side before letting go.

My wrist makes a loud snapping sound and I cry out in agony, swinging aggressively with my other arm. He catches this one as well, pinning it against his chest. The movement pulls me toward him and he looks down at me with contempt, his rancid breath filling the space between us. I gag.

"Charlotte," he rasps, his deep voice crunching like tires on gravel. "Kaleb sends his regards."

Before I can react, the hooded figure raises a dagger and plunges it into my heart.

6

I CAN'T MOVE. I CAN'T speak. I can't breathe.

I am alone in the darkness, my shoulder blades aching where they struck the pavement, but that pain doesn't compare to the scorching heat of the silver dagger embedded in my chest. The yellow light from Olivia's porch gleams sickly at the edge of my vision and I wish I could close my eyes against it, but I can't. I'm frozen, the burning silver pinning me in place like a moth to a pin board.

The stars—which, under normal circumstances, I would find to be a stunning accent in the deep blue of the night sky—stare down at me where I lie on my back, their cold, distant eyes watching dispassionately as I burn.

Gazing at them, I am reminded for a moment how beautiful the universe is.

On another, completely unrelated note, I idly wonder what Hell feels like. It can't be worse than this.

A wound made by a silver weapon is bad enough, but to be stabbed in the heart with one is an entirely different story. Kaleb once warned us that in such a case, it would act as a paralytic, immobilizing a vampire for as long as it remained in his or her chest. It had worried me then, but I had no idea it would feel like this. Like my entire body is burning from the inside.

I'd take the sun over this any day.

Blood soaks languidly across the front of my Aerosmith t-shirt, my paralyzed heart leaking out. The silver shoots a steady stream of fire through my veins until every finger, every toe, every nerve is crackling with heat. It takes only a few minutes for my hands to go completely numb.

I mentally scream for Rose, for Xander, for *someone* to find me and remove the dagger from my chest. I'll take anyone if it means I can be released from the searing prison of my paralyzed body.

Well, maybe not *anyone*.

What if Tristan comes outside?

"Lottie?" Rose's voice breaks through the silence after what feels like centuries. "Are you alright?"

I try desperately to reach out to her, but I should know better. The dagger isn't going anywhere and, as long as it's embedded in my heart, neither am I.

"Charlotte, what the hell?" Rose's face appears above me, blocking out the disinterested stars.

Finally.

Rose yanks the dagger from my chest and I suck in a huge, suffocated breath. It takes a few seconds for the feeling to return to my hands, but I finally feel the burning stiffness retreat, my skin tingling before the pain disappears like static from a sleeping limb. I prop myself up on one elbow, wincing strongly as I'm reminded of the snapped bones in my wrist, and clutch at my bloody t-shirt over the hole in my chest. I can already tell it's going to leave a nasty scar.

Rose squeezes my shoulder, her dark eyes wide and anxious. "What happened?"

"There was a guy," I croak venomously, "in a black hoodie. He came up behind me and—and stabbed me, that *bitch*."

"What guy?" Rose asks, her tone all business. "A vampire? Is he nearby? Did he say anything?"

"One question at a time, Rose," I grunt as I force myself into a sitting position. My skin is still prickling and I rub my arms with bloodied hands. My wrist screams. "I have no idea who he was. Some inbred creep following daddy's orders."

Rose stares at me for a few seconds, open-mouthed. "What is *that* supposed to mean?"

I grimace. "He said that Kaleb sends his regards." The stranger's voice echoes menacingly in the back of my mind, and a bolt of anger licks through me.

Kaleb already made his point. He showed up at our house, uninvited, and threatened me in front of our family. *My* family. Why in Hell's name would he send a stranger to stab me on a dark street in front of another stranger's house?

Rose stills, her hand flexing on my shoulder. "You're joking, right?"

"Do you think I would make a joke at a time like this?" I ask sardonically. When Rose raises an eyebrow, I shrug. "To be fair, I have been known to make jokes in much more dire situations. But this is different, Rose. I just got impaled by someone working for *Kaleb*. What if the guy had been packing a wooden stake instead?"

Rose frowns, pressing a soft palm against the still-bleeding wound in my chest. I wince. *"Nullum corpus,"* she says quietly. "Kaleb never kills."

"Except when he does."

Rose's worried eyes meet mine and we share a knowing look. The last time Kaleb hurt someone we loved, she wasn't lucky enough to walk away.

"I'm calling Xander to bring the car," Rose says, ignoring my groan of protest. "You're obviously not going back inside looking like a murder victim, and I think the others will want to hear about this."

◊　◊　◊

"Let me get this straight." Pippa paces back and forth by the stone fireplace in the living room, wisps of platinum hair escaping from her long braid. "You're telling us that Kaleb—the same Kaleb who plans everything down to the most meticulous detail and probably has specific pairs of underwear for each day of the week—sent a buff crony to follow you to a random house in the suburbs, stab you on the sidewalk, then just...leave you there?"

"Asshole," I mutter.

Xander rubs his temple and stares tight-lipped into the fire. After Rose and I related the night's events to him, he insisted we call Nik and Pippa to discuss the situation. Within minutes, they were both in the living room, looking distressed as I recounted the story a second time.

Victoria is conspicuously absent, probably upstairs meditating or doing one of her ever-growing lists of yoga flows. She usually tries to avoid getting involved in what she calls our "nasty family business." Now that I think about it, I can smell the faint scent of burning incense wafting from the direction of her bedroom.

Nik scratches his jaw. "Something seems off about it, doesn't it?" he murmurs. "We all know Kaleb is a bastard, but this isn't his style. If he wants a point made, he'll make it himself. And I don't think he would—" The words catch in his throat. He takes a quick swig from his flask before switching gears. "He has ignored us for more than a century. Why does he care about Charlotte's behavior? Why now?"

"Exactly," Pippa says, sinking into a plump armchair. "We've known Kaleb a long time—a *very* long time in Nik's case—and he's never been one to make a scene. Well, except for" —she shrinks back slightly— "the Rayna incident."

Nik tenses and takes another drink.

"But what do we actually know about Kaleb now?" I ask, resting my hand over my heart. The skin there is hot around the still-healing hole—silver wounds always take longer to heal—but feels much better since I changed into fresh clothes and practically inhaled a blood bag. "A hundred and twenty-one years is plenty of time to change things up."

"Yeah, but not that much," Pippa counters.

"Lottie's right," Rose says, speaking for the first time. She pulls the sleeves of her sweater over her hands with a considering look. "We have all changed in the last century—why not Kaleb?"

Xander perches on the back of Rose's armchair and draws a hand over his mouth. There's something distant in his eyes, a pensiveness that catches my attention. He sighs loudly through his nose.

"I'll talk to him." His phone appears in his hand and I raise a eyebrow.

"Don't tell me you have his *phone number.*"

"Sure, that sounds like a great plan." Pippa scoffs loudly and throws Xander a mocking look. "'Hey, Kaleb? We would love for you to explain your sudden reappearance in our lives, and were wondering if you've started stabbing people you don't like.'"

"Anything sounds stupid if you say it with that attitude," Xander says. "It would be better than the alternative."

I narrow my eyes. "Which is?"

"Spinning our wheels trying to read his mind," Xander replies tersely. "Besides, what he has to tell us can't be worse than what we already assume."

"Famous last words," Nik mumbles.

I snatch the phone from Xander's hands. "Not tonight," I say, ignoring the glare he shoots me. "I don't want Kaleb showing up here again. I'm not sure I have enough willpower left to keep myself from doing something incredibly fun but incredibly stupid."

"You want to snap his neck, don't you?" Pippa whispers next to me, a smile playing at her lips. "If you did, I wouldn't stop you."

"Kaleb has nothing against me," Xander says, "and he wouldn't dare try to hurt me." He finishes the sentence with the boastful confidence of someone who has already fought that battle, and won. "I'm going to talk to him, Charlotte. I don't need your permission."

Nik squints at him, and I mentally note that while Xander may be able to take Kaleb in a fight, he's no match for Nik.

"Maybe you should listen to your sister for once," Nik offers dryly. "She's the one who got stabbed, after all. It would be novel of you to give her a voice."

I flinch. "Nik—"

"No," Xander says, fixing a threatening—yet cautious—gaze on Nik, "it's alright, Charlotte. I want to hear what Nik has to say."

Rose, Pippa, and I exchange wary glances. Nik and Xander were once closer than brothers, but their relationship has been unstable for the last hundred years or so. While Nik is older, stronger, and more experienced than Xander, it's Xander who filled the role of pseudo-Alpha to our little group after Kaleb left us. I'm still not sure how Nik feels about it. Or Xander, for that matter.

Nik flushes, clearly uncomfortable at being put on the spot. "I just think we should be careful. We don't want to provoke Kaleb when everything is still so fresh."

Xander considers him for a few seconds before resigning. "Fine," he says, plucking his phone from my hands and slipping it back into his pocket. "Then what do you suggest we do?"

"Let's egg his house," Pippa says.

"Not helpful, Pippa," Xander snaps. "And besides, I don't think that would do much good. Kaleb doesn't live in a 'house,' per se."

Pippa's eyes widen. "You know where he *lives?*" she exclaims, and Xander stares at her with the instant regret of someone who has said too much.

Xander makes a bold decision. "Of course I know where he lives, Pippa."

The room erupts into chaos, Xander and Pippa arguing over one another about Kaleb, Nik offering his own anxious commentary as he sees fit. Rose watches them all carefully with her head resting against Xander's arm, absorbing information with the focused intensity of a gambler listening to the day's lottery numbers.

It's a wonder we ever get anything done around here.

While the others grill Xander on his knowledge of Kaleb's living situation, I find my mind wandering. Sure, I want details. But there are more important things to worry about than the secrets Xander keeps from us. I know there are too many to count.

It makes me yearn for the days *before:* before blood, before death, before immortality. Back when we shared everything, secrets included.

Rose catches my eye from across the room. I must look like death warmed over (so to speak) because she clears her throat loudly. Xander, Nik, and Pippa all turn to stare at her.

"Okay," she says, straightening. "It's been a long night. How about we all sleep it off and revisit the issue later? I know I could use some rest."

I flash her a grateful look.

Pippa glares at Xander once more before rising from her seat. "Rose is right," she says, approaching me for a quick hug. "Don't do anything stupid while we're gone, okay?"

"Yes, Aunt Pippa," I say with mock seriousness. "No stupidity for me."

She rolls her eyes, then looks back to Xander. "That goes for you too, Mr. Control Freak. We don't need any more drama today."

Xander scowls.

Nik stands and takes my hand. "Don't worry, Lottie," he says softly. "We won't let anything happen to you." He kisses my forehead, and his familiar tenderness calms a bit of the anger buzzing through me. Pippa and Rose follow him into the foyer, the three of them vanishing through the front door and into the crisp early morning.

I breathe into the silence for a moment, watching logs pop and crackle in the fireplace, and try to force back the anxiety bubbling beneath my ribs. Kaleb has come for me two nights in a row; what's to stop him from coming a third time? One little non-murder slip-up at a Halloween party hardly seems enough to warrant multiple death threats.

Though I'm still unsure of what Rayna did to warrant an even greater wrath.

At least one thing is for sure: if Kaleb kills me, I'll have no one to blame but myself.

Sighing, I turn to my brother. I don't envy him for the position he often finds himself in. We're not the easiest group to deal with, but he still manages not to kill us every day. I have to give him credit for that.

"Why don't you want me to talk to Kaleb?" Xander asks in a low voice. His eyes glitter in the firelight. "He won't hurt me."

"Like he didn't hurt *me*? Or *Rayna?*"

"And if I told you I already sent him a message—"

"Then I'd say you're a damn fool."

Xander sighs, turning his emerald gaze on me. "I need you to trust me, Charlotte. Can you do that?"

Kaleb's stoic face hovers at the edge of my subconscious, his pale eyes bright with malice as he stands, rimmed in sunlight, under the portico. I hear my name in his smooth, British voice, hear it grind in the throat of the man who stabbed me in the heart. A chill shivers up my neck, and I hug my arms to my chest.

"If trusting you involves trusting Kaleb, then no. I can't."

Xander purses his lips, then asks, *"Tabie choladna?"*

I stare at him, unsure if I heard him correctly. It's a reference he hasn't made in...hell, I don't know how long. A secret code we used as children when we were afraid, when we needed comfort from the other and we didn't want our mother to worry.

Are you cold?

I consider my answer for a few long minutes, watching as the low flames turn to embers. "Yes. A little."

Xander rises immediately and offers his hand. "Come."

We walk upstairs arm-in-arm, Xander holding me close as we escape into the darkness of his bedroom. Images flash in my mind as we tuck into his bed: Tristan's terrified eyes, Rayna's wicked grin, Kaleb's emerald glinting at his throat. I curl into Xander's side and bury myself under the blankets, dousing my worries in the dark ambivalence of sleep.

7

A TIMID KNOCK AT THE door rouses me and I groan, burrowing deeper against Xander's side. I don't know if I can handle one more unexpected visit from He-Who-Betrayed-His-Family or any of his minions. I'm half-tempted to ignore the knock until it sounds a second time, stronger than the first.

The knock isn't syncopated like Kaleb's. In fact, it isn't familiar at all.

Mumbling curses, I throw the covers off and steal a hoodie from the closet. I look back at Xander, his hair mussed from sleep, and smile when I see Victoria curled on his other side, a porcelain, Chinese goddess against the deep olive of his skin.

Xander's eyes flicker open. "Would you like me to come with you?" he asks, his voice low.

"I'm not a child, Xander." He narrows his eyes as I slip his hoodie over my head, and I add, "Just keep your ears open, will you?"

Xander nods, pulling the blanket over Victoria's shoulder; she nuzzles against his cheek and he plants a gentle kiss on her forehead. Something twinges inside my chest.

What I wouldn't give for a love like theirs.

I shuffle down the stairs as a third knock sounds.

"I'm coming, I'm coming," I grumble, swinging the door open and squinting against the sudden glare of afternoon sunlight.

"Charlotte."

Tristan stands on the porch in a burgundy jacket, two paper cups in his hands. His hair is tousled and his cheeks are kissed with pink, no doubt from the cold wind whipping across the porch. I'm instantly overtaken by good, old-fashioned mortification. I don't want to know how terrible I look in my day-old jeans, Xander's black hoodie, and what I'm sure is a glorious display of bedhead.

"Tristan!" I say a little too loudly, ruffling my hair in an attempt to hide the fact that I was in bed at three o'clock in the afternoon. There is a low growl from Xander's room. "What are you doing here?"

Tristan holds one of the cups out to me. "I brought coffee," he says, trailing off at the end like a question. "Last night was a little awkward, I think."

"You can say that again," I mumble, taking the cup he offers. There's a cardboard sleeve around it that says GOLDEN GATE GRINDS in bold black letters.

"I'm sorry about Noah's murder story," Tristan says, scratching his cheek. "And for what happened with Olivia. I wanted to make sure you were okay since you never came back inside, but I don't have your number. I figured that stopping by would be the next best thing."

"Um, thanks," I say, inhaling the nutty aroma of unsweetened coffee.

"I didn't know if you take cream or sugar or anything—"

"Black is fine," I interrupt. "Cream doesn't sit well with me." I take a sip of the bitter liquid and shudder slightly. It has been a long time since I've had anything to drink besides alcohol or human blood, and the taste of coffee is stronger than I remember.

I'm glad Tristan didn't bring something more substantial. Though I can technically eat, it comes back up within minutes.

Better that Tristan doesn't see that.

He rocks from heel to toe with one hand in his pocket, the other still clutching his cup. The wind lifts tendrils of sandy hair around his temples, his golden eyes sparkling like sunlight on the ocean's surface.

I'm going to do something stupid.

"You said you wanted a tour, right? How about now?"

Tristan blinks at me, his expression betraying a hint of excitement. "Really?"

Xander grumbles from his bedroom. "Don't you dare."

Watch me.

"Why not?" I say brightly, and Xander responds with disapproving silence. "Come on in."

Tristan strides over the threshold and closes the door behind him, plunging the foyer into darkness.

"It feels like I just walked into a tomb," he jokes. "Can I—?" He doesn't finish the question, choosing instead to throw aside the curtain hanging over the front windows.

I bound quickly to the side before sunlight bursts into the room, narrowly avoiding its scathing, golden light. "We tend to be a little nocturnal around here."

Tristan takes in the vaulted entry with a few sweeping glances. His eyes snag on the large modern chandelier overhead. Light from the arched clerestory windows glints playfully off its crystals, reflecting white hot daggers into my eyes.

"How much did that cost?" he asks without taking his eyes from the chandelier.

"That's your first question?" I jab, folding my arms across my chest. Something about Tristan makes me want to mess with him. He's so soft, so trusting. Completely different from anyone I have met in the last two hundred years. Granted, almost every new person I meet these days is a vampire. "I get it now. You're just using me for my money. What are you, some kind of gold digger?"

"You caught me." Tristan grins. "I was hoping if I got a tour of this place, I'd be able to make off with something valuable. And, like any normal, self-respecting thief, my first thought was the ten-foot chandelier that undoubtedly weighs a few tons. An easy target, if you don't mind me saying."

I scoff. "Alright, I'll throw you a bone. The chandelier cost about twelve grand. It came from Milan."

"That has to be a lie."

"It isn't."

"I don't believe you," Tristan says, squinting at me. "No one would pay *twelve thousand dollars* for a single chandelier."

"Victoria would," I say. "She loves beautiful things."

"Who's Victoria?"

"Xander's fiancée." Tristan stiffens minutely at the mention of Xander, and I don't blame him. My brother wasn't exactly welcoming last night. "She designed the entire remodel when we moved in. She has a knack for that kind of stuff."

"Ah, of course," he says, and there's a strange inflection behind the words.

"What do you mean?" Something small tightens in my chest. "You're not crushing on my brother, are you?"

Tristan looks taken aback. "Xander? No, I don't swing that way. It's just that, from what you've told me—and after meeting him—Xander seems like one of those perfect guys that makes the rest of us men look bad, you know? Tons of money, art skills, good looks, and, of course, a fiancée. And all at twenty-four."

I grin at him, my chest loosening slightly. "Wait until you meet the fiancée. She's what you might call a 'bombshell.'"

"Don't tell me that," Tristan groans dramatically. "How are any of us supposed to compete in this world when perfect people exist?"

I really hope Xander and Victoria are listening. They never pass up an opportunity to be complimented, even if it is more out of exasperation than genuine awe.

"That's a question I've been asking myself for years."

Tristan examines me for a few seconds before his mouth stretches into a wide grin, his eyes brightening as the skin crinkles at their corners. Sunlight from the window paints him in golden backlight, the freckles over his nose and cheeks blooming like raindrops on dry earth.

I swallow. "So. What do you want to see first?"

◊   ◊   ◊

"Are you kidding me?" Tristan exclaims as we enter the game room. "Are you *kidding me?*"

After changing into fresh jeans and a sweater and running a brush through my knotted hair, I walked Tristan through the house on a terribly-guided tour. The Pruitt Mansion was built back in the 1920s by Thomas Pruitt, who obviously had more money than he knew what to do with. The classic manor checks all the stereotypical mansion boxes, from the oversized, overflowing library loft to the sweeping oak staircase.

I suppose the game room could be considered a college boy's paradise: gray walls lined with framed movie posters, a wet bar, a red-felted pool table, and a huge, overstuffed, black sectional sitting in front of a massive movie screen. Pinpoints of light sparkle in the navy-painted ceiling, creating the illusion of the night sky. An ice-maker crackles loudly through Tristan's stunned silence.

"I take it you like this room," I observe.

"This is the *dream,*" he breathes, crossing the room to collapse heavily onto the sectional. "I bet you guys throw some amazing parties in this place."

"I wish," I say, plopping down next to him. "Xander is very particular about his parties, and would rather gouge his eyes out than invite a bunch of humans over to trash the place." I bite my lip, internally laughing at my own joke.

"We humans do tend to make a mess of things," Tristan says with mock severity. "But this place was *built* for parties. Maybe you should just plan one without Xander."

"He would murder me," I say, then add, "Literally. It is a shame though, especially given the pool out back..."

"You have a pool?"

"Of course. What kind of self-respecting mansion doesn't have a pool?"

Tristan smiles softly, and his eyes crinkle again. I notice a tiny white scar on his left cheek that sinks when he smiles, giving him a permanent dimple.

"I really think you should plan a party," he hints.

"Yes, maybe I should," I agree, smirking. "And instead of inviting humans to make a mess of things, maybe I'll invite, I don't know, a coven of vampires."

I expect Tristan to laugh—or at least smile—but he doesn't.

"I suppose you could," he says pensively, tapping a finger to his lips. "Though vampires may prove to be an even bigger problem. I wouldn't want to clean up after a party like that."

"You would need a gallon of bleach, at *least,* and..." I trail off as Tristan's mouth stretches into a wide grin. My heart flutters.

"God, you're easy to tease," he says, resting his elbows on his knees. "Do you always take everything so seriously?"

Embarrassment prickles through me and I suddenly feel out of my element. Teasing in this house usually involves cutting remarks and a fair amount of physical violence, not clever quips about the practicality of cleaning up after supernatural house parties.

"I guess I'm just a serious person."

Tristan raises an eyebrow. "You don't strike me as a serious person."

"I don't strike you as a lot of things," I say. "Yesterday I didn't strike you as a serial killer."

My attempt at humor falls flat, Tristan's grin sinking into a soft frown, and I groan inwardly. Something about Tristan is infuriatingly hard to read, and I silently wish Xander would appear so I could make an excuse to kick Tristan out. The memory of the Halloween party flickers in my mind and I shove it away, but not before I'm reminded how stupid it is of me to be spending time with someone who watched me turn into a murder monster a few nights ago.

I release a resigned sigh. "Are you okay?"

"I'm fine." Tristan's voice is distant and low, but when he looks at me his eyes are clear. "I just keep thinking about Noah's vampire murder story. Pretty freaky, right?"

Something in his expression cuts into me and I shrink away from him, sure for a moment that he can see straight through my weak facade.

"You know vampires aren't real, right?"

Oh, the lies I tell.

"Well, of course," Tristan says, one hand fiddling with something on his wrist: a black guitar pick tied with a thin cord, etched with a few tiny words I can't make out. "But it's still a little weird, isn't it? The idea that someone is out there *pretending* to be a vampire? My sister and I used to go to that café for brunch every Sunday. I guess it hits a little too close to home."

A chill settles behind my ribs and I hug my arms over my stomach. How am I supposed to talk to Tristan about this? How can I sympathize when I'm the one who killed that girl in the first place?

I make a desperate grasp for a change of subject. "You have a sister?"

"Yeah," Tristan says automatically, before his mouth curves into a sad smile. "Well, I *did*. She...died. About eight months ago, now."

Good hell.

I think immediately of Nik—of the years of pain he experienced after losing Rayna—and a terrifying sympathy sweeps over me. Tristan may only have been alive for a few decades, but losing a sibling at any point would be devastating. I try not to imagine what it would be like if Xander were simply...gone.

I'm not sure I would survive it.

"I'm so sorry, Tristan. I didn't know."

"It's okay," he says, still twisting the guitar pick on his wrist. "You don't need to apologize. It's not like it's your fault."

I can't relate to Tristan losing a sibling, but I understand loss. My mother died when I was nineteen, the day I was Turned. My best friend was killed by her own partner. I watched as her brother slowly lost himself, and as my brother tried to pick up the pieces. I have fallen farther than I thought possible, and I have clawed my way out.

I wonder how far Tristan fell. Or if he's still falling.

"So," I say stiffly, ignoring my better judgment, "you've seen my house. Now tell me about yours."

Tristan's eyes warm with gratitude. I gather that he isn't keen on talking about his dead sister. I wouldn't be either.

"Oh, it's just a little apartment near the Financial District," he says, his tone brightening again. "Nothing special. I live there with Noah and Jason. We're—*they're*—going to school at San Francisco State. I was until last semester, and now I'm...taking a break."

I stare at him, but he doesn't elaborate. It seems that every new subject I breach with Tristan leaves me with more questions than answers.

"You know, you didn't need to come all the way over here just to bring me coffee," I say, skirting the topic of school. "It's not like we're actually friends or anything."

"It's only a ten-minute drive." Tristan seems shyly unapologetic. I hear his pulse strengthen slightly. "And I'd like it if we were friends. Friends check in when they're worried about each other, so this is a start, right? I hope it isn't too weird."

Something spasms under my ribs. Probably a burst of hunger in reaction to Tristan's quickening heartbeat.

"No, not weird. It's..." I pause, searching for the right response. "It's nice."

Tristan tilts his head to the side, silently mocking my word choice. His pulse continues to strengthen and I freeze, the dull throbbing of blood echoing loudly between us. I can see it pumping just below the smooth skin of his neck, and a pressure in my gums alerts me to the fact that I may be too hungry for this type of closeness.

"Hello, Tristan." Xander's voice pierces through the room, making Tristan jump. "I wasn't aware we were expecting you. Again."

Tristan isn't fazed. In fact, he looks almost determined. He stands from the sectional and I follow him reluctantly. "I'm sorry for stopping by unannounced. Charlotte left early last night and I wanted to make sure she was okay."

"That's very kind of you," Xander replies through tight lips. "Charlotte is fine, and I'm sure she appreciates the coffee, seeing as it's growing cold on the kitchen counter."

Tristan stares at him and I sigh. I know Xander would rather not have a human in the house, but does he have to be such a jerk about it?

"Now, if you'll excuse us," Xander continues, "my sister and I have an important family matter to discuss."

Tristan looks at me questioningly, but I just shrug, wishing I could die again so I wouldn't have to stand in this game room any longer.

"Well," Tristan says, "I should probably be going, anyway." He turns to me. "I'm glad you're alright, but maybe I should call next time. I assume you have a phone number."

I feel Xander's eyes boring holes into my skull as I snatch a pen from the side table and scribble my number on Tristan's hand like a schoolgirl in the nineties. "That would probably be best."

With a shy smile, Tristan closes his hand and holds it over his chest. "I'll talk to you soon." He brushes past Xander and up the stairs, opening and closing the front door with a definitive *click*.

"What was *that?*" Xander asks.

"What was what?"

Xander narrows his eyes. "Nothing. We need to talk."

8

PRAGUE, BOHEMIA
AUTUMN 1835

"WHAT SHOULD WE DO?"

Alexander's voice is thin but sharp, cutting through the quiet night like the tip of a rapier. Yellow light from the harvest moon shines down on us, bathing the countryside in dim gold and highlighting the unfortunate amount of blood pooled on the dirt path at our feet. Its sticky scent chokes the air, and I hold my breath so I am not distracted. Though it is difficult to focus on the task at hand when we cannot even decide what it is.

Alexander's eyes flicker to me then back to Nikolas, who stands with a hand over his mouth, his mind working as he stares down at the mess.

I feel for the poor man on the ground. It's a pity for him that he caught Alexander off guard; my brother tends to be a touch overprotective—something Kaleb is attempting to train out of him—and when the man approached me in the dark, he reacted in what he felt was an appropriate way.

It wasn't until the man lay dead that we found one of my gloves in his hand. He had simply been trying to return it.

"Well?" Alexander's attempt to mask his fear is unsuccessful. "What should we do, Nikolas?"

I draw breath to speak and nearly choke on the scent of blood, clinging to Nikolas to maintain what little self-control I have. It always seems to disappear when Rayna is absent.

"We must find Kaleb," I say thinly. "He will know what to do. He told me that he and Rayna would be visiting the Town Square tonight—"

"No," Alexander snaps. "Kaleb cannot know. If he found out I—" He swallows hard, running an anxious and bloodied hand through his hair. "Please let us take care of this on our own."

I frown at the apprehension in Alexander's voice. "He will forgive you, as he has before—"

"It must appear as an accident." Nikolas speaks for the first time, his gaze still fixed on the ground. "Do you understand?" His eyes snap up to meet Alexander's, who stares back at him dumbfoundedly. "Alexander. Do you understand?"

My brother blinks a few times before nodding briskly, watching Nikolas with bated breath.

"Good. Now," he says, "what is Kaleb's rule?"

Alexander's jaw tenses. "Leave no bodies."

"If there is no body, then no rule has been broken. Would you agree?"

Comprehension flashes in Alexander's eyes.

"Charlotte, darahi," *Nikolas says, turning his amber gaze on me. "I need you to find a piece of flint."*

I stare up at him in confusion, but his expression is sincere. I nod once.

Nikolas crouches down and gathers the dead man into his arms, blood instantly soaking into his ivory sleeves and the front of his waistcoat. "Meet us there when you find something," he says, motioning toward a small building in the distance. "Come, Alexander. It is time to start a fire."

He strides off in the direction of what I assume is a barn, and

Alexander follows. I stand for a few moments in stunned silence then dart into a nearby copse of trees, searching between gnarled roots and trying desperately to remember what flint looks like.

Nik and Victoria are waiting for us in the loft that overlooks the entry. It's one of my favorite places in the house: oak bookshelves with gold supports line the walls, each covered in various books, decorative objects, and houseplants. One wall displays an impressive collection of paintings—including *Starry Night* by Vincent van Gogh and Gustav Klimt's *The Kiss;* Victoria insists they are reproductions, but I have my suspicions—and the lounge furniture is decorated in shades of champagne, caramel, and deep emerald green.

The two friends chat quietly—Nik in dark jeans and a short-sleeve button-up, and Victoria in her characteristic black leggings and an oversized sweater—each carefully positioned to avoid the warm afternoon sunlight streaming through the clerestory windows. It sounds like Nik is giving Victoria an impromptu Czech lesson, but her pronunciation is terrible. It's comforting to know she isn't good at *everything*.

Both look up expectantly as we approach.

"Hi, Lottie," Victoria says with a sly smile. "It sounds like you were having quite the time with that Tristan boy."

Nik raises an eyebrow at Victoria, swirling a glass of whiskey in one hand. "The question is," he says, "did she kiss him?"

"Excuse me?" I ask as Victoria collapses into giggles. "I did not *kiss him*. Why is everything about kissing with you, Nikolas?"

He shrugs, a mischievous glint in his eye. "We're immortal, Lottie. We have to do something to pass the time." Victoria laughs again, while Xander pinches the bridge of his nose.

"You may have humans fawning all over you with that bone structure," I drawl, folding my arms, "but not all of us were sculpted by Michelangelo himself. I don't have the luxury of constant affection to dull the monotony of immortality."

Nik shrugs again, his lips twitching at the corners. "You can't blame me for being born with such astonishingly good looks."

"Okay," Xander interrupts, "enough of that. Charlotte, don't listen to Nik. We all know he attracts a fair amount of human attention, but I wouldn't exactly call his looks *astonishing.*"

Nik rolls his eyes, but his mouth stays neutral as he sips from his glass.

I take a seat next to Nik and Xander sits in a lounge chair, drawing Victoria onto his lap.

"So," he begins, toying with a strand of Victoria's hair, "we have a bit of a problem. Lottie, your little accident yesterday made last night's news."

I cross one leg over the other. "And? It's not like I haven't been on the news before. You remember the Golden Gate Park fiasco."

"How could I forget?" Xander says, his mouth twisting downward. "That story went on for months. But this is different."

Nik frowns. "Different how?"

"Different because there was a second murder last night." My heart jumps uneasily in my chest. "This one was on the Embarcadero, near the water. It was definitely done by a vamp: drained of blood, broken neck, very public. Just like yours, Charlotte." He glares pointedly at me, and I am instantly on the defensive.

"Hey, don't look at me. I haven't left the house since I got home from Olivia's, I *swear.*"

"I know that, *repa,*" Xander says, and I grimace at the old nickname. "You were a bit incapacitated by that hole in your chest. Besides, I'm not concerned it was you. I'm concerned that another vampire may have seen that news story and become...*inspired.*"

Victoria frowns at the idea, chewing on her bottom lip. I'm surprised she is here for this conversation, since she usually avoids getting involved in any kind of drama. But she doesn't leave, worrying instead at the edge of her sweater with French-tipped fingers.

Come to think of it, I'm not sure why Nik is here, either. Once Nik started drinking—like, *really* drinking—he became a different person. An alcoholic, distorted version of his old self. Trying to get coherent thoughts out of him is like trying to pull a boot from knee-deep mud: not impossible, but often more trouble than it's worth.

Xander used to trust Nik with his life. Now I'm not sure he trusts him with anything.

My brow furrows. "Are you saying I have a copycat?"

"More or less."

"Awesome."

"No, Lottie," Nik interjects, scowling into his drink. "Not awesome. One news-worthy vampire attack looks like a sick joke. Two and it starts to look more like a serial killer, and you know how obsessive humans can be about that kind of thing."

I tap my fingers rhythmically on Nik's denim-clad knee. If this blows up like Golden Gate Park, we could have a slew of wannabe sleuths on our hands. And the last thing we need is a bunch of humans poking around the San Francisco underground.

"So, what does this mean?" I ask warily, wishing I had a drink of my own. I snatch the glass from Nik's hand and finish it off in a quick swallow. He glowers at me then slips the flask from his pocket.

"It could mean nothing," Xander says. "But I'm not so sure. There has been an odd spike in new Turnings over the past few months, and I worry that some vampires may be growing belligerent toward Kaleb."

I narrow my eyes. Kaleb may be the Alpha vampire of San Francisco—the city's head honcho, the one who makes the rules and keeps the fragile peace—but I am almost positive that Xander is moonlighting as a rebellious, underground Beta. When we moved here at the turn of the century, he instantly began making a name for himself, calmly asserting dominance in precarious situations and training abandoned, fledgling vampires like it was his job. After a few years, the vampires who didn't like Kaleb started reaching out to Xander when problems arose.

Xander has never admitted anything to me directly, but I'm not *completely* blind. I like to imagine he is flashing Kaleb a giant middle finger every time he gets a call.

I grimace. "And we care about Kaleb's problems because...?"

"Because," Xander replies, "we live in the same city as Kaleb. And if Kaleb has a problem with vampires in the public eye, then we all do."

"Why haven't you said anything?" Nik asks Xander with a troubled expression. "If there are rebels and wild fledglings loose in the city, it would be in our best interests to know."

"I haven't said anything because, until now, it hasn't been an issue," Xander explains with a tone that grinds like nails on a chalkboard.

Defiant energy crackles between them and I suppress a sigh.

Boys.

"Well," Victoria says brightly, easing her way into the conversation, "we know now, right Nikolas? That means we can keep an eye out and let Alexander know if we see anything suspicious."

The boys soften almost immediately. I envy Victoria and her incredible knack for diffusing tension.

"Right," Nik says, but doesn't take his eyes from Xander. I assume there was more he wanted to say, but the moment has passed. "Let's just hope this is an isolated incident. We don't need another media fire like Golden Gate."

"Yeah, that one was on me," I say sheepishly. "But I'm sure this won't be *that* bad."

◊ ◊ ◊

The rest of the afternoon passes uneventfully, Xander and Victoria retreating to Xander's bedroom while Nik and I sit together on the sofa in comfortable silence.

I can't help but think back to the incident in Golden Gate Park. I didn't *want* to kill that girl but, like the girl outside the coffee shop, she was in the wrong place at the wrong time. Unfortunately for me, her family had money, and they dragged out a very public, very emotional investigation that spanned most of the summer.

Needless to say, there was a lot of suspicion involving the word "vampire" thanks to the holes in her neck and her startling lack of blood. The police and media were constantly hypothesizing a reason behind the murder—a robbery, a prank gone awry, a psychopath on the rampage—but they'll never know the real reason.

I was left unsupervised.

Rayna wouldn't have let that girl die. I wish every day that she were still with me.

At least I still have Nik. Not that he's doing much better than I am.

Regardless of Nik's languid mental state, I do enjoy spending time with him. He sits stoically next to me, swirling his refilled glass of dark whiskey with one hand, scrolling mindlessly through his phone with the other. A steady stream of stranger's faces flashes on his screen and he swipes left or right quickly, an occasional bright trill punctuating the silence.

"What are you doing?"

"Oh, nothing," he says, his eyes flickering sideways as he locks his phone with a soft *click*. "Just dulling the monotony of immortality, as you would put it." He takes a long swig from his glass and his eyes soften as the alcohol saturates his bloodstream.

Sometimes I miss the old Nik, with his sharp eyes and quick wit. He had such life to him, once. Now he seems more like a dying ember than a roaring flame.

"Is there something you need, *darahi?*"

"No," I say. "You're intriguing, is all."

"I won't argue with you there." The warmth that touches his expression could almost be mistaken for a smile.

My phone buzzes where it lies next to me on the sofa and I'm tempted to ignore it. After all, Nik isn't *completely* out of it today, and a part of me wants to talk to him more about what happened at Olivia's house last night. He has always been the best listener in the family, and manages not to judge me for my poor decisions most of the time. Though that might be because his poor decisions almost outnumber mine.

My curiosity finally gets the best of me and I glance down at my phone screen; it displays a text message from an unknown number.

> Hey, Charlotte. Are you busy tonight? There's a party at Pier 39 that we're going to check out. You in? -Tristan

I drop my head unceremoniously onto Nik's shoulder. Tristan left my house less than three hours ago and he's already inviting me to another party. Doesn't he realize that spending time with a disastrous vampire gremlin like me will only lead to trouble?

"What's the matter?" Nik asks. "Human boy got you down?"

"You could say that," I grumble. "I met Tristan *yesterday*—well, if you don't count the Halloween party—and he has already asked me out for coffee, invited me to hang out with his friends, shown up at my house unexpectedly, and he just texted me about another party tonight. I barely know the guy!"

"Maybe you have more vampire magnetism than you thought," Nik teases, then his tone turns sincere. "Or maybe he recognizes how amazing you are and wants to get to know you better. You know, like a normal college boy."

"Yeah, right," I scoff, sitting up and fixing my mussed hair. "I highly doubt that normal college boys are so forward."

"You would be surprised."

"I guess you would be the expert in that arena. You've kissed enough of them."

"All very innocent," Nik smirks, taking another sip of his whiskey. "'Kiss, Compel, release.' That's the old adage, isn't it?"

"'*Feed*, Compel, release,' you absolute libertine."

Nik grins a grin that doesn't touch his eyes, and we fall into silence again. The silver coin resting at the base of his throat catches my eye, glinting in the dying light. I think of its twin lying untouched on my nightstand, and a tiny jolt of pain cuts through my chest.

"I think you should go," Nik says suddenly, his eyes bright. "To the party, I mean. I'll come, too. It will be fun."

"Charlotte," Xander growls from his bedroom down the hall. "You are absolutely *not* going to another party."

Nik mouths a silent, "You're in trouble now," and I shove him sideways before picking up my phone.

I'm in! Meet me here and we'll go together.

Tristan's reply takes only a few seconds.

Awesome! See you at 7:30?

Sounds good!

"Sorry, X!" I call. "I already said yes."

Xander's silence is more reproachful than any words he might say.

◊   ◊   ◊

After Nik leaves to "freshen up"—which loosely translates to, "put on clothes more suited to sweeping unsuspecting humans off their feet"—I find Xander lounging alone on the living room sofa, rhythmically tapping a charcoal pencil on his knee. A fire crackles lazily in the fireplace, its dull yellow glow illuminating the warm tones in Xander's dark hair, its soft heat permeating the room with the comforting smell of charcoal and embers.

Sometimes it feels like if I close my eyes, I'll wake up from this hellish, vampire nightmare back at our tiny cottage home in Belarus, Xander teaching me to ride a horse or helping me up when I trip over Mama's pumpkin vine.

I miss those moments.

"Što vy dumajecie pra?" Xander asks, glancing sideways at me.

"I'm thinking that our lives are much too complicated. And that I miss home."

He sighs quietly and pats the cushion next to him. I almost ignore him but think better of it, crossing the room and perching on the sofa a few feet away from his resting hand.

Xander frowns softly. "I miss home, too," he says. "Things were much simpler there."

"Yes. But that was before."

We sit in heavy silence for a few minutes before Xander rises to his feet. "Come on. We better get changed if we don't want to miss the party."

I stare up at him. "We?"

"Yes, *we*. You didn't think I would let you and Nik go alone, did you?"

"But you *hate* parties. You didn't even come on Halloween to mess with Kaleb."

"Exactly," he smirks. "Which is why I think I deserve a night out. Victoria is coming too." He stalks toward the staircase then glances over his shoulder. "As are Pippa and Rose. We'll take my car."

"I am going to kill you, Alexander," I growl, and his dry chuckle echoes through the foyer.

"I'd like to see you try."

9

"THE MORE I LEARN ABOUT your brother, the more I'm convinced he made a deal with the devil," Tristan whispers, and I stifle a laugh.

When Xander pulled his matte black Maserati in front of the house earlier, I thought Tristan might have a heart attack; I was afraid I would have to scrape him off the ground where he had melted into a metaphorical puddle of envy and hero worship. Compared to Tristan's Mazda, Xander's car looks like the Space Shuttle. That is, if the Space Shuttle were all black and had a secret compartment for storing an emergency supply of blood bags.

The four of us exit the car and a brisk wind catches my hair, whipping it into my face where a few strands find their way into my mouth. I spit them out and look toward the sky, where a layer of ominous-looking clouds threatens the moon and chokes out the stars.

Xander and Victoria lead us to the pier arm-in-arm, their footsteps perfectly synched, and Tristan leans close to me, his olive green coat brushing stiffly against my shoulder.

"I mean, any guy with *that* house and *that* car and a fiancée that looks like she walked off the set of *America's Next Top Model* must have something up his sleeve."

"You could say that," I shrug. "Like I said, Xander is smart with his money."

Tristan scoffs. "I assume he knows the exact asking price for one human soul. Which is why he doesn't have one."

Xander whispers something to Victoria and they both laugh quietly, their shoulders shaking in unison.

"I promise Xander didn't make a deal with the devil," I say, glaring at the back of his head, "but I will have to get back to you on the soul thing."

The water-worn boardwalk of Pier 39 is one San Francisco tourist trap that I usually try to avoid. If a vampire were to cause a problem here, there's a very good chance they would get caught by either the human police or Kaleb's secret entourage of loyal, fault-finding douchebags. I've experienced both. And I don't know which is worse.

We reach the giant carousel at the end of the pier and, despite the November chill and the threat of an oncoming storm, the area is filled with a chaotic sea of people, its edges stretching back to the storefronts and disappearing into the shadows between buildings. A huge lighting rig has been set up over the Center Stage, flashing purple and blue and green, and a stream of Top 40 hits blasts from two massive black speakers. The overpowering scent of seafood, grease, and sweat fills the air—though it is slightly dampened by the hovering scent of incoming rain—and I stifle a gag.

We pause at the edge of the crowd and Xander leans toward me. "Well, this is delightful."

"Shut up," I growl, elbowing him in the ribs. "You're the one who insisted on joining us."

"There you are, my favorite hotties!" Pippa's bold voice cuts through the noise as she makes her way toward us, fully clad in black leather and a pair of thigh-high boots. Nik and Rose are with her, Rose in a V-neck teal sweater and Nik looking handsome in dark jeans and a military jacket with gold buttons. He winks at us and I feel Tristan's gaze shift from Nik to me, then back again.

"I assume the biker chick and brooding guy with Rose are friends of yours," Tristan murmurs, eyeing the intimidating trio as they approach. "They look like they all walked off the set of a cheesy eighties movie."

"That sounds about right."

"Hey, baby girl," I say as Pippa greets me with a kiss on both cheeks. I would have rather called her a thirsty, hedge-born, English wannabe but I'm not sure that would go over well with Tristan standing two feet away.

"And who is this?" asks the thirsty, hedge-born, English wannabe, her gaze raking Tristan from top to bottom. Her tongue flicks over her lips like a viper.

"Tristan," he says through a soft grin, holding out a hand. "Tristan Carr."

I suppose I should have asked his last name.

"This is Pippa," I say to Tristan. "She has the manners of a demon, so you can ignore her. You already know Rose" —she waves— "and this is Nik."

Nik flashes him a disarming smile—the kind that might make one question his or her sexuality—but, as with Pippa, Tristan seems unfazed.

"Nice to meet you both," he says, just as a muscular, dark-haired figure appears behind him.

"Tristan, my man!" Jason bellows, throwing his arm around him. "We thought you'd never show up!"

Pippa regards me with narrow eyes, as if to say, *You didn't mention the sexy human blood bag would be joining us.*

Tristan quickly introduces Jason to the group, as well as Noah, Bree, and Olivia, who have all appeared from within the writhing mass of dancing humans. Rose exchanges a little wave with a navy-clad Bree from across the circle, and Nik regards them all with poorly-masked intrigue. Olivia's nose is in the air—I wonder if she ever lowers it—and Noah's wide eyes hover on Nik for a few seconds before dropping to the ground.

Pippa grabs Jason by the edge of his jacket. "Might as well get this party started. Care to dance with me, pretty boy?"

Jason opens his mouth to reply, but is whisked into the crowd before he gets the chance.

Tristan frowns after them. "I'm not sure if Jason can handle her."

"Trust me," I say. "He can't."

Rose takes Bree and Olivia by the wrists and follows Pippa, both human girls laughing in surprise, and Noah darts after them. Xander and Victoria disappear in the opposite direction.

"Come on," Tristan says, taking me by the hand. I flinch at his sudden touch, at the warm pulse throbbing in his palm.

Nik smirks and I motion for him to follow. There's no way I'm going in there alone.

After squeezing through the throng of music-drunk teenagers, we reunite with the group, all of whom are dancing in a haphazard but enthusiastic circle. Though I wouldn't exactly call it dancing: it's more of a rhythmic bouncing, the song's beat not lending itself to anything but awkward sidestepping.

Nik slips past me, kissing the top of my head before gently brushing Rose's arm. She tenses briefly, her eyes wild, before recognizing Nik's touch; he offers his hand and she takes it, allowing him to spin her in a few quick circles. She laughs, attempting to spin Nik in return, but he is too tall to fit under her arm. Instead, he twirls her into the air and sets her gracefully back on her feet.

Olivia gapes at Nik as if seeing him for the first time, and he offers her a rakish grin. Her mouth pops open, and I mentally brace myself to catch her if she faints.

"What's his deal?" Tristan asks, eyeing Nik dubiously.

"That's Nik for you," I shrug, watching as he and Rose dance in a few more sweeping circles. "He's just...like that."

Nik wasn't always this way; he was once softer, brighter, more adventurous. But after we lost Rayna, his edges hardened, creating a protective armor of sarcasm and overconfidence to mask the desolation underneath. Though looking at him now, grinning and dancing confidently with Rose, it's hard to believe that pain exists at all.

Unless I get close enough to see his eyes. Nik quoted someone, once: "The eyes are the windows of the soul." And the glass in those windows shattered lifetimes ago.

The music suddenly slows and softens, morphing from an upbeat dance anthem to a stereotypical love song, and the lights from the scaffolding fade from icy blue to rosy pink. Dull horror sweeps over me as humans begin breaking off into pairs—Pippa commandeers Jason a few yards away; she catches my eye and makes a suggestive motion with her hips—and the tumultuous sea of bodies slows to form the soft waves of open water.

I see Nik kiss the back of Rose's hand before sauntering into the crowd, a lewd gleam in his eye.

"Nik!" I call, but he's already gone.

Harlot.

Xander leads Victoria into a patch of open floor space and pulls her close, her pale cream dress fluttering as they spin in practiced circles. A few people stop their awkward sidestep to watch them, Xander's effortless footwork leading Victoria into flourishing twirls. Their foreheads touch briefly and Xander kisses Victoria once before spinning her away, then pulls her back into an impressive dip. A tiny bubble of envy blooms in my chest; I know for a fact that I have never looked that graceful while dancing. Or while doing anything, for that matter.

Tristan looks down at me, a hopeful glimmer in his eyes. The freckles on his cheekbones stand out vividly in the neon pink light and I have a strange urge to reach out and touch them, to feel the points where they add sun-kissed shadows to the smooth skin of his face…

"Would you like to dance?" he asks, and a loud crack of thunder echoes the shock that jolts through me. The sound is met by a few excited squeals from the partygoers, and I welcome the moment's distraction.

"Who, me?"

"Yes, you."

His eyes meet mine with warm intensity and an unfamiliar feeling shivers in my chest. It's followed by a flash of lightning and another peal of thunder; I wonder how much longer this party will continue once the storm hits. From the sound of it, it's going to be a big one.

"Absolutely not," I say. "I'm a terrible dancer."

"Fortunately, I am *also* a terrible dancer, so you have no one to impress."

I consider him—his half smile and encouraging eyes and the wisps of sandy hair fluttering over his forehead—and make what is bound to be a horrible decision.

"Fine. Let's dance."

Tristan takes me by the hand, expertly weaving through the crowd to a bare bit of floor. I feel the strength of the racing pulse in his palm and attempt to ignore the instinctual call of hunger that lurks, ever-present, in the back of my throat. Humanity swirls around me and my eyes close against the creeping heat, the pressure in my gums, the hollow pit in my stomach.

I am starting to realize how far we've strayed from my friends when Tristan pulls me toward him and wraps a firm hand around my waist. I gasp quietly. He is close.

He is *very* close.

"This isn't so bad, is it?" Tristan asks as he spins us in slow circles. "I'm sure you've been to worse parties."

"I have." *Like the one where I drank your friend.* "And I'm starting to think you lied about your dancing abilities."

He laughs, releasing me into a twirl before pulling me close again. So close. "There's a chance I took a ballroom dance class once. But don't tell Jason," he says, leaning in like he's sharing a piece of confidential information. "He'll never let me live it down."

"I won't say a word. Cross my heart."

"And hope to die," Tristan finishes with a wink.

My chest tightens abruptly around my atrophied heart. I know Tristan meant it as a joke, but the words strike too close to home. I can't hope to die; I'm already dead.

"Charlotte?"

I look up at Tristan to find him watching me warily, though his arm is still wrapped comfortably around me. I may have been quiet for a bit too long.

"Sorry," I say. "I'm just imagining Jason in ballet tights."

"You should see him in football pants. It's not much different."

I laugh loudly and unattractively, clapping a hand over my mouth. A sparkle of life alights in Tristan's eyes and, for a brief moment of weakness, I am hypnotized.

Tristan spins me again, releasing me into a quick dip before continuing in a simple waltz. His cheerful energy fills the air between us, his smile illuminating his face and creating dimples in his tanned cheeks.

As the song nears its end, Tristan draws me closer until our bodies are touching, his forehead brushing mine. My mouth is inches from the blood pulsing under the smooth skin of his neck. Hunger claws at my throat. I close my eyes, forcing it back.

Leave, Charlotte. Rayna's deep voice rings in my ears. *Now is not the time to misbehave.*

She's right, of course. I came here in an egregious attempt to annoy Xander, but it has backfired terribly. Xander is having the time of his life, and here I am, seconds away from a potential disaster, fighting to keep myself from going into full monster mode on this unfortunate golden boy.

I *should* leave, but I don't. I stay, my body pressed into Tristan's like an inebriated sorority girl, and focus on reining in the heat threatening my chest, my cheeks, my lips. Maybe it's the music or the darkness or the familiar, rapid pulse of blood through Tristan's veins, but suddenly I feel...*something*. Something different. Something almost forgotten.

I might even say *human*.

"I'm glad you came tonight, Char," Tristan says, snapping me from my trance. "And your friends. They seem really cool."

"Char?" I repeat.

"I'm kind of a sucker for nicknames; is that okay?"

"Hmm." His eyebrows pinch together and the sarcastic retort I was planning dies on my lips. Genuine people are impossible to tease. Instead, I say, "It beats the name Xander called me when we were kids."

"And what was that?"

"*Repa*," I say, and Tristan looks at me with questioning eyes. "It means 'turnip.'"

Tristan throws his head back in laughter, exposing the expanse of unblemished skin at his throat.

Please stop that. You're just begging me to do something I'll regret.

"That's *terrible*," he says through a grin. "But it's still better than my childhood nickname."

I open my mouth to ask what could possibly be worse than 'turnip,' when the song swells into its last chorus, mimicking the unfamiliar swelling in my chest. Tristan slows as the last notes fade into a new song, and he pulls me closer. I feel bizarrely calm, intoxicated by the music and the warmth of Tristan's presence and the metallic smell of human blood.

It has been a long time since I've been this close to a human in a way that didn't involve vampirism. It surprises me how much I instantly crave it. I may be constantly judging Nik for his promiscuous behavior, but he may be onto something.

Tristan must be able to read my expression, because he leans forward and rests his warm temple comfortably against mine. Heat bursts into my cheeks and creeps its way toward my eyes. Tristan's hand presses into the small of my back and coaxes me upward; I lean into him, letting go of my inhibitions, allowing myself to be close to someone—to a human being—in a way that I have almost forgotten.

The woody scent of Tristan's cologne mingles with vanilla lip balm and the deep, savory aroma of fresh, flowing blood.

So much blood.

I jerk backward as the scent slams into me, carried on the rain-dampened wind, and my senses are suddenly on high alert. Tiny raindrops prickle against my skin like hundreds of icy needles.

Somewhere in the darkness, at a cramped human party with only one easy exit, blood has been spilled. And a lot of it.

10

WHAT A BUZZKILL.

"Char," Tristan starts, "are you—"

I raise a hand to silence him and he trails off, eyes alight with confusion. The raindrops are falling more heavily now, dusting the shoulders of his coat with watery constellations.

"I'm sorry, Tristan. I have to go."

He calls after me but I don't look back, darting through the crowd and ignoring the cries of partygoers as I shove them aside; many of them are heading back up the pier now that the storm is picking up, and I feel like a lone salmon swimming upstream. If only I could move *faster.*

I'm not sure what worries me more: the fact that someone at this party is most likely dead, or the fact that I'm only following the scent of blood because I have an overpowering and desperate urge to drink it.

In my rush across the floor, I don't see Xander heading in the same direction. I slam into him and he grabs my arm to steady me.

"Do you smell it?" I ask and he nods, his expression wild but focused.

The music has returned to its former party beats, bass notes throbbing in an excited rhythm, now punctuated by deep cracks of thunder and their accompanying bright flashes of white. Xander follows me closely, his hand still grasping my arm, and we make our way down the set of shadowed stairs behind Bubba Gump's Shrimp Factory. The music is slightly muffled here, and I can hear the water slapping against the pier—made more violent by the wind—as we round the corner toward the marina.

The fishing boats tied at the docks sway sickeningly in the stormy waves and, though my feet are planted firmly on concrete, the sound of crashing water combined with the scent of blood makes my vision swim. We snake around the end of the pier, the path lit by only a few wan street lamps. There, leaning against a metal gate leading onto one of the docks, is a slumped, human-shaped shadow, a dark pool staining the ground underneath it. Standing over the body is a tall, hooded figure.

Just like the one who stabbed me.

"Hey!" I call, detaching myself from Xander and breaking into a run. Lightning flashes. The figure takes one look at me and bolts down the walkway, disappearing around the corner into the misty dark.

He may be fast, but I'm faster. I leave Xander behind as I sprint down the narrow path, leaping into the air and landing squarely on the stranger's shoulders. He stumbles to the ground, his head striking the concrete with a loud *crack* as I grind his face into the pavement.

Adrenaline courses through me and I snarl, yanking the red hood from his head and anchoring my hand against his throat.

Lighting sizzles above us with a simultaneous, deafening crack of thunder, offering me just enough light to catch a rain-soaked glimpse of the mystery vampire. One side of his face is torn and ragged—dark blood leaks onto his cheeks and soaks into his hairline—but the skin is already knitting back together like a fleshy zipper. He looks young—a Turned age of maybe twenty or twenty-one—and a mop of damp brown hair curls over his pale forehead.

Though his appearance is unexpected, nothing surprises me more than the indignation in his eyes as he glares up at me.

"First of all, *ouch,*" he chokes out, clawing at my hand on his throat, but his wet skin slides uselessly against mine.

I want to kill him. I want to destroy another of Kaleb's hooded cronies before he can destroy me, before these copycat murders can escalate any further. But when the boy's eyes meet mine, there is a plea in them: *Don't hurt me,* they say. *Let me live.*

Something like mercy tugs at my chest, and I loosen my grip on his throat. But only a little.

"Who are you?" I demand. "Why are you killing people?"

"What? I didn't kill anyone!"

I snort, leaning my face close to his. "And why should I believe you?"

"I—" He swallows stiffly. "I smelled the blood. I couldn't—"

His eyes widen, his gaze fixed on something over my shoulder, and I'm suddenly aware of a presence behind me. I whip my head around to see Xander standing above us, rain dripping from his sodden curls, his lips parted hungrily. The tips of his fangs brush his bottom lip and his eyes are shadowed. From my vantage point on the ground, he looks even taller than usual, his black-clad body extending upward like a skyscraper with its lights out.

"Who are you?" he asks the boy in a commanding tone. Rainwater trickles down his forehead and he wipes it away brusquely. "What is your business here?"

"Ty," the stranger croaks, his Adam's apple moving against my palm. "My name is Ty. I didn't kill anyone, I promise."

Xander considers him in silence for a moment, then turns a stern eye on me.

"Release him, Charlotte."

My jaw drops. "Excuse me?"

"Now."

I stare down at Ty's bloodied grimace and another bolt of lightning illuminates the night, making his eyes flash silver; there is something in them—something almost genuine—that gives me pause, but I keep him pinned despite Xander's command.

"Why the *hell* would I let him go?" I snap. "I just found him standing over a dead body. And after the other murder last night, doesn't that seem suspicious to you?"

"It does. But I believe him." Xander purses his lips and folds his arms definitively. "He didn't kill anyone. Well, not on purpose, anyway. Not tonight."

I shake my head, keeping my hand closed tightly on Ty's throat. "You're insane."

Xander's face betrays nothing. "Look at him, Charlotte. He isn't fighting back, and you obviously outran him." He looks at Ty, then back to me. "He's new."

A lightbulb clicks on inside my head, and I look down at Ty. His eyes jump wildly from me to Xander, his fangs bared defensively as his slim hands pull weakly at my arm. Xander is right: he hasn't fought back.

"Yes," Ty says quietly, his eyes boring into mine. "I didn't kill anyone. Let me go and I'll explain."

With a reluctant sigh, I remove my hand from Ty's throat. He inhales deeply and coughs, rubbing his neck where my fingers left a pattern of plum-colored bruises.

"How long have you been a vampire?" I ask, standing and brushing my hands together. I look down at my clothes and notice that my knee is bleeding, dripping down my leg and staining the front of my sodden jeans.

"I'm not exactly sure." Ty props himself up on one elbow and his brow furrows. "All I know is that I was sick for a while—I thought it was a stomach bug or something; couldn't keep anything down—then I got a taste of blood and...well, since then things have been...weird." He flinches at the last word, his shoulder ticking upward.

Xander stares at him coldly. "Meaning?"

Ty frowns but doesn't answer. Instead, he looks stoically at the ground before hoisting himself to his feet.

Xander exhales slowly, worry creasing his brow. He mentioned an uptick in new fledglings lately; could Ty be one of that number?

"You said you happened upon that dead body," Xander says. "That seems, for lack of a better word, convenient."

"Yes, I swear," Ty replies. "I was at the party trying to, you know, *find something to eat.* Then I smelled the blood."

Xander glances at me and raises an eyebrow, sharp resolve hardening the emeralds in his eyes. I groan internally.

"Him?" I sneer. "You can't be serious."

Newly-Turned vampires can be a bit messy, especially when Sired by a vamp who metaphorically dumps them on the side of the road to become someone else's problem. Xander has taken it upon himself to train the ones he comes across—showing them the ropes, teaching them to control their hunger—which usually involves me disappearing for a while. I'm not exactly a great role model.

"He's harmless," Xander counters. "Besides, I think we owe Kaleb a favor after your missteps this week. Helping to remove an impetuous fledgling from the streets isn't going to hurt your situation."

Ty glowers at us through another rumble of thunder. "I'm standing right here, you know."

"And?" Xander turns back to face Ty, who looks taken aback. "You obviously need some vampire lessons. We don't need a fledgling like you wandering around the city and stirring up trouble.

There's enough to worry about as it is."

Ty's expression morphs into one of mock fascination. "Vampire lessons? What are you guys, the vampire police?"

I laugh. "The vampire police? First of all, that's a stupid name. We prefer the Undead Feds. Or, if we're feeling frisky, the Vamp Tramps."

Ty's mouth stretches into a slow grin, and it looks disproportionately menacing with the still-healing road rash and blood covering half his face.

Xander clears his throat disapprovingly. "Meet us at Hyde Street Pier tomorrow at midnight," he says. "Come alone and wear good shoes."

"Okay?" Ty frowns at Xander, obviously unsure about agreeing to a meeting with the strange vampires who just chased him down. His eyes flicker to me and he gives me a once-over. "But only if you're there, hot stuff."

I grimace.

"Go home," Xander cuts in, "and get some sleep. We'll see you tomorrow."

Ty raises an eyebrow at Xander but doesn't protest. "Yes *sir*," he says, jamming his hands in his jacket pockets as he turns and disappears into the stormy darkness.

"That was strange," I say after a few long seconds. "Do you think he'll actually show up to your weird little mentor session?"

"He will," Xander says confidently.

I'm about to ask Xander what makes him so sure, but my question is interrupted by Nik appearing from around the corner.

"I saw the body," he breathes. "What happened?"

There is a ruffled air about Nik, his hair a dripping mess of auburn waves. I ignore the purplish veins rimming his eyes and the warm flush over his cheekbones and look instead to Xander, whose eyes are narrowed minutely.

"Fledgling," Xander says.

Nik's shadowed eyes widen. "A *fledgling* did that?"

"No," Xander says. "We'll explain later." He slips his phone out of his pocket and taps the screen a few times before putting it away again.

"What was that?" Nik asks. "Who are you texting?"

"Kaleb," Xander says nonchalantly, and Nik's eyes spark.

"You have *got* to be kidding me."

"He needs to know what's going on. We just found another body—the third murder in as many days—and he is in charge, after all. You wouldn't think it a problem if the Alpha were literally anyone else."

"But it *isn't* someone else," I growl, feeling the ghost of a dagger in my chest. "It's *Kaleb*. And I thought we had agreed *not* to talk to him about the murder thing."

"Yeah, well, plans change." Xander looks at Nik—whose dark expression is unreadable—and his gaze lingers for a moment on the flush over Nik's cheeks. "Let's get out of here before this escalates any further. Someone is going to find that body, and you know how I hate cops."

◊　◊　◊

My phone buzzes on the bathroom counter and I glance down from the mirror—I have been attempting to comb out the soaking knot of my hair for the last twenty minutes—hoping it's not Tristan.

It is.

The buzzing stops and three missed-call notifications flash on my screen, accompanied by a few short text messages. I check the time—2:04 AM—and groan, yanking on my hairbrush and wincing as it tears a few hairs from my head.

I have no desire to talk to Tristan right now. What am I supposed to say? *Sorry I disappeared, my vampire senses were tingling?*

This time, he leaves a voicemail.

"Hey, Char. Charlotte. Um, I'm just checking in to make sure you're okay. And your friends! Your friends, too. After you ran off we couldn't find you guys and...well, I'm not sure what happened, but it was kind of chaotic. The police showed up and shut down the dance. Just...call me back. When you have a second."

I scowl at my reflection in the mirror. For some reason, Tristan has decided he wants to keep tabs on me. I don't know if he senses the same recklessness in me that Xander does or if he's just an idiot. Either way, I might need to accept the fact that I now have a human shadow.

"Answer your damn phone." Xander appears in the doorway of my bathroom, arms folded over his chest. A charcoal pencil is tucked behind his ear and his hands are dusted with black powder.

"No."

"Then turn it off. If it doesn't stop, I'm going to throw it into the ocean."

"Fine by me. Hell knows it might do me some good."

Xander strides into the bathroom, his eyes glinting, and snatches my phone from the counter. "If that's how you feel."

"Hey!" I cry, but Xander has vanished into the hallway. "Give it back!"

I dash out of my room just in time to see Xahder slip through the doorway of his studio. I bolt in after him and stop dead in my tracks.

The studio is a huge room that sits alone in the northwest corner of the mansion. When we remodeled the house, two adjoining walls were replaced with floor-to-ceiling windows that look over the bay; the city night shines through them now, the storm having cleared, the lights from the Golden Gate Bridge glittering on the surface of the dark water. One remaining wall is a huge corkboard with sketches and color studies pinned in careful grids, and the other is a gallery wall displaying the framed pieces Xander is most proud of. Among these are an impressionistic watercolor of Victoria, a massive pen-and-ink sketch of the Paris skyline, and an oil painting of our cottage home in Belarus.

In the center of the room is a large table covered in art supplies, everything from charcoal to watercolors to crayons and a freshly-sharpened set of colored pencils. A large easel holding a giant pad of thick paper stands resolutely near the table, Xander mirroring its stance.

But it's not the size of the pad of paper that catches me off guard. It's what is *on* it that makes my heart stutter painfully in my chest.

A fresh charcoal portrait of my face smiles from the page, my arm around Nik as he laughs through a bright, fanged grin. On my other side is a girl my age with a square jaw and messy hair and narrow eyes that burn with confidence. The portrait radiates life, in the way Xander's work always does, and I brush my fingertips against the girl's charcoal shoulder.

"Rayna," I murmur.

Seeing Rayna's face is startling, but it's more upsetting when I realize the scene is happy. *Too* happy. There is a comfortable excitement in all our faces that has become unfamiliar. Nik looks especially lively, and I wonder how Xander was able to capture that emotion in him with such clarity.

But if he can draw Rayna's face from memory, then surely he can draw Nik's happiness, too.

"I've been thinking a lot about the past since...well, since Halloween," Xander says, wringing his black-dusted hands. "It's been a long time since I've drawn her—some of the details are getting fuzzy. There's something wrong with her nose, and she had such high cheekbones. I can never quite get them right."

"She looks perfect," I say, glancing up at him. "But I do have one critique."

He frowns, handing my phone back to me. I slip it into my pocket. "And what is that?"

"You should be in this picture with us."

"I don't do self-portraits, Charlotte. You know that."

"It's never too late to start." I return my focus to the drawing. "It feels wrong to see the three of us without you and Ka—" I choke on his name, wrapping my arms around my stomach.

Kaleb was part of our family once. A leader, a friend, a brother. Sometimes I miss him.

But only sometimes.

Xander takes a deep, understanding breath and touches my shoulder hesitantly. For a few blissful seconds, I feel the distance close between us. We stare at his latest work, and I half expect Rayna to wink at us and flash her infamous grin.

But I'll never see that grin again. Kaleb made sure of that.

"I'm going to kill him someday."

"Who?"

"Kaleb."

Xander sighs. "Not if Nik gets to him first."

My phone buzzes in my pocket and Xander rubs his temples. "Good hell."

"I'm *sorry*," I grumble, hurrying to silence it. "It's not my fault he keeps calling."

"He's going to think you're avoiding him on purpose," Xander says. "You have to answer the phone eventually or he won't leave you alone."

"That's exactly the point, Xander. I *am* avoiding him on purpose." He fishes his own phone from his pocket and taps on the screen, a worried crease forming between his eyebrows. I try not to think about who he might be texting. "And besides, why do you care? From what I can tell, you would have no problem with him disappearing forever."

"I'm not blind, Charlotte," Xander says. "I see the way you look at him. You like him."

"I most certainly do *not,*" I scoff, but the idea stirs something behind my ribs.

Images of Tristan appear in my mind: his sandy hair wisping over his forehead, the way his golden eyes captured the colors of the party lights, the soft bow of his lips stretching into a dazzling grin. Everything about him is a welcome contrast to the other boys in my life: Xander's essence of shadows, and Nik's dark, molten anguish. In comparison, Tristan's disposition is akin to summer sun bursting through the clouds after a two-hundred-year storm.

He definitely might be a little bit alluring.

"Okay," I concede, "I don't *hate* him. But he's persistent and cocky and has absolutely no sense of personal space—"

"You know he likes *you,* right?" Victoria peeks through the studio doorway, a mischievous sparkle in her eye.

I glower. "He does not."

"Come on, Lottie," Xander says. "Even you aren't *that* dense."

Victoria smiles slyly and slips into the room. "It's painfully obvious."

"You are both out of your minds," I say, though a flash of warmth flickers under my skin. I shake it away. "He has only known me for two days! Well, not counting Halloween." Xander's eyes narrow slightly. "And if you think he's so cute," I add, purposely steering the conversation away from myself, "then why don't *you* date him, V?"

"Because then I'd have to dump this exquisite brother of yours, and I don't think his poor heart could take it." She sidles up to Xander and wraps her arms around him, reaching up on her tiptoes to peck him on the lips. Xander sighs deeply.

I gag. "Get a room, you two."

Xander shoves his phone back into his pocket and sweeps Victoria into his arms. She lets out a surprised giggle and nuzzles into his neck.

"Don't mind if we do," Xander murmurs, planting a kiss on Victoria's forehead as he carries her into the hall.

"Gross," I say, though I can't help the pinprick of neon jealousy that flickers in my chest. I can't remember a time anyone looked at me the way my brother looks at his fiancée.

On second thought, maybe I can. But Nik and I were never destined to be anything more than what we are now.

"Lottie, dear," Victoria says in a lilting voice as they disappear from view, "please talk to that boy. Alexander isn't the only one who wants to throw your phone into the ocean."

11

I BOLT OUTSIDE THE INSTANT I hear Victoria's bedroom door slam shut, followed by the soft murmur of breathless voices and a low moan from Xander.

There is no way I'm staying inside to witness whatever Victoria is doing to my brother. I prefer not to think about it.

The night is cool and I inhale deeply, relishing in the salty tang of the ocean air as it blows over the San Francisco hills. Ripples from the pool's surface cast shimmering reflections onto the ivory-colored columns lining the yard, the underwater lights changing lazily from purple to blue to pink. A few lone crickets chirp from leafy hiding places and fill the darkness with their soothing rhythm.

The sound of the insects combined with the ever-present roar of the ocean and city traffic almost drowns out the ruckus now happening in Xander's bedroom.

Almost.

I collapse onto one of the cushioned chaise lounges by the pool's edge and stare down at my phone. Tristan's name flashes like a distress beacon and I'm tempted to change it to something less normal, like "Human Boy With a Strange Obsession" or "The One Xander Hates" or "That Guy." Maybe then it would be easier to ignore him.

Tristan barely knows me, but maybe his persistence is more than just keeping tabs. Maybe Xander and Victoria are right.

I cringe. I'm being such a *girl*.

My phone buzzes in my hand and I contemplate drowning it in the pool. But I can't put this off forever.

"Hello?"

"Charlotte, thank *God*. I was starting to think you were avoiding me." Tristan's voice is teasing, but it carries the unmistakable breathlessness of relief.

"I'm not avoiding you," I say, even though I am.

"Did you get my message?" he asks. "About the police shutting down the party? I wasn't sure if you were still there when that happened."

"Um," I start, forming a quick cover story in my head. "Yeah, we were there. We just—I needed to talk to Nik about something. Then the police showed up, and we all got herded out of the party. It was crazy."

There's a short pause before Tristan answers. "Nik. Right. Is he—are you two...?"

"Me and *Nik?*" I scoff. "Not even a little bit. That would never happen."

Not again, anyway. Memories flash in my head from our tryst in Paris. And again in London. And in New York. But we don't talk about that.

"Oh." There's a beat. "So, you're sure you're alright?"

"Yes, Tristan. You don't need to worry about me. I'm tougher than I look."

"I never said I was *worried*," he says. "Just a concerned citizen doing his due diligence to make sure his...*friend*...got home safely."

"We're friends now?" The idea doesn't repulse me. In fact, my chest flutters at the thought.

"I think so." It sounds like a question. A quiet, hopeful question.

I almost laugh. "Okay," I say. "Friends."

"Awesome," Tristan says, and I can hear his grin. "Then, as your friend, can I apologize for the last few nights? The hangout at Olivia's was a disaster, what with Olivia cutting her hand and Noah not shutting up about vampires." His voice catches strangely on the last word. "And the pier party…well, I have no explanation for what happened there."

This time I do laugh. "It's not your fault. If anything, it's mine. I tend to be a magnet for disaster."

"Then I guess I'm in for an adventure every time I see you."

I frown, watching as the wind forms ripples on the pink-lit surface of the pool, and immediately second-guess myself. What Tristan might call an adventure, I call a night of hunger, mystery, and unapologetic violence. A normal Tuesday night for a vampire. But for a human…

"Understatement of the century," I murmur, brushing a few wild strands of hair out of my face. I haven't changed clothes since I tackled Ty at the pier, and dark blood from my skinned knee stains my pale jeans a shade of black. I've been covered in blood a lot lately. And that's saying something, coming from me.

If Tristan—a very fragile, very mortal human boy—thinks we're going to be *seeing* each other, then I'll need to make a few things abundantly clear.

"Listen," I say. "At the risk of sounding completely insane, my friendship comes with a few ground rules."

Tristan waits a few seconds before saying, "Okay, shoot."

"First, you're not allowed to show up at my house unless you call first. No spontaneous coffee dates."

"I guess I'll have to head home then."

"What?" I ask loudly, adrenaline pulsing through me. I whirl in my seat to stare in the direction of the front door. "You're here?"

"Relax," Tristan says, his voice sparkling with humor. "I'm *kidding.*"

I release a shuddering breath. I'm already on thin ice with Xander; I can't imagine what he would do if Tristan showed up here *again*. Right now. Not that Tristan would have any idea of the debauchery happening upstairs, but *I* would know.

"You're terrible," I groan, and he chuckles. "Okay, rule number two. My friends will try to push your buttons—*especially* Nik and Pippa—but you *cannot* retaliate. They will eat you alive."

He sighs loudly. "Retaliation is a favorite hobby of mine," he says with mock sadness, "but deal."

"Lastly, you have to trust me." I pause as a car rushes by on the street in front of the mansion, loud music blaring despite the late hour.

The words feel foreign on my tongue. *Trust me.* Trust me not to lie. Trust me not to make a mess of things.

Trust me not to kill you.

"If I don't answer my phone," I continue, "I have a good reason. You can't call me at all hours of the night. Xander threatened to throw my phone into the ocean."

"I wouldn't want to upset Xander," he muses, his voice thick with sarcasm, before he sobers. "I can trust you. Absolutely."

Doubt flickers in my mind but I push it away, smiling at Tristan through the phone.

"Good. That being said, can you trust me enough to finally go to sleep?"

"I think I can do that. I'll talk to you tomorrow?"

"Tomorrow."

I have no idea what tomorrow will bring. But maybe it will be something good for a change.

◊   ◊   ◊

I'm jolted awake by someone pounding on my bedroom door.

"Get up!"

"I'm *sleeping*," I snap.

"Not anymore," Xander says, pounding again. *"Get up.* You're famous."

"What?" I ask, untangling myself from my mess of blankets. "What do you mean I'm *famous?*"

"Come downstairs and I'll show you."

He strides down the hallway, his footsteps fading quickly as he descends the stairs.

I throw my legs over the side of my bed and pick up my phone, which greets me with three text messages from Tristan.

Good morning :)

I'm heading to an amazing deli for lunch. Do you want to come?

Have you seen the news?

Late afternoon light slips through the edges of my blackout curtains and I sigh. I'm not used to spending time with people who aren't nocturnal. It takes me a few minutes to figure out an appropriate response.

Sorry, Tristan. Busy day. Things are a bit crazy right now in the life of Charlotte.

He replies immediately, and a smile threatens my lips.

Oh, I know how you feel. I'm currently getting demolished in a very intense game of MarioKart. It's not looking good.

Noah says hi, by the way.

"Charlotte, are you coming?"

I stick my tongue out in Xander's general direction but follow his voice, slipping downstairs into the game room where the TV is showing the evening news.

It's a disaster.

There are photographs of the party, videos of police officers ushering terrified partygoers from the pier, teenagers pushing and shoving each other in a desperate attempt to get away from the threat of a vampire serial killer.

At least, that's what they're calling it.

"Based on the information we have received from the San Francisco Police Department," a well-dressed, blonde reporter calls from her place in front of the roped-off pier, "the victim was found at the marina here on Pier 39 just before midnight. This murder comes just one day after similar bodies were found on both Beach Street and Embarcadero near Pier 43. Many are noting the similarity to another murder in March of this year at Golden Gate Park, where a twenty-two-year-old woman was found dead by her brother in the Shakespeare Garden. Could this be the work of a new serial killer? More to come as the story unfolds."

A hashtag flashes at the bottom of the screen:

#SanFranciscoVampire

"You have a hashtag," Victoria says from her seat on the sectional. "I like it. Very catchy."

"*It wasn't me,*" I say, sitting down next to her. "I mean, the first one was me. And so was Golden Gate Park," I add with a grimace. "But the others weren't. I don't want a stupid hashtag!"

Xander flips the TV off, sinking back into the leather sectional with a sigh. "Regardless of who did it" —I open my mouth to comment, but he silences me with a glare— "this isn't good." He fiddles with the steel rings in his ear. "I suppose it's a good thing I'll be meeting with Kaleb tonight."

I gawk at him. "Tonight? I'm surprised the emotionless ice king found time for you in his meticulously-planned Alpha schedule."

"Kaleb finds time for anything that will benefit him," Xander says carefully. "And I have first-hand information about two of the three murders in his city."

I wince at the way Xander says *his city*. Like San Francisco is Kaleb's game board, and we're nothing but pawns dancing around at his beck and call, ready to be sacrificed at the drop of a hat.

Or of a match.

"Kaleb sucks," I mutter, the ghostly memory of white-hot silver licking through my chest; it takes only seconds for it to morph into a fresh, potent anger. "I'll be coming with you, of course."

Xander's eyebrows shoot toward his hairline. "You absolutely will *not*."

"Just try to stop me."

Victoria glances at Xander and brushes two fingers softly along his jawline. "Better to bring her with you than for her to follow you there," she murmurs.

Xander considers her for a moment before nodding, turning his head to kiss her palm. I feel a sharp pang of shame watching them interact as though I'm not here; *We can't trust her,* their expressions seem to say. *We pity her. She needs someone to keep an eye on her.*

I pick up my phone and type a quick text to Nik.

A few seconds later, Xander's phone rings.

"Nik," he answers, frowning. "What—"

"You're meeting with Kaleb tonight and you didn't *tell me?*" Nik's deep voice blares through Xander's earpiece, his words as clear and sharp as if he were in the room with us. "What is wrong with you? Why do you refuse to tell me what's going on?"

Xander's gaze moves slowly to me, his eyes brimming with raw fury. I sneer at him and rise from the sectional, ignoring Victoria as she looks up at me sadly. She may have Xander wrapped around her finger, but her tactics don't work on me. I feel only a tiny twinge of guilt as I stalk toward the stairs, deliberately knocking a few pool cues from their case on the wall while Nik loudly chastises a stunned and murderous Xander.

I stand in the foyer for a few minutes, listening to the remainder of the conversation from a safe distance. It is loud and frustrated and peppered with a collection of curses that would have made my mother faint, and it ends with Xander begrudgingly accepting that Nik will be joining us at Kaleb's tonight.

I realize belatedly that texting Nik may have been a bad idea.

Xander storms up the stairs, glowering, and I prepare myself for verbal annihilation. But it doesn't come. He simply stares at me, assesses my current wardrobe, and says:

"Get dressed."

"What?"

"Did I stutter? I have a fledgling frat boy to deal with and you're coming with me."

I gape at him. "Not my job. Come find me when you're ready to talk to Kaleb."

Xander's jaw tenses and his eyes narrow furiously. "If you insist on joining me in my dealings with Kaleb, then I see no reason why you can't help me with this." He strides through the foyer and makes his way upstairs, pausing on the bottom step to look down his nose at me. "Now go make yourself presentable. Rose will be here in thirty minutes, and you look like death."

12

"For Kaleb."

The woman nods curtly.

She slips quietly through the tunnel, emerging into the smoky club with the note clutched in her manicured hand. Her stiletto heels carry her to the bar where the bartender pours a drink from a gold shaker into a cut-crystal glass. She slides the envelope across the bar top.

"For Kaleb," she says, and walks away.

The bartender winks and motions to a girl with bright tattoo sleeves. She carries a tray on her shoulder, balancing an army of drinks with practiced precision, and grins at the club's guests as she moves toward the bar.

"For the boss," the bartender says, and slips the note into the girl's hand.

She weaves back between tables and sofas, heading straight toward the boy with platinum hair where he lounges, grinning, between two humans. He looks up when he sees her, excuses himself, and stands.

"For Kaleb," the tattooed girl whispers, and hands the note to the boy in gray.

He offers a small salute then saunters through the club, through the back hallway, only stopping when the girl with one eye—the one guarding the carved double doors—insists on it. He hands her the note without explanation, then turns and disappears back into the haze.

The girl shoves the doors open, where Kaleb talks casually with a curly-haired young man. He pauses mid-sentence, and his lips press into a tight line.

"What is it, Catherine?"

Catherine crosses the room and drops the note on his desk. "For you."

She disappears through the door as Kaleb slices the envelope with a gold letter opener, not bothering to look back. Not seeing the haunted expression on Kaleb's face as the note's contents finally find their mark.

13

I'VE NEVER LIKED HYDE STREET Pier.

It may be a cultural landmark, or whatever, but I have never understood humanity's fascination with boats. They are nothing but weird-looking cars that drive on water instead of asphalt. Plus, the idea of being on a big ship in the middle of the ocean is my own personal idea of Hell. If Heaven had intended for humans to live on water, it would have given them webbed feet.

I do, however, love the sound of water lapping against the sides of the ships at night. There is something beautifully creepy about it, even if it feels like the dark water could reach over the edge of the pier and pull me down to the ocean floor with no witness but the omnipresent face of the silver moon.

Crisp wind whips over the pier, causing large waves to crash against the anchored boats with a surprising amount of force. I shudder.

There are two reasons we're here tonight. First, we needed a dark, deserted place to show the new kid his secret vampire super-powers. Second, there is still a rogue vampire on the loose and I know Xander is using this as an excuse to keep an eye out for him.

We wait in silence on a painted green bench near the Balclutha—the huge cargo ship docked permanently as part of the maritime museum—Rose sitting between Xander and I like a referee in a boxing match. I was annoyed to hear she would be coming—just what I need, two control freaks chastising me all evening—but I shouldn't have been surprised. Rose has more self-control than any of us, and if we're trying to teach discipline to a fledgling, it's only natural she would join.

It does make me wonder how often she accompanies Xander on his little moonlighting adventures. And how many times he has deliberately left me behind.

The faint sound of sneakers scuffling on pavement alerts me to Ty's approach. He emerges from the shadows, his hands shoved in the pockets of the same red jacket he wore last night. His expression is confident but his posture betrays his apprehension as we stand to greet him.

He moves into the light from a single orange street lamp and I get a good look at him for the first time. It was nearly impossible to see anything last night with the storm, not to mention the ragged road burn on Ty's face after I ground it into the asphalt.

Oops.

Ty stands wiry but strong, with ashy brown hair styled in short, ruffled waves. His nose is a little too wide for his face, but his carved cheekbones and full lips and sharp jawline more than make up for it. He narrows his eyes at Xander, and I notice a fringe of long, perfect lashes.

Oh, no. He's *hot*.

Xander steps forward. "Hello, Ty. Thanks for coming."

"Yeah, sure," Ty says. "Though it didn't really feel like I had a choice." He winks at me, then raises an eyebrow when he notices Rose hovering in the background. "You brought *help?*"

I smirk. "Rose is here to keep you in line."

"No offense, sweetheart," Ty laughs, turning to Rose, "but I'm pretty sure I could take someone like you in a fight."

Rose plasters on a wicked grin. "We'll see about that."

Xander glowers at Ty. "Don't pick fights with people you know nothing about. Rose could dismember you in a heartbeat."

Ty stares at him. "Am I being punked?"

"No," I snap. "We're here to teach you how *not* to be a menace to society. And we can't do that if you don't shut your mouth."

Xander stiffens next to me, and I flinch.

I know he doesn't want me here. I know that, in his mind, the "we" I'm referring to is him and Rose. I'm an ornament—here for no more than decoration and intimidation—and if I would shut *my* mouth, we could get on with it.

Besides, the fact that I'm here at all is more of a punishment than anything. I'm being *punished* for telling Nik about Kaleb, for insisting I be involved in their weird little rendezvous, for not wanting to be left out.

For worrying about what might happen to Xander if he were to meet with Kaleb alone.

"I'm not making any promises," Ty says. "So, who's in charge around here? I have to assume it's you, tall guy, since you seem to be the one giving orders."

"Actually, that would be Kaleb Sutton," Xander says, and Ty looks at him with curious eyes. "He is San Francisco's Alpha, and you don't want to piss him off. You're lucky we found you before he did."

"Why is that?"

"Because," Rose interjects, and Ty turns his steely gaze on her, "Kaleb isn't as nice as we are. If you know what's good for you, you'll do everything you can to avoid him."

Ty raises a mocking eyebrow. "It sounds like the vampire mafia or something."

"You're not far off," I say, keeping my tone as neutral and inoffensive as possible. Heaven forbid I say something off-kilter and make Xander *angry*. "Most Alphas are basically mob bosses, and Kaleb is no different. He has spies everywhere and a small army of loyal followers who will do whatever he asks."

Like stab someone in the heart.

"Best to avoid him, then. Got it." Ty's eyes flicker between the three of us. "If you're not in charge, then who are you?"

"My name is Xander Novik. This is my sister, Charlotte, and our friend, Rose. We've been vampires…well, for a little longer than you have."

"How long?"

"We were all born in the 1800s," I say. "We've been around the block more than a few times."

"Wow," Ty says wryly. "That makes you what, around two hundred years old? Keeping it tight, girl."

My mouth pops open in disgust. I know I should be annoyed by his unwelcome appraisal, but I'm not. I probably would be if he weren't so good-looking.

"You have a lot of nerve saying that after last night, when you were given irrevocable proof that I will beat you in a fight."

Rose coughs to cover a laugh.

"Yeah, thanks again for that," Ty says, his lip curling. "It took all night for my face to heal up. I was worried I might look like a monster for the rest of my life."

I grin at him. "Well, you *are* a monster, so is that really such a bad thing?"

Ty tenses and Xander eyes me reproachfully.

"What?" I ask. "I'm not wrong, am I? He's in good company."

"I apologize for my sister and her stunning lack of maturity," Xander says, glaring down at me. I glare back. "We didn't invite you here to insult you. First thing's first: what can you tell us about last night?"

Ty shifts his weight from one foot to the other. "It's like I said:

I was at the party, I smelled the blood, I found the body. Then I was attacked by She-Hulk, here."

"I like to think I'm more of a Wonder Woman," I say.

"And you don't remember anything else?" Xander asks. "You didn't hear anything or see anyone suspicious?"

"Now that you mention it, there may have been someone else back there." Ty's brow furrows beneath the wisps of ashy hair fluttering over his forehead. "But I can't be sure. I was a little distracted by, you know, the pool of blood."

Rose takes a step forward. "Close your eyes."

Ty considers her for a few long seconds before following her instructions.

"Now," Rose continues, "for your first lesson. As a vampire, you have the ability to recall memories in vivid detail; sights and sounds and smells you didn't notice the first time around. Returning to the scene of a memory can make the recollection stronger, but it isn't necessary unless you need something incredibly specific. Now focus. Think back to last night: to the party, the blood, the pier. What do you remember? *Really* focus."

Ty's eyebrows pinch together in concentration. "I see the docks. There are seven boats tied up. One is taller than the rest. It's called Madame Curie."

"Good," Rose says. "Keep going."

"A truck is parked behind the buildings. California license plate 4LVR762. It's backed up to a green door. Someone carved 'A+J' into one of the wooden posts at the dock. And...there's a man." Ty pauses. "It has to be a man. He's tall and muscular. Broad shoulders. But I can't see his face. He's wearing a black hood."

Rose and I share an uncomfortable glance. Kaleb's cold, blue eyes flash in my mind and I brush them away.

"He ran up the pier when I showed up," Ty continues. "He was fast—*insanely* fast—so he must have been a vampire."

"Perfect." Rose smiles at him as Ty opens his eyes.

He blinks a few times, then meets Rose's smile with a crooked grin of his own. "Cool."

"Cool?" I ask. "That's all you have to say about your newfound vampire superpowers? Cool?"

Ty shrugs, his grin stretching wider. "I've never been one to get overly excited about things. Though with a teacher like you, I might change my tune," he adds with a wink, his gray eyes flashing in the lamplight.

I swallow stiffly, and Rose mercifully steps in.

"Memory recall isn't the only thing you can do," she says. "You now have supersonic hearing, super speed, super strength, rapid healing, and, my personal favorite, the ability to Compel."

Ty looks at her inquisitively and a small smile plays at the corners of her lips.

"Compulsion alters the way a human thinks," Rose says. "It can be used to make someone remember an event differently or forget something altogether. You will also be able to get humans to do certain things or act a certain way. It requires a good amount of concentration—you really have to believe what you're telling them. If you don't believe it, they won't either."

"I can tell someone to do something and they'll do it?"

"Only humans," I say. "It doesn't work on vampires."

"So," he says, meeting my gaze, "if I said, 'Charlotte, snap your fingers,' you wouldn't do it?"

I roll my eyes. He may be obnoxious, but there's something in those gray eyes that tugs at me. I can't help but humor him. "Technically no, but" —I snap once— "there. A sneak peek of what Compulsion is like. Though it isn't quite that easy. You have to capture the human's attention and maintain eye contact until the Compulsion takes effect. Otherwise, it doesn't work."

"Interesting," he murmurs, smirking. "That will be fun to play with."

"No playing," Xander snaps. "Vampirism isn't a game, Ty. It's dangerous. It's a constant battle between your new nature and your sense of self-preservation. If you want to survive, you have to be careful. Everything is a matter of life and death, no matter how small."

"Geez, I bet you're fun at parties," Ty says acerbically, and Xander's lips harden to a tight line. "I get it. Survive, don't get caught, yada yada. But you guys have to have fun *sometimes,* right?" He looks at me. "At least *you* look like you know how to have fun."

"I'm probably the only one here who does," I smirk, and an idea forms in my head. "Wanna see?"

Without waiting for an answer, I turn and sprint toward the Balclutha. I clear the railing at the edge of the pier and leap into the air, soaring weightlessly for a few moments before landing in a crouch on the deck of the ship. I look back to see Ty grinning through his fangs.

Xander looks furious. I wonder if he regrets bringing me yet.

"Move, Lottie!" Rose calls, racing to follow me. She executes a beautiful pair of twists in the air and lands on the deck like a gymnast, both arms raised above her head.

"Show-off." I look down at Xander and Ty. "Come on, newbie! I'll give you a million bucks if you can clear the edge of the boat on your first try."

Ty raises his eyebrows and seems to mentally prepare himself before sprinting toward us with a startling amount of confidence. He flies through the air and slams hard onto the rail of the ship, his hands clawing at the wood before he manages to haul himself onto the deck where he collapses with a disgruntled grimace.

Rose and I break into laughter. Xander, on the other hand, is not amused.

"Bravo," I say, awarding him with a slow clap. "You might just make a passable vampire yet."

◊ ◊ ◊

We spend another hour with Ty, walking him through the dos and don'ts of being a vampire. We explain our abilities—Compulsion, speed, strength—what will hurt us—silver, hawthorn, hallowed ground—and what will kill us—a stake to the heart, holy water, sunlight, fire, decapitation. Ty listens intently, and takes each new piece of information in stride.

When the conversation winds down, Ty draws one hand over his mouth. "Honestly, I thought this was going to be much worse. But all I'm hearing from you guys is that I'm immortal and can do a bunch of cool things. It doesn't sound so bad, really."

"Being a vampire is about more than just what you can do," Xander says flatly. "It's a state of being. If you want to stay out of trouble, you have to be careful. Don't let humans see you, stay out of the sunlight, and try not to piss anyone off."

Ty's mouth quirks. "Then I should probably avoid you, shouldn't I? Because I definitely seem to be pissing you off."

"I'm not the one you have to worry about," Xander says. "Like it or not, there are vampires out there who would sooner kill you than give you a second chance."

"Like that Kaleb guy you mentioned?"

"Yes," I say, exchanging a nervous glance with Rose. "Like that Kaleb guy."

For a few shining moments, I had completely forgotten about my current nemesis. A chill crawls its way up my spine, as though he is spying from a distance.

Who's to say he isn't?

I suddenly find myself watching the shadows.

"The best way to avoid being caught by 'that Kaleb guy,'" Xander explains, snapping me back to attention, "is to learn to feed properly. Am I right in assuming things have been messy for you?"

133

Ty purses his lips but says nothing.

"Right," Xander says decisively. "We'll need to fix that. I guess you'll be coming to our place for dinner tomorrow night. Give Charlotte your number and she will text you the details."

"Done." Ty grins at me, his silver eyes flashing, and a tiny, fluttering pressure blooms beneath my ribs.

14

NEW YORK CITY, NEW YORK
SUMMER 1897

FROM OUR VANTAGE POINT ON *the roof of the Chelsea Hotel, it is easy to imagine that we are perched on one of the twin bell towers of Notre Dame, watching boats drifting lazily down the starlit Seine below us.*

Instead, steamboats putter by on the dark Hudson River, spewing black smoke into the air. I frown at the wan yellow moonlight glinting off the water and long for our days in Europe.

"Do you miss it?" I ask, taking a sip of wine. My heavy skirts are bunched around my thighs, showing a tempting amount of ankle and knee under my ivory stockings.

Rayna glances at me in confusion, tucking a long strand of amber hair back into her mussed chignon. Her skirt is also bunched around her thighs, but with the scandalous absence of stockings, her legs are ghostly pale in the moonlight.

"Miss what?"

"Paris," I say dreamily. "The art, the language, the architecture... New York is anemic in comparison."

Rayna scoffs. "Leave it to you to take the beauty out of New York, Charlotte," she teases, looking back out over the black water. "I appreciate the newness of this city. We can do whatever we want here. Fewer people, fewer rules." She ignores the glass of wine in her hand and instead takes a swig straight from the bottle. "I will miss it one day."

"Maybe Kaleb will let us stay here a while longer," I muse, leaning against Rayna's shoulder. "It has only been twelve years, after all. We have stayed in other cities much longer."

"Perhaps," Rayna says, nudging me playfully. "Then you might grow to love this city as I do."

We sit for a few minutes in silence, breathing in the smoke and grime of Manhattan.

Rayna perks up suddenly and turns to face me. "Suppose we were leaving New York tomorrow. How would you spend your last night in the city?"

Her question catches me off guard and I pause, searching for an answer.

"I'm not sure," I say finally. "Why? Has Kaleb said something to you?"

"Not at all," she replies, a wild glint in her eye. "I am simply feeling adventurous, and we are due for a little fun."

"Well, I suppose I might climb the Brooklyn Bridge, or swim the East River. I would like to try that new roller coaster on Long Island. And we still have not visited the Statue of Liberty."

"You would swim the East River?" Rayna asks, cocking an eyebrow. "That seems unlikely, given your irrational fear of the ocean."

"It is not irrational," I counter. "The ocean is heartless. She will swallow you whole if you don't respect her."

"Come, Lottie," she says. "Ladies' Night, just the two of us. We have only a few hours until sunrise, so we best be going."

I gape at her. "We can't do all those things in one night!"

"Is that a challenge?" Rayna grins wickedly.

"Perhaps it is," I grin back.

We end the night perched on the verdant copper torch of the Statue of Liberty, our dresses soaked, our laughter filling the open sky. We drink wine from the bottle and toast to our inescapable immortality as light leaks lazily onto the eastern horizon.

◊   ◊   ◊

By the time we return to Chelsea, our linen dresses have dried into crumpled heaps. The impending sunrise paints the treetops in soft gold, the leaves shivering in anticipation of the morning. Light bleeds slowly through the streets, waking its residents with the promise of a new day. I feel a slight twinge of fondness in my heart; perhaps I will miss this city after all.

"Thank you, Lottie," Rayna says as we approach her doorstep, "for an amazing night. It has been too long since we have enjoyed such things. I hate for it to end, but I have a very important date."

"You must tell Kaleb that he is not allowed to steal you away every *day.*"

"I could tell him that, but you know how needy he can be." Rayna smiles, and I know she is as excited to spend her days with Kaleb as he is with her. I have never seen a couple more in love.

Though Nikolas and I may be giving them a run for their money.

"Fine," I concede, "but Alexander expects you for dinner, and Nikolas will kill you both if you miss the fireworks."

"We will be there," she says brightly, then draws me into a hug. "Thank you again, my Lottie. Tonight was a marvelous adventure."

The familiar pressure of her arms around me is comforting. I never had a sister, but I have found one in Rayna; I don't know what I would do without her.

"I will see you tonight," I say, pulling away. "Sunset. Do not be late."

She winks. "Never."

◊   ◊   ◊

The crackling of flames is deafening.

I met Nikolas outside his Chelsea townhome, and we decided to surprise Kaleb and Rayna by walking with them uptown. When we arrived in Greenwich Village just after sunset, we were met not by the cozy, familiar facade of Kaleb's apartment building, but by a choking cloud of gray. A small crowd of concerned passersby has already gathered; Kaleb stands stoically in their midst, his charcoal suit coat blending seamlessly with the billowing smoke, his fingers methodically fiddling with its buttons.

"Kaleb!" I cry, running to him. "What happened?"

"There is a fire," he says simply, keeping his gaze fixed on the burning building. His building. Despite the heat of the flames and the stifling warmth of the summer evening, his words send a chill through me.

Nikolas appears at my side, the flames illuminating the red in his hair. "Where is Rayna?"

Kaleb says nothing, but the muscles in his jaw tense perceptibly. My stomach drops.

"Kaleb?" Nikolas says, his voice rising in panic. "Where is my sister?" When Kaleb does not respond, Nikolas turns a stricken gaze toward the building and terror transforms his features. "Rayna!"

He lunges forward but I catch him by the arm, and just in time: a large portion of the building crumbles away and falls, burning and crackling, to the ground at our feet. There are a few scattered cries as onlookers dive out of the way. Nikolas stands, horrorstruck, allowing the debris to shower him with embers before he collapses to his knees.

"Kaleb," I start, but I can't seem to find the words. "How— Rayna—what happened? Tell me she was not inside. Please. If you cannot tell me anything else, at least tell me that."

Kaleb finally tears his eyes away from the wreckage of his once-home, fixing me with a glacier-blue gaze as hard as diamonds. He continues to button and unbutton his coat.

"I cannot tell you that," he says, "because it is not true."

"Kaleb," *I whimper, but my tone does nothing to soften the severity in his eyes.* "Maybe she got out. Rayna is resourceful. What if she—"

"She was inside, Charlotte," Kaleb says coolly. "I am sure of it."

"You—she was—what?" I stammer.

"You heard me correctly, my darling," he says, his hands falling to his sides. "Rayna is dead. And I am the one to blame."

I stand, numb, holding Nikolas's trembling shoulder as Kaleb turns his back on us, striding purposefully down the street and into the unforgiving dark.

A guttural scream tears from Nikolas, cutting through the burning night as he watches his world go up in flames.

15

I SHOULD HAVE KNOWN KALEB would live in the stereotypical secret lair of a supervillain.

For a good part of the twentieth century, the Sutro Baths sat on the San Francisco coast, just south of the Golden Gate Bridge. It used to be a huge, glass-enclosed public pool fed by the ocean's tide, but after it burned down in the 1960s, it descended into ruin. All that remains are the stone foundations that still capture water and the crumbling facades of a few long-forgotten outbuildings. The old pool sits nestled below the main road, devoid of any plant life except for the sparse grasses and algae that grow at the water's edge. It has become quite the tourist attraction and people can be found wandering the area at all times of the year.

Nik and I follow Xander down a steep dirt trail leading from the road to the Baths. Xander's disapproval at our presence is palpable, but at least he actually allowed us to come with him. I draw a small amount of comfort from the fact that he won't be going into the belly of the beast alone.

If tonight accomplishes nothing else, at least I will be able to yell at Kaleb for sending someone to stab me.

The night is surprisingly clear despite yet another storm brewing on the horizon, the enclosed cove sheltering us from the relentless wind. A building down the coast glows with a collection of bright orange street lamps, casting a fiery reflection on the surface of the abandoned pool.

"Is this really where Kaleb lives?" I whisper loudly, picking my way past a pile of crumbling rocks. "I feel like we're approaching the lair of a James Bond villain."

"Yes," Xander hisses, following the curve of the stone cliffside. "Now hush."

On one side of the ruined Baths is an open-ended tunnel cut through a stone outcropping. Water floods it when the tide is high, but now, at low tide, it is empty except for a foamy layer of wet sand. The air is humid and surprisingly warm in the tunnel, the mixed scent of salty seaweed and mildew overwhelming.

There are a few local legends about this tunnel: that it is haunted by some kind of demonic beast, or that it is frequented by strange blood cults. The rumors aren't surprising; something about being here in the dead of night is disconcerting. The darkness of the tunnel seems to permeate the air, seeping into my skin and raising the hair on my arms.

Xander stops halfway through the tunnel and turns to face the wall, pressing two fingers to a crevice in the weathered stone. After a minute or so of silence, there's a loud *click* and a door-sized portion of the wall swings inward. A bronze-skinned woman stands just inside the opening, looking very *femme fatale* in a black cocktail dress and stiletto heels.

"Novik." She nods at him, then turns condescending eyes on me and Nik. "Who are they?" she asks in a sharp South American accent.

"Yara," Xander says acidly. "This is Nik, and my sister, Charlotte. Kaleb won't mind."

Yara's eyes sweep down to my feet and back up. She must decide I'm not a threat because she turns abruptly and disappears inside.

"Come."

Yara leads us a few steps into an old-fashioned elevator closed off by an antique gold gate, which groans loudly when she opens it. The lift inside is paneled with mold-dampened wood and a single flickering bulb on the ceiling creates a horror-movie vibe.

"I think Kaleb needs to find a new decorator," I mumble.

Yara glares daggers at me. "It's not often that we have non-member visitors, so this elevator doesn't see much use," she says. "Apologies for not rolling out the red carpet."

This elevator? Kaleb has more than one elevator? I open my mouth to fire back a retort, but one glance from Xander and I close it again. We are in enemy territory, after all. The last thing we want to do is start a war.

The elevator lurches upward, and we ascend into the rocky cliff-side. I am sandwiched between Nik and Yara, who studiously ignores us until we shudder to a halt. She wrenches open the gate and leads us through a sequence of doors, each opening into a small vestibule more ornate than the last. Hallways branch from each one, disappearing around dark corners, and I can barely contain my curiosity. *What is Kaleb hiding under here?*

By the time we reach a pair of huge, gilded doors, we're standing in a small room with marble floors and damask walls, golden light glowing from antique sconces. An elevator door—newer and more elegant than the one we used—is cut into the wall between two bookcases, each weighed down by huge encyclopedia sets.

"Would it have been so terrible to let us use that elevator?" I ask.

Yara glowers. "That one is for members only. Last I checked, none of you" —she looks pointedly at Xander— "are on the list."

With one more withering glare, she unlocks the doors with a large brass key and escapes into the room beyond.

My jaw hits the floor. Now, this. *This* is a secret lair.

We emerge into the most lavish, ridiculously over-the-top club

I have ever seen. The room is large and dim, the air smelling of cologne, alcohol, and cigar smoke. Dark, polished wood spans the floor, hidden partially by Oriental rugs and clusters of velvet-covered furniture in shades of emerald and gold. Wood paneling adorns the walls and is broken up by large oil paintings in gilded frames depicting battles and men in uniform and women in sweeping dresses of silk and lace. There is a massive stone fireplace on one wall and a bar on another, behind which is a glass display with hundreds of old-looking bottles of alcohol. Light from the three gilded chandeliers glints off the bottles and casts a golden glow through clouds of smoke. A crystal glass on the edge of the bar is etched with three words in elegant script: *The Caged Bird.*

Despite its obvious elegance, something about this room feels... *off*. It isn't until I notice Xander's disgusted expression that I recognize the scent of human blood mingling with the haze of intoxication. Somehow, the room's grandeur managed to distract me from noticing the people in it. Or what they were doing.

Small groups of vampires lounge on the furniture, all in beautiful suits and dresses, looking like the members of an undead mafia. Next to each vampire is a human, each wearing the same blank expression of long-time Compulsion.

I watch as a platinum-haired vampire with sharp cheekbones sinks his teeth into the neck of a petite brunette girl, her head lolling to the side as her hooded eyes meet mine. She grins, leaning into his touch, and a horrifying realization hits me.

This is a subjugate club.

"Oh, *gross,*" I mumble, averting my eyes.

The vampire community has a long history of subjugacy: the practice of keeping one or a few specific humans on hand as personal blood bags. Alphas and Betas used them as a status symbol for a while in the mid-1800s, and some vampires decided it would be a good idea to open what we called "subjugate clubs," where vampires without their own subjugates could still enjoy the benefits of an easy, familiar food supply.

The idea lost popularity after a few decades, but some vampires have kept the tradition going.

Apparently, one of them is Kaleb.

A few of the vampires eye us dangerously, their smiles challenging, as if daring us to intervene. The platinum-haired vampire licks blood from his lips and grins at me before digging back into the brunette's neck.

Yara is halfway through the room before she notices we're not following. "Hey," she barks. "Kaleb is a busy man. You're wasting his time standing there like slack-jawed imbeciles."

Xander glares at her but catches up in a few long strides.

Yara leads us through the room and past the huge bar, where a brown-skinned vamp with short, coiled hair expertly mixes a cocktail in a gold shaker. There is something almost familiar about him.

His eyes widen when he sees Nik, and he offers him a hesitant smile.

I turn to Nik, expecting a demonstration of his classic flirtation techniques, but he's rigid, deliberately ignoring the smiling bartender. The muscles in his jaw are strained, his lips pursed.

"Nik," I ask, touching his arm. "Are you okay?"

"Hmm?" His head snaps in my direction. The anxious look leaves his eyes and is replaced instantly with his usual nonchalance. "Yeah. I'm just not looking forward to seeing Kaleb. Again."

"Tell me about it," I mutter, linking my arm with his. "If you feel the desire to, say, punch Kaleb in the throat, you know I won't stop you. In fact, I may do that myself."

Nik's mouth quirks into a sly smile. "I'll keep that in mind."

Yara continues past the last group of chairs—a waitress with colorful tattoos and soft blue hair eyes us suspiciously—and down a long hallway, where we're met by a pair of huge, walnut double doors. A frowning blonde girl stands in front of them, her strong arms folded across her chest, her hair plaited into two tight braids. It takes all my willpower not to stare at the gnarled scar cutting from the middle of her eyebrow down to her jaw. Her right eye is white and unseeing, and when she looks at me, I find myself shrinking away.

"Alexander," she says in a deep British accent. She and Yara could compete for the coldest greeting.

"Catherine." Xander inclines his head and matches the girl's challenging glare. I'm almost sure I hear a touch of mockery in his voice.

"It's Cate," she says flatly, though her posture is nothing short of hostile.

Yara groans. "Cate, get out of the way," she says with a flick of her hand and Cate obliges, allowing Yara to push the doors open with a flourish.

Kaleb's office is surprisingly large, with emerald carpet and a golden chandelier, and it is completely lined with dark bookshelves. I can't say I'm surprised: he was always a bit of a nerd, and he had a penchant for collecting interesting things. The shelves boast an impressive collection of books that range from brand new textbooks to centuries-old leather first editions, and interspersed with the books are an assortment of strange-looking objects: a black urn, a crystal skull, an Egyptian figurine, a bronze tiger with sapphire eyes. The furniture includes only a collection of rose-colored lounge chairs, a coffee table, and a massive, mahogany desk.

A handsome teenage-looking vampire with a mess of brown curls and too-long legs is perched on the edge of the desk, dressed impeccably in a gray waistcoat with matching slacks and burgundy cap-toe shoes. He is talking intently with a distressed Kaleb, who sits in an oversized desk chair, a smoldering cigarette pinched between his fingers. Their conversation stops abruptly when we enter, a scowl transforming Kaleb's expression as he notices me, then Nik. The younger vampire, on the other hand, lights up.

"Xander!" he calls in a smooth London accent, crossing the room in a few strides. "I was hoping you'd show up before I left for the evening." His eyes flicker to me. "And Charlotte! How long has it been? A few decades or so?"

I offer an uncomfortable smile. "Hey, Henry. More like a century."

When he grins, his fangs extend over his bottom lip. I shudder.

Back in London, Boheme—Kaleb's club—was the talk of the town. He, Xander, and Nik spent most of their time there, and I know it was a frequent haunt of most male vampires in the United Kingdom. The only one I ever met was Henry Albright, who often caught me and Rayna trying to sneak into the "No Girls Allowed" club through a poorly-guarded back window. It was his job to inform Kaleb of any trespassers, but Rayna being the boss' girlfriend had its perks. She always managed to convince Henry not to turn us over, and we usually got a free bottle of booze out of it. He seemed so sweet, like an enthusiastic puppy dog.

According to Xander, Henry replaced Nik as Kaleb's second-in-command—his Beta, I suppose—after Rayna's death. I'm not really sure what to think of him now.

He stiffens when he notices Nik staring at him.

"Nikolas," he says. "I suppose I'll leave you to it." An awkward beat passes before he brushes past us and through the double doors, but not before winking and flashing another huge, fanged grin. His footsteps fade and the room descends into a tense silence.

Kaleb clears his throat and flicks his hand in Yara's direction, effectively shooing her out of the room. She glares at him before slipping back into the hallway, closing the doors behind her.

"Hello, old friends," Kaleb says brusquely, inhaling once more on his cigarette before smothering it in a crystal ashtray. He stands and smooths his hands down the front of his navy, velvet blazer, the topaz ring winking from his finger as he methodically fiddles with his buttons. The emerald at his neck glints like a third eye. He crosses to the fireplace and settles into one of the lounge chairs. "Shall we?" he says, smoke swirling from his lips.

Xander sits in the chair next to Kaleb's, looking altogether too comfortable as he kicks one heel onto the opposite knee, his black skinny jeans and sweater standing out sharply against the pale pink upholstery. Nik perches on the edge of his chair, looking crisp in dark jeans and a denim jacket. He takes a quick swig from the flask in his pocket before resting his elbows on his knees. I take the chair next to him.

Kaleb regards us carefully, looking at each of the boys in turn before his cool gaze lands on me. I stare back at him, fuming, before he turns his attention to Xander.

"Alexander," Kaleb begins, motioning to me and Nik, "I was under the impression that this would be a private meeting. Surely we could have done without an audience."

"They have their reasons for being here," Xander counters, fixing Kaleb with a glare that could melt glass.

Kaleb frowns for a moment, then shifts deeper into his chair. "Very well, then. There's no sense in beating around the bush," he says, clapping his hands together. "What is going on in my city?"

The British lilt to his voice seems especially pompous tonight. Can I punch him yet?

"What's *happening* is that you stabbed me in the heart," I growl, and three heads swivel toward me in surprise. Kaleb's eyes alight with confusion while Xander is, as usual, furious.

This was not my plan.

"What I mean is, you had one of your *cronies* stab me. With a silver dagger. Did you have to make your point in such a violent way?"

"Charlotte," Xander hisses, his eyes flashing.

"What? That's why we're here, isn't it? To figure out what the hell Kaleb has been doing the past few days? Am I just supposed to sit here and pretend like he didn't order someone to put a hole through my chest, not to mention my favorite Aerosmith t-shirt?"

"Lottie." Nik's voice is soft but strong. "Xander's right. Not now." I can hear the strain in his voice. Whether from fear or anger, it's hard to tell.

I stare at him for a few long seconds before fixing my gaze on Kaleb again. His face is the picture of ambiguity, but the muscles in his neck are tight.

"You're being surprisingly quiet," I bark. "What do you have to say for yourself?"

"I'm sure I don't know what you mean, dear Charlotte." Kaleb's head cocks to the side. "You were stabbed?"

"Yes," Xander cuts in, eyeing me dubiously. "A few nights ago in the suburbs. A vamp in a black hood got her with a silver dagger and told her that you sent him."

Kaleb's eyes narrow. "That is...concerning."

"What is?" I ask snidely. "That your crony has no tact? Or that you got caught in your own web?"

Kaleb's eyes flicker to Xander, then back to me. Studying me. If it were anyone else, I would say he was surprised by my accusation. But I know better.

Kaleb is the best liar on the planet.

"Lottie, you must know that wasn't me. I would never send someone to put a dagger in your heart. It's barbaric."

"First of all, you lost your nickname privileges a century ago," I snarl. "And second of all, since when has an action's barbaric nature ever stopped you?"

"Charlotte." Kaleb's voice might as well be a razor for how sharply it cuts through the smoky tension. "I know you love to blame your misfortunes on me. However, I can assure you that if you *were* stabbed by someone, it was because of your gross ineptitude and extreme disregard for your own safety or the safety of our family. It is not my fault that you're an absolute, bloody disaster."

His words shatter what little discipline I have. I leap from my chair, my skin on fire and my throat crackling with rage. "*Our* family? You disgusting son of a—"

Nik clamps an anxious hand around my wrist and I whirl on him. "Don't," he murmurs. The muscles in his shoulders are straining with the effort of staying still. I'm suddenly worried that he might do something stupid.

"Nik, you *know* it was him—"

"Enough," Xander snaps. "Stop hurling accusations or you're gone, Charlotte."

I tear my eyes from Nik's worried expression to glare at Xander, who stares at me with a loathsome amount of parental chastisement. I sink back into my chair.

"And Kaleb," Xander says through a murderous smile, "if you ever speak that way to my sister again, I will rip your heart out through your throat. Got it?"

Kaleb has the decency to look apologetic, but somehow maintains his air of arrogance. "My apologies, Charlotte, Alexander. And Nikolas," he adds reluctantly. "I have been under a fair amount of stress over the past few days, what with the recent murders making headlines. Do pardon my lapse in poise."

"Why are you stressed about the murders?" I ask, thinking of the vampire who stabbed me and the identical culprit Ty saw at the pier. "You're the one committing them!"

Kaleb scoffs. "Good Lord. Is that why you're here? Do you think *I* am the one responsible? You all must be dafter than I remember."

"We don't think you're murdering anyone, Kaleb," Xander interjects, glowering at me.

"Speak for yourself," I grumble, and Nik nods in agreement.

"Besides," Xander continues, "we know who was responsible for the first murder. The one at the coffee shop."

Kaleb leans forward, his interest clearly piqued. "Who?"

Xander's eyes roll deliberately toward me.

Kaleb exhales slowly and pinches the bridge of his nose. "Please tell me you're joking."

I shrug, though I feel no remorse as Kaleb visibly struggles to maintain composure. "It's not like you didn't know that already."

"What about my reaction gives you that impression, Charlotte?"

"Why else would you have sent someone to stab me?"

"Enough about the stabbing." Xander's voice slices between us like a blade. "We've already established that Kaleb was not responsible. Our purpose here is not to lay blame, but to find out who has been killing people. And maybe *then* we'll figure out who stabbed you, *repa*. Can the two of you manage to be civil for a few minutes?"

Kaleb's cold eyes are wide as he regards Xander and, for the first time since we arrived, I feel a prickle of old fear in my chest. Kaleb has never taken well to being told what to do, and I imagine it has only gotten worse in the last century. I will say this about Xander: he has guts.

A log pops in the fireplace, throwing ash onto the parqueted hearth. We sit quietly for a minute or so, Nik worrying at the cuff of his jacket. I reach over and rest a hand on his arm; I may be angry with Kaleb, but nothing compares to what Nik must be feeling. He has barely looked at Kaleb since we sat down.

"If Charlotte was behind the first murder," Kaleb muses quietly, toying with the ring on his finger, "then this makes my theory all the more worrisome."

"What theory?" Xander asks.

Kaleb sighs and rubs his temples, looking at each of us in turn before replying.

"My theory about Konstantin," he says hesitantly, and my blood turns to ice.

16

RAYNA ONCE TOLD ME ABOUT the first time she met Kaleb.

It was Prague—sometime in the 1730s—not long after she and Nik lost their parents. They were young—no more than sixteen at the time—and were shopping for food at a small market with the meager amount of money they had. While Nik perused a cart of fresh vegetables, Rayna was distracted by a pair of young men who were dressed impeccably in breeches and tailored silk coats, staring at her with two sets of bright, pale eyes.

One of them was Kaleb.

The other was Konstantin.

Everything changed for the Vesely twins that day. And I wish I could say it was for the better.

Kaleb watches the three of us carefully, the old name falling from his lips with a calm reverence. But no, not reverence. Submission. Fear.

Konstantin.

Nik stiffens in his chair, his usual dull heat doused by the cold bolt of terror that transforms his expression. While he has never given me specifics about his relationship with Konstantin, I've spent enough time with him to know that something happened between the two of them. Something dark and painful and completely off-limits. I tighten my grip on his arm.

"Please," Nik says quietly, lifting his gaze to meet Kaleb's for the first time. "Please don't joke about that, Kaleb."

Kaleb's eyes soften, just a little. "I wish it were that simple, Nikolas."

The two boys hold tense eye contact for a few moments before reluctant understanding flickers between them. Though Xander and I never met Konstantin, Nik and Kaleb knew him well. And, from what I've been told, he wasn't exactly a ray of sunshine.

In fact, he seemed more like a harbinger of death.

Nik frowns and reaches for his flask, taking a quick swig before pocketing it again. "What makes you think Konstantin is involved?" he asks. "He's been quiet since before we moved to Paris."

Kaleb's jaw tenses. "About that," he says, gazing into the fire while he adjusts the buttons on his cuff once, twice, three times. "I may have omitted a few details regarding our reasons for leaving Paris. And London, for that matter."

We gape at him, and I connect the dots slowly.

"Konstantin found you in Paris? *And* London?" I ask. Kaleb's expression is unreadable. "You said he was gone. That he wasn't a threat to you. *Rayna* said—"

"Rayna said a lot of things," Kaleb interrupts, and I grimace at the way his lips caress her name, as though he actually cared for her. "That doesn't mean they were true."

He stands and begins pacing, buttoning his blazer mechanically. "Rayna and I may not have spoken as freely to you as we should have," he continues, "about Konstantin's presence in Europe. Since the moment Rayna left him, he never stopped looking for her. Or for me." He swallows, something distant sparking in his eyes. "We thought we were safe in Paris, but we stayed there too long...and he caught up."

Xander plants both feet firmly on the floor, watching Kaleb

intently. "Why do you think he has anything to do with the murders?"

"Because," —Kaleb stops pacing, leveling his gaze on Nik— "I received a message from him earlier this evening."

Nik covers his mouth with one hand. I can feel him shaking.

"Good hell," I breathe. "How many bombs are you going to drop on us tonight, Kaleb?"

"What did it say?" Nik asks tensely. He sits with his shoulders curled forward and, despite his size, he looks small. "How do you know it was from him?"

"It simply said, 'I found you.'" Kaleb frowns, running a hand through his hair. "It is the same message Rayna received in New York before—"

Kaleb catches himself, but he has already said too much.

Nik stares at Kaleb, his eyes narrowing sharply. "Konstantin knew we were in New York?" he asks, his tone betraying his confusion. "You told us we were safe there. Why didn't we leave—" Something flashes in Nik's expression. "But *you* left, didn't you, Kaleb?"

Nik stands slowly, his hackles rising, heat devouring the fear on his face as his eyes turn molten. When he draws himself to his full height, even I feel the urge to shrink away, the combination of his breadth and the fanged snarl on his lips a menacing reminder of the monster hiding just under the surface. If I didn't know him, I would be terrified. And with good reason.

Kaleb doesn't look *terrified,* per se, but he has frozen in place, one hand on the back of his chair. Xander, on the other hand, seems unruffled, though there is a tension in his body that suggests he may launch himself into action at any moment.

"Do you mean to tell me," Nik hisses, "that Konstantin found us in New York, and instead of doing the decent thing and, I don't know, *telling us about it,* you *killed my sister* then ran off to save your own skin?"

I blink a few times as Nik's words hit home. If what he is saying

153

is true, then Kaleb was never the backstabbing traitor that I thought he was.

He was a *coward*.

A backstabbing, traitorous coward, but a coward nonetheless.

Kaleb watches Nik cautiously, shifting so that the coffee table stands between them. There is a sudden wariness in his eyes, and I can't blame him for it; Nik is much bigger than Kaleb. If it came to a fight, Nik would annihilate him.

I'd love to see him do it.

"Is that what I'm hearing from you, Kaleb?" Nik growls. Shadows darken the hollows beneath his eyes to a threatening shade of deep plum, his fangs flashing behind his upper lip. "Was Rayna slowing you down? Did you get sick of her? Did you think it would be easier to get away without the *dead weight?*"

Over the years, I've learned to differentiate between Nik's emotions, seeing as most of them are hard to distinguish from one another. He usually hovers somewhere between drunken apathy and existential dread, but sometimes his old confidence will shine through, usually when he is worried or excited or angry.

But what I see now is more than anger. It is an emotion I have seen only once before, on the night Rayna was burned alive. On the night his world turned upside down.

Nik stalks toward Kaleb with the coiled animosity of pure, unbridled fury.

It's the most emotion I've seen from him in decades. It may be terrifying, but at least it's *something*.

Xander shifts to the front of his seat while Kaleb retreats a step backward, his gaze full of warning and glued to Nik's face. His eyes flicker, for only a moment, to the coin around Nik's neck.

He frowns, holding up a staying hand. "Nikolas, I—"

"No," Nik snarls, the sound tearing from him like thunder. The room shudders. "I don't want to hear it. You are a *coward,* Kaleb

Sutton. You never cared about Rayna. You never cared about *any* of us. The only person you have ever cared about is yourself, and I'm done letting you get away with it."

Nik leaps forward and slams into an unsuspecting Kaleb. The two boys careen into Kaleb's empty chair, flipping head over heel and landing clumsily in a snarling heap.

"Nik," I gasp, bolting across the room as he lands a powerful punch to Kaleb's jaw.

Earlier, the idea of Nik punching Kaleb filled me with excitement. But seeing it play out in front of me fills me with something else entirely: *dread.*

I dig my hands into Nik's arm and try to pull him away, but I might as well be a kitten trying to tame a raging tiger. Kaleb lies flat on his back, his hands clasping at the front of Nik's jacket to keep him at bay, but he doesn't seem to be fighting. He looks stubbornly upward as Nik lands another punch, this one straight into his nose. There is a sickening *crack* and Kaleb winces, letting out a low groan as blood gushes onto his face.

"That's enough!" Xander roars, grabbing Nik by his hair and throwing him off Kaleb. "We're not here to settle old scores. We are not impulsive children!"

Nik stumbles to his feet, hunched over and eerily still, his gaze distant and his hands clenched into fists at his sides. Kaleb props himself onto his elbows, blood dripping heavily from his broken nose and coating his lips and chin in red. Purplish bruises bloom around his eyes and over his cheekbones. He glares at Nik with a surprising amount of defiance considering the fact that he just got his ass handed to him.

"You got blood on my blazer, Nikolas," Kaleb says coldly, hoisting himself to his feet. "It was new."

"No one cares about your stupid blazer, Kaleb," I snap, then, "Are you alright?"

Kaleb and Xander look at me with twin expressions of bewilderment. When my brain finally catches up to my mouth, I feel a little bewildered myself.

"Not that I care," I add hastily, folding my arms.

Xander rolls his eyes. "Kaleb," he says with thinly-veiled exasperation. "Since he won't, I'll apologize for Nik's outburst. Though, to be fair, it was completely warranted."

Nik's eyes flicker to Xander and linger there for a few moments before dropping to the ground.

Kaleb raises a wry eyebrow, but we don't get his thoughts on the matter. After setting his broken nose back into place with a disgusting crunching sound, he pulls a handkerchief from his pocket and attempts to staunch the blood still dripping down his face.

"As I was saying," he muses, as though the last few minutes never happened, "there may be a chance that these murders have something to do with Konstantin. Though how it relates at all to Charlotte being stabbed, I don't know."

"Could Konstantin have been the one who stabbed her?" Xander asks.

"We can't be sure," Kaleb says thoughtfully. "All we can do is be cautious and keep our eyes open. That being said, I think it would be best for the three of you to leave. I've had enough of you for one night, and I need to speak to my cleaner about removing blood from velvet."

I scoff. "Like you've never cleaned blood from your clothes before."

"*Charlotte.*" Xander grabs me by the arm. "Kaleb is right. It's time to go."

He drags me toward the door and Nik follows numbly.

"Do let me know if you learn anything else," Kaleb calls after us. "I would like to prevent this issue from getting out of hand."

Xander pauses in the open doorway—the hallway is empty, and

I wonder absently where Cate and Yara have disappeared to—and glances back over his shoulder.

"It's already out of hand, Kaleb," he says dryly. "If you had any leadership skills at all, it would never have been a problem in the first place. Yet here we are."

The blood on Kaleb's chin shines in the dimness and his icy eyes widen. A myriad of emotions passes over his face—anger, defiance, shock—before the door closes behind us, awarding Xander the satisfying last word.

17

NIK IS BROODING, WHICH DOESN'T surprise me. He sulks behind Xander as we make our way up the sidewalk leading to the house. A splatter of Kaleb's blood colors the knuckles of his right hand.

I should be happy right now. In fact, I should be *elated*. I've waited over a century to see Kaleb receive a touch of comeuppance. But there are two things keeping my excitement at bay, and I'm not sure which is worse: the fact that I actually defended Kaleb tonight, or the idea of Konstantin in San Francisco.

I haven't thought much about Konstantin for at least a decade, maybe more. It's not like I knew him personally, or anything. Rayna spoke about him in the past tense, like he was a threat that no longer existed, so I learned to think of him as nothing but a scary story. All I needed to know was that Kaleb, Rayna, and Nik parted ways with him shortly before they found us, and that was that.

Apparently, there was a little more to it.

It isn't until we walk through the front door that Xander acknowledges either me or Nik. We follow him inside, at which point Xander turns heel and slaps Nik hard across the face.

"*Jaki čort,* Alexander!" I gasp as Nik stumbles backward. His mouth drops open in surprise and he glares at Xander, fury igniting the fire in his eyes.

"Yeah, Xander," Nik roars. His bottom lip is split, staining his teeth bright red. *"What the hell?"*

"You're an *idiot*," Xander snarls, "and I'm tired of walking on eggshells around you. I know you're mad at Kaleb—we *all* are—but that is no excuse for your behavior tonight. Even Charlotte managed to keep her cool, and you know how rare that is."

"Thanks for that," I mutter.

"Shut up, Charlotte," Xander snaps, then turns back to Nik. "This is exactly why I didn't want to involve you. I knew it would end in disaster. As usual, my instincts were right."

"Xander—" I start, but he silences me with a sharp glare.

The confidence drains from Nik like heat from a doused flame. "I didn't think—"

"No, you didn't," Xander says icily. "I have always thought my life would have been better if you had taken over when Kaleb left us, but after what I saw tonight, I think we're best where we are."

Nik frowns. "I just—"

"I don't want your excuses." Xander's eyes are shadowed. "You've proven once again that you can't be trusted. You're a drunken fool with no inhibitions and even less self-control." Nik looks like he's been slapped again. "Let's pray that Kaleb has any sense of decency and doesn't tell anyone about your little outburst. I hoped he might be grateful for our—for *your*—help, but at this point, we'll be lucky if he allows you around him again at all."

Nik rubs his cheek absently, the anger in his eyes dimming as Xander's words hit their mark. I have a strong urge to scream at my brother, but in the last half hour, he has managed to verbally obliterate both Kaleb and Nik, which means I should probably keep my mouth shut.

"Alexander." Victoria appears at the top of the stairs in a blush, velvet tracksuit, her dark hair cascading over her shoulders. After spending the last hour in a dim, smoke-filled gentlemen's club, her presence is angelic. She descends the stairs quickly and places a light hand on Xander's arm. "Go cool off. It sounds like your night has been stressful enough. There's no need to add insult to injury."

Xander stares at her, his wheels turning, before shooting Nik one more withering glare and stalking off toward his studio.

I exhale in relief. There is only one person on Earth who can order Xander around like that and keep their head, and her name is Victoria Song.

After a few moments of uncomfortable silence, Victoria sighs loudly. "Well," she says, clapping her hands together, "the sun will be up soon and I was just heading downstairs to watch a movie. Charlotte, would you like to join me? You're welcome too, Nik." She glances at his blood-spattered clothes and grimaces. "After you've cleaned yourself up, of course. You can shower upstairs if you'd like."

Nik looks down and frowns at the large drops of Kaleb's blood decorating the front of his baseball tee and denim jacket.

"Thanks, V," Nik says quietly, "but I think I'll just head home." He darts quickly out the door without looking back.

Concern crackles through me. I may be exhausted—my mind reeling after everything that happened tonight, from Ty to Konstantin to Kaleb and Xander's judgmental emerald eyes—but where Nik's heart is involved, I will always find the strength to help him.

I made him a promise a long time ago, and I'm not about to break it now.

"Nik!" I call, bolting after him.

He is halfway down the front walk by the time I catch him. The first touch of dawn kisses the eastern sky with just enough light to illuminate Nik's hair, his shoes, the tight set of his shoulders.

"Nik," I say again, worried that if I speak too loudly, he may startle. "Are you okay?"

Nik turns slowly to face me, the last glimpse of Xander's

handprint fading from his cheek. The cut on his lip has closed but a dark spot of blood still remains, dripping sluggishly down his chin. I reach to wipe it away and his lip quivers.

I look up at him and see that, though his eyes are narrowed in defiance, they are shining.

"Nik," I whisper, wrapping my arms around his chest. He returns the gesture readily.

"When will it stop, Lottie?" Nik breathes, his voice shaking. He buries his face in my hair. "Every time I think I've moved past this... will I ever stop hating him? Will I ever be able to forgive Kaleb for taking my sister from me?"

"I don't know, *darahi*," I say, "but if it makes you feel any better, I hate him too."

"He was my best friend. My *brother*. He was Rayna's..." He trails off, sagging against me, and I mentally finish his thought: *He was Rayna's one love. Her life. Her everything.* "And then he mentions *Konstantin*. If he's right—if Konstantin is in San Francisco—we're in a lot of trouble. And I mean, a *lot* of trouble." He takes a shuddering breath. "It's all so much. I don't know if I can do this anymore."

Alarms sound in my head and I pull myself free, taking Nik's face firmly in both hands. One cheek is still warm where Xander slapped him. He leans into my touch, a deep crease forming between his eyebrows.

"Nikolas. We both agree that Kaleb is the lowest form of scum. Rayna didn't deserve what he did to her, and you have every right to be angry with him. And you know what? I don't believe a single thing he said tonight. Don't worry about Konstantin. It's just Kaleb trying to pin the blame on someone who can't defend himself." Nik's mouth quirks subtly and a bit of my anxiety subsides. "I'm glad you punched him in the face. Maybe it will knock him down a peg or two."

Nik smiles softly but his eyes still shimmer with familiar anguish.

"One day Kaleb will stop surprising us," I continue, "but until then, we have to be strong." I emphasize each word carefully. "Rayna would want us to be strong."

I touch the coin resting at the base of Nik's throat over a thick, pearlescent scar. The silver instantly burns my fingers but I endure it for a few painful moments. When Rayna was alive, she wore an identical pendant at Nik's request: a constant reminder that, though they were immortal, they were not invulnerable.

Rayna wasn't wearing hers when she died. Maybe if she were, she would have remembered. Maybe she would still be here.

Nik nods, covering my hand with his own. "Okay, *darahi*. For Rayna."

I remove my fingers from the silver coin, relieved that they are no longer burning.

Nik hesitates for a beat, then wraps me in another tight hug. A wave of exhaustion sweeps over me and I breathe into him, releasing all the anxiety and tension that has been building for the past few days. Nik's solid presence grounds me and I feel a welcome sense of calm, even as I hear Xander scribbling furiously through the open window of his studio.

These boys may be idiots, but they're *my* idiots.

"I'm sorry about Xander," I say, my voice muffled against the rough denim of Nik's jacket. "He was way out of line."

Nik is silent for a moment. "I'll get over it," he mumbles, but I suspect he'll be brooding for the next few days. Last time this happened, he disappeared for a week. "I'm sorry too," he murmurs against my hair. "I wasn't thinking. I shouldn't have behaved the way I did, even if Kaleb did deserve it."

"It's okay, Nikolas. Nothing you do is beyond my forgiveness. And while I may have been joking when I told you to punch Kaleb, it was extremely satisfying."

I don't mention the fact that, for a few brief moments of

weakness, I may have actually feared for Kaleb's life tonight.

Nik releases me with the flash of a familiar, confident smile. "It *was* satisfying, wasn't it?"

He presses a gentle kiss to the top of my head then wipes a hand roughly over his eyes before making his way toward the street. As he climbs in the driver's side of his white Audi, he strips off his jacket and uses it to furiously wipe the blood from his knuckles and chin. I watch as he downs the contents of his flask and pulls away from the curb, drawing another hand over his face.

I am going to kill Xander.

I stomp back into the house, fuming, only to find Victoria waiting patiently by the basement stairs.

"So," Victoria muses, ignoring my feral glare as she wraps a commanding arm around my shoulders, "I'm thinking a good rom-com. Maybe something with princesses. What sounds good to you?"

I glower. "Anything to prevent me from murdering my bastard brother."

Xander's scribbling silences for a moment then resumes at double speed as Victoria and I descend from the morning-lit foyer into the comfortable darkness of the basement.

◊　◊　◊

Girl time with Victoria usually consists of chick flicks, nail painting, and endless gossip: Victoria, though she hates being involved in Xander's drama, loves stirring up her own. She has dirt on most members of the local vampire community—from blood dealing to scandalous affairs—which seems to account for most of our one-on-one conversations lately.

Today, however, Victoria brings up none of her usual discussion topics. She just sits quietly, playing with my hair as I lie with my head in her lap, while we watch a movie starring a famous actress whose name I never bothered to learn.

When the credits roll, Victoria slips upstairs to check on Xander, who is no doubt holed up in his bedroom with the blackout shades drawn. It's not often that he lets his emotions get the best of him, but when they do, it usually takes only a few hours for him to retreat into his own head, judging himself more harshly than anyone else will.

Well, except for maybe Kaleb.

Which brings me back to that mess. I groan and fall sideways onto the sectional. If Kaleb *was* telling the truth last night, it brings up another question entirely: why would *Konstantin* send someone to stab me? And why would he attach Kaleb's name to the crime? I've never even met the guy. What could I have done that would draw his attention?

I had hoped visiting Kaleb would clear up my confusion, not make it worse.

Xander's unmistakable footsteps echo in the stairwell and I sit up, wrapping my arms around my knees. I feel guilty, somehow, like I'm the one who did something wrong.

My brother steps into the room and sinks down next to me with a soft sigh, letting his arms bounce into his lap. He's wearing a beat-up pair of charcoal sweatpants and a black t-shirt, complimenting a head of mussed curls. There is a dark shadow of stubble on his chin and along his jawline, indicating that he hasn't shaved since yesterday. And Xander *never* forgets to shave.

"Wow," I muse. "You're wearing your Grumpy Pants."

His brow furrows, the geometric tattoo on his inner forearm twitching as he wrings his hands. "My what?"

"You only wear those hideous sweatpants when you're upset about something."

"Well, I *am* upset about something," he says, his green eyes glowing dully. "I'm upset about Kaleb, and about Nik. And apparently, I have to be upset about Konstantin, which is something I never expected. I thought he would have given up by now. But I am occasionally wrong."

"I could have told you that," I say, and Xander purses his lips. "In your defense, those are all very valid things to be upset about. Though slapping Nik probably wasn't your best move. In fact, it didn't even make it onto a list of 'best moves.' It was idiotic and cruel and just about the last thing Nik needed after confronting Kaleb for the first time in a century."

Xander runs a hand through his already-rumpled hair. "Yeah, you're probably right."

"What was that?" I ask brightly, cupping a hand around my ear. "Can you speak up? I didn't quite catch the magnificent words that just came out of your mouth."

"You're hilarious." He exhales loudly. "The thing is, I don't know what to do with him, Lottie," he confesses. "Nik, I mean. He should have taken over after Kaleb left, not me. He's so much older—"

"I don't think eighty years matters much in the grand scheme of things."

"True, but it's not just about his age. Nik is *better.* He has always been stronger and smarter than me. And his compassion was unmatched. He really was something. But after Rayna..." He frowns, worrying at a stray thread hanging from the waistband of his sweatpants.

Xander doesn't need to continue. After Rayna died, everything changed. *Nik* changed. He became unrecognizable: a ghost of his former self, broken and lost in a downward spiral of alternating rage and hopelessness.

I feel a sudden pang of sympathy for Xander, forced into leadership by necessity, trying to hold everything together while our family crumbled to pieces around him.

"*Nie chvaliujciesia,* Alexander," I say, taking one of his hands.

His frown deepens. "Though you may not realize it, you were born for this job. You've somehow managed to keep us together for over a hundred years—even Nik—and that's quite the accomplishment, considering the lot of demons you've had to work with."

Xander squeezes my hand with cool fingers. "If Konstantin is in San Francisco, then I worry my job may have just gotten a lot harder."

I roll my eyes. "The only person who thinks Konstantin is here is a no-good, traitorous murderer who definitely killed his own girlfriend and abandoned the only people who ever cared about him. I'll believe Kaleb when Hell freezes over. I'm still convinced he's the one who had me stabbed the other night."

"It wasn't Kaleb."

"I beg to differ."

"It's not his style," Xander counters. "We know him better than that. It felt suspicious when you told me about it, and it feels suspicious now."

Annoyance flares in my chest. "Then who was it? Even if you're right and Kaleb didn't have me stabbed, how can we be sure his Konstantin theory holds any water?"

"I don't know, Lottie. But for now, we need to lie low. Kaleb has lookouts all over the city. Until we know exactly what's going on, it's best for us not to draw unnecessary attention."

The mood instantly dampens. "No more screwing up for me. Got it."

Regret flashes in Xander's eyes. "Charlotte—"

"Nope, I hear you loud and clear."

I stand brusquely, yanking my hand away from Xander's even as his fingers close more tightly around mine. He purses his lips and drops his gaze to the floor.

"Don't forget we're having a frat boy for dinner tonight," he says as I shuffle up the stairs.

"Sounds delicious."

I'm in the foyer when Xander says quietly, "Make sure he gets our address."

My bedroom feels too bright after the dimness of the basement, even with its dark blue walls and blackout shades. I collapse face-down onto the bed, not bothering to change out of my jeans.

I close my eyes, ready to sink into a sleep that could rival the dead, but Xander's words echo quietly in my head.

I grab my phone—the bright screen nearly blinds me—and scroll through my contacts until I find Ty's name, typing a quick text with our address. My phone buzzes seconds later with a response.

Sounds good. Do you need me to bring anything?
A side dish, perhaps?

If he keeps this sarcasm up, Ty might not live through dinner.

I'm almost asleep when my phone buzzes again, this time signaling a phone call. Not wanting to talk to Ty—or anyone, for that matter—I chuck it across the room. It bangs into the wall then falls to the floor with a dull *thud*, where it buzzes three more times before quieting. I wrap the sheets around me and let my limbs grow heavy as my mind descends into nothingness.

18

IT'S A BEAUTIFUL, CRISP MORNING *in Belarus. Late summer brings with it a golden warmth that seeps into everything around our small cottage, from the wildflowers lining its outer walls to the small stable to the pumpkin vines swirling verdantly in the vegetable garden.*

I sit outside the front door, waiting for the sunrise, and watch Aleksandr where he kneels at the far side of the large garden, yanking carrots from the ground and stacking them into a neat pile. His olive skin is striking against his pale linen shirt and wide-brimmed straw hat. He notices me watching him and grins, wiping the back of his wrist across his forehead.

He calls out to me, chastising me for ignoring my chores, but I stick my tongue out in response.

I am perfectly allowed to ignore my chores today. It is my birthday, after all.

Aleksandr scoffs loudly, but there is laughter in his eyes.

I remember that his fiancée, Mira, told him she would bring me a surprise for my birthday. She recently returned from a holiday in Sweden with her family, and I can't help but hope for a piece of foreign chocolate. I open my mouth to ask Aleksandr when she will arrive, but I am interrupted when Mama calls from inside.

"Ksusha!" I peek through the door of the cottage and am met by the mouthwatering scent of something sweet baking in the oven.

Mama is a small woman with soft, curly hair and wide hips and delicate, calloused hands. She stands at our wood dining table kneading a ball of fresh dough. I watch for a moment, awed by her rhythmic and practiced movements, her hands pressing and flipping and folding the dough to perfection. I ask Mama what she is making, but she only grins and asks me to fetch milk for breakfast.

I hope it is rhubarb pastries.

Our stable is tucked against the small wooded glade behind the cottage. It houses our chestnut mare, Natalia, and our dairy cow. Mama let me name the cow when we bought her and I, being a child at the time, decided to give her my middle name, Marya. Aleksandr called me Madam Karova—Madame Cow—for almost two years after that.

Marya moos softly as I approach, and I remove a metal bucket from where it hangs on a wooden post. There are wildflowers growing nearby and I can hear the lazy buzzing of bumblebees as they collect pollen on their chubby legs. I take a deep breath, relishing in the sweet scent of the flowers, the crisp dewiness of the early morning, the warm summer scent telling of abundance and comfort and happy days ahead.

Mama cries out from the open window before I have a chance to sit.

"Mama?" I call, but she doesn't answer. Concerned, I set my bucket on the ground and slip around the side of the cottage. "Mama?"

The front door is open and I can still smell the thick, sugary aroma wafting from the oven. I walk inside, expecting to see Mama picking up a broken dish or nursing a stubbed toe.

What I see instead is...well, I am not sure what it is.

Mama lies on the ground, held up in the arms of a young man. His face is buried in her neck and something dark is spreading down *the front of her apron, staining it black in the dim light.*

The man's head snaps upward as I approach, exposing the nauseating wounds on Mama's neck, her skin colored a vivid red. Though he is obscured by morning gloom, I sense the smile that splits the man's face. The shadows flinch.

I scream.

The man drops Mama to the floor where she lies unmoving, her eyes wide and glassy. He rises to his full height and takes a few staggering steps toward me, his left shoulder twitching violently upward once, then twice, the same arm hanging limply at his side. Mama's large kitchen knife protrudes from his heart, but it doesn't seem to bother him; his pale shirt is tattered and soaked in fresh blood, covering dark, older stains that send a chill surging through me.

I attempt to scream again but the shadow clamps a blood-covered hand over my mouth; whether the blood is his or Mama's, I do not know. His skin is smooth as silk, a disturbing contrast to the sticky blood that coats it. Some drips into my mouth and I gag.

"Shh, shh," he soothes, locking his eyes with mine. "Маўчы."

An immediate calm washes over me and my body relaxes in his grip, almost against my will. My instincts are screaming to run, but I can't. The shadow told me to be still, and that is what I will do.

"Ty pryhožaja malieńkaja ptuška," he purrs in a silky voice that might have been beautiful under different circumstances. His shoulder twitches upward again, bringing with it a frustrated snarl. "Vybačajcie, što nie znajdu dlia vy miesca."

His Belarusian is choppy and accented, but I understand: You are a pretty little bird. I am sorry I have no place for you.

Without warning, he jerks me toward him and bites into my neck. Horror pulses through me accompanied by a wave of nausea. The pain is unbearable, sharp teeth tearing open my skin, a skeletal hand digging into my skull. The strength begins to ebb from my body and I melt into the shadow, wishing I could fight back, do anything to get away from him.

"Deman," I choke out, just as Aleksandr bursts through the door.
"Ksusha!" he cries.

I try to call out to him, to tell him to run, but I can't. The words evaporate on my tongue. All I can do is pray as the shadow finishes with me, his good hand gripping the lower half of my face and twisting ferociously.

I do not scream; I haven't the time. There is a loud crack and my world is engulfed in darkness.

"Charlotte, ustavać!"

I bolt upright in bed, checking to make sure my head is still attached to my neck. Some might view the perfect memory recall of a vampire as a blessing. For me, it's more of a curse. I can't always control where that perfect memory will take me.

Occasionally, it has the audacity to replay the morning of my death. An annoying reminder that I have no idea who killed me—and that I'll never be able to return the favor.

"Charlotte," Xander calls again. "Get in here!"

"Two minutes!" I yell, groaning as I roll out of bed.

I stumble into the bathroom in the dark and flip on the light switch, blinking as my eyes adjust to the light, and I catch my haggard reflection in the mirror.

Yikes.

My hair is flattened on one side and my white t-shirt is marked with a few random splatters of blood that I assume belonged to Kaleb. I frown at the memory of Nik punching him and immediately chastise myself: *Am I feeling sorry for Kaleb now?* I shudder at the thought, then yank the shirt over my head and toss it into the trash can.

I splash cold water on my face, using my damp hands to give my hair a bit of life, then find a fresh charcoal V-neck from my closet and throw it on. For good measure, I clean the smudged mascara from under my eyes and apply a fresh coat.

Feeling rejuvenated, I head out to meet Xander where he is seating a redhead girl in a green, corduroy dress at the dining room table.

"Took you long enough," he grumbles, then turns his attention to the girl.

"You'll be comfortable here," he says with an alluring smile. "Don't move."

The girl looks up at him with a pair of soft brown eyes and nods slowly, like an infatuated puppet on a string. A pile of dark towels is stacked on the table in front of her, probably as a precaution in case things get messy.

"Will you get the other one?" Xander asks, motioning toward the opposite end of the room.

"The other one?" I turn to see a dark-haired boy in a white t-shirt and jeans standing obediently by the doorway, staring ahead with a confused look on his face. "Rolling out the red carpet, are we?"

I take Confused Boy by the arm and notice a fresh bite mark on his neck, the copper scent of blood wafting from the wound.

"Did you already eat?" I ask Xander, swallowing hard.

"No, Victoria did," he says, then frowns at my undoubtedly pained expression. "Are you going to behave tonight? Don't make me regret involving you."

"I'll be fine," I snap, turning to Confused Boy. "Hey, handsome," I say, patting him on the cheek. "You're going to be a good boy and sit here patiently, got it?"

"Okay," he murmurs and breaks into a lazy grin. "You're really pretty."

"Yeah, alright," I reply, coaxing him into a chair.

"I should probably tell you," Xander says, tugging at the hem of his sweater—the nervous habit makes him look young— "there was another murder last night. While we were with Kaleb."

My skin prickles with unease. "I was hoping this wasn't going to turn into a nightly thing."

"Apparently, that's exactly what it's turning into." He pauses. "They found the body at Hyde Street Pier."

Adrenaline jolts through me. I *knew* I felt those piercing eyes watching us. Despite my tiny internal victory, the floor still sways a bit under my feet.

"What?"

"I'm not sure if it has anything to do with us or if it was just a coincidence. But the news is saying it happened within an hour or two after we left."

"The real question is, how did the lying coward know we had been at Hyde Street Pier?"

"Charlotte," Xander growls. "For the last time, stop blaming this all on Kaleb. It wasn't him."

"So, you admit that he's a lying coward."

"Charlotte."

"Why are you defending him so stubbornly?" I ask, my voice rising in anger. "Why won't you just *listen to me* for once?"

Xander opens his mouth to make what I'm sure would have been a scathing remark, but I'm prevented from annihilation by a knock at the door. My anger cools instantly as I become aware of the pair of fledgling ears listening outside.

Xander frowns and shoves past me to answer the door. *"Repa."*

"Jackass."

Xander has mentored a good number of fledglings since we came to San Francisco. I'm not sure if he feels responsible for helping keep the peace or if teaching vampires somehow satisfies his god complex, but either way, it's a bit of a process.

This is the first time Xander has allowed me to join what I like to call the "First Meal"; I'm usually sent away or locked in my room so as not to "set a bad example" for the fledgling. It's a good call on his part.

While I sit alone in the dining room, the scent of Confused Boy's blood fills my nose and makes my mouth water. But tonight, I have to behave. As much as I hate to admit it, the past few days have been a disaster, and I don't know if Xander could handle another slip-up like the one on the wharf.

Or at Kaleb's club.

Or at the Halloween party.

Confused Boy and Redhead sit quietly in their chairs, staring forward with unfocused eyes. I can't help but imagine what their lives might be like, sleeping at night and eating churros at the wharf and, I don't know, going to school? I wonder where Xander found them. Were they walking in the park? Checking out the view from the Lyon Street Steps? Or were they unlucky tourists who asked a vampire for directions?

"Hey, hot stuff." Ty struts into the dining room with irritating bravado, wearing a long-sleeve gray shirt, light jeans, and white sneakers. A pair of tiny diamond hoops glitters in his ears. "Nice place you've got here."

"We get by," Xander quips. "Now *sit*."

Xander points to the chair next to Confused Boy, and Ty seems to notice the humans for the first time. He waves a hand in front of the boy's hypnotized eyes.

"Guy looks a little stoned," he muses.

"It's called Compulsion, Ty," Xander says with a condescending eye roll. "We discussed this last night. Or have you already forgotten?" Ty narrows his eyes, but Xander doesn't blink. "This is the easiest way to feed without getting caught or leaving a mess." Xander pulls up a chair next to Redhead. "That's rule number one, after all."

"What is?"

"*Nullum corpus.* Leave no bodies."

Ty raises an eyebrow. "Leave no bodies? That's *so* cheesy."

"It's not cheesy," I interject. "It's important. Besides, it's not even our rule. It's Kaleb's."

"This Kaleb seems like a real charmer," Ty says, taking a seat next to Confused Boy. He studiously ignores the bleeding bite mark on the boy's neck, but his eyes are bright and wild as he cranes his head to look up at me.

"Kaleb," I sigh, grabbing the back of Ty's collar in case he decides to do something impulsive, "is a piece of work. He's super old, super rude, and has an overdeveloped sense of importance. That being said, he *is* the Alpha and will make you pay if your actions threaten to expose us."

Ty smirks. "He sounds like the villain from an old melodrama. Cheesy rules, unearned power. I bet he has an awesome evil laugh. Maybe even a secret lair."

"Actually, he does. He lives in these weird tunnels underneath—"

"Charlotte." Xander's tone holds a warning.

I snap my mouth shut, aware that I was well on my way to saying too much.

"As I was saying," Xander says, reclaiming Ty's attention, "it's important to learn to control yourself. The more control you have, the better chance you have of surviving. Vampire 101: feed, Compel, release. You only kill if it is absolutely necessary, and sometimes not even then." He leans into Redhead, brushing the vibrant orange hair from her neck. "This is Rachel. I find that knowing their names makes it easier to stop feeding; it reminds me that they are human beings, just like I once was. Like we all were."

Wheels turn behind Ty's gray eyes. "Have you ever killed someone?"

Xander meets his gaze unapologetically. "Once or twice."

I snort. It has been decades since Xander has killed someone; he can thank Kaleb's training for that. But there was a time when my Casanova brother slashed and seduced his way through Vitebsk, unencumbered by an intact moral compass. "I know I will be going to Hell," he had said, "so why not enjoy myself until then?"

Xander was born to be a vampire. He always had a knack for attracting people—even before we were Turned—in the way a Venus Fly Trap has a knack for attracting flies. Everything about him is magnetic. He even has one of those faces you read about in young adult novels: perfectly messy dark hair and pouty lips and olive skin and piercing emerald eyes that sparkle like diamonds. Or whatever.

When he became a vampire, his magnetism cranked up to a thousand, while I stood uselessly on the sidelines.

Ty watches intently as Xander places a soft finger on Rachel's chin and turns her to face him, offering her an enticing grin. She melts under his gaze like an orange popsicle on hot pavement.

If Xander didn't have Victoria, I imagine he and Nik wouldn't be so different.

Xander's fangs slide from his gums and he bites slowly into Rachel's throat, then immediately withdraws to reveal two perfect puncture marks. Blood wells from the holes and drips lazily down her chest to soak into the collar of her corduroy dress. He wipes a finger through it and holds his hand aloft, his eyes accented by the inevitable dark circles that appear when a vampire smells human blood. "Care for a taste?"

Ty has gone completely rigid in his chair, the hollows under his eyes lined with deep plum veins, like angry bruises. I hold my breath, ignoring the creeping heat of hunger that finds its way across my own cheeks and into my eyes, and focus instead on the coolness of Ty's neck against my fingers, the soft humming from the overhead lights, the plush rug under my feet. Grounding myself, just like Kaleb taught me.

Ty, however, has received no such lesson. He takes a deep breath—a terrible idea—and bolts from his chair, lunging toward Rachel with his fangs at the ready. Xander is prepared, however, casually rising from his seat and clotheslining Ty with a strong arm against his chest. Ty hits the floor with a loud *thud* but jumps up quickly, glaring murderously at Xander.

I burst into laughter.

"Rule number two," Xander says, waving his bloodied finger in front of Ty's face. Taunting him. Ty glowers. "If you don't breathe, you can't smell the blood. A valuable lesson when you're—well, an idiot fledgling like yourself."

Ty snaps at Xander's finger, but I catch a playful glint in his eyes. Xander takes him by the arm and drags him away from Rachel, his knuckles white as he fights to keep him at bay. Ty may be thin and wiry, but there is still strength in him. He is a vampire, after all.

The muscles in Ty's neck strain as he looks down at Rachel and the blood that continues to stain her green dress. Xander pulls him backward a few steps and he resists, his eyes glinting.

"Charlotte," Xander says through gritted teeth, "how about a demonstration?" He licks his finger clean—savoring it—while keeping firm hold of Ty near the wall.

"Me?" I ask, startled. "You want *me* to demonstrate?"

Xander nods, indicating with his eyes that he's a little busy at the moment.

"Okay, sure." I shift closer to Rachel, relaxing slightly as the familiar anticipation of feeding bubbles in my abdomen. "Hey, Rachel." Her eyes search for mine, finally locking into place with a near-audible click. "You're doing great, just a little sleepy. This won't hurt a bit."

I watch with relief as she nods dreamily, her pupils wide and hypnotized. The last time I Compelled someone, he had just watched me try to kill his friend. Tristan's terrified, golden eyes hover in my mind, making my heart constrict uncomfortably.

I lick some of the blood dripping down Rachel's chest, then latch onto her neck over Xander's bite. Her skin carries the scent of cool air and growing things, marred by the bitter tang of cheap perfume. After a few swallows, I feel a warm hum spreading through my body and I sigh softly. My hand finds Rachel's arm and I dig my nails in, pulling her closer.

"Charlotte."

The girl's blood is hot on my tongue and she sinks against me, her head sagging sideways, her shoulders going limp. My mind quiets and my senses dull. It is only me and the blood, the rush of heat that fills my chest and the enveloping calm that follows.

"*Charlotte,*" Xander snarls, and I snap to attention. I detach myself from a near-unconscious Rachel and lean backward, wiping blood from my chin with the back of my hand.

"Sorry," I murmur to Ty. "There's a reason I'm not usually invited to Xander's little dinner parties."

"It's kind of hot," Ty says with a smirk. His eyes are still dark.

Xander's eyes practically roll out of his head. "Your turn. Let's see how you do with Wesley over there."

Confused Boy—Wesley—still sits obediently in his chair as Ty approaches him. "So, I just…bite him?"

"Don't tell me you have stage fright," I say.

Ty glares at me. "Not stage fright, exactly. But I don't like being evaluated." His tone is hesitant but his movements aren't; he braces Wesley's head with both hands and buries his fangs in his throat, his fingers digging into the boy's cheek as he twists his neck at an odd angle. After a few seconds, Wesley's eyes start to glaze over and his shoulders lose some of their stiffness.

Ty may have had a point. Watching him feed—*really* feed; the kind of raw, instinctual hunger unmarred by rational thought or inhibition—might be kind of, just a little bit…well, *hot.*

"And we're done," Xander says, and a tiny part of me is almost disappointed. He approaches Ty from behind and puts him in a chokehold, but Ty doesn't budge.

"Let go," Xander says, "but don't tear the skin. If you do, he'll bleed out." Ty snarls, shoving at Xander's arm, but Xander only snarls back. "Let. Go."

A low growl rumbles from Ty but he concedes, his mouth opening with a small pop as his lips leave skin. His work is quite a bit bloodier than Xander's, but I'll give him this: at least he didn't rip open the kid's jugular.

Which is more than could be said for Xander's first controlled feed. Kaleb had not been happy.

"Not bad," I say, using one of the dark towels to clean the blood from Wesley's neck. "Now you just need to learn how to stop without Xander putting you in a choke hold."

Xander smirks and, to my surprise, Ty responds with a smirk of his own. The hollows under his eyes have softened to a warm purple and his cheeks are flushed with a healthy dose of pink.

"That would definitely be an improvement," he says, squirming from Xander's grip. He skirts around the two humans and grabs me firmly by the wrist. Cold radiates from him as he leans close, making me shiver. "Now, if we're done, I'd love a tour."

"Come again?"

"Give me a tour. You can't expect me to come into a house like this and *not* be given a tour."

"I have already given one tour this week," I say. Tristan's eyes sparkle in my memory as I remember him observing each room with childlike wonderment; I smile a little in spite of myself. Ty's expression is imploring. "But I guess another wouldn't hurt—"

"No," Xander says, folding his arms across his chest. "No tour. I don't know you, Ty, and I don't like you. Do you really think I'm going to let you run wild in my house?" He turns his attention back to me, ignoring the scowl of complete indignation on Ty's face. "However, you can take him down to the fridge, Lottie. He'll need a stash to keep him satisfied. I'll finish up here."

I nod and Ty shrugs. "Fine. No tour tonight. But next time, yes?"

"Bold of you to assume you'll be invited back," I mumble.

I usher Ty out of the room as Xander settles next to Wesley, mumbling a few soft, Compelling words. The human boy gazes up at my brother like a love-struck teenager, his eyes brimming with a disturbing amount of trust and longing.

Xander braces Wesley's head with a strong hand to his jaw, and I watch with dark satisfaction as his fangs find the smooth skin of the boy's neck.

19

I LEAD TY DOWN THE stairs, past the game room, and into the wine cellar. Its polished concrete floor and stone walls keep the room at a constant cool temperature, the damp chill seeping through my clothes and tingling against my skin.

I flip the light on and Ty's gaze sweeps the room. "This is...a lot of booze."

"We've been collecting for a long time," I say with a shrug. "It's one of the only things we can drink besides blood. We have it on hand for those days when you think, 'I could really use some chocolate right now.' But you can't have chocolate. So..." —I motion vaguely around— "alcohol."

A touch of fascination warms Ty's eyes, turning the silver to a glowing platinum. There is something alluring about them—though it has nothing on the pure light that radiates from Tristan's eyes—and my heart flutters.

"As a vampire," I say, clearing my throat to dislodge the feeling, "you only need human blood about once a week, more often if you're weakened or hurt." I walk to a large metal door in one corner of the room and pull up on the latch. It groans loudly. "Thankfully, it's almost impossible to overeat, seeing as I get hungry at least once a day." I yank the door open with a metallic screech, revealing a small refrigerated room lit by humming fluorescent lights. Cold air engulfs us as we walk inside. "Fresh blood is always best, but if you're in a pinch, a blood bag will do."

The fridge is lined with metal baker's racks, each with a label: A-Positive, AB-Negative, O-Positive. Clear bins sit on the racks, each containing a small stack of blood bags.

Ty's eyes widen. "I see," he says, running his fingers along one of the metal shelves. He picks up a bag of B-Negative and examines it closely before returning it to its bin. "Alcoholics *and* hoarders. Immortality has not been kind to you."

I know he's joking, but Ty's words pack a surprising sting. In two centuries, I've watched my mother die, watched relationships flourish and fail, watched as those closest to me became echoes of their former selves. Time is as relentless as ocean waves, tossing us in an endless torrent until we forget what it was like to live on solid ground. Until we lose everything we once held dear.

I can't imagine how Nik feels after three centuries—or Kaleb after nearly five.

"Immortality is kind to no one."

Ty's smile twists into a frown as I make my way to each shelf, collecting a bag of each blood type and stuffing them into a small duffel I pull from a cabinet in the corner.

"Here," I say, shoving the duffel into Ty's hands. "All the blood types taste a little different, so blood bags are nice if you're craving something specific. These should keep you satisfied for a while until you've figured out how to feed without killing anyone."

"Have *you* ever killed anyone?" he asks, taking the bag. His eyes meet mine curiously, bright rings of sterling in the cold, white light of the room.

"Of course," I admit. "When you're a vampire, it's inevitable. And I've been a vampire since 1824."

"When was the last time?" His tone is light, but it holds an uncomfortable edge.

"I don't have to tell you that."

"What am I going to do, call the police?" he sneers, his lip curling just enough to reveal a faded scar cut into his upper lip. "Come on, Charlotte. Tell me."

Why do I get the feeling that he's trying to flirt with me?

And why is it working?

"Three days ago," I blurt out, feeling both relieved and exposed as the truth tumbles from me as if by its own accord. "But it was an accident. I'm sure you've figured out by now that you shouldn't spend too much time in the sun." Ty nods. "Well, I did. And mistakes were made."

Ty's expression is sharp but unreadable, and I can't tell if he's curious or concerned. Either way, he hides it well.

"It's good to know that even experienced, old women like you make mistakes."

"Hey!" I yell, shoving Ty backward where he collides with the door jam. He erupts into bright laughter that crackles with energy and sends a thrill through me.

"Ty, you are something else." I grin at him. "You're taking this vampire stuff surprisingly well."

"That's because I have an amazing teacher," he says, taking a step toward me.

"I wouldn't say Xander is *amazing*—"

"Not Xander," Ty says with a dismissive wave of his hand. "He's a bit boring, isn't he? Life isn't all about being perfect and careful." His eyebrow quirks upward, instantly transforming his expression from humorous to mischievous. "I'm talking about *you*, Charlotte. You make everything seem normal. Maybe even a little fun." He takes another step, closing the gap between us.

I cringe at his sudden proximity. "If that's what you're getting from us, then you have your wires crossed. I'm not sure anything about it could be described as 'fun,' so much as 'deplorable' or 'unfortunate' or 'rated M for mature.'"

"Maybe it's been so long since you were human, you've forgotten what fun feels like," Ty says, his voice low, and drops the duffel bag onto the floor. He traces the tips of his fingers along my jaw, his eyes sparking.

I freeze. "I think you might be misreading the situation—"

"Kiss me."

The air leaves my lungs in a huff. "I beg your *unbelievable* pardon?"

"You know you want to, Charlotte." His voice is dark and smooth as obsidian, enticing in a way that weakens my knees. "Do it. Kiss me."

Hunger swells low in my abdomen and I think back to the party at Pier 39, to the desire for physical, human contact that awakened when I danced with Tristan. Ty is most decidedly not Tristan, and most decidedly not *human,* but I can't deny his magnetism, the confident set of his shoulders, the hypnotizing glow in his eyes. Heat builds under my ribs until it feels like a cord is pulling taut, yanking me forward, and I find Ty at the other end.

We crash into each other like thunder in darkness, lightning crackling between us as our lips collide. Ty crushes me against him, his hands tugging at my hair, pressing into my lower back. I know this is a terrible idea—that I'm acting in the way Nik might after meeting an attractive stranger for the first time—but my tiny sense of morality is drowned by the remnant of Wesley's blood on Ty's lips.

My hunger turns ravenous as his hands slide under my shirt, cool palms finding my hip bones and shoving until I slam into the wall. I gasp as my shoulder blades strike cold metal. My heart stutters as Ty presses against me, his hips capturing mine, his lips languorous and commanding.

I take it back. This is an *incredible* idea. Ty can *kiss*.

Fevered excitement pulses through me and I slide one hand up his neck, my fingers finding purchase in the thick, ashy hair at his nape. Ty groans, his tongue tracing my lips, his mouth exploring mine greedily, and I feel a distant, uncomfortable sensation.

But it doesn't last long.

Ty's hand snakes around my back, his fingertips dipping below the waistband of my jeans, and all coherent thoughts leave my mind. I let my head fall backward and Ty kisses along my jaw and down my neck, leaving a trail of electricity in his wake.

His mouth curves against the hollow of my throat as he deliberately and unapologetically bites me.

With his *fangs*.

On my *neck*.

Wrong. The word pulses in my mind like a bell striking the hour. *Wrong, wrong, wrong.*

The last time a vampire bit me, I woke up dead.

Disgust surges through me and I shove Ty away with all my strength, sending him flying into one of the metal shelves, a bin of O-negative blood bags toppling to the floor. He stares at me wide-eyed but not at all repentant.

"Too far?" he asks, flashing a grin.

I clamp a hand onto my neck, feeling the bloodied holes made by Ty's fangs. The room suddenly feels less like a walk-in refrigerator and more like a sweltering broom closet. I sink back into the wall but can't seem to put enough distance between me and Ty's bloody, fanged grin.

"Vampires don't bite *other vampires!*" I shriek, suppressing the urge to gag. "It's disgusting and unnecessary and, if we're being totally honest, *cannibalistic!* What the *hell* is wrong with you?"

"What?" Ty asks, inching back toward me. I hold a hand out to stave him off, and he frowns. "It's not like you haven't been bitten before. I thought we were having fun—"

"*Get out of my house,*" I snarl, picking up the duffel of blood bags. I add a few more for good measure then chuck it at Ty; it slams into his chest and he catches it deftly.

"But—"

"*Out.*"

Ty glares in defiance before slipping past me, disappearing into the hallway outside the wine cellar.

I gape after him for a few seconds, hopelessly trying to erase the last few minutes from my memory. *What has gotten into me?*

I must be really desperate.

I follow after Ty reluctantly, catching up to him as he reaches the front door. He turns to look at me as I approach, his expression hard.

"I'll never do that again, Charlotte. I swear."

"You won't get the chance." I stalk over to the door and throw it open, my hair stirring in the breeze from outside. "Now *go.*"

Ty looks through the doorway and his expression morphs into subtle surprise. "You've got company."

I whirl around and nearly jump out of my skin. Tristan stands on the dark porch in a pair of fitted jeans and a leather jacket, his hand raised as if to knock. His face brightens when he sees me, the expression like morning sun peeking over the horizon.

"Hi, Char," he says. "I hope this isn't a bad time."

"Not at all," I say. Ty clears his throat loudly and I groan. "Sorry. Tristan, this is, uh, Xander's friend—"

"Ty?"

"Hey, man," Ty says. "Fancy meeting you here."

"What—" I start, but the question dies on my tongue. It's a few seconds before I find my words again. "You two know each other?"

"He's one of Jason's buddies," Tristan says, his eyes trained on Ty. "We've hung out a few times."

Ty plasters on a smile. "A few too many, if you ask me."

Great. Just when I thought my night couldn't get any worse.

"Ty was just leaving," I say, forcing my tone to stay calm. I remember the bite mark on my neck and hastily clamp a hand over it. "Weren't you, Ty?"

Ty raises an eyebrow but plays along. "Good to see you, *Char.* Oh," —he waves the duffel bag in the air— "and thanks for the snacks." He winks at me then melts into the night, but not before fixing a dubious eye on Tristan.

When I'm sure Ty is gone and—hopefully—out of earshot, I look at Tristan, who is squinting against the growing darkness.

I feel a surprising stab of guilt; my cheeks are still hot, my mind reeling from my kiss with Ty. But I shouldn't feel guilty. It's not like there is anything going on between me and Ty.

There's nothing going on between me and Tristan, either.

"Tristan," I sigh, exasperated, "I thought we agreed that you wouldn't show up here unannounced. *Ever.*" My eyes dart sideways to the dining room where, mercifully, Xander has cleaned up after our quick dinner. The dining chairs are perfectly tucked under the mahogany table, its surface polished and gleaming innocently. If Tristan would have shown up only a few minutes earlier...I don't want to think about it.

"No, you said not to show up without *calling* first," he says with a sly smile. "And to be fair, I did call. Twice. It's your fault for not answering your phone."

I think back to this morning when I threw my phone against the wall, and glare at him.

"That's fair." I fold my arms over my chest. "So, why are you here?"

"Your hospitality is astounding," he says, a glint in his eye. "Is this how you greet all your guests?"

"Tristan—"

"Okay, okay." He fumbles around in his jacket pocket and pulls out a small, blue flashlight. "I'm planning a little adventure tonight and I thought you might want to join me. You know, to get to know each other better. As friends."

I blink. "And that adventure requires us to bring a tiny flashlight?"

"Technically no," he laughs, "but it creates an *illusion* of adventure, don't you think?"

I know I shouldn't go to an undisclosed location with yet another mysterious boy I've only known for a few days, but my good sense seems to be taking an extended vacation. I consider sending Tristan away, but I can't help my curiosity: what does an adventure look like to this freckle-faced golden boy?

I haven't seen Xander since I came upstairs, but I can hear him talking in his studio. It sounds like he's on the phone.

Always, always on the phone. And this call sounds particularly tense.

Perfect.

"One second," I whisper, darting into the kitchen to slip on a pair of boots. I grab a jacket for appearances, pausing to wet a paper towel and hastily clean the blood from my neck, then slip outside with Tristan, closing the door quietly behind me.

Tristan beams at me and we walk silently down the front steps. The moon is luminescent in the sky, white light glancing off Tristan's hair, the manicured hedges lining the street, the keys in Tristan's hand as he unlocks his Mazda. He opens the door for me and motions me inside, the light catching his eyes and making them flash silver in the dark. Nausea heaves in my stomach as I think of Ty's silver eyes, bright and wild and confident as he touched me. Kissed me.

Bit me.

"Char? Are you getting in or what?"

"Oh, yeah," I mumble, sliding into the car. Tristan shuts the door and I take a deep breath, forcing the memory of Ty from my mind.

Tristan jumps into the driver's seat, his mouth curving into an excited grin as he starts the car and shifts it into gear. The black guitar pick winks from his wrist, but before I can make out the words etched into its surface, he leans heavily on the accelerator. The car lurches forward and I release a surprised yelp, making Tristan laugh.

Damn that laugh. And damn how infectious it is. I feel like I should be annoyed, but I only find myself laughing with him.

"So," I say, making a show of fastening my seatbelt, "are you going to tell me where we're going?"

"You'll find out."

20

"Okay, seriously. Where are we going?"

Tristan leads me down a winding dirt path lined with trees, peeking over his shoulder to offer me a sly grin. The air is cool but comfortable, and the scent of damp earth fills the air as our feet brush noiselessly through the dirt. As far as I can tell, we're completely alone, wherever we are. Tristan remained vague the entire drive here, despite my relentless questioning.

Now that we're apparently almost there, I think he may be taking me into the woods to murder me.

He will be in for quite the surprise.

We emerge from the trees and the starry coast opens its arms to us. The horizon stretches into blackness while pinpricks of light from the Golden Gate Bridge twinkle in the distance to our right, dancing on the water like a colony of multi-colored fireflies. Moonlight glints on the surface of the ocean, rippling lazily in the ever-changing current.

"This is where we're going," Tristan announces proudly, gesturing at the rocky beach ahead of us.

The barren coastline smells of salt and tangy, fishy seaweed. "I'm sorry, where?"

Tristan adjusts the straps of the guitar and canvas bag slung over his shoulders, leading me around a rocky outcropping until I finally see—well, *something*. On the ground in front of us are a few hundred small stones laid out to form a large, circular maze. One edge of the circle kisses the coastline where a jagged rock juts out into the ocean, creating tight corners where the water crashes relentlessly. I shiver.

"It's...a pile of rocks."

"It's an *organized* pile of rocks."

"Ah, that makes it *much* more interesting."

"This is the Land's End Labyrinth," Tristan says. "I like to come here at night to play music or write or just...think." He moves closer to the shore and motions for me to follow. I take a few reluctant steps forward. "Sometimes I get sick of all the noise. It's quiet here."

Almost on cue, a wave slams against the rocks, sending a shower of sea spray into the air.

"You call that quiet?" I ask, jumping backward to avoid getting misted by brine. "You should check out my bedroom in the middle of the night. Complete and total silence."

Tristan turns to face me and raises a playful eyebrow. "You want me to check out your bedroom?"

"What? No!" I say, and Tristan laughs. Embarrassment brings an unwelcome heat to my cheeks and I feel the overwhelming urge to jump into the ocean. "It's just—what I *meant* was—I don't know. Shut up."

"You said it, not me." Tristan takes me by the arms. "Close your eyes."

"Why? You're not going to murder me, are you? Xander always says not to trust a man I've just met, especially if he kidnaps me and takes me to a dirty beach after dark."

"Charlotte," Tristan says, his expression earnest. "Just trust me."

Trust me, trust me, trust me.

We've been using that phrase too liberally, I think.

I oblige and close my eyes, Tristan disappearing from view. But I feel him still, his strong hands on my arms, the warmth radiating from his skin.

"Now," he whispers, his breath tickling my cheek, "*listen.*"

So, I do. I listen to the dull roar of the ocean waves as the moon works her tidal magic. I listen to the wind whispering through trees, carrying with it the sound of tiny insects flitting through the evening air. I listen to Tristan's heartbeat, strong and steady, reflecting in the pulse thrumming in his palms where they rest against my upper arms.

There is nothing else. No scuffling footsteps, no vibrating engines, no voices or sound effects or incessant ringtones. Just the sound of Mother Nature's instruments, mingling together to paint an aural picture of life untouched by human influence.

I suddenly understand what Tristan means: it *is* quiet here.

"Wow," I murmur, opening my eyes. Tristan's mouth quirks into a crooked smile—one that nearly puts Nik's to shame—and my cheeks prickle with heat.

"What did I tell you?" he says, his hands still firm on my arms, one thumb tracing circles on my skin.

"I—this is—" Tristan's casual touch disorients me, and I swallow. "Cities really suck, don't they?"

Tristan laughs again and, this close, I notice one of his teeth is turned slightly sideways. Somehow, it only makes his smile more endearing.

"I'm getting too used to them, I think," I say, removing myself from Tristan's grip. His arms fall purposeless to his sides. "After living in cities for most of my life, the hustle and bustle becomes the new normal: the cars, the smog, the noise." I take a deep breath. "It's nice to escape it for a while."

"Most of your life?" Tristan asks, tucking his hands in his pockets. "Not all?"

"No, not all." I stare out over the water and am hit with a sudden bout of homesickness. "I was born in Belarus, actually, in a farming village outside Vitebsk. We lived in a little cottage on a huge plot of land, and Xander tended the garden while I helped my mother bake bread to sell at the town market." I close my eyes, remembering the way the long grass rippled in the wind, the sparkle of the sun glinting on the nearby river, the sugary aroma of Mama's pastries in the oven. "Things were simpler then. Sometimes I wish I could go back."

"It sounds beautiful." Tristan touches my shoulder gently, and his eyes shimmer with sympathy.

Longing pools in my chest: longing for home...and longing for something else entirely.

"It was."

"Can you teach me how to say something in Belarusian? I can't guarantee I'll be good at it, but I can try."

My gaze drifts back to the water where it slaps against the jagged rocks. The incessant ebb and flow of the ocean is mesmerizing; I breathe with it, feeling the unmistakable pull of the darkness as my lungs fill with salt-soaked air.

"*Akijan-biazdušnaja suka*," I say, grimacing.

"*Akijan-biazdušnaja suka*," Tristan repeats in a terrible California accent. "What does that mean?"

"The ocean is a soulless bitch."

"Oh, come on," Tristan says, his head tilting to the side. "Don't tell me you're afraid of the *ocean*."

"Of course I am. Just look at it! It's dark and foreboding and sea-witchy."

Tristan moves to stand next to me, his shoulder bumping into mine, and stares down into the water. "You're not wrong," he says. "It *is* dark and foreboding, though I don't see any sea witches. I may be biased since I've lived in Cali my entire life, but there's something calming about it, don't you think?"

"No, only creepy. The ocean at night is heartless and unforgiving.

If you don't believe me, take a swim and ask her. I'm sure she'll let you live."

"Why the chip on your shoulder? Bad experience?" Tristan's voice is soft but mischievous, and something flutters beneath my ribs.

"No, it's just—"

But I don't finish my sentence. Without warning, Tristan's shoulder nudges me hard, the motion jerking me forward toward the dark water. I feel a jolt of pure terror as I anticipate falling under the icy waves.

Goodbye, cruel world. It was nice knowing you.

I'm saved from a horrific death—or rather, an extremely unpleasant dip—when Tristan's arms wrap tightly around me, pulling me back from the edge of the abyss in the nick of time. His canvas bag swings around him and thumps against my hip.

I yell a few profanities that would make my mother turn in her grave. Tristan laughs.

"Why would you do that?" I ask shrilly, adrenaline coursing through me as I clutch the front of Tristan's laundry-scented shirt. "Are you *insane?*"

"You have to admit it was funny."

As my startled heartbeat slows, I realize that I'm very close to Tristan. *Extremely* close. My arms are curled to my chest and my body is curled into his, cradled against him like a terrified child. I might be embarrassed if he wasn't so *warm;* his arms hold me securely against him, strong and comforting, and I close my eyes for a few seconds, working to calm the fear rattling around in my ribcage.

"You know I wouldn't have let you fall, right?" he asks, squeezing me tighter before pulling away, sincerity darkening his expression. "You'll always be safe when you're with me."

I look up at him, all soft skin and cheekbones and gold hair turned silver by the moonlight, and am suddenly aware of how fragile he is. How *human*. If I had fallen in the water, I would have been fine. Traumatized and more than a little revengeful, but fine. If the situation were reversed, Tristan might *not* be fine. He could be beaten against the rocks by strong waves or drown in a riptide or be sucked out to sea and die of hypothermia.

I haven't worried about such things for centuries. And now I can't *stop* worrying about them.

I take a few steps back from the edge, dragging Tristan with me. "Let's just make sure neither of us falls in, okay?"

Tristan chuckles. "Sounds like a plan." He takes a few confident steps into the maze—well, it's not so much an actual maze as it is a two-dimensional *representation* of a maze—sitting down in the dirt at its center and patting the ground. "Join me."

I sink down next to him, still reeling from my near-death experience. The cold of the earth seeps through my jeans as I look out over the never-ending ocean and Tristan removes the canvas bag from his shoulder, producing two bottles of beer. He shifts closer to me until our knees touch, sending a little shiver through my leg, and I take one of the bottles when he offers it.

"So, Char," Tristan says, digging in his bag for what I assume is a bottle opener, "what makes you tick?"

"That's an odd question," I ask, popping the cap off my beer with a confident flick of my fingers.

Tristan watches me bewilderedly. "Well, you're an odd person."

I feel a strange sense of *déjà vu*, which morphs wickedly into the memory of Tristan outside the Majestic, bold and terrified and un-Compelled, struggling frantically to get away from me—the monster who tried to kill his friend. The memory of his eyes, so golden in the marquis lights, looking at me with such poignant fear that I wish I could erase the expression from my mind.

That's an odd question.

Well, if I saw what I thought I saw, then you're an odd person.

"Come again?" I ask.

"I said that you're an odd person," Tristan repeats, motioning toward my bottle. "You just opened that beer with your bare hands."

"Oh," I say, blinking to dislodge the unpleasant memory. "Yeah." I reach to pop the cap off Tristan's beer as well. "It's, uh…a trick Xander taught me."

"I'll add that to my list of things that make you not normal."

"You don't have a list. And it's *ab*normal."

"I absolutely do have a list. And I know."

"Show me."

Tristan takes a sip of his beer then sets it on the ground in front of him. "When the time is right." He moves the guitar from his back to his lap, fiddling with the silver tuning pegs.

"I didn't know you played the guitar."

Tristan glances sideways. "You didn't ask."

His fingers softly pluck the strings and a melody takes shape; it feels familiar somehow, though I don't recognize the tune.

"So," Tristan says, speaking over the rhythm of the music, "what makes you not normal?"

Where do I start?

"Not much," I say, twisting my beer in my hands. "I'm nineteen, I live in my brother's house, and I sleep a lot. I play the piano sometimes, and I run for fun. Is that enough?"

"Not even close," Tristan says as he changes chords. I notice white scars crisscrossing the knuckles of his right hand; I wonder where he got them. "You forgot to mention the fact that you speak multiple languages, you live in a literal mansion, your friends all look like supermodels, and you're one of the funniest people I've ever met."

"You think I'm funny?"

"Absolutely."

"That's new," I say, taking a quick drink. I grimace as the sickly-sweet taste of hops makes its way down my throat. There's a reason I don't drink beer. "Usually when people describe me, they say things like 'disastrous' or 'good-for-nothing' or 'Charlotte, you're such a mess, please stop leaving your dirty socks all over the house.'"

Tristan grins warmly at me. "See? Funny."

I roll my eyes to mask the smile threatening my lips. "What about you? What makes *you* not normal?"

"Nothing," Tristan says definitively. "I'm twenty, I live with two guys I've known basically my entire life, and I also sleep a lot. I play the guitar—obviously—and I can proudly say I've never run a day in my life."

"But running is the *best*."

"Sure, if you're a masochist. My sister always tried to get me to run with her, but if *she* couldn't get me to do it, then no one can."

I pause with my bottle halfway to my mouth. "The sister that's, um—"

"Dead?" Tristan's tone is surprisingly calm, considering his blunt word choice. His fingers don't miss a beat: the guitar's rhythm continues, unhindered. "Yeah, that's the one. I think she went out every morning to run on the beach, which, in my opinion, is even worse than running on pavement."

"A girl after my own heart," I say.

"It's kind of funny, actually. You and I both have siblings who are artists."

"Really?"

"Alison was *incredible*," Tristan says, and something tugs at my memory. Alison. *Alison.* Where have I heard that name before? "She was finishing up her Master's Degree when—" Tristan stops, a deep crease forming between his eyebrows.

"You know," I say, feeling a twinge of sympathy, "Nik's sister, Rayna, died too." I think of Nik's anguish after Rayna died, of the days filled with alcohol and the dreams filled with death. Tristan may not be a centuries-old vampire, but I see Nik in his demeanor: in his soft confidence, in the despair that darkens his eyes. "It was very unexpected, and it was terrible. For all of us. She was like a sister to me."

Tristan's expression softens and he offers a sad smile. "I'm sorry, Char," he says, pausing mid-song to swing the guitar onto his back. He places a warm hand on my knee and I almost jerk away, but the pressure is oddly comforting. I catch a quick whiff of musky cologne and vanilla before the wind whisks it away. "I didn't know that happened to you."

I take a long swig of beer, and I'm almost getting used to the musty flavor, enough to savor it as it tickles my tongue. We don't talk much about Rayna anymore; she simply hovers like an amber ghost, a presence in every conversation, in every thought. I find myself recalling the beautiful parts of her—her cunning eyes, her patience, her lust for adventure—and wonder if Tristan loved his sister as much as I loved mine.

"We all have our traumas," I say, taking one more drink before setting my bottle in the dirt.

"I guess we do," Tristan murmurs, reaching to tuck a strand of hair behind my ear. The calluses on his fingertips are rough against my skin as they trail heat over my cheekbone. Against my better judgement, I lean into his touch.

Tristan's eyes spark and he presses his palm against my cheek, leaning toward me until our breath mingles. The moonlight highlights the freckles on his face, the constellations decorating his skin like flecks of paint. I feel it again, that desire to touch him—to *know* him—and anticipation flares in my chest, banishing my self-control. I inch closer, lifting my hand to brush two fingers along his jaw.

For a few seconds, we freeze, and I worry that I've gone too far—that I've made a mistake that can't be undone. But Tristan exhales slowly, his golden eyes smoldering, and it's all the permission I need to trace my way to the soft curve of his lips.

Alison? Alison, are you there? Alison!

The memory screams through me like a gunshot. I jolt backward and knock over my beer, the liquid soaking quickly into the pale dirt.

"Charlotte?" Tristan asks, alarm plain on his face. "Are you okay?"

Panic explodes like a firecracker in my chest. "I don't—I don't know."

"I'm sorry. Did I do something wrong?"

His words barely register as my brain sorts through two hundred years of fragmented memories. It takes only a few seconds for the ghost of an image to appear, clawing out of my subconscious like a vengeful spirit.

The memory of Golden Gate Park.

I leap to my feet and Tristan follows with a worried expression, the guitar bouncing against his back. "Charlotte?"

My panic ignites to hysteria and I suddenly have to get away. To *run*. To get as far from Tristan as possible.

"I have to go," I say, taking a small step away from him.

"Char, wait—" I turn to run but Tristan catches me by the wrist, flipping me around to face him. "What's going on?"

The concern in his eyes sends a pulse of anger through me, accompanied by familiar shame. Just another boy who thinks he knows better than me. Who *pities* me. Who thinks I'm going to do something stupid.

"Tristan, let go of me," I say, my voice wavering. "I have something I need to do, and you're not allowed to be mad at me for it."

"Mad?" Tristan repeats, his eyes burning with wild confusion. "*What are you talking about?* I'm not mad at you, Charlotte. I'm *worried* about you. You're constantly running off when you're with me. Is everything alright?"

I open my mouth to reply, but my mind is already in Golden Gate Park, straining to recall the details I have been repressing for months. If I can get away from Tristan—return to the place where it happened—it will be clearer. All I have to do is get to the garden.

But I can't move. I'm frozen in place, Tristan's staying hand gripping my wrist as I fight against the growing fear in my chest.

"Char," he pleads. "Don't go."

"Tristan, *please*. Just...trust me."

He frowns at me for a few seconds before reluctantly dropping my hand.

I back away slowly, my chest tightening at the hurt in his eyes, then sprint around the rocky outcropping and back up the dirt path.

21

I RUN.

I run up the trail, tearing through the trees, crossing streets without looking.

I run faster than I've ever run before.

It takes me less than two minutes to reach the Shakespeare Garden in Golden Gate Park. The brick pathway looks haunting in the cold moonlight, lined on either side by empty flower beds and small rows of bare trees. The smell of rotting leaves fills my nose. I walk to the small sundial in the center of the path and touch it with trembling fingers.

I consider leaving, but I can't. I have to know.

I focus my energy on the brick under my feet, the crisp autumn chill, the scent of decaying leaves and cold, hardened soil. My eyes close, my breath slows, and I let the memory take me.

It feels like February, though March arrived weeks ago. It's too cold for March. A chilly, wet fog seeps through the air and into my clothes as I make my way quickly and soundlessly through the San Francisco streets, wishing Rayna were here with me.

Some days are worse than others, and this is one of them: the anniversary of the day Kaleb and Rayna found us, lost and desperate, in the brittle Belarusian spring of 1825. I remember Kaleb's soft eyes clear as day, his gentle hands as he escorted us from the tavern where Xander and I had—for lack of a better description—eaten dinner. Rayna was waiting outside, her expression stony, her arms folded across her chest. She took one look at us and rolled her eyes, turning heel and disappearing down the street.

"You can keep them for one week, Kaleb," she had called over her shoulder in Belarusian, which I realized later was only for our benefit. "After that, they are on their own."

I knew right then that she and I would be friends.

I remember how Kaleb used to look at Rayna like she was the most important thing in the world. Until she wasn't.

Tonight, my desperation for Rayna consumes my every thought, my every movement. I long to hear her laugh, to see her devil's grin, to race with her through the streets or to climb to the top of the tallest building we can find.

But Kaleb took my Rayna away from me. And I will never see that grin again.

In a sudden burst of rage, I punch a tree, making the trunk shiver and the branches prematurely release a few budding leaves.

I'm in Golden Gate Park now, standing under a large wrought iron gate, the words Shakespeare Garden *arching above it. Storm clouds threaten the sky, bringing with them the deep rumble of approaching rain.*

On the brick path leading into the garden, a young woman with a mess of red curls is hurriedly packing up painting supplies in the dying light. A canvas is propped on an easel in front of her, the fading sunset taking shape in expertly-placed oil paint. She is talking animatedly on the phone while she struggles to fit a handful of brushes and tools into a small pouch.

Lightning flashes overhead, followed by a loud clap of thunder, making the girl jump. She curses loudly and shakes her hand; I smell the blood before I see it, splattering red onto the weathered brick like spilled paint. Heat explodes behind my eyes and a snarl builds in my throat.

I run.

The girl cries out as I wrap my arms around her from behind, burying my teeth in her throat. She thrashes against me, trying to call for help, but I clamp a hand over her mouth.

I can't stop. I'm angry. I miss Rayna. I hate Kaleb.

And I'm hungry.

Icy droplets of rain begin to fall, biting into my skin, kissing the back of my neck as I hold the struggling girl. It sends a chill through me, as though I am being watched—and judged—by the storm, but it's too late for me to feel any remorse.

After a few long moments, the girl goes slack in my arms, her phone clattering to the ground. The call is still connected and the tinny sound of a boy's voice buzzes from the earpiece.

"Alison? Alison, are you there? Alison!"

The voice is Tristan's.

My eyes snap open and I stagger backward, dry heaving as my stomach turns over in horror. I stare at the ground in front of me, fully expecting to see Alison's dead body lying at my feet, but she isn't there. I'm alone with my memory and the few rotting leaves skittering over the worn, orange brick.

I run all the way home. I don't pause. I don't breathe. I don't think.

I tear through the front door of the house, my boots squealing with each step as I cross the polished stone floor of the entry, and collapse to my knees in front of the empty fireplace. A twisting pressure builds beneath my ribs, accompanied by an unfamiliar and overwhelming sense of guilt.

It was *me*. I caused the same heartache in Tristan that Kaleb caused in Nik: the pain of losing his sister, the anguish that comes from never getting closure. I could see it in Tristan's eyes, hear it in the numb timbre of his voice.

How many others have felt the same pain? How many lives have I ruined in the past two hundred years?

The pressure continues to build and I wrap my arms around myself, trying to hold it all in, to stave off the weight of my sins for even a few moments longer. But it's too much.

I scream.

There is a flurry of distant movement followed by a rush of footsteps.

"Charlotte?" Xander falls to his knees next to me, urgent hands bracing my shoulders. "Charlotte, *što zdarylasia?* Are you hurt?"

I curl into his chest. Maybe I can hide here and lose myself in old memories of my brother and Belarus and the time *before*. Maybe I can forget.

"*Sistra,* please," Xander says, stroking my hair. "Tell me what's wrong."

"Golden Gate Park," I choke. "It was—" My stomach heaves again, and I clutch the front of Xander's sweater.

"What about Golden Gate?" he demands, but concern edges his voice. "Be clear, Charlotte. What is wrong?"

Horror pulses through me in a steady rhythm, repressed memories flashing in my mind in a montage of blood and death. All dispassionate, all in the name of survival.

A teenage boy in London.

An elderly woman in Prague.

A young couple in Paris.

Who cried for them?

How many tears have been spilled by my hand?

Somewhere along the way, I watched myself become the monster that killed my mother. And I did nothing to stop it.

"The girl at Golden Gate," I say, "was Tristan's *sister.*"

Xander inhales deeply. "Oh, Lottie," he whispers, pulling me closer.

He says nothing else, but holds my head to his chest as I sob.

22

"How many times are you going to run away from that boy before he straight-up ditches you?" Pippa asks.

After what felt like hours of sobbing over my newfound existential crisis, Xander finally managed to calm me down with a pitiful amount of physical affection and an entire bottle of whiskey. The alcohol, coupled with pure exhaustion, has triggered an alarming bout of emotional numbness in me. I haven't felt much of anything for the past few hours except a distant, dull anxiety.

I wonder if this is how Nik feels all the time.

Xander, having exceeded his Charlotte-tolerance level for the night, dumped me at Pippa's about an hour ago. I suspect it was more for his benefit than mine, seeing as he ran out of things to say within twenty minutes of my meltdown. He doesn't always know what to do with me when I'm upset, but to be fair, I don't know what to do with myself, either. So here I am, seeking consolation from a long-legged heathen who is arguably more emotionally unstable than I am.

Tonight is going *great*.

I'm curled in one corner of Pippa's black, leather sofa. Her open-floor-plan penthouse overlooks the water near the Oakland Bay Bridge and is decorated with modern, uncomfortable furniture in shades of black, gray, and electric purple. The linear marble fireplace is lit but is housed behind a pane of glass. It does little to warm the room.

Pippa listened intently while I recounted my evening with Tristan, frowning once my story was done. "*Uffer dda,*" she had muttered in Welsh. "I don't know what I was expecting, but I was hoping for something...juicier." She had then walked to the kitchen, pulled a bottle of vodka from a shiny, black cabinet and returned to her seat. I downed half the bottle in a few swallows before she stole it back with a look of contempt.

"I don't know," I groan now, rubbing my temples. "He's probably starting to wonder what kind of secret vigilante nightlife I'm living."

Pippa takes a swig from the near-empty bottle of vodka and settles deeper into her purple Barcelona chair. The neck of her black t-shirt is wide, gaping open to reveal one white-skinned shoulder, and her legs seem unnaturally long in a pair of bright green booty shorts. The burn scar that covers her entire left forearm is a shocking red against her pale skin; she rubs it absently and her lips purse.

"What?" I ask.

"You're exhausting," she says, plunking the bottle down on a glass side table. "If it were me, Tristan would have been a one-and-done type of deal. I can't believe you haven't even kissed him yet."

"What is it with everyone? First Nik assumes I want to kiss Tristan, and now you're jumping on the bandwagon? Is nothing sacred?"

"Well, don't you?" Pippa smirks.

I frown. "Don't I *what?*"

"Don't you want to kiss him? Or, you know" —she wiggles her eyebrows— "other things?"

"I...haven't thought about it."

Pippa makes an obnoxious sound like the buzzer on a gameshow. "Wrong answer. Try again."

Tristan's grinning face flickers to the front of my mind, his strong arms pulling me back from the sinister darkness of the ocean, his calloused fingers caressing my cheekbone, the scent of vanilla laughing from his lips...

My heart betrays me with a flutter, and Pippa grins.

"Okay, fine," I concede, throwing my hands in the air. "Maybe it's not the most *repulsive* idea in the world. But even if it was an option at one point, it sure as hell isn't happening now. I killed his sister. There's no coming back from that."

"Well, your chances are dwindling. Either kiss him or ditch him. You're batting zero here."

"It's not that bad."

Pippa raises a judgmental eyebrow. "Yes, it is. Let's just say that this is better than the time you seduced the owner of that speakeasy and then stole all his money, but worse than the time you slept with Nik."

"Hey, *you're* the one who seduced the guy at the speakeasy. I just snuck into his safe when he was otherwise occupied."

"Tomato, to-mah-to."

"And you're insinuating that I only slept with Nik once," I add, smirking. "You do remember that Nik and I *actually dated,* right? More than once, for years at a time? There isn't much we *haven't* done together."

Pippa practically chokes as she takes another swig of vodka. "*Charlotte,*" she chastises. "We don't discuss such things in my house."

"You're one to talk. You've slept with him, too!"

She grimaces, her deep blue eyes glinting in the light from the fireplace. "Thank you for bringing that memory to the surface. But Nik is basically your brother, which makes your repeated *copulation* exactly one thousand percent grosser than our single regrettable night of weakness."

"But he's *not* my brother," I shrug, confident in my reasoning. "Plus, he's objectively hot. And a *very* good kisser. Among, you know" —I mock her earlier eyebrow wiggle— *"other things."*

She gags theatrically and sinks back in her chair. "You disgust me. And you know what? I've changed my mind. Your weirdness with Tristan has *nothing* on Nik. Rayna would agree."

I scoff. "Are you kidding me? I think Rayna wanted the two of us together more than we did."

Pippa shakes her head. "You four and your creepy little incest family."

"Five," I say automatically, then recoil.

"Ah, yes," Pippa says, tucking her legs onto the chair beneath her. "We can't forget Kaleb." She pauses, a question in her eyes. "Wasn't Xander supposed to meet with him?"

"Yeah, we went last night. Didn't Xander tell you?"

"We?"

I wish I could keep my mouth shut. "Xander, Nik, and I."

"Why is no one telling me anything?" Pippa demands, gesturing wildly with one hand. "And why wasn't I invited?"

"If it makes you feel any better, I wasn't invited either. It was only supposed to be Xander, but I kind of ruined that plan when I insisted on going with him. Then I told Nik, so—"

"Nik insisted on going, too."

I nod. "Xander was not amused."

Pippa sighs in resignation. "Fine. At least tell me what happened."

"Well," I say, dropping my gaze to the floor. The purple abstract pattern decorating the ivory rug is suspiciously reminiscent of blood spatter. "I confronted Kaleb about stabbing me and he denied it. *Adamantly.* But he's the only logical suspect, so it must have been him. Which means these nightly murders must be him, too."

"The only *logical* suspect?" Pippa's brow furrows. "Does that mean there is an illogical one?"

"No, not exactly," I say, but she sees right through me.

"Out with it, Novik."

"Fine. Kaleb thinks Konstantin is in San Francisco."

I curl more tightly into myself, frowning at the mention of Konstantin. I may not be convinced of Kaleb's theory, but somehow speaking it aloud seems to breathe life into the idea. I glance quickly over my shoulder to confirm we're still alone, as if speaking Konstantin's name could summon him from the depths of whatever Hell he has been hiding in.

Pippa nearly knocks the bottle of vodka to the floor as she reaches for it, steadying it just in time. "Konstantin? That's what he's going with? *Konstantin?*" She shakes her head with an exasperated sigh. "Kaleb will do anything to pass the blame, won't he?"

"I think he's full of crap," I say. "The whole meeting was a disaster. I blame it on the overabundance of testosterone and combined four centuries of repressed loathing that were together in that room."

"A disaster, huh?" Pippa's eyes glint mischievously. "Please tell me you punched him. Oh, I would *love* to hear that you punched him."

"I didn't," I say, pausing for dramatic effect, "but Nik did."

"Yes!" Pippa exclaims, pumping her fist in the air. "I bet that was fun to watch. Did Kaleb bleed? Did he beg for mercy?"

"Nik broke his nose," I laugh, feeding off Pippa's excitement. "Kaleb didn't even fight back. He just laid there like a deflated punching bag. There was blood everywhere."

"I would have paid money to see that."

"It would have been worth it."

"Oh!" Pippa bolts upright in her chair. "Speaking of Nik, I can't believe I forgot to tell you. Yesterday, I needed a good scotch, so I went to his house."

"Naturally."

"But when I got there, he was already with someone."

My interest is piqued: Nik *never* has visitors. I lean forward, resting heavily on the arm of the sofa. "Who?"

"I don't know!" Pippa squeals, wiggling in her seat like a restless child. "But it wasn't a casual meeting. Nik and this mysterious someone were *making out.*" A hint of her Welsh accent surfaces as it does when she gets excited. "The hot-and-heavy, alert-the-authorities kind of making out. I didn't go inside, but I could hear enough through the door."

"How *dare* he hide this from us!" I say in mock offense, clapping a hand over my sternum. "I think we have the right, as his past sexual conquests, to know about his current romantic entanglements."

"Gross," Pippa says. "But you're absolutely right, that *traitor.*"

"So, then…who was it? Do you think it's someone we know?"

Pippa's eyes grow distant. "I honestly have no idea. Which is weird because I *always* have an idea."

"There are at least a few hundred vampires in San Francisco," I muse, "and we only know a few of them. One of them is Kaleb, so that's a hard pass. Then there's Henry, also highly unlikely. And Ty, but Nik hasn't even met him yet." Or has he? Not that it would matter. I think I know where Ty's interests lie. "Or maybe it's a girl. I'm never sure, these days."

An uncomfortable knot forms in my stomach at the thought of Ty. I wonder for a moment if I should tell Pippa about our kiss, but I nix the idea immediately. Besides, it's none of her business. And it's not like it will ever happen again.

"Ty's the new kid, right?" Pippa asks. "The one from the pier?"

I nod, not meeting Pippa's eyes. The ghost of Ty's fangs prickles on my neck and I shiver.

"Maybe it's a human," Pippa muses, her eyes widening in excitement. "What if it was one of Tristan's friends?"

My heart sputters. "What? No. At least, I hope it isn't. The last thing Tristan needs is to have one of his friends tangled up with someone like *Nik*." I think back to the party at Pier 39, when our two groups met for the first time, and a moment flashes in my memory: Nik's eyes dark with blood from a recent feed, the ruffled look about him when we found the body. "Come to think of it, he did seem a little distracted after the party the other night."

"That's what I'm saying! If it started at the pier," Pippa says, twirling a platinum strand of hair between her fingers, "we can rule out the hot centurion dimwit you tried to murder. Because he was *very* preoccupied."

My mouth falls open and I narrow my eyes. "And you judge *me*, Philippa—"

"Hush," Pippa interrupts with a flick of her wrist. "Our situations are very different, my dear. If it wasn't the centurion boy, then that just leaves Catty Blonde, Doe Eyes, or Tight Shirt."

I think for a moment, picturing Tristan's friends. "You mean Olivia, Bree, or Noah?"

"Do I look like someone who takes the time to learn names?"

We sit in silence for a few minutes, my mind working as I stare at the electric flames flickering over river rocks in Pippa's fireplace. Could Nik really be hooking up with one of Tristan's friends? And if so, which one?

What are we dragging these poor humans into?

Pippa breaks the silence. "I think you should talk to him."

"Who, Nik?"

"No, stupid. Tristan."

I hug my arms around my chest and stick out my lower lip. "I don't want to. What am I supposed to say to him? 'Sorry I ran off for the *fourth* time. I was just concerned that I killed your sister. Turns out, I did! Can we still be friends?'"

Pippa rolls her eyes. "You'll have to figure that out yourself." She rises from her chair only to sink onto the sofa next to me, snuggling into my shoulder. "This whole thing really sucks, Lottie, but it comes with the territory. You're bound to make some mistakes with unintended consequences when you're an undead monster, albeit a beautiful one."

Her slender fingers squeeze my hand, and I lean my head against hers. Pippa may have the bedside manner of a piece of sandpaper, but I can always count on her to be realistic in uncomfortable situations.

"That's easy for you to say, baby girl. Not everyone has your confidence."

"I know you deny it," Pippa says, ignoring my comment, "but it seems like you might actually like this guy. I say go for it. You only live once, right?"

I know Pippa means it as a joke, but there is sadness in her voice. Yes, I did live once, but that girl died in 1824. Can what I have now be considered a life if I'm already dead?

My phone buzzes sharply on the glass table next to me, making both of us jump. I snatch it up to a text from Ty.

> I'm going outside today. How long do you think
> I'll last before the sun kills me? Currently taking
> bets. Winner gets a kiss.

I sneer at the word *kiss* and contemplate ignoring him altogether. The last I saw of Ty, he was disappearing into the night with a duffel full of blood bags and the taste of my blood on his lips. I can still see his eyes devouring me, feel the sharp bite of his teeth as they broke skin.

That being said, and considering how long it has been since I've kissed anyone, I have to admit that Ty was exceptionally good at it.

A few texts won't hurt.

> I'll give you eleven minutes. If you last twelve,
> I'll give you fifty bucks. NO KISS.

"Who's that?" Pippa asks, straightening and yanking the elastic out of her hair. She sits in a very unladylike way, her green shorts leaving little to the imagination.

"Ty," I say, frowning as he texts me again.

> Twelve minutes? Easy. But if I last thirteen, you
> DEFINITELY owe me a kiss, babe.

"Why does he have your number?"

"He's Xander's newest project, but I really wish he wasn't. He's gross."

"Gross how?"

Yes, Charlotte. Gross *how?*

"He keeps calling me stupid nicknames like 'hot stuff' and 'babe,'" I say with a verbal question mark, setting my phone back on the table, "and is the cockiest son of a bitch I've ever met."

"Ooh, can *I* have his number?"

"Pippa."

"What?" Pippa says through the elastic between her teeth, twisting her hair into another messy knot. "You know what I like."

"Unfortunately, I do."

I tug on my hair, braiding and unbraiding it as I picture Ty's arrogant smile and its accompanying lewdness. What could have possessed me to kiss someone with such an obvious agenda? Something in his eyes, maybe. He has the most brilliant, silver eyes.

Pippa secures her hair and stands, her arms stretching above her head. I've always been jealous of Pippa and her supermodel physique, all long legs and strong hips and narrow ribs.

"So," she says brightly, her sapphire eyes glowing, "are you going to talk to Tristan?"

"What, right now?"

"Yes, right now. Call him."

"I'm not calling him with you eavesdropping like a bat-eared she-devil."

Pippa takes a few steps toward me and I shrink under her determined gaze. "Fine," she says coolly, sauntering forward with her hands behind her back. "Then *I* will."

She plucks my phone from the table and darts across the room, tapping a few times on the screen.

"Hey!" I leap after her and tackle her to the ground, but not before I hear ringing from the earpiece. Pippa tries to shove me away, but I dig a knee into her chest. "What are you doing, you demon?"

"Helping with your boy problems," she grins. "You really should put a passcode on this thing."

I grab my phone and jump to my feet, just in time to hear Tristan answer the call.

"Hello?" His voice is muffled, most likely with sleep considering the early hour. I imagine him wrapped in a comforter, bleary-eyed and messy-haired and rumpled and warm.

Pippa props herself up on her elbows, watching me with the focused intent of an ocean-eyed panther. I shoot telepathic daggers at her.

"What the hell am I supposed to say?" I mouth angrily at her.

"Figure it out," she mouths back.

"Hi, Tristan," I say brightly, forcing a smile that only Pippa can see.

"Charlotte?" he mumbles. "It's six in the morning." His voice carries the gruff darkness of sleep, rumbling softly through the earpiece in a way that makes me feel...something.

"Is it really?" I ask, feigning innocence. "I'm sorry, I haven't slept all night. I guess I didn't notice the time."

"That seems about right. You all have the weirdest sleep schedules. Hold on." I don't have time to wonder who Tristan means when he says, "you all." There are a few seconds of rustling, during which I assume Tristan untangles himself from his covers and sits up. When he speaks again, his voice is clearer. "What's up?"

I take a deep breath, exhaling loudly as I attempt an explanation. "I didn't mean to run off like that last night. It's just—" I begin, but my confidence wavers. *It's just that I killed your sister.* "I remembered something important I needed to talk to Xander about—"

"I know," he interrupts curtly.

"You—what?"

Pippa is listening intently now, having risen from her seat on the floor. She stands next to me and presses her ear against the other side of my phone to emphasize her already-obvious eavesdropping. I shove her away.

"Xander texted me. He said that you were home, that there was something important you had to take care of, and that you would call me later."

"Oh," I reply lamely, something akin to gratitude blossoming in my chest. "That was...nice of him." After a beat, I add, "Are you okay? You sound upset."

Tristan is silent for a few seconds before replying. "I'm fine, Char." His voice is deep and soft, sleep elongating his vowels. "I mean, it is a little weird that every time I see you, you seem to run away from me. But you asked me to trust you, right? So I am."

I recall the hurt in Tristan's expression when I left last night. But here he is, forgiving me. *Trusting* me.

Guilt simmers like acid in my chest. I almost killed his friend at the Halloween party. I Compelled him to forget me. I nearly lost control in a room filled with his friends. I've run away from him every time I've seen him. I killed his sister.

I *killed* his *sister.*

And I'm not going to tell him about any of it.

Pippa wraps her scarred arm around mine, turning an encouraging and suggestive eye on me.

"Ask him out," she hisses.

I elbow her in the ribs. "Why would I do that?" I hiss back.

She glares at me. "Because you're batting zero, and it's been far too long since you've made it to first base."

If only she knew.

"Charlotte?" Tristan's tone is uncertain. "Are you still there?"

"Sorry," I respond. "Just taking care of a fly on the wall."

Pippa sticks her tongue out and stalks toward the kitchen.

"Literal or metaphorical?" Tristan asks, a hint of the usual humor returning to his voice.

"I wouldn't call a six-foot blonde girl a *literal* fly. But she's definitely nosy as hell."

"Hi, Tristan!" Pippa yells from the kitchen, where she has started mixing a cocktail with the determined vigor of a bartender during happy hour.

Tristan laughs. "Is that your friend from the pier party? Jason won't stop talking about her. If you want her out of your hair, I'm sure he'd be more than happy to volunteer his services."

Tristan's easy demeanor is contagious, and I feel some of my guilt subsiding. He may not have a reason to trust me, but I've given him no reason to hate me, either. The reasons are there, he just doesn't know about them. Yet.

"Do you want to come over later?" I ask, surprising myself.

Pippa halts her drink-making mid-pour and gives me an enthusiastic thumbs up.

"I actually have plans with Jason and Noah tonight, but I can reschedule—"

"No, that's okay," I interrupt as disappointment bites through me. "What about tomorrow?"

"Tomorrow sounds great," Tristan says, a smile in his voice. "You can show me that pool of yours."

"I'll be sure to tell Xander that you're coming this time."

"Perfect. Now, can I go back to bed? Some of us like to sleep in."

"Yeah. I'll talk to you later?

"Sounds good."

Tristan hangs up with a small beep, and I try not to imagine him sliding back into bed, wrapping himself in a down comforter, his face relaxing to innocence as he drifts off to sleep.

Pippa slides a glass of orange *something* across the counter to me and I dart sideways to snatch it up before it topples to the floor.

"See?" she asks, raising her own glass. "That wasn't so hard."

"You are literally the worst person I've ever met."

"That's ridiculous. You've met Nik." Pippa downs her orange drink in two huge swallows. "But hey, I'll own the insult as long as you engrave it on my tombstone."

23

I WALK HOME.

I could call Xander to pick me up—seeing as he's the one who dumped me at Pippa's in the first place—but I've had enough of him in the past few days to last a few months, at least. It would be different if he actually made an effort to be kind.

He wasn't like this before Rayna died. I'm still not sure why her death affected him so strongly. It's not like the two of them were close.

I make my way slowly through the darkened streets of the Financial District, weaving between buildings and steering clear of the sparse, early traffic. The first pale hints of dawn peek over the eastern horizon, bringing with it the dewy scent of morning and illuminating the fog as it rolls over the distant bay.

After a few minutes, the Grace Cathedral looms up in front of me, gray dawn light casting soft shadows on its matching towers. I've always loved the striking resemblance of the building to the Notre Dame Cathedral in Paris, but Grace lacks the painstakingly-detailed carvings and the beautiful, ageless quality of Notre Dame. Still, the two elegant churches have one very important thing in common: they are both on hallowed ground. And hallowed ground doesn't agree with me.

This morning, Grace Cathedral is lit by more than just the approaching day. A chorus of red and blue lights flash in chaotic rhythm from a collection of police cars huddled near the front steps. The road is blocked by an ambulance and a number of orange traffic cones, the sidewalk closed off by a makeshift fence of yellow tape. I cross the street to avoid the small group of reporters from local news stations that are camped just outside the barrier, yelling at officers and medics as they pass by in an attempt to learn new information regarding the body.

The *body?*

A uniformed officer passes the group and a woman's voice cuts through the noise. "Excuse me, sir? What can you tell me about the recent development in the San Francisco Vampire case? Is it true you may have a suspect?"

My stomach leaps into my chest and I freeze in the middle of the road, waiting for the officer's response. I don't hear it, however; a wine-red Mustang screeches to a halt a few feet from me, filling the air with the scent of burning rubber, and I stumble backward in surprise. I expect the driver to get out of the car—or at least yell a few profanities through an open window—but he just idles in the deep shadow of the cathedral, watching me from under the brim of a baseball cap as I find my way quickly to the opposite sidewalk. The squealing of his tires as he peels out makes my ears ring.

I consider yelling a few profanities of my own, considering he nearly ran me over, but the driver is out of earshot in seconds, flying around the corner at breakneck speed.

Exhaust from the Mustang surrounds me, suffocating the red-and-blue lights from the police cars in a nightmarish haze of gray. The reporters are all talking over one another now, hurtling questions at a cluster of overwhelmed officers. I catch snippets of sentences: "cannot confirm" and "another body" and "San Francisco Vampire murders" and "statement later today."

Standing on the sidewalk, staring up at the dawn sky, I nearly scream.

The murderer was *here*. And it couldn't have been long ago, if there are still police officers scouring the scene and reporters just catching wind of the story.

If I had left Pippa's house thirty minutes earlier, I could have caught him in the act. But there's still time.

After all, how far could Kaleb have run?

Before my mind can formulate a plan, my phone buzzes in my pocket, startling me. The bright light from the screen blinds my eyes and I sneer at the name on its surface: Xander. I have no desire to talk to him. So, in standard little sister fashion, I let the call go to voicemail.

Another reporter's voice—this one a man's—rises above the others. "What can you tell us about the latest victim? Can we place any significance on this location?"

An officer moves to make a comment, but I'm interrupted—again—by my phone buzzing. I answer it with a snarl.

"What do you want?" I snap, my eyes fixed on the officer speaking to the crowd.

"Good morning to you, too," Xander drawls. "Where are you?"

I try to formulate a response while listening to the officer, but I've never been good at multitasking. A few of his words register in my mind—"seems to have no connection to the locations of the other murders"—as I sputter a reply to Xander.

"Can I—can I call you back?"

"We don't have time for your games, Charlotte." Something in Xander's tone grabs my attention, successfully pulling it away from the literal murder scene across the street. He sounds tense, almost worried. "Are you still with Pippa?"

I could clap back with a witty retort, but the *something* in his tone kills any desire I have for sarcasm. "No, I'm on my way home," I say. "Listen, I'm just passing Grace Cathedral and—"

"Come home."

"I'm working on it," I growl. "Will you listen to me for *ten seconds?*"

"Just come home. We'll talk then."

The call ends with a soft *beep beep,* and I stare at the lock screen on my phone. It displays a rare photo of me with Xander, his mouth stretched into a wide grin that makes his green eyes sparkle. One of his hands scrunches my lips together, making me look like a disgruntled fish. It's obvious why he was laughing.

Victoria took the photo on one of our good days. The six of us—Xander, Victoria, Nik, Rose, Pippa, and I—took a trip north to Muir Woods, where ancient redwood trees create a natural cathedral that stretches into the heavens. Even Nik seemed to be in a better mood than usual, and we managed an entire night with no arguing, no accusations, no worrying. It was the perfect picture of what our family should be, the dream of what it could have been if our world hadn't been turned on its head.

But all dreams eventually come to an end.

The next day, Nik disappeared. We didn't see him for a month.

I slip my phone back into my pocket, taking one last look at the somber huddle of police cars before heading in the direction of home.

◊　◊　◊

An unfamiliar gunmetal Mercedes is parked in front of the house when I arrive. It has a strange sentience, its cold, unseeing headlights watching me condescendingly as I pass. I ignore the chill that prickles up my back as I slip up the front porch steps.

Unfortunately, the chill only intensifies when I see who is waiting for me inside.

Xander lounges on the living room sofa, talking quietly with an emerald-clad Kaleb, who has made himself comfortable in one of our leather lounge chairs. There is an easy familiarity in their body language, the tones of their voices, that fills me with rage. I wonder how Kaleb would react if I shoved him through the window.

I stalk toward the two boys, fully prepared to make my feelings public, but Kaleb stands as soon as he notices me, holding his hands at his sides with his palms facing forward. A gesture of surrender.

"Charlotte," he says, his icy eyes tight. "I know I'm the last person you want to see in your home, but I would not be here without a good reason."

I ignore him completely, instead giving Xander my full attention. "What the *hell* is Kaleb doing in our living room?"

Kaleb glowers. "I'm standing right here, darling."

"An issue that will be remedied shortly, I can assure you."

Xander exhales loudly from where he sits, unmoving, on the sofa. "If you will listen to him for *ten seconds,* Charlotte, I'm sure Kaleb can answer that question."

I recoil, then fix an acidic gaze on Kaleb. He stands tall and confident, the combination of his green blazer, emerald pendant, and chestnut hair combed into its perfect coif reminding me of a redwood tree: imposing and ancient and immovable.

If a tree falls in my living room and I pretend not to hear it, will anyone know I'm the one who knocked it over?

"I don't trust you," I growl, "and I don't like you in my house. Especially after what I just saw at Grace Cathedral."

"*Our* house," Xander mumbles, then snaps to attention. "Wait—what do you mean? What happened at Grace?"

"There was a *body,*" I say, narrowing my eyes at Kaleb, who sinks back into his lounge chair with a softer, more polite version of a huff. "Another one. Though I'm sure Kaleb already knew that."

"Enough with the accusations." Kaleb frowns, pressing a finger to his temple. "It's growing tiresome."

"Your *face* is growing tiresome."

Kaleb stares at me with contempt, as if to say, *You can do better than that.*

Xander groans. "Honestly, Charlotte."

"You never have had any sense," Kaleb says, twisting the topaz ring on his finger, "have you, Lottie?"

"It's *Charlotte*. And I like to think my sense died with Rayna."

Kaleb's eyes spark and his expression falls to one of misery and loathing. I may as well have punched him in the face. I curse the missed opportunity.

"Alright, enough." Kaleb sighs in resignation. "If you're looking for proof of my innocence, Charlotte, I will offer you this: I arrived here shortly after Alexander left you with Philippa. If I had committed this murder at Grace Cathedral, then I would have been in two places at once, and even I am not so gifted."

I consider him for a few moments, watching for a tell, for *anything* to prove he might be lying—though if Kaleb has ever had a tell, it remains invisible to me—and finally turn to Xander.

"Well? Is that true?"

"Yes," Xander says, watching Kaleb with stern eyes. "It's true."

Part of me is furious, knowing that Kaleb spent hours in *our* house, with *my* brother, drinking *our* wine. At least I assume as much, based on the collection of empty bottles on the coffee table.

Another part of me is—and I hate to say it—*relieved.*

But that tiny bit of relief does nothing to quell my anger. I stomp the short distance to the sofa and sit down next to Xander, leaving a good foot of space between us. After a few seconds, he lifts his arm and rests it on the back of the sofa behind me, his fingers tapping the gray fabric nervously.

"Now then," Kaleb says, kicking one ankle onto the opposite knee as he slides a cigarette out of his breast pocket, "may we proceed?" When I nod, he continues. "Good. Though I'm afraid to admit you will not like what I'm about to say."

I may not be on speaking terms with Kaleb, but there was a time when we were family. Closer, even. The cadence of his voice is as familiar to me as Xander's, and I learned long ago to notice the inconsistencies, the tiny changes in his tone that indicated anger or disgust or fear. This morning there is a tremble, just below the surface, alerting me to the fact that whatever Kaleb is about to tell me, it's going to ruin my day.

"We have a bit of a problem," he says matter-of-factly, "and it involves you, dear Charlotte."

"Okay," I say, settling myself deeper into the pile of textured pillows adorning the sofa. White-hot anticipation claws at my chest. "And what is that?"

Kaleb lights his cigarette with a brass lighter and takes a long, exaggerated drag before responding. "There is a video," he says slowly, smoke swirling out from between his lips, "of your *incident* the other day."

My heart jumpstarts, disbelief and embarrassment pulsing through me like shards of glass. I glance sideways at Xander, but his expression betrays nothing.

"That's...not possible," I manage, but the words are more of a wish than a statement.

"Unfortunately, it's very possible," Xander says, fixing a wary eye on me, "and very real. It's, uh—it's quite damning."

Xander offers me his phone, the screen glowing with a bold red headline that reads:

NEW LEAD IN SAN FRANCISCO VAMPIRE CASE

"It's a catchy name, isn't it?" I chuckle dryly, but Kaleb and Xander say nothing.

I skim over the article until I see a disclaimer about disturbing content hovering over a blurred rectangle, and hesitantly tap on it.

It isn't the clearest video—the camera is shaky, and there are voices in the background; a memory surfaces of a group of boys across the street, laughing at some shared joke, one with a phone held aloft in his hand—but the scene is unmistakable. I see myself sitting on the sidewalk, my face obscured by the edge of my hood, speaking with a young woman in jeans and a pale blue blouse. After a few seconds, I yank her toward me and bury my teeth in her neck, though it's impossible to tell exactly what I'm doing from this angle. I could be stabbing her for all anyone knows. She goes slack and sinks to the ground, just as Xander's Maserati pulls onto the street, obscuring the view.

I've never seen myself kill someone before. My stomach lurches.

"That was..." I start, swallowing my discomfort, "educational."

"As I said," Kaleb says, "we have a problem." He inhales deeply on his cigarette, the heavy scent of smoke tickling my nose. Victoria might kill Kaleb herself if she found out he was smoking in her living room, though if she is burning incense—as she usually does in the early morning—there's a good chance she can't smell it. I pray that's true, for Kaleb's sake. "I thought you had matured past such impulsivity."

"Because you've never been impulsive," I retort, "Mr. I-Murdered-My-Own-Girlfriend. Would you like me to list off a few times when your impulsivity got you into trouble?"

Xander sighs.

"You have me there," Kaleb replies, surprising me with a tiny quirk of his lips. I scowl at him. "But I'm not the one under scrutiny at the moment, am I?"

There is a flash of what could be considered good humor in his glacier-blue eyes, and a long-forgotten pang of fondness stabs through my chest.

"No, you're not," I reply, returning Xander's phone. "I messed up. I'll admit it. But bad things happen all the time. If I could have predicted it would blow up like this, I may have handled the situation differently." When neither of them seems convinced, I switch tactics. "This can't be worse than Golden Gate Park."

My stomach lurches again at the thought of Golden Gate: the media storm that lasted months, the mess that Xander—and, now that I think about it, most likely Kaleb—had to clean up.

And all of it because I killed Tristan's sister.

At least there wasn't a video then.

"That was different," Kaleb says. His nonchalance suggests that, despite the fact that we haven't spoken in over a century, he knows everything about Golden Gate Park. I've always had a sneaking suspicion that his involvement is what finally halted the investigation. "It was a single murder; a freak accident. We have all made the odd mistake and killed someone we shouldn't have." There is a tense pause, and something dark flashes in Kaleb's eyes. He taps his cigarette in a crystal ashtray on the side table. *Has that always been there?* "What we have now is deliberate. Premeditated. In addition to your little 'accident,' Charlotte, there have been four murders in five days. That does not bode well for our secrecy."

"Five," I correct him. "There have been *five* murders in five days."

"Ah. Right." He takes another puff of his cigarette, this time exhaling the smoke in a few perfect rings. "My scouts didn't pick up anything tonight. I was hoping Konstantin had taken a break."

"First of all, Kaleb," I snap, "I'm still not *totally* convinced that this isn't you pulling an elaborate prank. Second, if it *isn't* you, I'm not convinced that your Konstantin theory holds any water."

Kaleb raises a critical eyebrow. "I'm not playing tricks, darling. Why would I ruin my reputation just to bother you?"

"You've done more for less."

"*If* this is Konstantin," Xander interrupts, speaking to Kaleb, "what are we going to do about it?"

"As I mentioned before," Kaleb says, "I received a message from

Konstantin mere days ago. The same message he sent to Rayna in New York. It can't be a coincidence." I glare daggers at him and he turns away, glancing out the window where the sun has finally pierced the horizon. "Needless to say, we have our work cut out for us."

Xander frowns at him. "Meaning?"

"*Meaning* Konstantin is not easy to follow, let alone catch." Kaleb inhales once more on his cigarette before snuffing it in the ashtray. Residual smoke flutters around his head as he speaks. "If you think I'm a tricky bastard, imagine a vampire who gained power over all of Eastern Europe before he had reached his first century of life. He was already close to two hundred years old when he saved me, and he had the ferocity and ruthlessness of one whose sole purpose had always been survival."

I blink at him, then turn to Xander, who simply shrugs.

Konstantin *saved* Kaleb? My investment in this conversation just doubled. I'm desperate to ask a follow-up question, but I don't get the chance.

"Konstantin is used to getting what he wants," Kaleb continues. "And whatever he wasn't given, he took. He was as charming as he was ruthless, mischievous as he was cruel. He has been looking for me since we parted ways and I have managed to evade him, though it has not been easy. I thought I was safe in San Francisco until—" He cuts off, his eyes glinting at me. "Until Halloween."

I fight to maintain eye contact with him mainly out of spite, but the intensity in his expression finally breaks me. My gaze snaps to the coffee table—to the empty bottles of wine—and I swallow hard, guilt pressing against my sternum.

We're talking about *Konstantin*. So, why do I feel like I'm the one on trial?

"As it stands, Charlotte," Kaleb says, "your little stunt at my party was the catalyst that began this whole affair. I'm unsure how you're connected, but Konstantin didn't make a move until you misbehaved. He seems to have taken a particular interest in you."

I narrow my eyes. "What does that *mean?*"

"I originally thought the locations of these murders were random and coincidental, but now I am not so sure." Kaleb lowers his gaze, twirling the topaz ring on his finger. "Embarcadero, Pier 39, Hyde Street Pier...these are popular tourist destinations. Perfect places to leave a body if one is hoping for attention. But Alexander tells me you have visited all these locations in the past few days. Is that correct?"

"Yes," I say carefully. "What are you saying? That Konstantin is *following* me?"

"Based on the current evidence, it seems likely."

"That doesn't make any sense," I say, biting my lip, but panic rises like flames in my chest. All week, I have felt like I was being watched, like someone was lurking in the shadows. Until now, I had assumed it was Kaleb, but what if it was someone else? What if the bright eyes watching me weren't Kaleb's, but Konstantin's? I curl back into the sofa and hug my knees to my chest, finding comfort in my own closeness. "Besides, I hadn't been to Grace until this morning," I say in an effort to discount Kaleb's claim. "Not until the body was already there."

"Yes," Xander muses, resting a hand on my shoulder, "but you were with Pippa, and her penthouse is near Grace. It's possible that Konstantin chose something nearby since Pippa's building isn't exactly in the public eye."

"Awesome," I grumble, feeling Kaleb's cold eyes on me. I look up at him and fight to keep the tremor from my voice. "So, you're telling me Konstantin—a vampire I have *never met*—is somehow tracking my every move just to torment me...why, exactly?"

"I don't know, darling," Kaleb says with unexpected gentleness, "but we are doing our best to find out. Until then, it may be prudent of you to lie low. Konstantin has always followed a very specific set of rules. He cannot play the game if one of his pawns is removed from the board."

"Excuse me? I am no one's pawn."

"Of course you're not. But, if there is one thing I learned from Konstantin, it's that everything is a game of chess to him." Kaleb picks up his cigarette butt and crushes it between his fingers, dusting them in fine ash. "He misses nothing, carefully manipulating each piece to do his bidding, whether they know it or not. And he always plays black." He examines his ash-whitened fingertips for a few seconds. "I was a player in his game for centuries, and it was my hope that I had successfully removed myself. Obviously, that is not the case."

The cold foreboding in his voice raises the hairs on my arms. A mental picture unfolds in my mind: San Francisco as a game board, stretching for miles in a black-and-white checkered grid of skinny houses and sprawling parks. Xander as a stoic bishop, Nik a clever and unpredictable knight. Rose, Pippa, and Victoria taking turns as watchful rooks. And me, a lowly pawn in Konstantin's game, used and discarded in pursuit of some greater, unknown purpose.

If Konstantin always plays black, that means Kaleb is playing white. I'm almost sure there's something significant about the colors, some advantage one has over the other. Some reason why Rayna always, *always* played black. But, for the life of me, I can't remember. That, in itself, is disconcerting.

"I don't want to be on Konstantin's metaphorical chess board," I say a little too loudly, a small jolt of annoyance flickering through me. "I don't even *like* chess. What does any of this have to do with me, anyway?" The annoyance rises to more of a panicked desperation, my voice rising with it. "Why does he care about anyone but *you*, Kaleb? If he wants you, he can have you. Good riddance."

Kaleb sinks backward in his chair, regarding me with a look of mild bewilderment. I feel a tiny stab of guilt, but it lasts only until Kaleb opens his mouth again.

"You don't have a choice," he says coldly. "Once Konstantin

has you in position, there are only two ways out: you either win or you die."

"Then I guess we can thank you for ending Rayna's game for her." Kaleb's expression hardens to ice.

"Charlotte," Xander hisses. *"Behave."*

"No." I stand from the sofa and am met by a sharp glare from Xander. "This has been a lovely meeting, but I'm afraid I've reached my nightly limit for mind-blowing revelations. I'm going to bed."

"Lottie, wait," Xander insists and he catches me by the wrist, his green eyes glittering. "I—*we* need your input. If Konstantin is following you..." He trails off and his eyebrows pinch together, his fingers tugging at the hem of his sweater.

"You've never needed my input before. I fail to see how this is any different." I yank my arm free of Xander, leaving his hand to fall dejectedly into his lap. "Tonight started off on a great note, until—" I choke on the words. *Until I found out about Tristan's sister, Tristan's sister, Tristan's sister.* Was that only a few hours ago?

Kaleb looks up at me with scrutinizing eyes, their ice blue catching the dawn light and piercing straight through me. The effect is brilliant, *blazing,* and I shrink away, staring down at his wingtip shoes. His eyes have always held a certain power, an uncanny ability to understand more about me than should be possible. I'm sure, right now, he can see it: my guilt, my fear, the illusion I've painted for myself. Because, while I would rather die than admit it, all this talk of Konstantin is starting to worry me.

When I meet Kaleb's eyes again, concern has softened them to the pale blue of midday sky. Heat prickles under my skin, and I suddenly feel exposed. Vulnerable. *Seen.*

"Let's just say," I say, clearing my throat to mask the unknown emotion swelling in my chest, "it has been an absolutely horrendous night. If you need me, I'll be sleeping for the next year."

I hurry toward my bedroom, relief flooding through me as I

disappear from their probing gazes.

Whatever Kaleb and Xander have going on, I'm over it.

My dark bedroom is a welcome escape after a night of absolute hell, and I release a shuddering sigh as I close the door quietly behind me. I try to rid my mind of the nagging feeling of being watched but, now that I've awakened to the idea that Konstantin is following me, I can't seem to shake it.

I throw back my covers, check under the bed, tear open my shower curtain, and push aside the clothes hanging in my closet. Nothing. Just some dust bunnies and an old Aerosmith ticket stub and a silver coin on a leather cord.

Rayna's coin.

It must have fallen from my cluttered nightstand and been kicked under the bed, left to gather dust with a few forgotten pairs of socks. I hold it up, careful not to let the silver touch my skin, and watch as it rotates in a few lazy circles, glinting in the limited light peeking around my curtains.

Rayna would trust Kaleb. Of *course* she would. Even now, if she were to somehow rise from the grave and appear here in full, corporeal glory. "Screw the fact that he murdered me, Lottie," she'd say in that dark, wicked voice of hers. "Kaleb always has his reasons."

Sure he does: he's a selfish bastard. That's all the reason I need.

I walk into the bathroom and hang Rayna's coin on a hook near the sink with my other necklaces, then sulk to my closet and close the door, yanking every extra pillow and blanket from the upper shelves and throwing them unceremoniously on the ground.

As a child in Belarus, I made a habit of hiding in our small pantry when I encountered a problem I didn't know how to solve. Once, when I ripped my favorite dress, Mama couldn't find me for almost two hours. She and Xander spent the afternoon searching the small forest behind our cottage while I snacked on dried berries and cheese, falling asleep on the flour-dusted floor. By the time they found me,

Mama was hysterical. Xander, a usually-charming fourteen-year-old at the time, was beside himself with anger, scolding me for worrying Mama.

I spent the evening alone with a thread and needle, mending my dress to the best of my ability. Mama could have done better, but I wouldn't ask her for help. I didn't deserve it.

I learned two important things that day. One, that I was capable of doing things for myself. And two, if I ever made a mistake, Xander would be there to chastise me for it.

The dusty, stale air of my closet envelops me in an embrace of pitch blackness, and my anxiety subsides, just a little. I breathe into the silence and sink to the floor, collapsing onto a nest of pillows and blankets. When I close my eyes, moments flash in my mind: Ty's languorous grin, Tristan's strong arms, Pippa's wiggling eyebrows, Kaleb's ash-covered fingers, Alison's blood on my hands.

Alison? Alison, are you there? Alison!

Something else shimmers behind my eyelids, something fleeting and barely there and, I'm almost positive, *important*. A glimpse of red, maybe. Or silver? But the memory is gone as quickly as it came, disappearing into a dark fog as sleep engulfs me like a freezing ocean wave.

24

"*Checkmate.*"

Nikolas groans and dismissively topples his king. He and Kaleb have been at it for hours now. They sit across from one another at the game table in the parlour, an ornate wooden chess board between them, each taking his turn at victory. Though, if I have been counting correctly, Nikolas has lost more games than he has won.

Rayna has been studiously observing over Kaleb's shoulder, her eyes flickering rapidly over the board. Occasionally she'll mumble something like, "Knight to King's Bishop three," and Kaleb will shush her, think on it, and obligingly follow her advice. Nikolas seems to lose quickly after that.

"You always win when you play white," Nikolas grumbles, glaring over the game board at a bemused Kaleb.

"Not always," Kaleb says with a quirk of his lips, leaning backward in his chair. "I often win while playing black, as well."

Nikolas throws the black king at him and Kaleb swipes a deterring hand, blocking the piece just before it strikes him in the forehead. It clatters to the ground near my feet and Kaleb glowers.

"Do not break my pieces, Nikolas," he says. "They are antiques."

"Oh, please," Rayna interjects, leaning down to wrap her arms

234

around Kaleb's chest. He presses a kiss to her cheek. "You've had that chess set for barely three decades. It is as much an antique as Alexander, over there."

Alexander, who lounges on the sofa with a sketchpad on his lap, fixes Rayna with a withering glare. She grins in return.

"Do lighten up," she sighs dramatically. "Your sour mood is ruining my joke."

Alexander grimaces before returning to his drawing.

"Another game, then?" Kaleb asks, already resetting the board. He lines up the pieces carefully, each perfectly centered in its square.

Nikolas, on the other hand, spends less than half a minute position-ing his pieces, finishing the work as quickly as possible. "Fine," he says, "but I would like to play white this time."

Kaleb smirks at him. "As you wish."

The two boys switch seats and Kaleb turns to me. "Charlotte, darling, be a dear and bring me that king, will you?"

I reach down and pick up the black king from where it has settled against my skirts, twirling it a few times in my fingers. The piece is made of oak and stained a dark ebony, but the cross on its head is untouched, adorning it in a crown of white. Luckily for Nikolas, its recent journey across the room seems not to have harmed it.

I stand and offer Kaleb the piece—he takes it from me with a warm smile—before returning to my seat, but not before Rayna catches me by the wrist.

"Watch with me," she says, and I scowl at her.

"I have no interest in playing chess, let alone watching it," I say, retrieving a small book from the coffee table. "I would much rather sit here and read" —I check the cover— "A Lady's Guide to Etiquette and Politeness." Rayna cocks an eyebrow and I toss the book back onto the table. "Yes, alright. If I had hoped to be convinc-ing, I should have chosen something with a different title."

Rayna drags me toward the game, where Kaleb has just finished straightening the black pieces. "It's your move, Nikolas," he says and leans forward, resting his elbows on the table with quiet intensity.

Rayna wraps an arm around my shoulders as Nikolas moves a pawn two squares forward. After a few needlessly tense seconds, Kaleb moves a pawn of his own. I am already bored.

"May I please *return to my book of etiquette?*" I say, squirming in her grip. "I promise I will read it. I may actually learn something."

"Hush, Lottie," Rayna whispers, her fingers digging into my arm. Nikolas moves one of his knights, Kaleb, a bishop.

"I fail to see how simply watching chess will teach me anything important."

Nikolas hesitates, his hand hovering above a pawn, before moving his bishop a few squares diagonally and to the left. Kaleb's eyes narrow slightly, concentration brightening his gaze.

"Ha!" Rayna hisses, "did you see?"

I look from Rayna's eager face to the board, then back to Rayna. "Of course I didn't," I say, frustrated. "I barely know the game! What could I have seen in five moves?"

"The game is one of call and response," she says, leaning close to me as the boys continue moving pieces with cold determination. "With every move, a new collection of possibilities emerges, new ways for both Nikolas and Kaleb to win. Nikolas made the first move, leaving Kaleb to adjust and readjust based on Nikolas's choices. That is the key to playing black—" Kaleb moves a pawn again, taking the white bishop. "Oh, lovely!" Rayna says, snapping her fingers once. "It will be a miracle if Nikolas finds a way out of this."

"Dammit," Nikolas mumbles, straightening in his chair. "I didn't see that."

"Thus, why you have a losing record, Nikolas." Kaleb hasn't taken his eyes from the board. "You have your own plan, but fail to anticipate mine. It is a beginner's mistake. One you make often."

"Ah, the mental game," Rayna whispers. "Just as important as the physical one."

"Rayna, you devil," Nikolas says, glaring at her as Kaleb takes his knight. "Will you please be quiet? You will cause me to lose this game."

"You are already losing," Kaleb says confidently, resting a chin on his entwined fingers, "but it is endearing of you to believe you could still win."

I wake to the sound of my closet door flying open, followed by the soft rustling of clothes landing on the floor. I bolt upright, fighting to blink away the heaviness of sleep, and I see a tall, dark silhouette in the doorway. My heart leaps into my throat, my mind recalling the memory of a shadow in our Belarus home, tall and bleeding and staggering toward me with a knife protruding from his chest...

"Rise and shine, *collwr*," a sharp voice demands.

Pippa.

Relief surges through me before Pippa yanks on one of my blankets, flipping me over like an uncoordinated pancake.

"Ouch." I bury my face in a pillow. "Ten more minutes."

"You have *five* minutes. Rose and Victoria are waiting in the car."

With a considerable amount of effort, I sit up and begrudgingly open my eyes again. Pippa is wearing *very* tight pants, a leather jacket zipped all the way up, and thigh-high leather boots—her *mischief* boots. I groan.

"Is this a shenanigan?" I whine. "I'm not in the mood for shenanigans." I haven't had a hangover in two hundred years but I'm pretty sure this is what it feels like. A dull ache reverberates behind my eyes; I can't tell if it's from Pippa's rude awakening or the multitude of intrusive thoughts bouncing around my skull. Either way, I have to fight the urge to sink back to the floor.

"Yikes, Lottie," Pippa grimaces, grabbing me by the wrist and yanking me gruffly to my feet. "You look like death. Well, more than usual, anyway." She flicks the light on and I hiss loudly.

"A little warning would have been nice."

"You're such a baby." Pippa flips through my clothing with tenacity, her jacket reflecting the incandescent light with a dull vigor. "T-shirt, t-shirt, t-shirt...aha!" Her hand fishes through the hangers and she triumphantly reveals a low-cut red blouse with sheer, cuffed long sleeves. "This will do."

"I might agree with you if I knew what we were doing."

"Rose called a Girls' Night," Pippa says simply, throwing the shirt at me.

Excitement bolts through me as I snatch it out of the air. Finally, an excuse to ditch my brother. My mouth slides open into a grin and Pippa matches it.

"Hurry up," she says. "The city is waiting."

◊   ◊   ◊

It takes me a few minutes to scrub away a full day's worth of anxiety, made manifest in stale clothes and knotted hair and tearstains on my cheeks. Now, as I look at my reflection in the bathroom mirror, it's hard to believe the last day happened at all.

At any given moment, I'm usually in jeans, a t-shirt, and Converse sneakers, which means the few pieces of nice clothing I own don't often see the light of day, figuratively speaking. The blouse Pippa chose hugs my waist and cuts a deep V down my chest, exposing more pale skin than I'm used to seeing. I had almost forgotten that I had cleavage. Topped with some red lipstick, a swoop of dark eyeshadow, and a copious amount of dry shampoo and hairspray, I actually look kind of *hot*.

My eyes trail downward to the edge of a new, angry scar over my heart that peeks out from behind my neckline. A permanent reminder that I'm a little bit more than human.

Vampires don't usually scar, given our ability to heal rapidly. It takes something more potent than a simple scratch to leave a lasting mark, like a wound made by hawthorn or holy water. Though one impulsive decision in the Central Park Zoo did leave me with three massive, parallel scars stretching across my abdomen.

The purplish, raised skin over my heart has *nothing* on that.

Still, seeing it so blatantly on display sparks a touch of self-consciousness in me. I attempt to adjust my blouse to cover it, but to no avail. Leave it to Pippa to choose the tightest shirt in my closet.

My gaze slides sideways to see Rayna's silver coin pendant—twin to Nik's—hanging next to the mirror. I stare at it for a long moment before removing it from its hook and untying the knot in its leather cord. The coin twists lazily in the air and the tiny griffin on its surface seems to wink, as if to say, *Remember me?*

I lift the cord and place the coin carefully around my neck.

The silver kisses the skin between my breasts and I wince as a stinging circle of red blooms beneath it. The pain is nothing compared to that of the dagger that created the scar just inches away, but it's surprisingly intense for such a tiny thing. Something about the miniature fire burning on my skin sharpens my senses, anchors me in the present, distracts me from the endless barrage of worries streaming through my brain.

Konstantin who?

I suddenly understand why Nik never removes his coin.

I wonder why Rayna removed hers.

I flash my fangs and feel my demeanor change from confident to powerful. Maybe I should wear red more often.

A text from Ty flashes on my phone screen.

> THIRTEEN MINUTES. You owe me fifty bucks and
> a kiss. Pay up, buttercup.

I roll my eyes, but type a quick text in response.

> I'm impressed, newbie. Most guys in your shoes
> would have given up after five. A kiss wasn't
> part of the deal, if you remember. But nice try.
> Consider this an IOU.

He shoots back a thumbs up emoji followed by a kissy face.

At least one thing's for sure: if Ty saw me right now, he wouldn't be able to keep his eyes off me. Their dull silver flashes in my mind, and I find myself wishing for gold.

A car horn blares from outside, alerting me to the fact that the girls have run out of patience. "Coming!" I slip on a pair of black ankle boots and roll up the cuffs of my dark jeans before darting into the hallway.

I don't see Xander in the foyer until it's too late. I slam into him, nearly knocking the bottle of wine from his hands, and he gives me an exasperated look.

"Sorry, X."

"You have *got* to start watching where you're going," Xander says with forced calm. "That's twice this week."

"Well, maybe you should stop walking through the foyer while holding breakable and potentially dangerous objects. You're an accident waiting to happen." Xander shoots me a caustic look, and I concede. "Fine. I'm incompetent. Now will you *please* move? The girls are waiting for me in the car. It's—"

"Girls' Night, I know." His mouth twitches into what could almost be a smile. "Don't have too much fun without us."

"Us?" I ask, and movement flashes in the corner of my eye. I turn to see Nik lounging in a chair by the living room fireplace, swirling amber liquid in a crystal glass. He looks like a carving of some forgotten Greek god with his strong shoulders and pained eyes and perfect hair. I give him a small wave and he returns it before his eyes drift to the coin around my neck. He freezes mid whiskey swirl and his expression softens markedly.

Something else moves on the other side of the room. I turn to see Henry perusing the dark oak bookshelves, dressed in narrow suit pants, a pinstripe waistcoat, and a white shirt with his sleeves rolled up. Anxiety flutters in my chest and I eye Xander quizzically. A warning shadow passes over his face and he narrows his eyes: *Be nice.*

I attempt to swallow my suspicion, but my mouth suddenly feels dry. *He may be Kaleb's Beta,* I remind myself, *but I have nothing against Henry. Henry is harmless. I think.*

"What is he doing here?" I hiss at Xander, and he leans close to me.

"That is none of your concern."

"Well, if Henry's here, you might as well invite Kaleb. Or hell, why not invite Ty as well? Or Tristan? *Really* make it a party."

"Charlotte," Xander scolds, his voice barely more than a whisper. "Will you *please* trust that I know what I'm doing?"

I glance up at him, ready to reply with a quick retort, but the expression on his face is so genuine that the words evaporate on my tongue.

Usually during Girls' Night, the boys get together for their own version of fun, though it has happened less since the Rayna incident. Xander and Nik are barely on good terms as it is, which typically results in a whole lot of drinking and some small amount of mischief.

Seeing Henry in the living room, ready to join the fun, is more than a little strange: it's downright unheard of. This is the first time anyone besides Xander, Nik, or Kaleb has been invited to Boys' Night. *Ever.*

"Um, alright," I say, pretending not to notice the relief in Xander's eyes. He may have been expecting a fight, but apparently, I'm feeling agreeable tonight. "Hi, Henry," I say, and he spins on his heel, his face splitting into a bright grin.

"Charlotte, hello!" he replies in his smooth London accent. His spider-like fingers caress the cover of an old book, cradling it like it is made of the most precious materials. A gold chain shimmers in his waistcoat pocket. *Is he actually carrying a pocket watch?* "I'm just admiring some of your collection here." He returns the book to the shelf and runs his fingertips over the spines of a few leather-bound volumes.

"I can't believe you have a first edition of Pride and Prejudice!" Henry continues, practically vibrating with excitement. I have a hard time believing one can get that delighted by old books; surely, he has something else on his mind. "Kaleb's collection seems lacking compared to yours."

I tense, and Xander puts a firm hand on my shoulder.

"Didn't you steal that from Kaleb?" I mouth. "Didn't you steal a *lot* of these from Kaleb?"

He bites his cheeks. "Yes, but Henry doesn't need to know that," he mouths back.

I roll my eyes and turn my attention back to Nik, who is still staring at the pendant around my neck. I catch his eye and give him a look that asks, *Are you going to be okay?*

The muscles in his jaw tense, his eyes glinting, but he nods before finishing off the rest of his whiskey in a single swallow.

Satisfied, though still wary, I move toward the door.

"I expect there to still be wine when I get back," I say, and Nik offers a crooked smile that does nothing to reassure me.

25

Rose still won't tell us where we're going.

We zip through the night-darkened streets in her red Mini Cooper, eighties music blasting from the speakers; Rose, Pippa, and Victoria are dancing and singing along like drunk sorority girls. I, however, can't help the longing that claws at my chest.

Girls' Night was Rayna's *thing*. After seven arduous months of being a vampire, living day-to-day with Xander as we struggled and hungered and hunted, Rayna took me on our first girls-only outing. I thought she was insane. We were *vampires,* not little peasant girls who could afford frivolity. But, as usual, Rayna knew something I didn't: vampirism only made everything more exciting. The night was simple—stealing alcohol from a nearby brewery, chasing the chickens from a farmer's coop, climbing to the top of a windmill and drinking wine straight from the bottle—but it was liberating.

After that, it became somewhat of a tradition. Every few years, when immortal life seemed too cruel or monotonous, Rayna and I would paint the town with reckless abandon.

Damn, I miss her.

The tradition lived on after Rayna died. When one of us calls for a Girls' Night, we don't question it. We drop everything and go.

Sometimes Victoria will sneak us into an elite club or Pippa will get us racing down the beach in nothing but our underwear. But tonight, it's Rose's turn.

She parks the car on the Embarcadero and we file out near the entrance to Pier 39. Pippa and Victoria chat animatedly as Rose flits ahead, but I hang back a few feet, a chill creeping over me. It has only been a few days since we were here with Tristan and his friends, but it feels like it has been decades.

The pier looks completely different now, the shops closed and the boardwalk empty. The only light comes from the glow of the waning moon, the only sound from our quiet footsteps and the steady lapping of the ocean water below the salty, weathered boardwalk.

As we pass the Center Stage, visions of the party come flooding back to me. I see Tristan grinning under the pink party lights; Tristan throwing his head back in laughter, his eyes sparkling with warmth; Tristan, his arms circling me as I melt into the soft curve of his chest.

Mingling with the warm memories are cold ones: the blood pooling under a lifeless body; Nik's ruffled appearance, his eyes shadowed and his fangs bright; Ty's hands tugging uselessly at my arm as I crush his windpipe beneath my hand.

The memories swirl around me like restless ghosts, dancing in the pale shadows.

"Lottie!" Rose calls. "Are you coming?"

The illusion shatters and I find myself standing alone on the empty pier. Wind whispers around me, lifting my hair, breathing life into the night. The shadows seethe. The back of my neck prickles. I'm vaguely aware of my hands clenching into fists at my sides as anxiety pulses through me, and I'm struck again with the eerie feeling of being watched.

Something glitters in the corner of my eye. I whirl around, my heart pounding erratically, but it is only the moonlight glinting off a metal railing.

"Lottie!"

I jump at the sound of Rose's voice, then bolt toward it, ignoring the chill that has crept its way into my bones. I find her and Victoria standing near the rows of anchored boats, pressed close as they take a collection of selfies. The two girls look like ethereal, undead angels in the silver light, Victoria in a fitted, ivory jumpsuit and Rose in a pair of high-waisted jeans and a royal blue sweater, her coiled hair framing her face in a thick cloud. At some point along the way, the dress code for Girls' Night became "an outfit you might wear in a heist movie." Never mind the fact that we always arrive home with our clothes either ruined or in need of a very thorough wash.

A motor rumbles quietly to life and I look up to see Pippa at the wheel of a white-and-blue fishing boat named "Our Lady Lola." She winks at Rose and the two of them share a conspiratorial grin.

Rose's eyes flash as she turns to me and Victoria. "Let's go."

◊   ◊   ◊

Apparently, Pippa can drive a boat.

And, apparently, the only one of us who didn't know that was me.

We're cruising across the bay toward Alcatraz—the building that was once a nearly-inescapable prison, now lit by a strategic collection of warm spotlights. The top of the lighthouse shines brightly and sends a shimmering beam of yellow across the surface of the water. Fog settles over the bay, the light creating an eerie, glowing cloud around the island.

The crisp sea air cutting across the deck clears my head—so long as I don't think about the obscene amount of dark, open water below us—as does the silver coin burning over my sternum. I take a deep breath, focusing on all the worries of the past few days, and exhale forcefully, pushing them all away.

Tonight is about me, my girls, and some good, old-fashioned breaking and entering.

Pippa slows the boat and we drift lazily toward the rocky cliff face on the south side of the island. When we're close enough, Rose hops from the deck and ties the boat to a jutting rock. Victoria and I follow, landing carefully in our boots, and Pippa comes last, slinging a backpack over her shoulders before leaping to catch the side of the cliff with both hands.

"Last one up has to kiss Kaleb," she grins through her fangs.

We all make various sounds of disgust, Rose's lips curling into a sneer. "Speak for yourself," she says, skittering up the rock like a lizard. "I won't be kissing anyone, thank you very much."

Pippa sneers. "Then don't be the last one up."

We emerge over the crest of the island and the Alcatraz prison looms up in front of us, a forlorn, lonely-looking structure in pale concrete and steel. It took less than a minute for us to reach the top of the short cliffside and, though I deny it vehemently, I was definitely last.

We skirt around dark pathways, a quartet of ghostly wraiths, climbing rocks and scaling cracked stairs until we reach the outer walls of the prison. The air is cool and damp, carrying with it the familiar smell of the briny ocean coupled with peaty earth and crumbling stone. My heart pounds excitedly, each sluggish pulse a loud punctuation in the silence.

"Okay," Rose whispers, gathering us into a huddle, "you all know the rules. The bigger the act, the better. If security catches you, you're immediately disqualified. Voting commences at dawn to determine the winner. And, as usual, *no boys.*"

"No boys," we reply in a hushed chorus.

Rose leads us to a nondescript back door hidden by a scraggly bush. She slips a pin from her hair and bends it into a key shape, sliding it into the lock and twisting it a few times until we hear a muted *click*.

"It's like they were *asking* us to break in," Pippa says with mock sadness, shaking her head. "That puts Rose in a very weak lead. Who's going to top it?"

I brush past her and shove the door open. The stale scent of mildew and sea spray fills my nose, and the air carries with it a damp chill that suggests the building is always cold, blocked forever from the sun's warmth by thick, windowless walls. Our footsteps echo loudly as we make our way through a dark hallway and into the main cell block, steel prison bars looming up on either side of us like rusting, metal bones.

"This is so *creepy*," Pippa breathes. "I love it."

"If I were human," I muse, brushing a few flakes of paint from the nearest wall, "this is the kind of place I would imagine vampires living; dark, cold, and completely devoid of any creature comforts."

Rose nods in solemn agreement, her expression growing haunted. "Strangely enough, many vampires do live like this. It's absolutely horrifying."

"How do they do it?" Victoria asks, sticking her nose in the air. "If I went one day without my memory foam mattress or electricity or a hot shower, I would *die*."

"You're already dead, V," I say, and she groans. "But enough talk."

I scan the room for security cameras, noting their locations before leaping into the air, hooking my fingers over the upper walkway. With a grunt, I heave myself over the edge and flip over the railing, watching with satisfaction as the other girls stare up at me with challenging gazes.

"And what exactly are you going to do up there?" Victoria asks, her black eyes sparkling.

"This." I fling myself into the air and twist in a backflip before landing, crouched, next to her.

"You think *that's* impressive?" Pippa scoffs. "Watch *this*."

We spend the next hour in the prison doing increasingly-complicated backflips, racing each other between cell blocks, scaling the walls barefoot to see who is the fastest climber.

I am flying midair between one upper walkway and another when something clatters near the entrance. My focus shifts and, instead of landing gracefully on the concrete walkway, I slam into the railing and plummet to the ground, landing hard on my shoulder with a loud pop. Pain rockets through me and I cry out, but Pippa clamps a hand over my mouth.

"*Shh.*" She cocks her ear toward the door. "I think we've been made."

The four of us listen in tense silence, adrenaline temporarily numbing the pain in my shoulder. After a few seconds, I hear the unmistakable sound of approaching footsteps. A flashlight burns through the darkness.

"*Hey!*" calls a gruff voice, and we spring into action.

I scramble to my feet, clutching my arm as we race through the cell block, through the hallway, and out the back door. The night engulfs us, fresh ocean air clearing the scent of mildew from my nose, and we collapse into a fit of nervous giggles. The city lights reflect and dance playfully on the water, creating the illusion that the black void of the ocean is filled with swirling pools of glitter.

"That was *not me,*" Victoria says with a sly grin, leaning against the crumbling wall. "I blame Lottie for slamming that cell door."

"No way," I counter. "Rose was the one who was *showing off* for the security cameras." I attempt to punch her in the arm, but my shoulder screams in protest. I wince.

Victoria's expression betrays her concern. "Let me see," she says, taking my forearm with one hand and probing my shoulder with the other. "I think it's dislocated. Let me just—"

She wrenches my arm upward, and my shoulder pops back into place with a loud *crack.*

I curse, my voice echoing off the prison wall, and the girls bite back their laughter.

"Thanks for that," I say through clenched teeth, shrugging a few times to test Victoria's work. "I guess that means I won Girls' Night, huh?"

"Lottie," Rose says. "You don't get to win just because you're the only one who got injured."

"Of course I do. That means I went bigger than the rest of you."

"You wish," Victoria says. "Pippa's balancing act was pretty impressive."

Pippa grins. "It was, wasn't it? Though I think Rose has me beat with that wall-climbing move. Where did you learn how to do that?"

Rose opens her mouth to reply, but is interrupted by her phone buzzing. She answers it with a grin.

"Hi, Nik," she says. "Enjoying Boys' Night?"

"Yeah, it's, uh—look, we're going to need some help here." Nik's voice hums through the earpiece, breathless and wild, and my nerves prickle. Muffled sounds echo in the background: heavy footsteps, a girl screaming, a chorus of vicious snarls. Someone laughs, deep and foreboding.

"Nik?" I say a little too loudly, aware that the security guard may still be looking for us. "What's going on? Is Xander with you?"

Rose waves me off and straightens, wind stirring the dark curls that frame her face. "Where?"

"The sooner you can get back to the house, the better," Nik says. "We need to—son of a *bitch*. XANDER." The call goes dead.

Panic bolts through me, and I see it mirrored in Victoria's eyes.

Rose tries calling back, but Nik doesn't answer. I call Xander. Nothing.

We all stare at each other in alarm before Rose takes off in the direction of the boat.

I sprint after her, swallowing the alarm clawing through my ribcage, and say a quiet prayer that my brother will be alive when we get back.

26

"IF IT'S NOT AN EMERGENCY, I don't want to hear it."

Xander's voicemail greeting rings in my ear for the fourth time, and I throw my phone on the floor of the car. I rake my fingers through my hair, trying to fight the dread boiling in my chest, but I only succeed in ripping a few hairs from my scalp.

He's fine, I think to myself. *Xander is fine.* But if he was fine, why wasn't he the one to call Rose? Why did Nik call her? Why didn't Nik call *me?*

The car screeches to a halt in front of the house and I practically dive out of the backseat, tearing up the front walkway while the girls trail after me. The windows are dark, the front door slightly ajar. Icy fear rattles in my chest as I push the door open.

The smell of blood assaults my nose, the scent cold and acrid and tinged with death. *Vampire blood.*

Adrenaline shoots through me, accompanied by blinding panic. *"Alexander?!"* I scream, racing in the direction of the smell. "Alexander, are you—"

I burst into the kitchen and stop dead in my tracks; the girls slam into me one after the other, and we stagger forward in a domino effect. Xander, Nik, and Henry surround the island, all covered in varying amounts of blood—Nik looks like a murder victim—but they're grinning. I might even say they've been *laughing*.

I sigh in relief. It's been so long since I've heard Nik laugh.

To make matters more interesting, *Xander* is laughing, too. My brother, who has smiled exactly three times in his entire undead existence, is grinning brightly beneath rose-colored cheeks, his fangs out.

Which can only mean one thing.

"Xander, how much have you had to drink?"

Xander's grin fades immediately and he blinks a few times in rapid succession, his eyes searching for purchase on my face. After a few seconds of forced composure, he studiously says, "No."

Pippa bursts into laughter and I sigh into my hand. Xander has never been much of a drinker, which means his alcohol tolerance is abysmal, at best. Since our vampire metabolisms burn off alcohol faster than humans, it takes a *lot* of wine to get one of us drunk. And if Xander has been trying to keep up with Nik—a vampire who has been drinking like it's the end of the world for the last hundred years—it's safe to assume that Xander has transcended his earthly body and is hovering somewhere between I'm-ready-to-pass-out and there's-no-telling-what-I'll-do-next.

Xander's eyebrows pinch together in confusion. "What did I say?" he whispers to Nik, his vowels long, his consonants soft. "Was it bad?"

Nik, seated on one of the oak bar stools, pats him on the shoulder, his mouth twisting in mock pity. "No, not bad." His voice is deep and warm, but clearer than Xander's. "Just wrong."

I glance at Victoria and mentally applaud her ability to keep a straight face.

"Charlotte, you're back!" Henry beams from the sink where he's scrubbing blood from his forearms. Dark red stains the sleeves of his once-white dress shirt. He glances at the others with a wine-darkened gaze and his eyes snag on Pippa, his grin turning languorous. "And you've brought friends."

Pippa gasps quietly behind me. "Who is this absolute snack in your kitchen?" she whispers into my ear.

"Is anyone going to tell us what the hell is going on?" I ask, ignoring Pippa's question. "Or do we need to wait until you've all sobered up a little?"

Xander scowls—well, it's more of a put-off frown than a scowl—and leans against Nik's shoulder, Nik shifting slightly to offer support to my brother's tall frame. The scene is made strange not only by the obscene amount of blood on their clothing, but by the easy familiarity—long missing—between the two boys.

"You should have seen him!" Henry chirps loudly in that proper London accent of his, and I frown at him.

"Who?"

"Nik, of course!" Having deemed his washing job acceptable, Henry dries his arms with a clean, white dish towel. It comes away pink and Victoria scowls. "The bastards were about to kill that poor girl when Nik swooped in and saved the day. He was *magnificent*."

Something about Henry's optimistic demeanor is almost threatening in its consistency. Why he is so happy all the time is beyond me. I would rather die a thousand deaths than be stuck forever at sixteen.

Though nineteen isn't much better.

"I repeat," Pippa says, her eyes wide and lusty, *"who is he?"*

Rose steps forward, watching Xander intently. "Was it him?" she asks, and everyone turns to stare at her. "Did you find him?"

A hush falls over the group. I meet Xander's eyes and he hurriedly looks away.

"Find who?" When no one answers, I slam my hand down on the counter—the boys jump—and glare daggers at Xander. *"Who were you looking for?"*

My brother still leans heavily on Nik's shoulder, his gaze now focused ravenously on Victoria—her expression oozes disappointment—and I roll my eyes in disgust before turning to Nik.

"Care to give us the details, Nikolas? You seem to be the only one with half a brain at the moment."

"I have an entire brain, thank you very much," Nik says, wiping a sluggish drop of blood from a cut on his eyebrow. "And I'm insulted you would suggest otherwise." I glare at him and he sighs in resignation. "We may have...gone after Konstantin."

The room tenses at the name, as though everyone—including the room itself—is holding their breath. No one says a word for what feels like hours; I let the silence stretch for longer than it should, the boys avoiding my eyes. Even Xander, who usually brushes away my judgement with a casual flick of his hand, has the decency to look sheepish. It's incredibly satisfying.

Finally, I growl, "You did *what?*"

"It was a good plan," Rose interjects, and my head snaps sideways, anger sizzling in my chest.

"You *knew* about this?" I hiss at her, and she recoils. "You knew they were going after Konstantin on their own, and you just *let them go?* We could have helped them, Rose! What were you *thinking?*"

"Xander—" Rose starts, and her voice drops to a low murmur. "Xander didn't want you involved."

The heat crackling under my skin dissipates into nothing, replaced by an icy rage that slithers its way up my spine. Xander's eyes flicker to Rose with a glimmer of indignation, but he's far too drunk to comment. I take a step toward him and he flinches, sliding sideways until he is standing behind Nik. *Coward.*

"This is not the time to play favorites, Alexander," I say. He narrows his eyes in contempt. "You don't have to like me, but I'm not completely incompetent. Did you really think the three of you were going to take down Konstantin by yourselves?"

I take another step and Nik's arm slices upward, blocking my path to Xander. I freeze in place, seething. "The next time you want to get rid of me," I snarl, "have the courage to say it to my face instead of sending your precious little servant girl."

Victoria gasps, and my heart drops into my stomach. I turn slowly to Rose, who stares at me, wide-eyed, like I slapped her across the face.

"Rose, I'm so sorry. I didn't mean—" I say, but she spins away and disappears into the hall.

"Now you've done it," Pippa murmurs.

I fix Xander with a murderous glare. "We'll talk about this when you're *sober.*"

Xander's jaw tenses, but he stays silent. *Good.* He better think long and hard about how he's going to explain himself out of this one.

"Kaleb thought—" Nik says, refocusing, "*We* thought we might be able to stop Konstantin in his tracks. We knew that he would be killing someone new tonight, so we figured we might as well test the waters. See if we could catch him off guard."

"Oh, so you're listening to Kaleb now?" I sneer. Nik flushes and his arm drops to his side. "And you just happened upon the right guy in a city of almost a million people? I find that hard to believe."

"Kaleb has scouts," Henry pipes in, leaning handsomely on the counter. "They've been keeping an eye out and caught some unusual behavior near Lombard Street. It wasn't Konstantin, but it had to have been his minions. We got there just in time! They sure put up a fight but Nik really put them in their place. Didn't you, Nik?"

Nik shrugs. He may be playing it cool, but I know better: the crooked smile, the eyebrow raise, the way he runs a bloodied hand through his hair...he is *thrilled.*

Victoria stares at his now blood-spiked hair in horror. "Nik, *please.* In this house, we believe in personal hygiene."

"The human girl got away, then?" I ask. "And you killed the attackers?"

"All but one," Henry says, his grin all teeth. Wariness prickles in my chest at the way his fangs extend below his bottom lip. *Who has fangs that long? And why are they so pointed? Does he sharpen them?* "He's in the basement."

"He's *where?*" Pippa asks, horrified.

"Please don't tell me we have a prisoner in the cellar," I say.

Xander smirks, a little of the clarity returning to his eyes. "We *definitely* have a prisoner in the cellar."

"Of all the things I could have expected from Boys' Night, Alexander," I groan, "this was not one of them."

Victoria practically drags Nik upstairs to get cleaned up, grumbling something about manners and house rules and, "If you so much as *think* about touching *that* railing with *those* hands, I will wring your beautiful neck." Pippa sneaks up after them, and Xander and Henry hover in the foyer.

I find Rose leaning against the wall just outside the dining room.

The hall is dark and quiet, the cool air refreshing after the nauseating reek of vampire blood in the kitchen. Rose's eyes are glued to the floor, and shame shivers through me when I see the stricken expression on her face. I approach her carefully, pausing a few feet away so I don't startle her; Rose doesn't react well to being startled.

I know I shouldn't say things like that to Rose. She has never talked to me about her past, but I catch whispers now and then— anxious words exchanged between her and Xander about a wealthy woman in France who mistreated her servants. A woman who disappeared shortly after Rose was Turned.

"Rose?" I say softly, but she doesn't move. I want to throw my arms around her—or maybe grovel at her feet—but I stay still, my hands shoved in my back pockets. Rose doesn't react well to unwelcome physical contact, either. "Rose, I'm so sorry. I shouldn't have said that. You know I think better of you. I got caught up in everything going on, and the boys were—" I sigh. "I'm sorry."

Rose's eyes snap up to meet mine, her pupils blown wide. She isn't breathing. I take a step backward, ready to call Xander if the situation gets *iffy,* but Rose just stares. After a few long seconds, she inhales sharply and her hand shoots forward, locking onto my wrist.

"I know you're sorry," Rose says coolly, her pupils retracting. "And I know you won't do it again."

She releases my wrist with a flick of her fingers, then stalks down the hallway and into the foyer. Xander murmurs a few words to her before I hear light footsteps ascending the stairs.

27

WHEN I FINALLY BANISH MY unease—I can still feel Rose's fingernails digging into my arm—I creep into the kitchen and snatch a blood bag from the fridge.

My spaced-out brother is waiting for me in the foyer, along with the disconcerting, grinning teenager whose presence in our house is still a complete mystery to me.

I chuck the blood bag at Xander, who fumbles with it for a few embarrassing seconds before steadying. *"Drink.* I have a feeling you'll need to be lucid for whatever is about to happen."

Xander glowers, but obediently pops the top off the bag and takes a huge swig before we head downstairs. Henry follows us, excitement bubbling from him like blood from a stab wound.

"Any reason Kaleb sent the demonic puppy instead of joining you himself?" I ask Xander, glancing over my shoulder at Henry.

"Do I really have to answer that?" Xander's words are still drawn out, but at least he's making sense. "After what happened with Nik?"

"Unfortunately," Henry says cheerily, "it isn't the first time Nik has punched him in the face, and it won't be the last. I know you think he isn't trustworthy, but I assure you, Kaleb has your best interests at heart. He is concerned about Konstantin, and he thought

I might be able to help."

"It seems to me like he's trying to *appear* helpful," I say, "while he cowers in his creepy subjugate brothel."

"It isn't a brothel."

"It sure *looks* like a brothel."

"Kaleb gets punched all the time, Charlotte," Henry sighs, patting me on the shoulder. The icy coldness of his long fingers seeps through my sheer sleeve and I shiver. "But he would prefer not to have his nose broken again, so he sent me tonight in his stead. Besides, Kaleb doesn't like getting his hands dirty if he can help it. I, on the other hand, do so willingly and without hesitation."

I glance uncomfortably at Xander—he shrugs, seemingly unconcerned—and think again of Henry's elongated fangs.

Our cellar sits in a dark part of the basement, the door hidden around an unsuspecting corner. I assume it was originally intended as an inconspicuous storage room, but is now empty, the brick walls crumbling, the stone floor dusty. A large padlock has been added to the door. Just in case.

Occasionally, as part of Xander's moonlighting, he deals with vampires who would rather kill him than be reasoned with. Sometimes a rogue needs to be housed in a controlled environment for a few days until Xander can get them to calm down, or until he deems them beyond helping.

Thus, our cellar-dungeon.

And the incinerator next to it.

We approach the door and Xander turns a huge key in the padlock, dropping his now-empty blood bag on the floor. Already his movements are tightening, his eyes clearing. The heavy oak door swings open with a loud creak and I peek inside.

The light is off, but I can just make out the figure sitting on a lone chair in the middle of the room, his arms and legs tied, his chin raised in defiance. The stale air is punctuated by the reek of drying vampire blood. Xander flips on the single lightbulb and the vamp's face is illuminated hauntingly from above; he has onyx hair, paper-thin skin, and a square, twisted jaw. There's a large cut on his cheek and his jacket is torn and soaked in blood.

When the stranger sees me, his scarred mouth quirks into a crooked grin.

"Hey, sweetheart," he croons in a familiar, rasping voice—tires on gravel—his eyes moving down to linger on my chest. "I see you have a nice little scar there from my dagger. Got you pretty good, didn't I?"

A fire ignites in my stomach and I lurch forward, but Xander catches me around the waist. "Easy, Lottie," he urges.

Henry looks from the stranger to me then back again, and a cold comprehension flashes in his eyes. His jaw tenses.

"You scumbag," I snarl at the vamp, straining against Xander's arms. "You disgusting trash person. Where do you get off, huh? Do you think it's fun to paralyze unsuspecting women? Did Kaleb even send you? Or are you just Konstantin's *bitch?*"

The man laughs, the sound grinding against my eardrums like nails on a chalkboard. "You have a fire in you," he says. "I like that."

Xander's arms flex against me and a low growl rumbles in his chest.

Henry steps nimbly into the room, winking at me before turning to the prisoner. He leans over with his hands on his knees—a parent preparing to chastise a child—his face close enough to the stranger's that his breath stirs his hair.

"Hey, mate," Henry breathes through a fanged smile. "I'm sure you know why you're here. I have a few questions for you and, if you would like this to be a pleasant meeting, I suggest you refrain from speaking to Charlotte again."

Every word out of Henry's mouth sends a chill through me. He may be smiling, his voice calm and sweet, but I know a threat when

I hear one.

"How about we start with a name," Henry continues. "Your back-country mother must have called you something."

The man thrashes once, but the ties hold fast. Acid glows in his eyes as he snarls, "And why would I tell you that?" through a tight-lipped sneer.

Henry shrugs and fishes something from his pocket. "I only asked as a formality. I had hoped you wouldn't be quite so obstinate." He opens the object in his hands, which I now see is a wallet, and makes a show of searching through it.

The man stares at him in amazement, struggling against his restraints in a vain attempt to check his own pockets. "What—how did you get my wallet, you gangly little Brit?"

"A magician never tells, and all that," Henry says with a dismissive wave of his hand. "It says here that your name is Jacob Ezra Kauffmann." He points to the driver's license showing through the wallet's little vinyl window. "Jewish, are you? I'm Jewish myself, on my mother's side." He squints at the card, then at Jacob, then back at the card. "Jake—may I call you Jake? You were born in 1976, is that correct? By the looks of it, your age seems to match your birth date. Newly-Turned then, I take it."

Jake opens his mouth then shuts it again, as though unsure of which statement warrants a response. In the end, he settles for a gruff, "Still lived a lot more years than you, kid."

Xander scoffs.

Henry laughs once, loudly, and claps a hand on Jake's shoulder. "My friend, you clearly know nothing of your newfound immortality. I am nearly two hundred years old. My parents and siblings are all dead and gone." He says all this with a wide grin, dimples pressed into his cheeks, but there is an edge to his voice—the gleaming edge of a blade, freshly sharpened. I shrink backward into Xander, and he rests his chin on top of my head. "I have seen more in my life than your pathetic little brain can comprehend. And you have the *nerve* to claim superiority over me?"

Jake's eyes are wide, his back straight, but I can see his confidence beginning to dwindle.

Henry's eyes glint with fevered light, and he tosses Jake's wallet into the corner. It lands with an unimpressive *slap*. "Now, Jake. Tell me: who do you work for?" He sighs dramatically. "Oh, it's that absolute *tosser*, Konstantin, isn't it? It must be. I have a hard time believing a dodgy git like you has the brains to mastermind such calculated murders."

Jake lashes out again, then freezes; Henry is holding a silver blade to his throat with a leather-clad hand. I blink, unsure of when he had the time to draw a weapon. Or to put on gloves, for that matter.

"Uh-uh-uh," Henry purrs, the silver caressing Jake's skin; Jake winces but retains the stubborn set of his jaw. "That's not any way to behave, is it? Xander was kind enough to invite you into his home. Are you going to insult him by causing a fuss?"

Xander's arms are an iron vice, but I'm no longer fighting him. Instead, all my attention is focused on Henry and the ease with which he holds the dagger, the exhilaration in his predatory smile, the tension in his legs, his back, his shoulders. He is close enough to Jake now that their noses brush.

"What is Konstantin doing, hm?" Henry continues in a silky voice. "Why is he in San Francisco? Kaleb—you do know Kaleb, right? Alpha, sharp dresser, takes orders from no one, will have you killed without a second thought? He would *love* to know why Konstantin is here. And it would make me so *very* happy to bring him such a valuable piece of information."

Jake flashes a wicked grin. "We had hoped Kaleb would be here himself. As you can see, I dressed for the occasion."

I note the torn knees of his jeans, the blood stains on his black hoodie, and raise an eyebrow. "If Konstantin had hoped you would impress Kaleb in that outfit," I say dryly, "he clearly doesn't know him as well as he thinks. You could show up in black coattails, your shoes polished to high heaven, the literal Hope diamond hanging on a 24-karat chain around your neck, and Kaleb would judge the length of your inseam."

Xander stifles a laugh while Jake ignores me, his gaze still fixed on Henry. But if he's expecting a reaction from his interrogator, he doesn't get one. After a beat, he adds in a terrifying monotone, "Konstantin is king. Konstantin will not stop until he recovers what was taken, and only Kaleb can return it. I will never tell you anything, for I have nothing to tell."

What little hope I had that Konstantin wasn't involved dissipates like smoke from one of Kaleb's cigarettes.

Konstantin is king. Kaleb's chess analogy rushes back to me. Though, when I think of the black king, it isn't the white-crowned piece from Kaleb's old set. In fact, it isn't a chess piece at all. It's a shadow.

Henry narrows his eyes for a few long seconds, then straightens and faces me and Xander. "You know, I believe him." He turns back to Jake and grins darkly. "I believe you, Jacob. You'll never tell us anything."

And with one smooth motion of fangs and hands, Henry quickly and cleanly severs Jake's head from his neck.

Silence hangs heavily over our bedraggled quartet—now a trio, I suppose—interrupted only by a dull *thud* as Jake's head topples to the floor. The bitter, stale scent of his blood is stifling in the small room. I press my forearm to my nose.

Henry sighs with satisfaction, smoothing his freshly-bloodied hands down the front of his waistcoat. As if it wasn't bloody enough already.

"Well," he says brightly as he tugs at his lapel, his mouth painted red, "that was successful, wouldn't you say?"

When I finally find the words, they erupt from me at top volume. "You just *ripped the guy's head off!*"

Henry smiles warmly, all traces of the predator gone. He pulls off his gloves, slipping them into his pocket, then produces a surprisingly clean handkerchief and wipes the blood from his face. "He told us exactly what we needed to know: that he works—well, *worked*—for Konstantin, and that he's the one who gave you that dashing new scar." His eyes flicker to my chest and harden for a millisecond before softening again. "Kaleb will be pleased."

I gape at him as he slips past us, gliding noiselessly out of view as his grin morphs into a deep frown. His rapid changes in mood are starting to give me whiplash.

After a few seconds, I peel myself away from Xander and stare up at him.

"That was unexpected," he says tensely as the last of the alcohol works its way from his system—his vowels are still too long, his eyes slightly unfocused.

"What just happened?"

Xander shakes his head to dislodge the haze, drawing a hand over his face. "Henry just decapitated someone in our basement."

"Oh, really? I hadn't noticed."

"He's good at what he does."

"Not to mention *completely insane.*"

"There's no need to yell, Charlotte." He presses two fingers to his temple, wincing at my admittedly shrill tone. "I actually agree with you on this one."

"Can we also agree that we're never letting strange children with a penchant for murder into our house again?"

"I can't make that promise."

I glance over at the now headless body sitting in our cellar-dungeon, the memory burning itself onto my retinas like an after-image of the sun.

"So," I say slowly, my mind working, "this guy—Jake—stabbed me outside Olivia's the other night. He told me that 'Kaleb sends his regards,' but he just confessed that he works for Konstantin, who won't stop until he 'recovers what was taken.'" His confession quells any—well, *most*—of the lingering suspicion I had about Kaleb's involvement, and I can't help the relief that sighs through me. I may want to pour red wine on all of Kaleb's furniture while he watches, but at least he hasn't given me yet another reason to hate him. "And you found a group of vampires trying to kill a girl at Lombard Street, but stopped them before they could. Have I covered everything?"

Xander thinks for a few seconds before nodding. "Yes."

"Okay, then I have a question. Why Lombard Street?"

The crease between Xander's eyebrows deepens. "What do you mean?"

"Why was he at Lombard Street? I thought we decided Konstantin was following me, choosing places I had been recently." Comprehension sparks in Xander's eyes. "I haven't been anywhere near Lombard Street this week, or even this *month*, for that matter. So, why there?"

There is a long beat as Xander's gears spin. "I...don't know," he admits, just as we hear Henry curse loudly above us.

Xander's startled eyes meet mine before we dash upstairs, only to find a disgruntled Henry, his phone held tightly to his ear, pacing in front of the living room fireplace. His free hand rakes through his hair in distress.

"When?" he hisses, his brows furrowing. He pauses for an answer and his black eyes flash. "Okay. I'll finish up here, then—"

Henry notices us and stills, his demeanor changing as a cheery mask slips down over his face like a guillotine. "I'll be back soon," he trills into the phone before hanging up.

"Is everything alright?" I ask.

"Of course!" he declares, though he carries new tension—a crack in his wide smile, a shadow in his eyes. "There's a small issue that requires my attention, is all."

Before I can help myself, I blurt out, "What was Jake talking about?"

Henry's features harden and he deliberately straightens the blood-ruined cuffs of his shirt. "I'm sure I don't know what you mean, Charlotte."

"Kaleb has already used that line on me this week," I say, halving the distance between us. I have to look up to meet Henry's eyes. It's nearly impossible to ignore my flight instinct when I see his lethal fangs up close—not to mention the leftover smudges of blood on his chin—and an agitated itch prickles through my body as my mind screams, *Run.* "Let's try that again. What did Jake mean when he said Konstantin won't stop until he finds what was taken? What is he looking for?" I pause, a new question taking form. It whispers from my lips: "What did Kaleb take?"

Henry's eyes flicker to Xander momentarily, his expression unreadable. "I don't know, Charlotte," he states, his tone dismissive. The predator is gone, but so is the child, replaced by someone with the confidence of centuries, his chin high, his eyes hard. The Beta. "Now, if you'll excuse me, I must be going. That is," he adds, shifting his attention to Xander, "if we're done here?"

Xander hesitates for a moment before giving Henry a clipped nod. Henry reciprocates the gesture and brightens it with a tight grin before disappearing into the glaring morning.

"Well, it looks like Henry won Boys' Night," I mumble as Xander slips back downstairs to clean up the mess.

28

KALEB TWISTS HIS PHONE NERVOUSLY between his fingers, unsure if he would rather punch the wall or throw the phone against it. Either way, the wall will be taking a beating, and he just had the wallpaper replaced. He'll have to find another way to rid himself of his frustration. After all, the paper is an antique—quite the chore to track down—and he hasn't the patience to find more.

Not now.

It has been so long. Kaleb thought it was over. In fact, he had been sure of it. But if he's learned anything in five hundred years, it's that nothing—not even death—can stop Konstantin.

Kaleb paces the floor of his lavish, windowless bedroom, his bare feet wearing creases in the lush wool carpet. A pity. He just had it steamed. He'll have Yara call the cleaners tomorrow. No, not tomorrow. Perhaps next week. He can't afford to let anyone else in the club now. If what Henry says is true, then things are much worse than he thought.

He has picked up his phone a hundred times in the last hour, debating.

It won't change anything, he thinks to himself. *What will this accomplish?*

But he can't do *nothing*.

He lifts his phone to tap out two words—and two words only—then waits an uncomfortable amount of time before pressing *Send*. The words glare up at him in sharp relief, harbingers in black and white, the point of each letter like a dagger in his chest.

He knows.

29

SLAM.

I wake with a start, bolting upright in bed before promptly toppling over the edge. My head strikes the bedside table with a jolt of pain, knocking the unlit candle to the floor next to me where it clatters loudly, rolling across the room and coming to a stop against the wardrobe.

"Ouch," I grumble, then dare a glance at Nikolas. But he isn't in bed.

His laugh sounds from across the room.

"I'm sorry, darahi,*" he grins, buttoning his shirt. His eyes are glowing, his hair still ruffled with sleep. The light peeking in from behind the curtains lines his profile in gold. "I knocked one of my journals from the bookshelf. I didn't mean to wake you. Though I will admit, I enjoyed the show."*

I rub the throbbing lump on the back of my head and glare at him ruefully. "I will forgive you only if you'll explain why you are awake in the middle of the day."

Nikolas finishes with his shirt then shrugs on a pale, linen coat. In the dimness of the bedroom, the fabric seems to radiate its own light, chiseling Nikolas in a coating of fine ivory. When he draws a hand through his hair, my breath hitches.

"A meeting," he says matter-of-factly, crossing to me in a few steps, "about the Boheme. Nothing too exciting, I'm afraid." I take the hand he offers and he pulls me to my feet, my nightgown settling back down around my knees.

"Could it not wait until evening?" I pout, wrapping my arms around his chest. "I thought Kaleb agreed you belong to me *during the day."*

Nikolas's mouth twists into a crooked grin and he takes my face in his hands. I breathe into him as he leans down, our noses touching, his lips brushing mine, gentle as a feather.

"You are a wretched little creature," he whispers, his thumb tracing circles on my cheekbone. I melt, rising on my toes for a kiss, but he stays just out of reach. "You do tempt me, my Lottie, but I have business to attend to. And I am nothing if not punctual."

He draws away, winking as he goes, leaving my lips parted against empty air.

I stand alone for a few minutes, listening for footsteps, for breathing, for any sign of movement. When I am sure Nikolas is gone, I dash to the wardrobe and retrieve my dressing gown, throwing it on hastily before sneaking into the hallway.

I may not be invited to the meeting, but there are other ways of attending.

Bright afternoon light hisses through the hall windows, stinging my eyes with white heat. I am not sure why all the curtains are drawn, but I stopped questioning Kaleb's reasoning for such things years ago.

A chorus of male voices drifts from somewhere down the wood-paneled hallways and I close my eyes, focusing on the way they echo through the quiet house. After a few moments I pinpoint them in Kaleb's office.

I groan inwardly. At least it wasn't the cellar.

Knowing Rayna will want to join me as I listen in on yet another men-only meeting, I knock quietly on her door at the end of the hall.

"Rayna," I whisper, the sound too loud in the heavy daytime silence. "Wake up! The boys are meeting without us again."

I wait for a long minute, but she doesn't answer; after knocking a few more times, I shrug and slip away. Knowing Rayna, she is likely already waiting for me in the attic.

By the time I climb the attic stairs, the meeting is well underway. Kaleb and Nik are talking in hushed, agitated tones, another male voice joining the chorus. I emerge into the dark room carefully, flailing for a moment when I walk into a suspended cobweb, and whisper into the shadows.

"Rayna?" No answer.

Frowning, I tiptoe across the dusty floorboards and flatten myself against the floor, peering down through a metal grate into Kaleb's windowless office. The fire burns low, casting dancing shadows over the damask walls and the four bodies sprawled over a cluster of lounge chairs. Kaleb sits closest to the fireplace with Nikolas scowling next to him, flanked on his other side by a brown-skinned man I don't recognize, though it is hard to see his face from this angle. I expect the fourth person to be Alexander. But it isn't him. In fact, it isn't even a man.

It is Rayna, wearing nothing but a gold dressing gown.

My mouth opens with a tiny pop. Rayna is never allowed at club meetings. Kaleb has made it abundantly clear that the club is run by the men, and only the men. It bothered me at one time, but I suspect it is less about our gender than about Kaleb's concern for our wellbeing. As though Rayna and I are unable to take care of ourselves.

"—may be unnecessary," Rayna is saying, waving a noncommittal hand in the air. "You're acting on a hunch, Kaleb. You have no real evidence—"

"What we have is evidence enough, darling. I won't risk it."

"But the club—"

"James will see to it," —Kaleb turns toward the stranger— *"won't you, James?"*

The stranger—James—nods once, his fingers drumming on the arm of his chair. "Of course, sir," he says, his voice deep and smooth and undeniably French. I choke back a laugh at the idea of anyone calling Kaleb sir. "It would be my pleasure."

Kaleb motions toward James and pointedly raises his eyebrows at Rayna. "You see? Everything will be taken care of."

"Kaleb, please." Rayna's voice trembles, but her eyes burn through the shadows. "I am not ready to leave."

Alarm jolts through me, followed immediately by hollow disappointment. Kaleb has said nothing about leaving London, and I find myself echoing Rayna's sentiment.

"I am not ready to leave, either," Nikolas interjects, his voice carrying the same tremble, the same despair. He runs a hand through his sleep-tousled hair. "But this is non-negotiable."

Rayna stiffens, glaring at Nikolas with a look of utter betrayal. "I do not appreciate your candor, Nikolas," she snarls. "And I will not sit here and allow my brother to make decisions for me. Leave, for all I care. You all can have a lovely holiday in America while Charlotte and I stay here. Hell knows she is better company."

She rises to her feet and storms out of the office, her dressing gown billowing behind her.

A beat of silence passes before Nikolas sighs. "That went well."

"She'll come around," Kaleb says, reaching for a crystal glass of cognac on the small table beside him. "She always does." He takes a sip of his drink before turning to James. "We will plan to leave within the week. In the meantime, I will begin the process of transferring Boheme's ownership to you. I trust you can handle it."

I can see only the edge of James's face, but I get the sense that he is smiling. "I handle most of the club's affairs already. It is time we make it official."

Nikolas laughs loudly and Kaleb—stoic, emotionless Kaleb—grins. "I suppose it is." He sets his glass down and stands, buttoning his coat. Even in the middle of the day, while the others are ruffled with sleep, Kaleb manages to look pristine. "That will be all, gentlemen."

The two of them nod at the clear dismissal and rise to leave, Nikolas beating James out the door in a few long strides. I jolt to attention, realizing—perhaps too late—that Nikolas will be returning to an empty bedroom. A cloud of dust billows around me as I stagger to my feet, brushing cobwebs and dirt from my dressing gown.

As I hurry down the attic steps, I hear Kaleb say, "And James? Once we leave London, our contact will be very minimal. But if you do hear from me, I expect you to come running."

Kaleb's words linger in my mind with a sense of foreboding, which I carry with me down the stairs, through the bright hallways, and across the sea to New York City.

After I take a long, scorching shower, I spend the rest of the afternoon not knowing what to do with myself. With Nik and the girls long-since passed out upstairs and Xander having retreated to his studio after an hour of disinfecting and incinerating, I find myself alone in the living room. My phone interrupts the blissful silence with a text from Tristan.

Hey, Char. How's your day?

And it all comes rushing back.

Xander's words ring in my head: *I find that knowing a human's name makes it easier to stop feeding; it reminds me that they are human beings, just like I once was. Like we all were.*

I heard Tristan yell Alison's name through the phone that night.

272

I knew her name. And it changed nothing.

The truth of it forces a fresh wave of nausea. Maybe Xander isn't as clever as he thinks he is.

I stalk down the hallway next to the kitchen and throw open the double doors to the ballroom. This, unfortunately, is one of the least-used rooms in the house. Xander doesn't like parties and our circle of friends is pathetically small, so we have never really had a use for it.

A shame, really. It's magnificent.

It boasts two massive crystal chandeliers, oak floors parqueted with tendrils of gold, carved crown molding and damask wallpaper and floor-to-ceiling windows hung with billowing white curtains. It's the only room we haven't remodeled. A coat of varnish on the floors, new wiring in the chandeliers, and it remained a sight to behold.

We really need to throw a party. I'm sure Tristan would like that. And so might Kaleb.

I shudder, annoyed by my brain's sheer audacity, and cross to the corner of the room where a grand piano sits quietly, dark and alone and clad in a vinyl cover that I promptly rip off.

The glossy surface of the piano gleams beautifully in the shade-darkened room and I touch it reverently, leaving a pattern of fingerprints along its edges. I haven't played in a few years, at least, but I'm getting restless. All this nervous energy and nowhere to put it.

At least if I played, I would have something else to focus on.

I spend a few long minutes readying the instrument: raising the lid, setting the music stand, adjusting the bench height. When I first learned to play, I was terrible. "An insult to musicians everywhere," Xander said. After enduring a few weeks of me pointedly plunking discordant keys, Xander finally gave in and helped me find a teacher. Or rather, talked to Kaleb about finding one.

After Rayna died, I played for hours at a time until my arms ached with the effort, until my fingers created deep indents in the soft ivory.

Better than putting indents in Kaleb's eyes.

I don't play much anymore, but Xander still has the Steinway tuned once a year, just in case.

Maybe one day I'll get around to thanking him for it.

I sit down on the bench, the black and white keys staring blankly up at me, and shrug my shoulders a few times, loosening the tension in my neck, my arms, my back. The motions are familiar, as is the feeling of my fingers on cool ivory as I begin to play.

My mind quiets. My eyes close. I am here, in the present, the piano reverberating in the emptiness. I am here, feeling the swell of music as it flows through me, filling my chest with a tension so beautiful that it aches. I am here. Alive. Alone, but not alone. Rayna's coin smolders against my chest. I play stronger.

I forget the past, the future. There is only here and now, a place where I can pretend that this is all a wonderful, torturous dream. That I'll wake to Rayna's grinning face or Kaleb's gentle nudge or Mama's rhubarb pastries.

I am here, I am here, I am here.

The last high notes of the song shimmer in the air like crystals and I rest my hands in my lap.

"That was beautiful, Lottie."

My eyes snap open to see Nik leaning against the doorframe, looking handsome in an all-black wardrobe that I assume he stole from Xander's closet.

Heat rises in my cheeks. "I didn't know you were there."

"I like it better that way." Nik's bare feet make no sound as he crosses the room. He sits next to me on the bench. "I miss hearing you play."

"Don't get used to it," I say flatly. "I'm just...well, I don't know what I am. Bored? Stressed? I needed to do something with my hands that didn't involve violence."

"I can definitely understand that." Nik grins his crooked grin.

"There was enough violence last night to last a lifetime. I really thought those creeps were going to kill us. They were *strong,* Lottie. Ruthless." His eyes tense. "I've never seen anyone fight like that. They just kept coming, like nothing could stop them. Almost like they were Compelled."

"Well, now that we know they worked for Konstantin, let's be glad that vampires can't Compel other vampires, or we would be in big trouble."

"Kaleb was right, then." A tremor rocks through him. "About Konstantin."

Konstantin is king. Konstantin will not stop until he recovers what was taken, and only Kaleb can return it.

"Yeah," I say, smoothing my thumb over the crease forming between his eyebrows. "Kaleb was right."

Nik slides the flask from his pocket and takes a quick swallow. I frown as the bitter scent of vodka fills the air between us. His drinks are getting stronger.

"I guess it's a good thing I beat the guy to a pulp, then," he says through a smirk, the alcohol numbing the nervous tremor in his voice. "I hate to admit it, but it felt *good.*"

"Good for you, Nikolas," I say, pushing my concern aside. "You deserved a night of unhinged violence. Sometimes it's the only way to release those manly, vampire emotions."

Nik rolls his eyes. "Henry may not be my favorite vampire in the world, but I will admit that being out hunting with him and Xander—feeling *useful* for once—was incredible. I almost felt like myself again. I felt alive."

And I can see it—in the excitement shining in his eyes, in the proud set of his shoulders, in the confident curve of his mouth.

"Maybe Xander needs to send you on stealth missions more often," I muse, smoothing his hair back from his face. He leans into my touch, an old habit that still manages to make my heart flutter. "It suits you."

"As long as he lets me do the punching, I might actually let Xander boss me around a little. Give him a taste of willing compliance."

It's my turn to roll my eyes. "Will you boys ever get over this problem of yours?"

Nik's gaze shifts to the floor. "We don't have a problem."

"That's the biggest lie I've ever heard come out of your mouth, Nikolas," I retort. "And that includes the time you convinced that poor girl in London that you were the king of France."

"It worked, didn't it?" he smirks, though nothing about his tone denotes good humor. A flash of wicked clarity shines through his expression for a moment before extinguishing.

"That's not the point," I sigh. "Is it too much to ask for the two of you to just get along?"

"That *is* the point, Lottie. And it is too much."

I purse my lips but say nothing. I'm starting to think that the day Nik and Xander become friends again will be the day Heaven starts letting vampires through its pearly gates.

Nik's eyes flicker down to my chest. "You're wearing Rayna's coin."

"What?" I ask, caught off guard by the sudden change of subject. "Oh. Yeah, I am." I take a deep breath. "I've been thinking a lot about her. It's been unavoidable, really, with Kaleb showing up every twelve seconds. I can't help but feel like she would know how to fix this mess. She always knew just what to do."

"You're not wrong about that," Nik says through a sad smile, then his expression turns somber. "You don't—you don't have to wear it."

Embarrassment prickles through me and I reach to untie the cord. "I'm so sorry, Nikolas. If you don't want me to—"

"Lottie, stop," he says, catching my hand in his. "Of course, *of course* I want you to wear it. I would love nothing more. It's just... it *burns*." He touches the coin around his own neck. "It burned for decades before I got used to it, and it leaves such an ugly scar..." He trails off, rubbing at the thick white scar at the base of his throat.

I consider him for a moment. "Yes, it does burn," I say, looking down at where the coin rests low on my chest. "But it reminds me of Rayna, in a way. She was always there, always reminding me of who I was, of why it was important to enjoy life while we endured it. She was my constant. This can be my constant now."

Nik's expression softens into a sad longing that nearly breaks my heart. *"Ja ciabie kachaju, darahi,"* he whispers, pulling me into a tight hug.

"Love you too, Nikolas."

We hold each other for a few minutes in silence, wishing for Rayna.

Nik's phone buzzes and he fishes it from his pocket. After looking at it for a long second, he plants a firm kiss on my forehead and stands, stretching his arms in front of him.

"I have to go," he says, waving his phone in the air. "Plans."

"What do you mean *'plans'*? With who?" I suddenly remember my conversation with Pippa. "Plans with *who*, Nik?"

Nik narrows his eyes mischievously and starts walking backward, one corner of his mouth ticking upward. "I'll never tell."

I gasp, jumping to my feet. "Nikolas Vesely, you tell me right now!"

He only laughs as he bounces from the room.

Nik *laughs.*

"Nik!" I call, gaping after him, but he's gone.

I pull out my phone, ignoring a pair of messages from Ty, and type a quick text to Pippa.

> CONFIRMED. Nik is definitely seeing someone, and he seems extremely happy about it. Unsure of identity. Further investigation needed.

With Nik gone, I sink back to the piano bench, racking my brain for who he might be running off to meet. I say a little prayer to the demonic powers-that-be that it's not one of Tristan's friends. Tristan has enough to worry about, what with his murdered sister and the vampire girl he can't seem to get enough of.

Tristan, Tristan, Tristan.

I frown, a thought occurring to me: didn't I invite him over? I'm starting to lose track.

It's hard to ignore Ty's messages—there are three now—but I do it gladly, instead opening a new message to Tristan.

> I'm surprised you haven't shown up today. You seem to like doing that.

A speech bubble indicating his incoming response appears almost immediately.

> You asked me to call first, remember? I haven't called, therefore I will not be appearing on your porch to whisk you away on another adventure. Though I sure would like to.

I glance out the window: it's almost dark, the sun dipping low on the horizon.

> I wouldn't say no to that.

> If you promise not to run off again, I think we can make it happen.

> No promises.

Curse you. I'll be there in twenty.

"Hey, X?" I call.

"Yeah?" he replies, his voice muffled by a few walls and his studio door.

"Tristan's coming over."

There's a pause, then, "Have fun."

"Ooh, the cute human is coming over?" Victoria's voice echoes from upstairs.

Pippa jumps in right behind her. "Is he bringing that absolute specimen of a man with him? You know, the one you drank? Pippa could use a drink herself."

"You *promised*," Victoria chides, "that you would stop referring to yourself in the third person."

"Pippa promised no such thing."

"Does this make him your boyfriend, Lottie?" Rose asks slyly, and I'm relieved to hear the familiar mischief in her voice. "How many times has he been to your house, now?"

"You are all vile little gargoyles," I groan, and am met by a chorus of muffled giggling. I had almost forgotten they were here. "Will my life never know peace?"

"We're here forever, Lottie," Victoria trills. "It's a good thing you love us."

My phone buzzes, announcing another text, this one from Ty.

Are you sick of the whole nocturnal thing yet?

Because two hundred years of that must suck.

You still owe me fifty bucks, by the way. Among
other things.

Are you home?

As if I would tell him. As if I would invite him anywhere near my house again. Not after last time.

I slam my phone face down on the piano. Ty will not be getting anything else from me if I can help it.

I lift my hands to the keys again and begin to play.

30

I'M IN THE MIDDLE OF *Hungarian Dance* by Johannes Brahms when I hear a hesitant knock on the front door, followed by the sound of it opening.

"Hello?" Tristan calls tentatively.

I would go to meet him, but then I would break my number one rule while playing the piano: never stop in the middle of a piece. Ever.

Instead, I yell in the general direction of the door. "In here, Tristan!"

After a few seconds, Tristan peeks his freckled face around the doorframe and the room seems to brighten. When he sees me, he breaks into an easy grin.

The last time I saw Tristan, he was staring after me as I ran from him—again—in a moment of wild desperation. His eyes were dark then, lit by only the cold light of the moon. Now, in the ambient glow from the deepening twilight, his eyes are radiant.

My heart does a slow backflip in my chest, something I once mistook for hunger. But after Pippa's revelation, I'm aware that it might be something else entirely.

Don't you want to kiss him? Or, you know, other things?

I focus on the last few measures of my song, finishing it with a flourish, and Tristan crosses the room to rest his elbows on the piano. He wears a hunter-green shirt, a canvas bag slung over his shoulder—the same one he had with him at the labyrinth. I wonder what it carries; drinks, probably. But the way it is stuffed to bursting suggests Tristan has more planned tonight than simply sitting on a rocky beach drinking sour beer.

Tristan props his chin on his fist. "I know you mentioned that you play the piano, but you said nothing about playing like *that*. You're really good."

The compliment slips from him with no prompting, and I fight the flush that creeps into my cheeks.

"Nik is better than I am," I deflect, though I can't remember the last time I heard him play. "Plus, he can sing. And, unfortunately, that is a talent I was not blessed with."

"Oh, come on. You can't be *that* bad."

"Yes, I can. But trust me—you don't want proof."

Tristan's laugh echoes through the empty room. Something about it exudes...warmth. I'm not sure how; it's just a laugh. But it fills the air with something bright and glowing and *alive,* like the first rays of summer sunlight burning through the morning mist. I want to bask in it.

I close the piano's lid and step out from behind it. Tristan's eyes widen.

"What?" I ask.

"You look...different."

"Are you trying to compliment or insult me? Because either way, you're off to a great start."

Tristan's eyes sparkle and he offers a sly grin. "I'm merely pointing out the fact that you seem to have actually gotten ready today."

I scowl at him, which only makes him grin wider.

To be fair, I did *try*. A little. After scrubbing the memory of Jake's decapitated head from my memory with a long shower, I needed to do something to keep it from resurfacing. So, I dressed in a seldom-worn pair of jeans and a white V-neck, then spent a fair amount of time putting on makeup and giving life to my hair.

"It's been known to happen."

He laughs again and catches my hand in his, squeezing it with warm fingers. I feel the pulse thrumming in his palm and I swallow.

Hunger or something else?

Tristan's eyes trace an imaginary line from my eyes to my jaw. They flicker toward the neckline of my shirt and I suddenly feel exposed.

"What's that?" Tristan asks.

I follow his gaze downward to Rayna's coin resting flat against my chest, the skin beneath it red and blistered, sizzling as the silver tries its best to poison me.

"Oh, that," I say with a dismissive wave of my hand. "It belonged to my best friend who...died." The word comes out sharper than I had intended. Tristan's hand twitches in mine. "I just started wearing it and I guess I'm a bit allergic to the metal."

"I would say more than a bit," Tristan mutters, his frown deepening. "That was Nik's sister, right?"

"Rayna. And I'm surprised you remember."

"It's not an easy thing to forget."

"I think she would have liked you," I muse.

"Really?" Tristan says, his gaze curious. "What makes you say that?"

I'm not sure how to respond. Rayna was harsh and brazen and spent more time getting into trouble than she did stoking new relationships. She would have rather ripped out her own fangs than make small talk with a stranger. But there is something about Tristan...

"I don't know," I reply. "It just feels right. She didn't like many people, though. Just me and Nik and Kaleb, her...boyfriend."

Tristan raises an eyebrow. "Not Xander?"

"Definitely not Xander."

Xander scoffs from his studio. "I assure you the feeling was mutual."

I stiffen, but Tristan is none the wiser. Odd, that he can't hear Xander's discontented grumbling or the girls whispering upstairs. It must be nice to be under the impression that our conversation is private.

Though, right now, I do wish Tristan knew that Xander can hear him, because he says, "I'm sure that bruised his ego, but he seems to have made a full recovery."

A chorus of poorly-stifled, astonished giggles erupts from Victoria's room upstairs.

"Oh, *snap*," Pippa snickers.

Xander only growls.

"The problem with Xander and Rayna," I say, biting back my instinct to shush our eavesdroppers, "is that they were too much alike. They were both—"

"Competitive?" Tristan cuts in. "Overbearing? Just unkempt enough that you might think they didn't try, but actually spent two hours in front of the mirror to give them that I-woke-up-like-this look?"

I stare at him for a few seconds of merciful (and dangerous) silence, and decide it's best not to engage.

"Good relationships are a balance of give and take," I say instead, "but they only took." *Not unlike the way Xander and I are now,* I think, then shove the thought aside. "Everything Xander did, Rayna had to do better, and vice versa. They would run each other into the ground trying to be the fastest or the strongest or the smartest. Until one day, they got into a huge fight."

"It kind of sounds like they might have been in love."

Xander gags.

"A *real* fight, Tristan. With fists." Tristan's expression turns skeptical. "And after that, they just sort of...stopped competing. I'm not sure exactly what happened, but they barely spoke for years."

The memory surfaces, spinning me back to a dark night in London, a heated argument, the sound of a fist connecting with a jaw. It caught us off guard—even Kaleb hadn't known what to do—and we watched helplessly as the two of them tore into each other in a snarling, wild-eyed, tangled mass of limbs and teeth. It had taken both me and Nik to wrestle them apart.

I was never sure who threw the first punch, but something tells me it was Rayna.

"Are you *sure* they weren't in love?" Tristan says, jerking me back to the present.

I open my mouth to snap back a retort, but Tristan's expression derails me. His tone is jeering, but it isn't reflected in the softness of his eyes or the way his mouth quirks down at the corners.

Pity, my mind whispers. *Always pity.* But there's a touch of concern there. Sadness, maybe. Or worry?

The emotion shivers into focus and my feet carry me backward a step, my hand slipping from Tristan's.

Sympathy.

What the hell am I supposed to do with that?

Lacking an appropriate response, I grimace, fiddling absently with a strand of hair. "Xander is going to kill me for telling you that."

Tristan stares for a moment at his now-empty hand then grins conspiratorially, light once again dancing in his eyes. "What he doesn't know won't hurt him."

He is answered by another low growl from the other side of the house. I take it as my cue to change the subject.

"Where are we going tonight?" I ask, patting the bag slung over his shoulder. Something clinks inside it. "Nowhere near the ocean, I hope."

Tristan eyes me slyly. "We're swimming."

My eyebrows shoot upward, panic flaring in my chest. "No, we're not."

His smile broadens. "After sunset. Just Charlotte, Tristan, and the Soulless Bitch."

"Tristan."

He glances pensively at the ceiling, ignoring my discomfort in an infuriating way. "That would make a great band name."

"*Tristan.*"

"Oh, come on," he says, throwing up an exasperated hand, though it's not very convincing when paired with the laughter in his voice. "What fun will it be if I tell you before we get there? Wouldn't you rather it be a surprise like last time?"

"Last time, you were cryptic enough that I thought you were luring me into the woods to murder me."

"Who's to say I *wasn't* going to murder you?" He shrugs and folds his arms, leaning back against the piano with an air of nonchalance. The bag falls against the glossy wood with a heavy *thud*. "Maybe I chickened out. Or maybe I changed my mind when you popped off that bottle cap with your bare hands. Maybe I have a lot of bottles that need opening and I figured your company would be much better than that of a bottle opener."

"I should hope I have more personality than a junky piece of metal," I grumble. "If not, you might start mistaking me for Xander."

Victoria laughs above us. *"Charlotte."*

Something that sounds suspiciously like a jar of pencils clatters to the floor in Xander's studio.

"No, I could never mistake you for Xander," Tristan says. "He may be pretty and more than a little troublesome, but he has nothing on you."

The girls laugh again, and I mentally vow to avoid Xander for the next few hours.

I consider Tristan's casual confidence, matching his stance as I lean against the piano next to him.

"Your loose tongue is going to get you killed one day."

Tristan rubs his chin. "How so?"

"For starters, you've really laid into Xander in this conversation, and he doesn't take well to verbal beatings." Tristan nods with mock seriousness, his bottom lip jutting forward in an exaggerated pout. "And you just managed to compliment *and* insult me in one blow. Luckily for you, I am not my brother, and my tolerance for verbal beatings is as finely-tuned as this piano."

Tristan's mouth stretches into a lazy grin while his eyes settle on mine, narrowing slightly. Searching. "You're always going to be trouble, aren't you?"

"Oh, trust me. I'm more trouble than I'm worth," I say, then realize the bold implication in Tristan's words.

Always. *Always.* How long does he plan on sticking around?

"Are you?" he asks.

"You have no idea."

"And why is that?"

"You don't want to know."

Tristan shifts to face me, one arm leaning heavily on the piano, and when he settles, his eyes resume their search. There is a challenge in them.

"Try me," he says.

I sigh through my nose and turn my gaze up to the ceiling, where shadows are gathering in the polished oak coffers. What about me *isn't* trouble? How can I possibly condense it into something simple, something that Tristan understands?

When I turn back to him, he is watching me intently, leaning forward as if on the edge of his metaphorical seat. I can smell the salt at his neck, the faint scent of aftershave and soft cotton and warmth, ruby-red, just under his skin.

"I never listen to my brother," I start, the words tumbling out in a rush, "even when I know he's right. I enable my drunkard ex, even when I know he's going to end up killing himself one day. I should

287

probably have about ten charges for breaking and entering." Tristan's eyebrows shoot upward. "Probably more. The one real relationship I had ended *terribly*. This coin around my neck is *driving me insane* but I refuse to take it off because it actually makes me feel something for once." I pause, breathless, then add, "And I'm a lousy singer."

Tristan listens, nodding when appropriate, and waits until I quiet to say, "You dated Nik?"

I stare at him. "Out of everything I just said—including the bit about *breaking the law*—that's the thing you choose to focus on?"

"Sometimes I'm right about things, and I enjoy relishing in that knowledge." And, to his credit, the knowledge doesn't seem to bother him.

"You've met Nik *once*. First, I never said he was my drunkard ex. And second, how could you have *possibly* guessed that we dated?"

Tristan's expression hardens before smoothing over into a familiar sly smirk, and he traces a finger on the shining surface of the piano, inching closer to my arm with each swirl. "A guy just knows these things."

"Tristan, you are what they call an 'enigma.'"

He brightens. "Thank you."

"Okay, your turn," I say, desperate to move away from the subject of Nik and dating him before Tristan starts asking the wrong questions, like *when* and *how long* and *did you two ever...* "What makes you trouble?"

The light in Tristan's eyes retreats, shadowed by the increasing twilight and a flicker of hesitance. "Is this going to be a thing now? Asking vague and slightly prying questions in a strange attempt to get to know each other?"

"You started it."

"Hmm. You're absolutely right." Tristan pushes off the piano and stares out the window for a few seconds, clasping his arms over his chest. The fading dusk highlights his hair, threading it with silver.

When he speaks, his voice is low. "I dropped out of school in March and have no intention of going back. My roommates are paying my cut of the rent and I'm currently surviving on Top Ramen and cereal and what little I have in my savings account. I haven't written a new song since Alison died. I can't stand wearing this guitar pick around my wrist" —he shakes his left hand in annoyance— "because she gave it to me and every time I look at it, it reminds me of her. But I refuse to take it off because it actually makes me feel something for once." He turns back to me, the dying light etching a rim of gray around his face, and offers a wistful half-smile. "Sure, it's excruciating, like my heart is shattering over and over again. But at least it's her. At least it makes me feel like she's here, in a backward, nonsensical way." He pauses, his grin returning. "And I'm an *amazing* singer."

Just when I think the gaping hole of guilt in my chest has started to close, it's ripped open again, the raw ache in Tristan's voice tearing at the edges with greedy claws.

I killed her, I killed her, I killed her.

"Damn our emotional jewelry," I croak, swallowing the guilt before it can bleed onto my tongue. "Do you think Alison and Rayna would understand if we burned their things and never looked back?"

"Definitely," Tristan nods.

"Absolutely," I agree.

"Alison would probably encourage it."

"But I'm still never taking it off."

"Neither am I."

The conversation lapses into uncomfortable silence and the ball-room suddenly feels stifling. Maybe the fresh air will be good for me, despite whatever ridiculousness Tristan has planned tonight.

I really hope he was joking about the swim.

"We should probably get going," I say, making for the door, but Tristan catches me by the wrist.

"Wait." He pulls me back toward him, interlacing his fingers with mine. I make a conscious effort to relax my hand. "About the other night, at the Labyrinth. Are you alright?"

I frown up at him. "I'm fine."

"Okay, I'm just making sure." All the humor has gone from him, replaced with a smothering concern. "You seemed really freaked out."

"I—I realized I forgot to do something important, but I figured it out."

Tristan's eyes are scrutinizing. "Is there anything I can do—"

"I don't need your *help*, Tristan," I snap, his words packing an unexpected sting. I try to wriggle my hand free of his, but he holds fast.

"It's not about *need*, Charlotte," he says gently but firmly, brushing the hair from my eyes with his free hand. There's a tightness in his voice that reminds me of Xander—the tightness that usually precedes a few minutes of yelling—and I brace myself for a rebuttal, but it doesn't come. "It's obvious that something is bothering you, and I want to help you fight it. Even if all I can do is distract you for a few hours."

Oh. That's...not what I was expecting.

I stare up at him—the freckled constellations sprouting over his cheekbones, the unnatural, molten gold of his eyes—and something blooms behind my ribs. Something that starts deep, like the flicker of a dying star, then spreads through me like the colored rays of an ocean sunset.

Something *warm*.

"You want to distract me?" I ask, my eyes dropping to stare at the buttons below his collar. If one more of them were undone, I would have uninhibited access to the tanned skin over his sternum, and the blood-filled heart just underneath it. My fangs jab through my gums, hunger scorching its way into my throat, but I force it back.

The truth is, I'm already distracted, and I shouldn't be. I should be worrying about Kaleb or Konstantin or fledglings or *murders*, but instead I'm standing in the ballroom, too close to a human boy

I barely know, while his fingers trace up my arm, leaving twisting tendrils of heat in their wake.

Tristan lifts Rayna's coin by its cord, twisting it between his fingers. "I've been told I can be very distracting," he says teasingly, releasing the cord and brushing his fingertips over my collarbone.

Oh no.

I dare a glance up and find him grinning through the gathering dark, a bright pulse of sunlight in an otherwise dead room. If I saw that grin every day, I might never long for the sun again.

Don't you want to kiss him? Or, you know, other things?

Maybe I only need to do it once—a one-and-done deal, like Pippa said. Just to get it out of my system.

It's worth a try.

Tristan moves closer to me—only *inches*—but it's enough. I catch a whiff of metallic blood as he rests his forehead against mine, accented by heady cologne and vanilla chapstick and something that may or may not be dryer sheets. I clench my teeth together, allowing Tristan to pull me toward him, his hands finding their way to the small of my back.

My heartbeat quickens, the sluggish pulse paling in comparison to the drumming of Tristan's heart. It is nearly dark now, the pale dusk leaking through the windows and painting Tristan in splashes of cool lavender. His bright grin is gone, replaced by something new.

When his eyes flicker to my lips, they are dark with desire.

And when he presses his body against mine, I let him.

For the first time since I met him, I'm not distracted by Tristan's humanity. I'm mesmerized by it.

Bang. Bang. Bang.

I leap back from Tristan, expecting to see someone burst into the ballroom, but we're alone. We stare at each other in alarm before I bolt into the hallway, Tristan following closely.

Bang. The front door flies open, slamming against the wall.

"Xander?!"

I stiffen at the sound of Ty's voice, but his presence isn't what concerns me. It's the way he calls Xander's name. The wildness in it.

Tristan and I hurtle around the corner into the entry to see Ty just inside the open door, his hair rimmed in twilight and his body reeking of human blood.

31

I CLAP A HAND OVER my mouth and nose to smother the scent, but it's too late. I screech to a halt as my abdomen ignites with hunger, my throat on fire, my eyes prickling with darkness. Tristan crashes into me from behind, launching me forward until I nearly run into Ty.

"Where's Xander?" Ty's eyes are shadowed and sunken in, the color under them almost black, and his lips are curled back over his fangs. His pale t-shirt is wet with blood. "I need to—"

He cuts off abruptly when he notices Tristan, who is staring at him in horror.

"Ty? Is that *blood?*" Tristan asks, squinting through the dark now engulfing the house. His heart is hammering in his chest, bringing a heated flush to his skin that makes me want to do something unsavory. And violent. I sidestep away from him. "Are you okay?"

Xander flies around the corner, sliding a few feet in his socks and coming to a surprisingly graceful stop. His hands are streaked with paint and a paintbrush is tucked behind his ear.

"What's going on?" he demands, staring from Ty, to me, to Tristan, and back again. His eyes are as dark as Ty's—bruises rimming them like smudges of black charcoal; an unfortunate, instinctual reaction to the smell of human blood—and the crease between them is more worry than anger.

I note Xander's tense posture, his eyes wild and his breath held, and feel a little better about the incessant burning in the back of my throat. Xander may have more self-control than I do, but he's still a vampire. And even vampires can be taken by surprise.

"I—got in a fight," Ty says, and it sounds like a question. He looks at Tristan pointedly, then fixes his attention on Xander. "There was a pair of...*people*. At Pier 39. They lured a guy into the space between two buildings and were, uh, hurting him. I managed to get rid of them, but they...*left him for dead.*"

The way he looks at Xander strongly suggests that the boy isn't actually dead, but that he may wake up very agitated. And very hungry.

"Oh my god," Tristan breathes. "Is he alright? Did you call the police?"

Xander ignores him, instead leveling his gaze on Ty. "Are you certain?"

Ty nods. "I saw it happen with my own eyes."

A muscle jumps in Xander's jaw, and his frown deepens into one of resolve. I sense Tristan's apprehension—nothing about this conversation is normal or comforting—but I refuse to turn to him. I don't know what my face looks like as I fight to force back my hunger, but I'm sure it's nothing short of feral.

I'm silently grateful for the dark.

"Girls," Xander says without taking his eyes from Ty's face.

Victoria, Pippa, and Rose slip down the stairs like phantoms and hover a few steps away, watching Ty with cat-like interest. The wariness in Ty's eyes tells me that he wasn't expecting to be greeted by the whole family. Well, excluding Nik. But he's off who-knows-where doing who-knows-what with someone whose identity he refuses to disclose.

"Pippa, Rose, go home," Xander commands. "Take Tristan with

you. Make sure he forgets what he saw here."

They nod, all business, and Rose approaches Tristan with a soft smile before linking her arm with his. I sense the panic rising in him, his heart racing into a frenzy, no doubt from the ominous implications of Xander's words. The salty, adrenaline-filled scent of him is starting to make the floor sway beneath me; I ball my hands into fists, digging my nails into my palms in a wild attempt to keep myself steady.

"Hold on a second," Tristan says, the timbre of his voice just too high. He shakes off Rose's arm and she flashes Xander a concerned look. "What's going on? Ty is standing here *covered in blood.* Why am I the only one here who seems concerned about that?"

"It's more common than you might think, golden boy," Pippa drawls, grinning at him. She's far enough away that when she flashes her fangs, they are barely visible in the dark. Still, I want to murder her for it.

Tristan stares at her anyway. "Is this some sort of elaborate prank? Are you in a secret fight club or something?"

"You could say that." Ty smirks, and I shoot him a glare.

"Of course not," I say stiffly, trying to conjure an excuse that doesn't sound completely insane. But I've got nothing, so I don't elaborate, which only makes me sound suspicious.

And Tristan isn't having it.

"I'll ask again—what is going on?" Tristan's voice is bordering on frantic, and I force myself to repress the hunger screaming in my throat as I snatch his wrists, pinning them against his chest.

"Tristan," I say, forcing myself to meet his eyes. "Calm down. *Please.*"

It's not Compulsion—not even close—but Tristan's shoulders sag obediently. He nods, his pulse slowing, the anxiety ebbing from him like a sunflower wilting in a drought. His expression, wild only moments ago, now betrays nothing but raw confusion. I slowly release his wrists and he rubs them absently—a blossom of purple is blooming on one of them and I silently curse myself—before shoving his hands in his pockets.

"Compel him, Charlotte," Xander growls from across the room.

"Like hell," I snap, and his eyes narrow. "I'm not doing that again."

Tristan's eyes flicker between Xander and me for a few seconds, suspicion warring with calm annoyance. "Okay, you got me. Haha. You're all very funny. Now can we *please* drop it? I'd rather be part of the joke than the butt of one." He glances around, squinting, and exhales. "And would it *kill you* to turn on the lights?"

"Tristan, don't—" I start, but his hand is already on the light switch. He flicks it on and is met by the wide, hungry stares of not one, but six vampires: eyes dark, pupils dilated, throats burning.

Xander says, "Rose," and she is on Tristan in an instant.

"Forget what you heard here," she murmurs in the smooth tone of Compulsion. I'm too stunned to stop her. "You and Charlotte had a lovely evening together, and now you will go home. You will not remember that Ty was here, nor will you remember his story. You will not remember this conversation."

Tristan's golden eyes glaze over as Rose speaks, then clear as he blinks the Compulsion away. He considers me for a moment before leaning in to press a quick kiss to my cheek. The blood pulsing under his skin sings to me, and the warmth of his lips nearly pushes me over the edge. If I clench my jaw any tighter, my teeth might shatter.

"Thanks for the lovely evening," he says dreamily, then walks past a blood-soaked Ty and out of the house, leaving the door open behind him.

Silence follows.

A few seconds pass as I try to compose myself, and I'm acutely aware of five sets of glittering eyes watching me. Pippa wiggles her eyebrows suggestively.

"Alright, none of that," Xander says. "We all know Charlotte is making some questionable decisions with her choice of arm candy, but you'll have plenty of time to mock her later."

Xander better watch his back or I'm going to put bleach in his shampoo again.

I glare at him, then at Rose. "The two of you are dead to me."

Xander shrugs. "It's not the first time."

Pippa and Rose say quick goodbyes to Victoria, then sneak out the door. I glower after them. Always the good girls, following the boss's orders, never questioning why he wants them to leave. Never hoping he'll let them stay.

Ty is surprisingly quiet. The blood on him is a shocking red, and there is more than I realized: it coats his forearms and hands, his shirt, the knees of his jeans. He's lucky he didn't track it in on his shoes. Victoria retreats upstairs with a glare at Ty that is half-withering, half-warning, leaving me alone with the two boys.

I glower at them, too.

"Thanks for that," I say to neither one in particular, then I turn to Ty. His cheeks are flushed and his hair is a wild mess. He probably ran all the way from the pier. "Next time you decide it's a good idea to barge into our house, covered in blood, yelling loud enough to wake the dead, maybe give us a little warning."

"I *tried*," Ty retorts, his eyes glinting like burnished silver, "but *someone* was ignoring my text messages."

I think back to where I left my phone on the piano, annoyed, coincidentally, by Ty's texts.

"We don't have time for this," Xander snaps, shouldering me aside. "Ty. You said you witnessed a Turning. Is that correct?"

"Yes," Ty says, though he still stares at me. Some of the cocky confidence has returned to his expression, and the intensity of it feels almost oppressive. I force myself to hold his gaze, but I can practically feel his eyes undressing me. "There were two vampires, a man and a woman. The man bit his own wrist and forced the kid to drink from it, then he snapped his neck and just left him there. I managed to get the guy hidden afterward, but he was bleeding pretty heavily, thus..." He motions to his ruined clothes.

"What were they wearing?" I interject, an idea snagging in my mind. "The vampires. Were they in black hoods?"

"Why does that matter?" Ty frowns.

"Answer her." Xander's face is stoic and shadowed and completely unreadable.

Ty looks taken aback. "Yeah," he says, considering Xander with distaste. "Now that I think about it, they *were* in black hoods."

It was the answer I was expecting, but not the one I wanted. A combination of adrenaline and panic bites through the hunger still gnawing at my stomach, creating an altogether very unpleasant sensation that I want to banish immediately.

I look up at Xander. His eyes are distant, his jaw working, his body frozen as though he is carved from black marble. There is a smudge of purple paint on his cheek and I reach to wipe it off before thinking better of it. My hand falls to my side.

"The fledglings," Xander says absentmindedly, rubbing a hand over his mouth.

Ty and I exchange a confused look. "What about them?" I ask.

"There has been a large uptick in new fledglings lately," Xander says in a leading tone, and I nod, unsure of where he is going with this. Ty watches him intently. "And we have good reason to believe that the black-hooded vamps are connected somehow to Konstantin."

Realization dawns on me less like a gradual wave and more like a brick being dropped on my head. "You think Konstantin is the one Turning new vamps."

Anxiety fizzes in my chest. Exactly how far does Konstantin's influence reach? How many vampires does he have under his command? And how many have been following me for the last week?

"Konstantin?" Ty asks, his gray eyes sparking with interest.

Xander frowns at him. "Konstantin is none of your concern, Ty," he says. "And if you're done here, you may go."

"I *may* go?"

"Yes, you may. Apparently, I have a mess to clean up. And if this incident has larger implications than a simple rogue Turning, I don't trust you enough to join me."

Ty recoils slightly, his head tilting to the side. "What is that supposed to mean?" Something akin to menace colors his words and I flinch. It's unlike Ty to exhibit anything but distaste or brazen self-confidence. In the few days I've known him, anyway.

"I've done everything you asked, Xander," he continues. "I came to your little vampire mentor session. I came to dinner and didn't make a mess. I haven't killed anyone even though I've wanted to. And now I come to you willingly and you push me aside like a broken toy you're done playing with?"

I stare at him, mouth agape, but my surprise is nothing compared to Xander's. He takes a few dangerous steps toward Ty, his green eyes ablaze.

"Listen here, you little prick," Xander snarls, jabbing a finger into Ty's chest. The shadows thicken under his eyes, making him look more monster than man. "I owe you *nothing*. I didn't ask you to come crying to me with your problems. I barely know you, and yet you demand information and inclusion. What makes you think you are deserving of either? You should be grateful I offered to help you at all. Not every fledgling is so lucky."

The look Ty gives Xander is black as ink before it morphs into a strained—albeit furious—smile.

"Of course," he says in a clipped tone, the forced civility somehow more hostile than if he were screaming. "I don't expect to know all your deep, dark secrets."

Xander stares at Ty for a few more seconds before asking, "Where is the boy now?"

"I hid him in a dumpster near the aquarium," Ty says matter-of-factly, and I grimace. He shrugs. "What else was I supposed to do with him, Charlotte? Leave him to be taken to a morgue? I'm sure that would have gone over well."

"You could have brought him here!" I practically yell.

"What, you expected me to carry him halfway across the city?"

Xander and I both say an exasperated, *"Yes!"*

Ty throws up his red-stained hands. "Well, excuse me for not knowing your seemingly-random, unspoken rules. Do you have a manual, maybe? 'How to be a Vampire in San Francisco Without Pissing Off the Noviks'?"

"Let me take care of this," Xander says, brushing aside Ty's insolence. "I will let you know if I have more questions for you. But until then, I want you out of my house."

"Our house," I murmur.

Ty sneers, combing a blood-crusted hand through his hair. "Fine, I'll go. But I'm not going to be happy about it. And Charlotte," he adds, turning to me, "if you don't want me to interrupt another *lovely evening,* then *answer your phone."*

He stalks out the door and slams it behind him, causing the chandelier's crystals to shiver above us.

"What is wrong with you tonight, Xander?" I yell, shoving hard at his chest. "Is there a reason every boy I know feels the constant and overwhelming need to be complete assholes to each other for no reason? You don't see Pippa yelling at every girl that pisses her off."

Instead of replying, Xander drags me into the living room and drops me roughly on the sofa. "I was on the phone with Kaleb when Ty showed up." I tense at the concern in his voice, so different from the fury of moments ago. "The vamp we caught at Lombard last night was a decoy. They found a body a few hours later at the Sutro Baths."

A charged silence follows, and I stare blankly at my bastard of a brother. I'm both confused and annoyed by Xander's sudden closeness with Kaleb, but that does nothing to dispel my concern over, well, everything. The decoy must have been what Henry was so worried about when he left the house this morning. And if Konstantin left a body at the Baths, it doesn't bode well for Kaleb's secrecy. I'm surprised by the worry that flickers through my chest.

I wrap my arms around myself and drop my gaze to the empty fireplace. "Does that mean Konstantin knows where Kaleb lives?"

"We don't know what it means," Xander says, perching on the edge of the coffee table, "except that he knows we're on his scent, which significantly limits our options going forward."

"Did we have options before?"

"Kaleb had a list. I'm not sure what his plans were, but he seems to be rethinking most of them."

My mind paints a picture of Kaleb alone in that lavish, underground office of his, an old-school scroll of parchment lying open in front of him, a quill pen in one hand. Black ink covers his fingertips and he stares, unseeing, at a list of ideas, each marked with an angry strikethrough.

There's no doubt that Konstantin has experience. He is old, after all. Older than Kaleb, even. And while Kaleb may think he has to figure this out on his own, he can't. He's not smart enough for that.

"What are we still doing here?"

Xander starts, his eyes brightening with confusion. "What?"

"*What are we still doing here?*" I repeat, enunciating each word like I'm speaking to a toddler. "Why aren't we out there hunting him down ourselves? You all played offense for Boys' Night, and I think it's time we played it again. If you're going to follow this lead of Ty's, I want to come with you. Konstantin doesn't know that *we* know about the fledglings. This could be our chance to get a jump on him." I stand abruptly. "Call Kaleb. He can meet us at the pier."

301

A strange glint sparkles in Xander's eyes. "You want to help Kaleb?"

"That's not what I said." Even though that's exactly what I said. And I hate myself for it. "I'm tired of waiting for Konstantin to come to us."

"You're not going anywhere," Xander says emphatically, rising to his feet. His height gives him an unfair advantage when we argue: it makes me feel small, like a rabbit staring down a wolf. "Konstantin is following *you*, remember? And we're not sure how. The last thing I need to worry about is you trying to dispense vigilante justice and getting yourself killed in the process."

"Xander—"

He claps a hand on my shoulder. "If last night's murder was a trick—a distraction—who's to say this Turning isn't, as well? Konstantin could be setting a trap. I don't want you anywhere near it."

The idea shocks me into silence. After all the terrible things Rayna told me about Konstantin, I wouldn't put it past him. She spoke often of the way he manipulated her and Nik, convincing them to do things they would never have chosen to do themselves. He's the reason they were running, the reason Kaleb killed Rayna, and the reason why Nik dies a little more with each passing day.

Rage boils in the pit of my stomach. "I'm going to rip Konstantin's stupid head from his stupid body."

"Charlotte, I appreciate your enthusiasm, but don't mistake it for strength." Xander moves his hand to the back of my neck, forcing me to meet his eyes. "We've discussed this. It's best if you lie low."

"Screw you," I snarl, my temper and volume rising, tears threatening the corners of my eyes. "Rayna, Nik, and Kaleb tried lying low, and look where it got them. Konstantin fractured us. He *ruined* us." I tear myself from Xander's grip. "And now he's coming for me and I don't know *why*."

My voice cracks traitorously on the last few words, and the

tears fall in earnest now, fear eclipsing everything else. Konstantin is coming for me and *I don't know why.*

"Go to your room, Lottie," Xander says softly, and all the tension seems to evaporate from him, an invisible weight settling on his shoulders. "I'll take care of this and be home in a few hours."

"Please let me come." I shrink away from the plea in my own voice. "I want to help. I *need* to help."

Xander regards me with pity. "I'm sorry, *repa*. But this is non-negotiable."

Always pity.

"I know why you don't trust Ty, but you can trust *me.*" My desperation is palpable now, pouring from me in a torrent. I take one of his paint-covered hands. Pleading. *Begging.* "I'm your *sister.*"

Xander's eyes close and he rubs his free hand over his forehead. His voice is hard when he says, "Unfortunately."

The word pierces my heart like a barb, and the tiny, hopeful part of me withers to nothing.

Xander disappears into the kitchen, emerging moments later in a long black pea coat and a pair of black boots.

"Stay here with Victoria. And stay out of trouble."

"Go to Hell," I hiss, fresh tears staining my cheeks. I don't wipe them away.

He shoots me a wry look. "I'm already there."

I bite hard on the insides of my cheeks and, like the obedient little sister that I am, I go to my room.

32

XANDER SHOULD KNOW BY NOW that my best schemes are hatched in my bedroom.

The plan starts forming in my head the instant I close the door, while Xander leaves the house in the midst of a heated phone call with Kaleb. They seem to be arguing about what Konstantin's next move will be and what the Turnings could mean and which of them is the bigger jackass. Though that last part may have been my imagination getting away from me.

I leave the light off; I won't be here long, and it's not like I need the light to see. The blackness washes over me, muting the fear and panic that lingers in my chest.

I shuck off my clothes and rummage through the closet for shades of black, pulling on dark jeans and a hooded long sleeve shirt, then dig around in the dresser until I find my knives.

Pretty things, my knives: five blades of solid silver with handles wrapped in leather and edges so sharp they cut through bone like butter. Or so I was told. They were a gift from Kaleb back in Prague when he insisted I learn to fight. He taught me the proper way to hold the knives and how to throw them with deadly accuracy. He showed me the exact insertion point on a vampire's chest that would cause the blade to graze the heart with each breath.

I never asked why he knew that. But tonight, it may finally come in handy.

I unroll the leather sheath and strap it to my right thigh, careful not to let the silver touch my hands. The tiny fire of Rayna's coin still burns on my chest; I don't need yet another self-inflicted distraction.

Though, if the distraction were Tristan, I might reconsider.

"Charlotte," I hiss into the shadows, hastily replacing the contents of my dresser. "You are not a teenager with her first crush. You're two hundred and thirteen years old, and you do not have time to be pining after a twenty-year-old college drop-out with no boundaries and a stupid grin and those damn *freckles*."

I slam my dresser drawer shut and tug on a pair of boots.

"Maybe if he were a vampire, it would be different," I continue, tying my laces aggressively. "But he's human. It's not like you can keep him. It's only a matter of time before he finds out what you really are, and you'll have to Compel it all away."

The thought strikes me with unexpected dread, and I deflate like a week-old balloon.

But this is not the time to feel sorry for myself. I have a plan, and it's going to work.

Konstantin has been following *me*, that much is certain. Though the question still remains: why? Did I unknowingly do something to offend him in the last century? Does he think I'm an easy target? Or does he think Kaleb cares enough about me that he can use me to get to him?

I laugh out loud. Kaleb hasn't cared for anyone but himself in a hundred years.

The reason doesn't matter, really. What matters is knowing Konstantin's plan, and he's been obvious. *Too* obvious. If he is leaving bodies at places I've been, then all I have to do is revisit them. He's bound to show up eventually, and when he does, I will remove him from our lives—*permanently*.

I mentally retrace my steps, focusing on the places that haven't already been targeted. Alcatraz does present a bit of a problem, seeing as I can't drive a boat, but if it's an issue for me, then it's probably—*hopefully*—an issue for Konstantin.

That narrows the list down to four: Olivia's house, the Land's End Labyrinth, the Majestic Theater, and the Shakespeare Garden.

I can find Konstantin, kill him, and be back before Xander even knows I'm gone.

"Knock, knock," Victoria says from the hall, and I startle.

"What?"

She leans against the door but doesn't open it. "Are you alive in there?"

I sink to the edge of my bed, sulking. "Xander insinuated that he would rather not have me for a sister, so yes, I'm just living it up."

"You know he didn't mean it."

I frown at her through the wall. "Do I?"

Victoria's fingers tap a soft rhythm on the door. "You and Alexander are lucky, you know," she muses. "You were born siblings, you were Turned together, and you've been by each other's sides for two hundred years. The rest of us had to say goodbye to our families long ago, but not you. Alexander can't imagine what life would be without you, and he doesn't want to find out."

I laugh once, a low, guttural sound. "He has made it abundantly clear that his life would be better without me in it."

"Lottie—"

"I'm tired, Victoria," I interrupt, letting exhaustion seep into my voice. "Can we talk later?"

"Of course," she says, but does a poor job of hiding her reluctance. "I'm going to grab a drink. Do you want anything?"

In truth, I could probably drink an entire bottle of whiskey. But I need to get out of here, so I say a quick and incontestable, "No."

Victoria is silent for a moment, then says, "Okay. I'll be in my room if you need me."

After what feels like an eternity, Victoria makes her way back upstairs.

It's now or never.

I slip quietly out of my room, careful to shut the door silently, then tiptoe through the foyer and out the front door, plunging into the black night.

◇　◇　◇

A tepid, salty wind howls through the streets, whipping hair into my face as Olivia's blue-and-white house comes into view. I take refuge in the alley across the street. All the lights are on inside and I can hear a chorus of female voices, all raised in laughter. I picture the cozy living room with the fireplace lit, Olivia and Bree snuggled with their friends and drinking peach schnapps, eating Chinese takeout with chopsticks and gushing over their latest mundane drama. The imagined scene is a bright alternative to where I sit in a grime-darkened alley, drinking in nothing but the scent of asphalt and concrete, waiting for a vampire psychopath to appear so I can murder him.

But he never comes. I wait for two hours without seeing so much as a rat.

◇　◇　◇

The Majestic is next. The venue is empty tonight, the marquis a blank slate, but the lights still cast a hazy glow over the sidewalk. Wind gusts fiercely over the bay, making the reflection of the Bay Bridge shiver nervously.

I make a few rounds—scanning the street, the garbage-filled alleys, the rooftops—before tucking myself into a stone alcove on an adjoining building. Despite the late hour, this part of the city is busy as ever, groups of college kids enjoying clubs, nearby theaters emptying after the final curtain. The clouds are swollen with unshed rain, casting heavy shadows over the city.

My heart leaps when I hear two sets of footsteps nearing my hiding place, and my fingers twitch toward the knives at my thigh. But it's only a pair of twenty-something humans, a boy and a girl, holding hands and moving quickly into a dark alley.

The boy presses the girl up against the wall and she slides her hands under his shirt. He moans.

I leave quickly after that.

◊　◊　◊

By the time I reach the Shakespeare Garden, it's almost one in the morning. Hunger blazes in my throat and I swallow it; I haven't eaten since our dinner with Ty, and I rarely go so long without a meal. Unlike Kaleb, I don't enjoy torturing myself with weeks between feedings. Needless to say, I'm starting to feel foggy.

Rain is finally falling, fat droplets soaking my hair and clothes, and the air is filled with the scent of petrichor and autumn rot and something heady and bitter.

Seeing the familiar orange brick path sends a wave of nausea through me, and Tristan's tinny, phone-muffled voice rings in my ears. *Alison? Alison, are you there?* Alison!

I make my way up the path toward the sundial, the memory of Alison swimming in my vision. Why did it have to be her? It could have been anyone in this stupid city, but it had to be *her.*

As my eyes adjust more fully to the tree-shrouded darkness of the park, I can almost see her body slumped on the ground, the life bleeding out of her.

And yet...

I look closer and *yes,* there is a body, but it is not the memory of Alison. The scene snaps into crisp focus as I recognize the heady smell, hidden until now by the scent of rain and decaying leaves.

Blood, freshly-spilled. The girl is lying in a pool of it, red trails swirling in the puddling water, snaking away from her like veins.

Konstantin was here. And I *missed him.*

I want to scream, or cry, or do *something.* But I just stare, dumbstruck, at the girl bleeding out a few yards away.

I spent too much time at Olivia's. Too long at the Majestic.

I'm an idiot.

But no, I'm not.

There was no pattern to Konstantin's location choices, no indication of where he would strike next. It could have been any of the four places. I just chose the wrong ones.

But a thought snags in my mind: didn't Kaleb say Konstantin was an obsessive planner? A game master. Someone who plans every move before making it. Why would he choose places at random?

Unless...

Unless he did it on purpose. To confuse us. To make it seem random, when it wasn't. Or maybe...maybe it wasn't Konstantin at all.

A shadow flickers near the girl. I tense and dart behind a tree, snatching a knife from its now-soggy leather sheath. The weight of it is comforting and I grip the handle tighter, ready for the psychopath to show his face. Not that I know what his face looks like, but I bet it's hideous.

The shadow shifts. It's a man—tall but not *too* tall—and he's soaked to the skin. He moves with a terrifying smoothness as he kneels and rolls the girl onto her back, his hands reddened by the blood on her shirt. They smooth her hair from her face, press against her neck, her cheeks. He lifts one finger to his mouth and licks it clean.

My heart pounds wildly; if it weren't for the rain, the sound would betray my presence, I'm sure. I raise the knife, aiming for his heart, when the shadow turns his head slightly, but enough. And I realize that this man can't be Konstantin. The set of his shoulders, the hard angle of his stubbled jaw, the shine of his polished wingtip shoes...they're familiar.

Achingly, horrifyingly familiar.

The world tilts.

The figure rises to his feet, his expression hard as ice, his hands covered in the dead girl's blood. Recognition shivers through me, sharp as the cut of his green velvet blazer.

The shadow isn't a shadow at all.

It's Kaleb.

33

VITEBSK, BELARUS
AUTUMN 1825

"KSUSHA, НЕТАНА DASTATKOVA."

Kaleb's Belarusian is getting better, but he still slips into Russian or Czech from time to time. An ordinary man might learn two languages in his lifetime, more if he's lucky or ambitious. But Kaleb is no ordinary man. According to Rayna, he speaks upward of twenty languages, which is absurd, in my opinion. How could one possibly keep track of so many words?

"It is useful," he once told me, "when one is bound to live forever. Immortality is a strange type of magic, granting unlimited time to its owner, but with no guidelines on how to spend it. Rayna, Nikolas, and I have explored much of Europe, its cities, the towns and countryside in between. Knowing the native language keeps us from standing out. And the less attention we draw, the better."

"Why?" I had asked, still bewildered by the idea of a life without end.

"Because, Ksusha," he replied, "it is anonymity that keeps us safe."

Now, as I struggle to learn the most basic English, I wonder if I will ever match Kaleb's affinity for languages.

"Ksusha," Kaleb says again, and I sit up from my meal, settling

back onto the pile of hay in the old, too-warm barn. The girl's head sags against my shoulder and I glare up at my self-proclaimed savior.

"I told you," I growl in my native tongue. "That is not my name anymore."

Since Mama was killed by the demon over a year ago, I have felt a strange disconnect between myself and my given name. After all, Mama gave it to me, and she died with it on her lips. Whenever I hear it, I have to suppress the chill that runs up my spine. I have yet to find another name that feels right.

Kaleb frowns and leans against the oversized doorframe of the barn, his arms crossed, his hair wreathed in a halo of moonlight. "Then what is your name?" His accent is sharp and proper, the edges of his words too crisp for my liking. "I must call you something."

I wipe the blood from my mouth with the back of my hand. "I do not know yet. But it is not Ksusha."

Kaleb's frown twists into one of annoyance. "Alright then, whoever-you-are. Nullum corpus. I do not want you to kill that poor girl."

"I wasn't going to kill her," I groan, "but it has been days, Kaleb. I am starving."

"Vampires do not starve." Kaleb raises a flippant hand, as if to demonstrate the absurdity of the idea. "Starving insinuates death, and we cannot die from lack of blood. Only wither, as you should well remember. We can survive very happily with one feeding a week; every other week if necessary."

I have grown used to Kaleb's speeches over the past few months. Each time Alexander or I misbehave, he gives us a stern talking-to, as if we are delinquent children and he is our chastising father. He may deny it, but he must hate us. Loathe us, even. We have become quite the chore. Or rather, I have. Alexander is...well, he has always been one for rules.

Personally, I do not understand Rayna's love for Kaleb. He is serious, calculating, and technical—while, admittedly, very nice to look at—and I find myself exhausted by the constant judgement in his voice. I am much more partial to Nikolas, with his auburn hair and soft, yearning eyes. Still, there must be some good in Kaleb, for how much Rayna loves him.

Grumbling, I look at my dinner where she lies, barely conscious, on my shoulder. I nudge the girl awake and she blinks up at me with bleary eyes. "The barn seemed a lovely place to be tonight," I purr, Compelling her just as Kaleb taught. If only Alexander and I had known the lovely trick months ago. "You ventured out here to sleep in the hay. When you wake, you will have no memory of what happened here." Her eyes glaze over dreamily and she slumps backward, sinking into an immediate sleep.

I look up at Kaleb, his silhouette blocking out the moon. "There. Are you satisfied?"

Something flashes in Kaleb's eyes. "Very good. Now come."

I rise from the floor, brushing dirt from my blue peasant's dress. Kaleb watches me critically as I walk toward him, his eyes sweeping from my head to my feet.

When I reach him, he swipes a few stray pieces of hay from my skirt, then offers me his arm. I blink in surprise. Kaleb has never so much as hugged me, let alone escorted me anywhere.

When I hesitate, he drops his arm and looks at me curiously, his ice-blue eyes penetrating, a question swirling in them.

"How would you feel about 'Charlotte?'"

"What?"

"As your new name." There is a hint of a smile in his voice, though his expression does not reflect it. "How am I to address you if you haven't a name at all?"

"Charlotte," I repeat. The sounds are foreign on my tongue, the vowels all wrong, but there is also a sense of rightness to it.

"It is an English name," Kaleb continues nonchalantly, though his eyes betray a touch of pride. "One I have always loved. It would *pair nicely with Alexander's choice to adopt a more common spelling of his own name. You do not have to use it, of course, but I feel that it might suit you."*

"Yes," I say, reaching forward to link my arm with his. I lean my head on his shoulder and he stiffens, but doesn't retreat. In fact, he almost returns the gesture. Almost. "Charlotte. Charlotte Novik. I love it."

The corner of Kaleb's mouth twitches. "It is settled then. Now, Charlotte Novik, we must find your brother. I fear one of the young women in the farmhouse has taken a liking to him, and he does have a tendency to break the young ones' hearts."

Kaleb leads me away from the barn into the cool autumn night, the full moon illuminating the countryside in a blanket of silver frost, and I think that maybe—just maybe—my self-proclaimed savior does not hate me so much after all.

As a newly-Turned vampire in the late summer of 1824, I found myself struggling. Not for survival—that was the easy part—but with the knowledge that in order to survive, I had to hurt people. Maybe even kill them. The only person I had ever hurt was my brother, in the way a sister does: punching his arm when he tattled to Mama, pulling his hair when I wanted to bother him. But I had never hurt anyone in earnest. Not until I was Turned. And my moral compass was cracking under the strain.

Xander did not have the same problem; he took to vampirism like a duck to water. From the moment we first woke, broken and orphaned and our throats burning for blood, he was a natural.

I died that day, but Xander was reborn.

His charm was intoxicating. Women—and men alike—were entranced by his elegance, the way he held himself, the dangerous quirk of his smile. Before we discovered Compulsion, it was Xander who lured humans from taverns and homes. Xander who told them everything would be alright. And they believed him. After all, he was young and handsome, and his lips carried promises of pleasures beyond imagination.

They followed without a second thought. And then we killed them. Every last one.

We left a devastating trail of bodies in our wake. By week three, I had forgotten all about my moral dilemma. By week ten, I lost count of the victims.

Kaleb found us after seven months.

It wasn't easy, drying us out. He locked us in a room, deprived us of blood, watched with disinterest as we snarled, then begged, then sobbed. It was torture—my throat screaming, my skin graying as my body leeched the blood from my veins, devouring it until my heart slowed, then stopped, then withered in my chest.

I have no idea how long we were in that room, but the day we stopped begging, Kaleb opened the door.

At first, I hated him. I hated the man with ice in his eyes who locked us away to rot. But Xander understood: Kaleb did what had to be done.

After that, he was our teacher. He trained Xander to use Compulsion and to exercise restraint. He taught us how to feed without killing, how to run and hunt and hide in plain sight. Without Kaleb, we would have been lost. I loved him for it, once.

The man standing in front of me now no longer resembles the man from 1825. And to think, only hours ago I had started to feel sorry for him.

"Kaleb?" I breathe, and his head snaps in my direction.

"Charlotte?" he asks sharply. "Is that you?"

"Kaleb, what have you done?"

He looks from me to the girl lying dead at his feet and horror flashes in his eyes. "No, Lottie, let me explain—"

But I'm already running.

I dash through the green gate and onto an asphalt path, rain pelting my face, blindly running, running, running.

Running from the memory of Kaleb's icy expression as his house devoured Rayna with tongues of flame.

In my haste, I fail to notice the closed wooden gate ahead of me and I slam into it, reducing it to a pile of debris and splinters. A few of the jagged wood pieces have found their way under my skin, but I continue on, cursing as one burrows deeper into my leg.

Kaleb catches me around the waist.

"Get off me!" I shriek, shoving hard against his chest.

"Charlotte—"

"No!" I continue struggling, but to no avail; Kaleb's grip is strong as iron. I jab the point of my knife into the skin beneath his chin—a satisfying droplet of blood blooms on the blade—and he glares down at me defiantly. "Get away from me, you disgusting, murderous, son of a *bitch.*"

"*Charlotte,*" he snarls, catching my wrist and twisting until my bones grind together. I cry out, dropping the knife, and it clatters to the ground with a metallic *twang.* "Will you please shut up and bloody *listen to me?*"

The intensity in his voice stuns me and I go slack in his arms. I reluctantly meet his eyes and am surprised to see wild desperation swirling in them. More surprising still are the bruises shadowing them, the veins below them swollen and purple, a darkness that makes the pale blue of his irises appear nearly white. His fangs glint behind his lips.

Wild. Worried. Out of control. So unlike him, that for a moment I can do nothing but stare.

"If I let go," Kaleb says carefully, "will you promise not to run off again?"

After a moment's hesitation, I nod.

"Good." He unwraps his arm from my waist, watching me

warily as he retrieves my knife from the ground and offers it to me, handle first. I snatch it up and shove it back in its sheath, which is now a ruined mess of water-logged leather. Kaleb frowns. "I would never have given you those knives if I knew you would treat them so poorly."

I wince as I yank a chunk of wooden fence from my leg, blood pulsing from the wound and staining my jeans. "You're lucky I didn't embed one in your neck."

"If you'll let me explain—"

"Explain what, Kaleb?" I snap as thunder rumbles in the sky. "The fact that none of this mess started happening until you showed up at our house? Or that you lied to us for *years* about the fact that Konstantin was following us? Or maybe you'd like to explain why I found you here, standing over a dead body, in the exact place I thought Konstantin would be."

Kaleb stiffens, rain streaming from his hair and dripping onto his cheeks. If I didn't know any better, I might think he was crying.

"I didn't kill the girl, if that's what you're asking," he says, rubbing a hand over his eyes. But they stay dark. Unfocused. "She was dead when I arrived, I swear to you."

"*Nullum corpus.*"

Kaleb's eyes narrow. "Lottie—"

"Leave no bodies," I say coldly. "That was your rule. Your most *important* rule."

"It still is."

"I don't believe you." When he doesn't respond, I continue, unhindered and shivering and *furious*. "You know, I have to give you a little bit of credit. You almost had me. That whole story about Konstantin and his petty revenge...it was convenient, wasn't it? To have another villain to blame it on? And you played your part so well: the long-lost brother appearing just in time to save the day. The Prodigal Son. And everyone fell for it. But not me."

A crease carves between Kaleb's eyebrows, and he worries at the pearl buttons on his cuff. Fastening, unfastening.

"Is this just a game to you?" I continue. "Has it always been a game? You already killed Rayna. Am I your next target? You obviously have no qualms about betraying those closest to you."

Kaleb sags. "I would never hurt you, darling," he says. "You must know that. Everything I've done is to protect you. To protect *all* of you."

Lightning flashes overhead, mirroring the fury crackling through me. "I'm sure you said the same thing to Rayna before you burned her alive."

The words find their mark and Kaleb recoils, stricken. I search his expression for guilt—defiance, even—but there is none. Just a dull exhaustion, sweeping down from his ice-chip eyes to his shoulders, his hands. They fall limply to his sides.

"Charlotte, please. Allow me to speak."

He takes a hesitant step toward me, and I force myself to stay still. I'm done being afraid of Kaleb Sutton. If I'm going to die, then I'll die standing my ground.

"You have thirty seconds."

"Then I'll be brief," Kaleb says, his frown deepening, and he manually forces his fangs back into his gums with unsteady fingers. "Alexander called me not long ago. He was frantic. He said you were missing and that you didn't have your phone." I hadn't realized; I must have left it on the piano. "It took us a few minutes to puzzle together the fact that if you were anywhere, you were looking for Konstantin, retracing your steps in an attempt to find him. It was a very idiotic thing for you to do, Charlotte."

I scowl.

"I arrived at the park only minutes before you did and found the poor girl dead," he says. "Recently, I might add. I thought I saw movement behind the trees—just a shadow—but I chose not to pursue it." When I open my mouth to ask *why the hell not,* he

318

holds up a firm hand, palm facing forward. "The rain had dampened the scent of the girl's blood, and I couldn't tell if she was human or vampire. For a moment, I was worried..." He pauses, his lips pursed. "I had to be sure it wasn't you."

I start. "What?"

"You should go home. Your brother is worried sick—"

"I don't care about Xander right now," I hiss, though my anger is fading, a deep ache taking its place. "But if I ask him, will he tell me the same thing? That you were here looking for me?"

Kaleb nods solemnly. "I promise."

Thunder crashes through the trees and a dam bursts in my chest, emotions flooding through me at staggering speed: frustration over my plan's failure, guilt over Xander's worry. But, stronger than anything, is a crushing wave of sadness as I stare up at Kaleb.

He was supposed to protect us. He *promised*. But then he killed Rayna, and the world turned on its head.

And then he *left*.

A century later, he was the Alpha of San Francisco. He managed to track down the phone number to our Chicago penthouse, speaking cordially with Xander while my brother fumed. And then we were moving to California. The moment I stepped foot in the new city—in *Kaleb's* city—I swore I would find the answer to my question, even if it killed me.

The question that has tortured me for the last hundred and twenty-one years.

"Why?"

Confusion brightens Kaleb's gaze as he smooths hair from my forehead with gentle, still-bloodied fingers. "Why what, Lottie?"

"She loved you, Kaleb," I whimper, clutching at his hand and pinning it to my chest. "*We* loved you. I don't understand how you could do that to us. How you could tear our family apart."

Kaleb's soft expression shatters. "That was never my intention,

Charlotte. You, Alexander, Nikolas, the girls...you meant everything to me. And to Rayna, as well."

"Then *why?*" I wail, and realize that I am crying. "Why did you kill her? *Why did you kill our Rayna?*"

I never thought much about what would happen once the question left my lips. I thought I would ask it, Kaleb would answer, and that would be the end of it. But the world seems to slow, the rain dulling to a soft roar in the background, and the seconds stretch to minutes, to hours. In the space between words, I feel an eternity's worth of anticipation building.

Kaleb stares at me for those few agonizing seconds, rain streaming from his cheeks, dripping from his hair where it curls at his temples. He closes his eyes briefly, and when he opens them they are hard. Hesitant, maybe. But determined.

"It was a last resort," he says grimly, and adrenaline surges in my chest. "A decision made with no regard for the consequences. I have played that night over millions of times, trying to make sense of it, but only one thing remains clear: Rayna's death was as much her fault as it was mine."

I shake my head, bewildered, and drop his hand. "What—what are you saying?"

"Konstantin was never going to stop, Charlotte." Kaleb's eyes focus on something past me, something far away. "Rayna felt that if she were gone, he would move on. That he would find someone new to torment, and that we would be safe. She was wrong, of course. But you know Rayna—her mind was the driest kindling, each new plan a lit match. Once the fire caught, there was no going back. Rayna's death was her idea. All I did was fan the flame."

He is standing close enough that when I lash out, my open palm connects firmly with Kaleb's wet cheek. His head snaps sideways with the impact and when he turns back to face me, his expression is miserable.

"*Liar,*" I snarl, my fangs bursting through my gums. "Rayna would never do that to Nik."

"I speak the truth," Kaleb says. The bruises beneath his eyes have softened to gray, making him look worn and tired. "Konstantin was after us. She knew that he would never stop searching for her as long as she was alive."

I open my mouth to reply, then close it again.

I remember running. For seventy years we moved from place to place, country to country, never remaining anywhere for too long. Rayna told me stories about Konstantin: how he Turned her, how he manipulated her, how she had been his lover, his plaything. And how she had left him for Kaleb.

When they left, Konstantin went on a murder spree, desperate to find her, to lure her from her hiding place. He left messages with his victims: *I will find you,* they said.

And, apparently, he did. More than once.

What could she do but run?

Kaleb watches me warily. Waiting.

The worst part of this is the fact that I *knew* Rayna: her quirks, her ambition, her mad schemes. And even as I try my best to deny it, Kaleb's confession rings true.

I can almost hear Rayna telling me that it's going to be alright, that she loves me and that it's not Kaleb's fault. She would expect me to forgive him.

But I *can't,* can I? Kaleb deserted us, all those years ago.

Then again, Rayna deserted us first.

My expression must reflect my warring emotions because Kaleb steps forward, taking my face in both hands. His touch is familiar in a painful way, and my nose fills with the diluted scent of the girl's blood still lingering on his fingers. I close my eyes and focus on the smell of the earth, the pounding of the rain, the soft pressure of Kaleb's palms against my cheeks.

"Everything Rayna did was to protect her family," he says earnestly, a quaver in his voice. "Especially Nikolas. And especially you, Lottie. She loved you both so much. Her presence in your lives put you in danger, so she removed her piece from the game board. And" —he swallows— "so did I."

If I was looking for a satisfying explanation, this wasn't it. I had expected something angry or reckless. Something that painted Kaleb as the villain and Rayna as the innocent, unsuspecting victim. That would have been horrible, but this is much, much worse.

Rayna is gone. Sure, Kaleb may have helped her along, but it was her idea. *Her* idiotic plan. Kaleb fled from New York, shunned by his family, and let us hate him, *despise* him, for a hundred and twenty-one years, all to keep us safe.

Because even with Rayna removed from the board, Kaleb is alive and well. And Konstantin won't stop until he's the only king standing.

"It was never about Rayna," I whisper, my voice cracking beneath tears. I bite my lip to keep it from trembling. "We've blamed you for so long, Kaleb. And Nik—"

"It is not for you to worry about, dear Charlotte," Kaleb says gently, his thumbs brushing over my cheeks. Agony bleeds from his eyes. "I made my bed long ago and have been lying in it since. I can only hope that one day you will find it in your heart to forgive me."

I don't know if I can. Not now, anyway. But Kaleb—the man who saved us, who gave us a home and a life and a family—has been suffering, broken and alone, since 1897. And that thought is enough to break my heart.

Without thinking, I wrap my arms tightly around Kaleb's chest. He flinches, hesitating for a few seconds before returning the embrace, crushing me against him as the sky continues its deluge. He sighs deeply, the tension draining from him with the rain.

"I miss you, *moj vyratavalnik*," I mumble against his chest, breathing in the cool, smoke-singed scent of him.

He presses a tentative kiss to the top of my head. "I miss you too, Ksusha." He tenses immediately, his arms flexing. "Apologies. *Charlotte.*"

"No, no," I whisper. "Ksusha is fine."

We stand there, enveloped in each other's arms, until the chilly rain has washed the blood from Kaleb's hands.

34

"*Charlotte.*" Xander yanks me into a rough hug despite my sodden state. "What were you thinking? You could have been *killed.*"

Neither Kaleb nor I had driven to the Shakespeare Garden, so we were forced to return to the house on foot (after Kaleb made an anonymous and well-rehearsed phone call to the police). By the time we arrived, we were both exhausted and waterlogged and in desperate need of a drink. I had stomped through the door, making straight for the wine cellar, but was instantly assaulted by my brother.

"Get off me," I gasp as Xander squeezes the air from my lungs. I shove him away. "I can take care of myself, you know. Besides, Konstantin was long gone by the time we found the body."

Xander's eyebrows knit together. "We?"

Kaleb moves to stand beside us and Xander's eyes flicker sideways, seeming to notice the Alpha for the first time.

"Kaleb," he acknowledges, and the two of them share a meaningful look. "You're sure everything is alright?"

"Everything is brilliant," Kaleb says, not without sarcasm. "Unless, of course, you count Charlotte's legs."

Xander looks down at my blood-soaked jeans and his eyes widen. "What did you do?"

"I had a run-in with a wooden fence, but I'm okay now. See?" I show him the skin through the holes in my pants, smoothed and nearly healed over.

Xander draws breath—I assume to scold me—but thinks better of it, releasing the air in a huff.

His gaze settles back on Kaleb, who ruffles his wet hair, scattering shining droplets onto the floor. The soaked-to-the-skin look really works for him. He seems more relatable, somehow, with his hair a disaster of dripping waves and his green, crushed-velvet blazer sagging in all the wrong places.

Ever-present, though, is his emerald pendant, gleaming proudly on his neck and managing to preserve what little regality he has left. It has become such an iconic thing, that necklace—an integral piece of *Kaleb*—that it would be strange to see him without it. He never did tell us where it came from.

"At least you're alive," Xander says to me, some of the familiar long-suffering returning to his voice. "Tell me what happened."

I give Xander a quick run-through of the night, from Olivia's house to the Majestic, ending with our discovery of the dead girl in the Shakespeare Garden. Kaleb interjects with details from his side, including the shadows he, infuriatingly, didn't pursue. We conveniently gloss over our full conversation—a mutual decision made with a single, shared glance—choosing to focus only on the details relevant to our search for Konstantin.

Victoria emerges from the kitchen while we talk, holding her usual glass of red wine, and Xander shifts closer to her as she approaches, like he's a magnet trained to her presence. He contemplates our story quietly, interrupting with the occasional *hm*.

"It sounds like an enchanting evening," Victoria says when we finish, raising a perfect eyebrow. "Especially after seeing the lovely little puddle of mud and rain you've tracked into my house."

"*Our* house," I mumble.

Xander gives us each a once-over and grimaces. "She's right. You both look like hell."

"Oh, Alexander," Kaleb muses dryly, placing a dramatic—well, dramatic for *him*—hand over his heart. "You do know how to make one weak at the knees."

I bite back a bark of laughter.

Xander's expression betrays nothing but mild annoyance. "Before we discuss anything further, you'll both need to clean yourselves up. Kaleb, you can use my room." He nods toward the staircase. "In the meantime, I have a few phone calls to make."

Victoria follows him as he stalks into the kitchen, pausing in the doorway to fix Kaleb with a dangerous glare. "Kaleb, be a dear and remove your shoes before walking on the carpet." With a tiny smile at me, she disappears around the corner.

Kaleb looks dazed. "Have I done something to offend Victoria? I barely know her, and yet it seems she already harbors a grudge against me."

"You can thank me for that," I admit. "But I'm not going to apologize for it. When we met her, I had a problem holding my tongue."

"I see nothing has changed."

My hand twitches into a tight fist, and I almost punch his arm. Thankfully, I stop myself, bending instead to peel the ruined sheath of knives from my thigh. "It doesn't help that the first time she met you, it was the day after your stupid party. You know, the day you threatened my life?"

"Right," Kaleb says, rubbing a palm on the back of his neck. "I may have gone a bit too far. I am sorry, Charlotte. I was only trying to—"

"Save it, Kaleb." I hold up a hand to silence him, the other clutching my knives as exhaustion settles in my bones. "If you think I'm going to sit here while you apologize for every lapse in judgement you've had over the past two centuries, you overestimate my patience. We'll be here all night."

Kaleb's powder-blue eyes narrow reproachfully, but he says nothing further. I take his silence as permission to keep talking.

"Look," I hiss, dropping my voice low enough that Xander and Victoria won't hear. "We may have had a *moment* just now, but that doesn't mean we're suddenly friends again. Hell, we're barely colleagues. Just because I understand *why* you killed Rayna doesn't make her any less dead."

Hurt registers in Kaleb's expression before it hardens again to solid ice.

"Of course," he says tersely, his jaw working.

I shake my head. "I'm done with you. For now," I add when his eyes stretch wide, and he relaxes again. "Xander's bedroom is upstairs and to the left." I gesture vaguely in that direction. "It's the one that has zero personality and, I don't know, about six hundred and eighty-seven plants. He and Victoria share the bathroom. Clean towels are under the sink, clothes are in the closet. I hope you like black."

Kaleb nods and turns toward the stairs.

"And Victoria wasn't kidding about your shoes," I say. "She will murder you if you get mud on the carpet."

◊　◊　◊

I take a scalding shower for two reasons: one, to distract me from my colossal failure of a plan tonight, and two, to steal all the hot water from Kaleb.

Kaleb, who saved me and gave me a home. Kaleb, who killed my best friend. Kaleb, who, until a few days ago, I hadn't spoken to since the nineteenth century.

Kaleb, who is upstairs, showering in my brother's bathroom.

I lean against the tiled wall, the water scorching my skin, and frown. Am I supposed to be okay with the fact that the man I had all but written off as my mortal enemy is in my house, probably using too much of Xander's sandalwood body wash? It's not like I can erase a hundred years of passionate and incredibly specific loathing. Regardless of the reason, Kaleb still took our Rayna from us. He still tore Nik into pieces, leaving his heart flayed and unrecognizable.

I'd like to think Rayna would understand if I didn't forgive him.

But I know better.

Kaleb was good once, in his own way. He helped Xander master his self-control. He stopped Pippa from ending her own life. He brought Rose back from the brink. He gave me a name, a family, a home.

And he gave me Rayna.

Granted, he also took her away. That seems enough to condemn him.

I sigh, rinsing the shampoo from my hair with vigor.

What would Rayna say?

Charlotte, stop being such a baby. You're an immortal being, and you should have learned to deal with death and disappointment by now. Get over it, hike up your skirt, and move on. Don't you dare leave my Kaleb alone forever.

Maybe asking Rayna was a bad idea.

In fact, while my anger at Kaleb has diminished slightly, I may be more upset with Rayna now.

Damn her.

I crank the water off and wring out my hair, my mind reeling. I can't re-evaluate my feelings about Kaleb by thinking about them forever in the shower. Only time will tell if I decide he's worth forgiving.

I dry off quickly, then slip Rayna's coin around my neck. It bites into my skin, but the pain is dulled now by the sharp sting of anger.

When I emerge from my room in black leggings, my hair dripping onto a gray sweatshirt that reads *Somewhat Responsible,* I'm met by an unexpected gathering of vampires that has materialized in the living room.

The furniture has all been pulled away from the fireplace to account for a few added lounge and dining chairs. Victoria has claimed a leather lounge chair, Xander perched on its arm, Rose on the floor and leaning against Victoria's legs; Pippa has opted for a dining chair near the sofa where Nik sits looking somber; Kaleb is sulking in the chair next to Victoria, looking exceptionally ordinary in black jeans and a black t-shirt, the emerald winking at his throat. He catches my eye then quickly looks away, pretending to examine something interesting on the back of his hand.

I'm not surprised to see Henry talking animatedly with Pippa (who is eyeing him hungrily), but am surprised to see Yara, stiff as a board, sitting next to an unfamiliar brown-skinned man with a collection of colored jewels in his ears. He surveys the room with quiet amusement, his eyes snagging repeatedly on Nik, who is ignoring him studiously.

The group falls silent as I round the corner, and I shrink under their gazes. I cross hurriedly to the sofa and sink down next to Nik, who opens himself toward me and wraps a steady arm around my shoulders.

"Ah, lovely," Kaleb pipes up, straightening in his chair. "The guest of honor has finally arrived. Shall we begin?"

"What exactly are we doing here?" Yara drones in her sharp accent.

Kaleb shoots her a withering glare. "If you will be quiet, Yara darling, then I will explain."

Yara meets his gaze unflinchingly and I get the impression that, while she may be part of Kaleb's inner circle, she doesn't seem to like him very much. Regardless, she says nothing else, folding her arms subserviently.

"Wonderful," Kaleb says, and everyone turns their attention to him. "As we are all aware, there has been a string of murders—very *public* murders—this past week in our city, and I" —Xander shoots him a sharp look— "*we* have reason to believe they are the work of Konstantin." The room bristles at the name. "Not only is he threatening the members of this circle specifically but, with each murder he commits, he threatens the very secret of our existence. We cannot allow these actions to continue or it could mean destruction for all of us.

"We have discovered a pattern," Kaleb continues, "regarding the locations of murders. Each seems to coincide with locations our Charlotte has visited in the past week: Pier 39, Embarcadero, Hyde Street Pier, Grace Cathedral."

"I didn't actually visit Grace—" I start, but Xander cuts me off.

"I thought we had been over this," he says to Kaleb. "We're aware of how all these places relate to Charlotte."

"Those are all very popular places," Henry chimes in brightly, and his eyes are sharp. Considering. "Most of us could have been to—or near—them in the last week. What makes you so sure it has to do with Charlotte?"

"Because," Xander sighs, "Charlotte killed the first girl. The one near the wharf."

Henry starts, his gaze drifting sideways until it lands on me, and his lips stretch wide into a disturbing smile. "Did she now?"

"And," I interject, aware of Yara staring at me with judgmental eyes, "because of the lovely little hole that Jake guy put in my chest. Or had you forgotten about the vampire you beheaded in our basement, Henry?"

Henry's smile vanishes and he narrows his eyes, his jaw working in slow circles.

"Yes, that," Kaleb says, "and because of the location of the last murder. Since Lottie visited the Golden Gate Park alone, it confirms our theory that Konstantin is following her specifically."

I swallow hard as nine heads swivel in my direction.

"It seems Konstantin has taken a liking to you," says the man with the jeweled ears. His voice is deep and warm, and it rings with a strong French lilt. A memory catches, then drifts away. "Though he took a liking to many."

"Who are you again?" Pippa asks with mock sweetness. "And why are you here?"

Kaleb's lips pucker. "Philippa—"

"It's alright, Kaleb," the stranger says, offering Pippa a genuine smile that resonates through his entire body. "I'm James de la Rue, an old friend of Kaleb and Nikolas. And I am here to help."

And just like that, the memory is back: a private meeting, Kaleb's fireplace crackling, the scene obscured by a wrought iron grate.

And James? Once we leave London, our contact will be very minimal. But if you do hear from me, I expect you to come running.

The man who took over Kaleb's club after we left London is *here,* in my living room, smirking like he owns the place.

Pippa raises one dark eyebrow. "An old friend, huh? By the way Nik is ignoring you, I might think you were an old lover."

Nik chokes on air, burying his face in one hand as James bursts into laughter. Victoria and Rose exchange a stunned glance, then turn to stare at Nik, who looks like he would rather be anywhere else.

Pippa grins, kicking one leg over the other. "Just how many people in this room have you slept with?"

Kaleb glares at her. "Philippa, now is not the time."

Pippa scans the group with devilish eyes, counting on her fingers. "Let's see...Lottie, me, and James makes three."

"Pippa, *please,*" Nik groans, pressing both palms over his eyes.

"Oh, come on, Nik. It's *funny*—"

"*Now is not the time,*" Kaleb barks, glowering at Pippa. Nik looks at him with an odd mixture of confusion and gratitude. "Or had you forgotten, darling, that there are more important things at hand than the details of Nikolas's sexual history?"

Pippa's eyes snap to Kaleb in annoyance, but she immediately shrinks back when she sees his icy expression. We may not run with Kaleb anymore, but he is still the Alpha of our city. And it's an unwritten vampire rule that you should never piss off the Alpha.

Pippa mumbles an apology, though it sounds more like a curse than anything.

Satisfied, Kaleb resumes his presentation. "As I was saying, we aren't sure why Konstantin is targeting Charlotte. But we're not concerned with the *why* so much as the *where* and *when*."

"Then we need to know where else Lottie has been this week," Rose muses. "So we know where to look next."

"Precisely." Kaleb turns to me expectantly.

"Well," I start, yanking the sleeves of my sweatshirt over my hands, "if we eliminate the places that have already been targeted, that leaves the Majestic Theater, a house on Pacific Avenue, Land's End Labyrinth, and...Alcatraz."

Kaleb's eyebrows flick upward. "Alcatraz? The prison?"

"No, Kaleb, the gift shop," I sneer. "Yes, *obviously* the prison." James snickers.

Kaleb stares at me, obviously waiting for an explanation, but I don't give him one. Victoria, Pippa, and Rose avoid eye contact in an attempt to hide their involvement, but it only makes them look guilty.

"Right." Kaleb finally says. "Charlotte, while your plan tonight was foolish and poorly executed" —I scowl at him— "you had the right idea. The evidence leads us to believe that Konstantin will be at one of these locations tomorrow night. All we have to do is be ready for him."

"Oh, is that all?" Yara says, her eyes sweeping arrogantly through the room. "Do you really think Konstantin will be so easy to catch? If you want to take him down, you'll need more than an accidental Alpha with a superiority complex and his group of dysfunctional misfits."

James makes a show of rolling his eyes, while Kaleb stares at Yara with an expression of poorly-masked loathing. Henry glares daggers at her. Even Nik seems appalled. Xander growls, but Victoria touches his leg with a warning hand.

I, however, receive no such warning.

"Hey," I snap, and Yara's head swivels languidly in my direction. Nik tenses beside me, then fishes for his flask and takes a quick swig. "There's no need to be rude. Some of these misfits happen to be highly functional."

Kaleb lifts a hand. "Enough, Charlotte." He considers Yara through narrowed eyes. There is a predatory look about him as he tilts his head to the side. After a few seconds of tense silence, he says, "For the life of me, I don't know why I continue to bring you to business meetings, Yara, darling. You have always been more suited for hosting."

Henry laughs once, then claps a hand over his mouth to stifle it.

Darkness flickers in Yara's eyes as she stares down an unruffled Kaleb, and for a moment I'm worried she might leap across the room and tackle him to the ground. But she submits, yet again, and leans back in her chair with a grimace.

To be fair, if Kaleb spoke to me that way, I don't think I would like him either.

Kaleb surveys the group icily and touches the emerald at his throat, as if to remind everyone of its presence. Even in casual clothes, he manages to be pretentious.

"To answer your question, Yara," he says, "no. I don't think catching Konstantin will be easy." Yara raises an eyebrow. "But it is the only lead we have, and we have to start somewhere. We will split up and cover all four locations. Obviously, Charlotte will stay behind—"

"Obviously, Charlotte will *not,*" I challenge. "If you think I'm going to stay here and cower while you all risk your lives, then you're a damn fool. Konstantin is after you too, if you've forgotten. And I know you'll be out there tonight, putting your life on the line with everyone else."

Kaleb glares at me dubiously, then looks to Xander for support, but he only shrugs.

"She has a point," he says.

"I'll go with Xander," I offer, and both stare at me in surprise. "We can take his car. All very safe."

Xander nods slowly. "Yes. Charlotte will come with me."

I know my brother is only agreeing with me for his own peace of mind—he would rather keep an eye on me than have me sneak out by myself again—but still. He took my side against *Kaleb*. That has to count for something.

"Fine," Kaleb says in a clipped tone. "Charlotte and Alexander, then."

"I call Henry!" Pippa shouts. Henry cocks an eyebrow, his boyish mouth twisting into a smirk. "I have access to a boat, and therefore to Alcatraz."

"This is not the time for frolicking, Philippa," Kaleb sighs, "but very well. Nikolas, you take Victoria, and Ambrosia will accompany me. Yara, James, I'll need you two back at the Bird to keep watch. I can't have it unguarded, and we have...*guests*...to entertain."

Nik narrows his eyes at Kaleb, who stares back with an expression blank as a cloudless sky.

35

WHEN KALEB DISMISSES EVERYONE, YARA practically bolts from the house. She obviously has more important things to do, like, I don't know, cleaning blood from Kaleb's overpriced furniture.

James stays long enough to ask Kaleb a few whispered questions, then he, too, disappears into the early dawn. But not before offering Nik a two-fingered salute and a grin that could soften stone.

Everyone else lingers for a few hours—including Kaleb and Henry, much to Nik's dismay—and we pull a few bottles of wine from the basement. The group disperses into separate areas of the living room: Xander and Kaleb are murmuring near the fireplace; Rose and Victoria are curled on the sofa, laughing at something on Victoria's phone; Nik is perusing the bookshelves; and Pippa and Henry are sitting at the card table, playing what looks like a very seductive game of Uno.

I watch from the corner of the sofa, a glass of wine in my hand, as Kaleb turns a critical eye on Pippa. "Please don't corrupt him, Philippa, dear," he calls across the room.

Pippa sneers at him. "Not any more than you have already corrupted him, Kaleb, *dear.*"

Kaleb bites the insides of his cheeks and turns back to Xander.

The exchange between the two is so effortless that I almost forget that Kaleb has been gone since 1897, and that his presence here is as alien as Henry's. But it doesn't *feel* wrong or uncomfortable. Seeing him talking with Xander, a pale mirror image of my brother in casual black, feels *right*.

Rayna's voice echoes in my head, some snippet of an old memory from our time in Belarus: *I understand your wariness of Kaleb. He can be cold—some may even say cruel—but for those of us who know his heart, nothing could be further from the truth. He loves fiercely, cares deeply. And if he must be cruel to protect those most important to him, then so be it.*

Kaleb chuckles quietly at something Xander says, a small smile tugging at the corners of his mouth. I find myself smiling with him.

Maybe he could belong here again.

I have no doubt that Xander, Pippa, and Rose would learn to accept Kaleb eventually. And after some intense self-therapy, I probably could too.

Nik, on the other hand...

I glance around the room and notice that Nik has disappeared. After setting my wine glass on the coffee table, I scurry from the living room to look for him. It takes a few minutes, but I finally find him in the corner of Xander's studio, leaning against one of the floor-to-ceiling windows with a sketchpad in his hand. It is open to a graphite drawing of Xander's that depicts Rayna in men's fashion from the mid-1800s.

She often grew tired of skirts.

"Nik?" I link my arm with his, following his gaze as he stares out over the glittering skyline. "Are you okay?"

"Hey, Lottie," he sighs, dropping the sketchbook onto Xander's desk. "I'm fine. There's just...a lot to process."

"You're telling me," I murmur, leaning my head against his shoulder. "I'm sure you weren't expecting to see an old *lover,* and that tends to add an extra level of discomfort."

Nik scoffs. "An old, *old* lover. And it wasn't much of a surprise. I saw him at Kaleb's club the other night. I figured he would show up again eventually."

"You did?" I ask, frowning up at him. "Where was I?"

"Right next to me." He smirks, but his eyes are distant, focused on something I can't see. His lip curls. "I assume you were distracted by the *activities* taking place in the club."

I think back to the smoke-filled room, the hypnotized eyes, the pale-haired vampire plunging his teeth into that poor girl's neck, and I shiver. It's one thing to dine and dash with humans you'll never see again. It's another thing entirely to keep them as pets. Since Kaleb and I are recently on tentative speaking terms, I might need to have a *word*.

"That's a fair assumption," I grumble.

"I was startled when I saw James the other night," Nik muses, "but honestly, I shouldn't have been. It makes sense that Kaleb would bring him here. At least he would have one person he could trust."

"He can trust *us*," I say softly, and Nik shoots me a sharp look. "You and me, Pippa and Rose. Even Xander. Kaleb has always had people he could trust. He's the one who severed those ties."

Nik's eyes examine me carefully for a few seconds before he turns away, slipping from my grasp to lean against the window. Dawn light sparkles over the bay, causing pinpricks of light to dance on his skin. He sighs.

"Kaleb might be able to trust us," Nik says, his voice cracking, "but I'll never trust him. Not again."

"Nik, you don't have to forgive him, but you can trust him with this. I promise." If the statement surprises him, he doesn't show it. "He wants to catch Konstantin as much as we do—"

"James, though," Nik murmurs remotely, as though he doesn't hear me. "*James* I trust. He has never been anything but good. He won't betray us."

"Kaleb isn't going to *betray* us—"

"How do you know, Charlotte?" Nik whirls on me, his once-calm eyes now blazing with rare fire. The sudden fury startles me and I take a step back, my legs bumping against the desk. "How can you *possibly* know what Kaleb is thinking? He has been back in our lives for less than a week, and he already has us trotting obediently at his heels like a bunch of whipped dogs. What happens when he's caught in a lie, hm? What happens when he gets tired of babysitting? *What's to stop him from killing you, too?*"

I recoil at the suggestion, clutching my hands to my chest and dropping my gaze to the floor. If only Nik *knew*. If only he had seen the agony on Kaleb's face, heard the misery in his voice. Maybe he would understand.

I glance back up at Nik and find horror etched in his expression.

"Lottie," he whispers, striding forward to gather me into his arms. "I'm so sorry. That wasn't—I didn't mean—"

"I get it, Nik," I mumble, curling into him. "I really do. But please. Trust me when I say that when it comes to stopping Konstantin, Kaleb is the best chance we have."

He flinches and presses his face into my hair, his hands clenching into tight fists against my back. "I know Kaleb is helping us, which is" —his voice catches— "great. But I still can't look at him without seeing flames."

"Kaleb is complicated." I bite my lip to keep from saying too much. Every part of me wants to tell Nik what I learned tonight about Rayna's death—that she was every bit as responsible as Kaleb was—but I can't. Not yet. Not until this Konstantin business is behind us.

"At least we can go back to ignoring him after this," Nik says.

A wave of guilt crashes through me as I remember Kaleb's sodden clothes, the strength of his embrace, the rain that dripped down his cheeks like tears.

"Yes," I agree, hating myself for it. "Yes, we can."

◊   ◊   ◊

I know I should be sleeping. I'm going to need all my energy to catch Konstantin tonight.

But how can I be expected to sleep when we might *actually catch Konstantin tonight?*

I have been literally and metaphorically bouncing off the walls all afternoon. Xander is ready to kill me, and I don't blame him. After an unfortunate incident with one of the library bookshelves—if we're able to salvage the books is anyone's guess—Victoria banished me to my bedroom where I've been holed up for an hour.

And I'm not sleeping.

The house is quiet enough now that when my phone buzzes, I almost fall out of my chair. I brighten when I see who it is: Tristan.

No surprise there.

The truth is, Tristan hasn't crossed my mind all day. Between the looming threat of Konstantin and navigating my ever-present family drama, I haven't had much time to think about anything else. Even if "anything else" is a human boy with honey eyes and freckled cheeks and scarred knuckles who has absolutely nothing to do with my current predicament.

Except for, of course, the Alison Incident.

"Hi, Tristan," I say with forced calm—my nerves are crackling like lightning.

"Hey, Char," Tristan responds, a smile in his voice. "How's it going?"

"Oh, you know," I say vaguely. "Living the dream, over here." If *the dream* means planning a stakeout to catch a psychopathic vampire with my brother, my best friends, and the ex-leader of our family who I cried with in the rain only hours ago, then yes. I am living it.

"That good, huh? Did you figure everything out with your family yesterday?"

I shrug, then feel ridiculous. It's not like he can see me. "More or less."

"I'm glad," he says, but there is skepticism there. Which is fair, because I'm barely convincing myself. "So. Are you busy tonight?" Tristan asks. "I thought it might be fun to get the whole gang together again. You know, everyone who was at the Pier 39 party. Minus the serial killer, of course," he adds jokingly, but there's an edge to his voice. "I know Bree and Rose have been hanging out quite a bit, and Noah—"

"Tristan," I interrupt, choosing to ignore the fact that Rose apparently has a new BFF. "Tonight isn't great. We have...other plans," I finish lamely.

"Oh, okay," Tristan says, doing a terrible job of masking his disappointment. "How about tomorrow?"

Tomorrow works. Konstantin will be dead by tomorrow.

"I think we could do that."

"Perfect! Your place, seven o'clock?" His confidence is unnerving. "I know everyone will *freak out* when they see your house. Plus, that ballroom of yours could use some love."

"Sure, why not?" I know Xander will kill me for this, but I can't resist. After all, we'll have something to celebrate. "Let's have a party."

There's a muffled but celebratory yes in the background.

"Hey, am I on speaker phone?"

A few muted giggles, a smack, and an *ow.*

"Of course not," Tristan says. What a liar. "I'll let the others know about the party. Have fun with your plans tonight, yeah?"

"I will."

I definitely will.

◊   ◊   ◊

With three hours until sunset, I realize that it will be impossible for me to stay sane alone in my bedroom, waiting for darkness to fall. I slip into the hallway and make my way downstairs. If I'm not going to sleep, I might as well eat.

The house is eerily quiet despite the presence of five extra people, who all made the collective decision to sleep here today, despite the fact that we only have the two guest rooms. Xander offered them to Kaleb and Henry after they returned from picking up "supplies" (whatever that means) while Nik, Pippa, and Rose are curled together in the corner of the game room sectional. I tiptoe past them on my way to the wine room.

A pile of O-negative blood bags is still on the floor of the walk-in refrigerator where I left it a few days ago, and one wire shelf is askew. The shelf that Ty crashed into when I threw him across the room. After he bit me.

Scowling at the memory, I straighten the shelf and replace the blood bags in the hopes that returning them to their rightful places might erase the feeling of Ty's teeth on my neck. It doesn't. In an attempt to kill time, I meticulously sort through every bin and organize the bags into tidy rows of four. Kaleb would be proud. When I'm done, I grab a bag of AB-positive—and a B-negative for good measure—then slink up the stairs.

I start across the foyer but pause when I see Kaleb lying on the sofa in the living room, his arms crossed over his chest and still clad in Xander's black clothes. A deep crease cuts between his closed eyes. It wouldn't be such an odd sight, except for the afternoon sunlight slicing through the clerestory windows at the front of the house: it pools on Kaleb's cheeks, highlights the tiny hairs on his arms, and paints his hair in a halo of gold. I suddenly crave the sun.

But there is something else about him. Something strange. And it has nothing to do with the light.

"Lottie." I jump as Xander's whisper punctures the silence, and the thought dissipates into nothing. He blends into the shadows where he sits on the raised hearth of the fireplace, his elbows on his knees, and he motions me over with a flick of his head.

Careful not to step into the shaft of bright sunlight, I cross the room and settle myself on the floor next to Xander's legs. I lean my shoulder against his thigh and he strokes my hair absently. The gesture is comforting, and I'm reminded of late nights in front of our fireplace in Belarus, Xander playing with my hair while Mama read us stories from our small collection of books.

"How does he do it?" I whisper, looking up at Xander. "Sleep in the sun, I mean."

"Centuries of practice," Xander says. He glances over at Kaleb and his cool demeanor shifts to thoughtfulness. "He said he wanted to keep watch."

Kaleb stirs and shifts slightly so the sun illuminates more of the flat planes of his face. He reminds me of a weathered bronze statue, cold and unyielding but radiant in the sunlight, like a dark angel.

"Kaleb was good, once," I say, removing the clasp from one of my blood bags and taking a long sip. "I hate to admit it, but I might even say he was *incredible.*"

Xander is quiet for a moment, and when he speaks, there is a twinge of sadness in his voice. Maybe even a touch of regret. "You're right. Kaleb has done countless incredible things. But he has also done many terrible things. Unfortunately for him, those are the things most people seem to remember."

I take another drink from my blood bag, relaxing as warm life flows through my veins, and my racing heart begins to slow.

"You really should sleep, Charlotte," Xander says, combing his fingers through my hair. "It's going to be a long night."

He's right, obviously. I'm exhausted. And if I'm exhausted now, there's no telling how useless I'll be later. I shift my body until my head is resting in Xander's lap and close my eyes, the image of a glowing Kaleb burning against my eyelids.

◊   ◊   ◊

I'm awoken by a soft hand on my shoulder.

"Charlotte," Kaleb whispers.

My eyes snap open and I find myself lying on the floor, a pillow resting under my head. Xander has disappeared. Kaleb stands over me looking somber, his face now painted in evening shadows instead of sunlight.

"Come, darling," he says, offering me his hand. "It's time."

Everyone has already gathered in the dining room, wearing individual versions of what I like to call "hunter chic": Xander and Nik are both in dark jeans and fitted sweaters, Pippa in her standard leather jacket and combat boots, me in jeans and a zip-up hoodie. Victoria might as well be a comic book assassin in tight-fitting clothes and an equally tight ponytail, and Rose's Doc Marten's look heavy enough to crush skulls. I wish I could say we all looked fabulous, but Kaleb shrugs on a charcoal, double-breasted duster that puts us to shame. If I saw him with no context, I might assume he was on his way to solve an unsolvable crime or woo the heart of a fair maiden.

"Right then," Henry chirps through a wide grin, his tone all business. He lifts a leather duffel from the floor and sets it on the table with a loud *thud*. Victoria flinches and eyes Henry acerbically, warning him against scratching the glossy tabletop. He winks at her. "I know you're all *exceptional* fighters," he says with a note of sarcasm, "but it doesn't hurt to have a bit of help." He unzips the bag to reveal a pile of wooden stakes and silver daggers in various sizes. "Everyone take your pick. If we run into Konstantin, it may take more than brute force to bring him down."

"And remember," Kaleb says, regarding us all coolly, "we don't know how many others are working for Konstantin. He may have a team with him. Don't let your guard down for even a moment."

343

We all nod earnestly and take turns rummaging through Henry's bag of deadly weapons, releasing the scent of old leather and wood and something surprisingly sweet. I choose a pair of narrow stakes, struck by the way their polished tips shimmer wickedly in the incandescent light. I tuck the stakes under my belt and tighten my knife sheath around my thigh. It may be warped and rain-stained, but it still works.

"Where did you get all these weapons, Henry?" I ask, watching as the others select their own prizes, each more ornate than the last. I'm pretty sure the handle of Pippa's dagger is made entirely of amethyst.

Henry smiles crookedly, his fangs glinting. "I'm a bit of a collector. One has to have hobbies when one is immortal."

"Don't tell me there's some kind of arsenal hidden in those caves of yours, Kaleb."

"No," Kaleb says. "We have no need for one. Henry *is* the arsenal."

Henry zips the duffel and drops it back on the ground without removing weapons for himself. I notice that Kaleb hasn't taken any either.

"The two of you may be good fighters and literally as old as time," I muse, raising an eyebrow—Kaleb purses his lips— "but you should probably arm yourselves. Especially you, Kaleb. What with Konstantin wanting your head, and all."

"Oh, darling," Henry grins and tugs on his waistcoat, brandishing two daggers seemingly from out of nowhere, "I am always armed."

The look Pippa flashes him is wildly inappropriate given the circumstances.

I turn to Kaleb and he opens one side of his coat. A gold hilt glints brightly at his hip. Xander rolls his eyes.

"If we don't know what Konstantin looks like," Rose interjects, quickly and efficiently changing the subject, "how are we supposed to recognize him? You're sure you don't have a photo or a drawing or something?"

Kaleb shakes his head. "Unfortunately, the last time I saw

Konstantin was just before the invention of the photograph. Since then, he has been more than difficult to track down. All I can say is that he is of medium build with brown hair. He'll be easily recognizable by his cold, unforgiving eyes that lack any trace of the humanity he once possessed."

"Kind of like *your* eyes, Kaleb," Nik grumbles, and I elbow him hard in the side.

Boys.

We all stand in awkward silence for a few seconds. Kaleb once told me that Konstantin was one of the first vampires to emerge during the Plague outbreak in Romania. I can only imagine the things he has seen in seven hundred years. How much humanity can someone retain when they live through so much pain and death? At some point, he must have learned to turn it off: the pain, the worry, the fear.

I wonder if the same thing is happening to Kaleb.

If the same thing will happen to me.

"On that poetic and distressing note," Xander says, looking markedly at Kaleb, "everyone please double-check that you have your cell phones" —his eyes roll toward me— "and that they are on *silent mode.* If you see or hear anything suspicious, send a text and we'll all come running."

Only Xander would worry about cell phone functionality in a room full of vampires holding wooden stakes and daggers.

"One more thing," Kaleb says, resting his fingertips on the tabletop. "When you arrive at your respective locations, check the area for humans and clear them out as soon as possible. We're trying to prevent a murder, and Konstantin can't kill again if there is no one to kill."

"Brilliant," Henry trills, clapping his hands together. "Let's get this show on the road, shall we?"

We leave the house two-by-two—an undead Noah's ark—and climb into four cars, caravanning down the dark street like a funeral procession.

36

"MAYBE THIS WAS A BAD idea."

When I decided to go after Konstantin by myself, I wasn't worried at all. Hell, I was actually *excited* about the prospect of finding him. But now, as I picture my friends—Nik and Victoria, Kaleb and Rose, Pippa and Henry—doing the same thing, I can't seem to shake the uneasiness twisting my stomach into knots. Even having Xander with me seems like too much of a risk.

I lean my head against the Maserati's window, clenching my hands into fists in a vain attempt to stop their shaking. The night is uncharacteristically dark, the street lights shining dim and yellow as we turn onto Lincoln Boulevard.

"Someone is going to get hurt, and it will be my fault."

Xander sighs for what must be the thousandth time since we left the house. "Charlotte, *enough*. If anyone is to blame for this, it's Kaleb."

"But Konstantin is following *me*. Apparently, I'm important." The statement sounds like a question.

I'm rewarded with an eye roll. "Don't flatter yourself. Konstantin is here for Kaleb, and no one else. This mission is about more than just an old feud: if Konstantin keeps this up, our whole world could be exposed, which would mean danger not only for us, but for every vampire in existence. There's no need to make it about you."

Xander parks just off the road near the trail to Land's End Labyrinth and turns off the Maserati's purring engine, plunging us into sudden, heavy silence.

"Are you ready?" he asks, staring through the windshield.

"I'm here, aren't I?" I say darkly, then throw open the door and step out into the night.

The air is damp with fog, but the breeze is almost warm as it blows through the trees, carrying with it the scent of sea spray and earth. I stretch my arms above my head and inhale deeply, doing my best to calm the anxiety prickling at every nerve ending.

It's late enough that the parking stalls are almost empty; a single car sits at the far end of the row, and I notice a lone figure walking briskly toward the trailhead.

"Hey," I whisper to Xander as he emerges from the driver-side door, "we've got company."

Xander glances at the figure, then nods his head in its direction and says, "Go on."

I pat all my pockets to make sure I have my phone, secure the stakes in my belt, and walk confidently in the human's direction.

"Excuse me," I call, catching up to him with a wave that mimics hailing a taxi, "do you have a moment to talk about the environment?"

The figure spins around, his shoulders tense under the weight of a pale wool coat. He meets my gaze with a pair of disoriented golden eyes, framed by thick lashes and wind-mussed hair and a ridiculous number of freckles. My heart stutters to a stop.

"*Tristan,*" I breathe. "What are you doing here?"

"Charlotte?" he asks, blinking in surprise. "What are *you* doing here? I thought you had plans with your friends tonight. Though I'm not going to complain if those plans have changed." His mouth slides open into that easy grin of his, but it doesn't have its usual effect. Its edges are hard, sharpened by the worry in his eyes.

Why? *Why* is he here? He's supposed to be home, playing video games or eating pizza or whatever it is that human boys do on Wednesday nights.

Instead, he's here. Standing right in Konstantin's path.

"You need to leave," I say urgently, squeezing his arm hard.

He winces and his smile vanishes like smoke in the breeze. "What?"

I start to drag him toward his car but he yanks his arm away. It's hard to tell under the blanket of night, but Tristan's appearance seems more ruffled than usual: there is a discomfited anxiety buzzing through him, elevating his heart rate, creating a thin sheen of sweat on his forehead.

Tristan isn't supposed to be *ruffled*. He's supposed to be confident and grinning and full of sunshine. Instead, the energy coming from him is tense, like a taut wire about to snap.

"Tristan," I say, frowning, "are you okay?"

Darkness swirls behind his eyes for a few seconds before he lets out a huff of air. "No, Char," he says, and I notice the phone in his hand. "I'm not okay."

Apprehension bubbles in my stomach as Xander approaches us, and Tristan's expression becomes guarded.

"Oh," he mumbles, and Xander looks almost affronted. Tristan carefully avoids his eyes. "Hey, Xander. Do you mind if I talk to Charlotte for a minute?"

Xander peers down at me with narrow, incredulous eyes, and I'll admit I share his reluctance. The longer Tristan stays here, the more danger he's in.

But I can't deny the flitting of Tristan's gaze, the tremor in his jaw.

Tristan touches my arm softly. "Please."

"Two minutes," I murmur to Xander, who is chewing on his bottom lip. "Then I'll send him home."

Xander steals a few piteous glances at Tristan. "Okay. You have *two minutes.*" He pauses, then adds sternly, "And no more."

I nod, and he presses a quick kiss to my forehead before melting into the shadows like ink in water.

"Char—" Tristan starts, but I shush him.

I snatch a fistful of Tristan's coat—he cries out in protest, but the seconds are already counting down—and drag him toward the Maserati, my eyes scanning our surroundings for any hint of movement. I say nothing until we're safe in the backseat, the door slamming behind us, too loud. I flinch.

"Charlotte, what the *hell.*"

Tristan glowers—I didn't know he *could* glower—and turns the phone over a few times in his hands. The shadows are thick and unyielding inside the car, the black-tinted windows filtering out even the starlight, but his eyes still manage to glow. We are both twisted sideways on the seat so we're facing one another, our knees knocking together. Tension pulses from Tristan like a second heartbeat, filling the cramped car with the burning scent of skin and sweat and adrenaline and *blood.*

I stifle a groan. As if it wasn't enough to know that, at any minute, a psychopathic demon hell-bent on revenge could show up and try to murder me. To make matters worse, Tristan has to be here, innocent and distracted and completely oblivious to the danger he is in. Not to mention the fact that this Tristan isn't the one I'm used to. This Tristan is different. *Off.*

He glances down and his brow furrows. "What's on your thigh? Are those *throwing knives?*"

"Oh, these?" I say with forced nonchalance, patting at the band of leather near my knee. "Yeah. They're for...a game we're playing."

Tristan's eyes narrow, obviously less than satisfied with my answer, but he doesn't press the matter. His eyes move to his phone and he taps the dark screen in a nervous rhythm.

"Tristan, tell me what's going on."

"Well," he begins slowly, his jaw tensing, "I got a text."

When he doesn't elaborate, I throw my hands in the air. "Come on, man. You're going to have to give me a little more than that."

There's a tiny rustle outside the car and I snap to attention, my eyes straining to see through the dark windows. When the shadows stay fixed, I focus back on Tristan, who is watching me with a deep frown.

"Char, are you alright? You seem a little jumpy. Are you sure this is a good time?"

I wish I could say no. "It's fine, Tristan," I say through a forced smile, but he doesn't seem convinced.

"Are you sure? Because we can talk later if there's somewhere else you need to be..."

The distress in his voice is palpable. Guilt prickles in my chest. *Why, why, why.*

I take one of his hands in mine, squeezing tightly.

"It's fine. Xander can wait." The words feel rotten on my tongue, and I silently plead into the void that Xander is okay out there.

Waiting for Konstantin.

Alone.

Tristan stares down at our entwined hands and swallows hard before offering his phone.

"Here," he says without looking up.

The screen displays a text conversation from a few hours ago; there are three messages.

> Would you like to know who killed your sister?
> The answer is closer than you think.

> Who is this? What kind of prank are
> you trying to pull?

I thought so. If you have been watching the news
lately, you may already have an idea. They just
released the most delicious little video.

I gape down at Tristan's phone, disbelieving. I read the texts again.
Then again. Hoping that, somehow, they will rewrite themselves.

The answer is closer than you think.

In fact, it's so close he can touch it.

Touch *me*.

I slide my hand from Tristan's and tuck it securely into my pocket.

"Who do you—" I start, then change course. "Tristan. I know
you're worried, but this is probably just someone messing with you.
How would anyone know something like that?"

I ask the question not only for Tristan's benefit, but for mine:
how *would* anyone know?

Tristan hangs his head and sighs. "The thing is, I think...whoever
this is, I think they might be onto something."

The adrenaline that rips through me is enough to revive a corpse.
"What do you mean?"

"I never told you what happened with Alison."

He slides his phone into his coat pocket then rests his hand
lightly on my knee. Despite the chilly evening, his skin is hot through
my jeans. I resist the urge to take his hand again—his thumb traces
circles on the dark fabric—and try not to think about the fact that
we've been here longer than two minutes. And that Xander hasn't
come to retrieve me yet.

"She was painting in the park at the time," Tristan says, "like
she did every Tuesday before coming to my place for dinner. It started
to rain, so I called to check in. I offered to pick her up. She said no."
Tristan sags a little, leaning heavily against the backrest. "I was on
the phone with her when she—"

He doesn't finish his sentence. He doesn't have to.

Alison? Alison, are you there? Alison!

"When I found her," he says quietly, "she had lost a lot of blood. And I mean, a *lot* of blood. And she had these marks—*bite marks* on her neck. Like some sort of sick joke." He spits the words with contempt. "Then everything started happening with this *San Francisco Vampire*...and it started to feel like less of a joke and more of an experiment. A test. To see if it would work."

I want to run. This is not a conversation I want to be having now, or *ever*, for that matter. But the gentle pressure of Tristan's hand on my leg anchors me to the spot, impossibly frozen in the growing heat.

"If what would work?" I ask.

"This crazy blood-sucking thing!" Tristan shucks off his jacket and throws it in the front seat. Hair curls at his temples, at the nape of his neck, sticking to his damp skin. "Alison was practically drained of blood. With all this vampire stuff on the news, and that video...it can't be a coincidence."

I feel suddenly small, dread settling on my shoulders and crushing me to dust.

It would be easier if I knew nothing. But I do know. And I can never tell him.

So I say what any normal human might say in this situation: "Vampires don't exist, Tristan."

"It's a cold case, you know," he says, looking past me with eyes shadowed by the memory. "They never found who did it. My parents poured everything we had into the investigation, and just...nothing. No trace. They found skin under her fingernails and a few pieces of hair on her shirt, but it led nowhere. They told us the DNA belonged to no one living. Like she was killed by a ghost." He pales, clutching at my jacket sleeve, and his eyes bore into mine. "But maybe the person who sent me those texts knows something. What if they're right? What if the San Francisco Vampire killed Alison?"

Shame sinks white-hot claws into my chest. *It was me!* I want to scream. *I killed her! It was my fault!*

But I say nothing.

A few things are starting to make sense, at least: Tristan's reaction when he saw me at Kaleb's party, his anxiety over Noah's vampire story.

He thinks his sister was killed by a wannabe-vampire serial killer. He isn't far off.

"You could be right," I say, though the lie sounds weak to my own ears. "Maybe this guy killed her."

"But who could know that? And why text me now, after all this time?"

Tristan wipes his forehead with the back of his hand. The salty tang of his skin stirs the air and I lean backward, putting as much distance between me and his blood-filled veins as possible.

I attempt to push back the apprehension creeping upward from my abdomen. The only people who know about my involvement in Alison's death are me, Xander, and Pippa, and I know for a fact that neither would be so cruel as to taunt Tristan with the death of his sister. Xander has never been one for psychological torture, and Pippa—well, Pippa may act tough, but she's basically a kitten in wolf's clothing.

It can be only one person, really.

I've never met him, I know virtually nothing about him, but only Konstantin could do something like this. I'm not sure how he can know about Alison, but this reeks of his involvement. It's the exact kind of emotional manipulation that nearly drove Rayna mad.

He's chosen another pawn, made another move.

My skin prickles at the idea of Konstantin's ever-present eyes on the back of my neck.

"This could be a huge breakthrough in the case," Tristan continues, his body practically vibrating with nervous excitement. His heartbeat cuts sharply through the silence like gunshots. "It could be the information that finally leads us to Alison's killer. Tonight could change everything."

He's right. After tonight, everything will be different.

Because after tonight, Konstantin will be dead.

But, I remind myself, killing Konstantin will do nothing to erase what I've done. No amount of penance on my part will bring Alison back.

Maybe this is how Kaleb feels.

My heart is a stone inside my chest, and for a second, I worry it has stopped completely. But the faint beat is still there, spasming like a dying bird, while Tristan's heartbeat pounds in a deafening rhythm. It's loud.

So loud.

It's all too much. Kaleb's eyes. Nik's fear. Konstantin watching, waiting, scheming.

And Xander, outside. Alone.

I squeeze my eyes shut and try to force away the sound, the metallic scent of blood and sweat pulsing from Tristan's skin, the fear, the fear, the fear.

But his heart is so *damn loud.*

"STOP."

I slam my hand against Tristan's chest and he gasps loudly, stunned into stillness as my nails dig into the thin material of his white t-shirt. His heart thumps under my palm—still too loud—but his posture softens, his heartbeat slows. He moves carefully, lifting one hand to rest it over mine.

"Charlotte?"

I am here.

I open my eyes to find Tristan staring at me, his irises glinting like gold coins, his pupils blown wide. There is no anxiety in them now, only concern.

A sense of wrongness pierces me like an arrow.

Tristan leans forward, crushing my hand beneath his, breathing into the space between us. "Charlotte, what's wrong?"

Everything. Nothing. And yet...

"I don't know."

He brushes the backs of two fingers along my jaw. The walls of the Maserati seem to close in around us, drowning the backseat in suffocating darkness; heat rises from Tristan's skin, burning in my throat as he draws closer, creeping into my cheeks with sharp vigor.

My hand is still splayed against Tristan's chest. His eyes flicker to my mouth.

I bite the insides of my cheeks.

This is what I want. Isn't it?

Then why does this feel so *wrong?*

Something stirs in my subconscious, but it's stifled by the kiss Tristan presses to my lips.

My eyes flutter closed as the car is plunged into muffled silence, the only sound the dull roaring of my own heartbeat in my ears. Tristan's mouth is warm and soft, lingering for a few quiet seconds before he pulls away—only inches—his eyes glowing with a dark light. He traces calloused fingertips over the hollow of my throat, along my jawline, his hand splaying open to press his palm against my cheek.

My lips prickle with the lingering taste of vanilla.

This is bad. This is *very* bad. I just...can't remember why.

Because Tristan just kissed me.

And I *desperately* want him to do it again.

One moment we are frozen, staring at each other through inky shadows, and the next, Tristan's urgent mouth is on mine, his fingers tangling in my hair, and my hands are clinging to him like I'm hanging from a cliffside. Like he is the only thing keeping me from plummeting over the edge.

Though it's clear I may have already fallen.

I have lost track of the kisses I've stolen in my long life, the number of lovers I've had. I've touched and been touched, broken hearts and been heartbroken. Some I remember more than others: Nik, Enson, the thief in Prague, the raven-haired gypsy in Belarus, the Welsh privateer with a thirst for adventure.

They were all unique in their own way, but similar, too. *My type*, I always thought. *The only type I fall for: gentle souls who are kind and caring, those whose love burns steady and low like smoldering coals.*

But there is something different about Tristan, something unfamiliar and exciting. Something in the way his hands clutch the back of my jacket, in the way his mouth devours mine, in the way he shivers as my fingers rake down his chest, like my touch might break him into pieces.

He is something *new.*

Tristan's kiss deepens and he draws me toward him, closing the space between us in a few fevered seconds. His mouth explores mine hungrily, enticing me with a coaxing tongue, with teeth that scrape against my bottom lip. Desire claws its way through me, igniting fires everywhere Tristan's hands find my skin: my throat, my jaw, the exposed point of my sternum.

He unzips my jacket. His fingers slip beneath the collar of my shirt. A soft moan escapes me—

I twist sharply and throw myself onto Tristan's lap, my knees straddling his hips and my fingers sliding to tangle in the soft hair at the nape of his neck. His eyes glitter with longing as he looks up at me, his lips parted and his cheeks flushed with rose. The effect is dazzling.

"*Oh,*" I breathe, mesmerized again by the humanity of him.

When I lean to press a kiss to the soft hollow beneath Tristan's jaw, he sighs.

"Charlotte."

His pulse stutters under my lips, hot and fevered and *alive*. It happens before I can stop it: my fangs explode through my gums, bringing with them the unwelcome sensation of frenzied bloodlust, raw and wild and uncontrollable. I press my body against Tristan's, digging my nails into his neck, staring down at the delicate skin where his pulse is visible, pounding an uneven rhythm just below the surface.

I can't. I *shouldn't*.

But the hunger burns.

I suppose one drink won't hurt.

I drag my tongue along his collarbone, relishing in the salty-sweet taste of him, and he shudders with pleasure as my fangs graze his skin—

And Tristan heaves upward, catching my face in both hands, his breath hitching as he crushes his mouth against mine with a desire reinvigorated.

And I forget.

"Charlotte," he gasps in the moments between.

"Charlotte," he whispers as his hands slip beneath my shirt.

"Charlotte," he breathes against my skin, his lips trailing down my neck and leaving devastation in their wake.

I scramble for the hem of Tristan's t-shirt and yank it up, exposing a tantalizing amount of skin stretched over hard muscle. My heart jumps in my chest. Who gave him the right to have abs as chiseled as Michaelangelo's *David?*

I press my palms flat against Tristan's stomach and trace my thumb over a diagonal scar cut into his abdomen, partially hidden by the waistline of his jeans. It isn't pretty—deep and thick and stained a mottled purple—but against the near-perfect smoothness of his skin, the fading gold of his summer tan, it reminds me of what he is: *human.*

Unable to help myself, I bend to touch my lips to the scar, just above his belt.

Tristan groans. "Oh, *god.*"

I kiss my way up his abdomen, weaving between his ribs, my hands exploring the sharp curves of his hip bones. Each kiss draws a breath from Tristan's lips, a shiver from his shoulders, his hands clenching fistfuls of my hair as he whispers:

"Charlotte."

I had almost forgotten how it felt to be wanted.

Thump.

I freeze, my lips parted over Tristan's sternum, and train my ear upward, but I hear nothing. Only the sound of Tristan's ragged breathing as he strokes my hair with trembling fingers.

"Charlotte?" My name rumbles through him like a growl, desire softening his voice to the consistency of warm honey. "Is something wrong?"

"Shh."

Tristan obediently falls silent, and I raise my head to look at him. His hair is a tousled mess of golden waves, his shirt hitched up over his ribcage—good *hell,* he is beautiful—and it takes all my willpower not to drag it off of him.

There will—hopefully—be time for this later, but all the heat in the car has been doused by that one tiny *thump.*

"I'll be right back," I whisper, rolling off Tristan's lap and onto the cold leather seat next to him.

He says nothing, but I feel his eyes on my back as I slip out of the car.

"Xander?" I hiss, peering into the darkness. Thick clouds have gathered, erasing the moon and blanketing the little glade in gray mist. "Xander, are you there?" Silence. "If you're messing with me, I swear I will rip that stupid ring out of your nose while you sleep—*ah!*"

A heavy weight lands on me and knocks me to the ground, pain jolting through me as my forehead collides with asphalt. Stars erupt in my vision as strong, bony fingers dig into the back of my neck and, all at once, the world goes black.

37

IT'S THE KIND OF DARKNESS that might incapacitate a human—thick and heavy, like my head is encased in concrete—but, luckily for me, that mortal ship sailed lifetimes ago.

My vision swims back into focus and I launch myself to my feet, my attacker stumbling to right himself with a few muffled curses. Blood trickles into my eyes and I hastily wipe it away, muttering a few curses of my own while my head throbs.

The assailant stands, hunched, on the stretch of grass between the parking lot and the trailhead, a dagger in his hand and a grin gleaming from beneath a black hood. My heart leaps into my throat.

"Excuse me, sir," I snap with more conviction than I feel. "If you couldn't tell, I was a little busy. Couldn't you have waited a few minutes before attempting to lure me to my death? Is chivalry dead?"

His mouth twists into a cruel, fanged sneer that sends a chill through me. This can't be Konstantin...can it? Could it really be so easy? But I see wisps of the other vampire's hair where it curls over his forehead—deep red, the color of late autumn—and my hope evaporates into the growing fog.

Not Konstantin. But if Konstantin's cronies are here, he can't be far behind.

"I love the uniform," I drawl, grinning through my fangs. "Very broody. What is Konstantin going for, exactly? Every drug dealer in a 1980s high school sitcom?"

The mystery vamp hurtles forward with a growl, and I brace myself as he slams into me at full speed. I use his growing momentum to knock him sideways, but not before the dagger in his hand slices up my cheek. The silver screams against my skin, drawing a snarl from my throat.

"Not...*cool,*" I say through gritted teeth. I grab him by the front of his jacket and throw him onto the ground, but he leaps to his feet, undeterred.

At least the fall managed to knock the dagger from his hand.

The boy's hood has fallen back and I'm surprised by what I see. He is young, his red hair falling into his eyes. I half expected all of Konstantin's cronies to look like Jake: hardened and bulky with scars cut into their faces. Instead, this kid looks less like an ex-Marine and more like he has history homework due on Monday.

When he lunges again, I'm ready for him, riding the wave of adrenaline already pulsing through me. I dart out of the way and knock him down with a sweeping kick to the ankles. Again, he jumps up, ignoring the fact that there is now a hole in the knee of his jeans.

I distract him with a low swing while I aim a sharp jab to his face, but he's faster than I anticipate. He twirls away from my attack, catching my fist in one hand while the knuckles of the other slam into my jaw with a sickening *crack.*

I stumble to the side, wrenching my chin sideways to pop my jaw back into place, and suppress a groan.

"You know," I growl, rubbing my cheek where blood still drips from the dagger's shallow cut, "it seems like you have some unresolved issues that you need to talk about. And I, being a bit unhinged myself, am not opposed to a good, old-fashioned therapy session.

What's the matter, hmm? Does someone need more attention from Daddy Konstantin?"

A snarl tears from the boy's throat and he watches me with glittering eyes, my blood staining the knuckles of one hand. "I need only what Konstantin needs," he says, his voice surprisingly bright and clear. And monotone. "For Konstantin is king. Konstantin will not stop until he recovers what was taken, and only Kaleb can return it."

Déjà vu hits me like another punch to the jaw, and unease pools in my stomach as I remember the gravel in Jake's voice when he repeated the same words.

I snatch the front of the vamp's shirt and yank him toward me until our noses touch. His breath is cool and reeks of sour blood.

"What does Konstantin want?" I hiss, desperation clawing its way into my chest. "What did Kaleb take?"

The boy grins—a gruesome, evil thing—and spits in my face.

Oh, *hell* no.

I tackle him to the ground. My fist connects with his cheek-bone—*crack*—before he throws me off of him, gliding gracefully to his feet.

The vampire growls again and runs at me. I catch him by the shoulders and we slam into each other, struggling wildly in one another's grip. I drive a knee into his stomach. He elbows me hard in the temple. My nails carve parallel lines across his cheek. His jaw snaps shut a breath away from my throat, and terror bolts through me.

No. I won't let another sicko get his teeth beneath my skin. Not again.

I claw at the boy's thick hair and wrench his head sideways, plunging my fangs into his neck. He cries out in surprise as his blood explodes into my mouth—acrid and stale—but the sound is cut short when I jerk my head sideways, tearing his skin into ribbons with one violent twist.

He stumbles backward onto the grass, clapping a hand to his neck in an attempt to staunch the bleeding, but it will take more than a few seconds for a wound like that to heal. And it will definitely slow him down.

I grin in triumph.

"Tristan, get back in the car!" Xander's voice cuts through the silence, and my eyes comb the darkness in search of him. I finally spot him near the treeline, locked in a fighting embrace with another hooded vamp, this one sporting a blonde pixie cut. She shrieks as Xander's fist connects with her nose.

Abject horror flashes through me at Xander's words, but it's doused immediately by the white-hot pain that cuts through my abdomen. I cry out and look down to see something silver buried in my ribs. A dark stain spreads across my shirt, and I can feel the thick liquid dripping down my stomach.

I yank the dagger from my torso, hissing as blood pulses from the new hole, soaking into the waistband of my jeans. The angled blade is familiar, as is its leather-wrapped handle.

"With my own knife? *Rude.*"

I throw the knife at the vamp but he ducks out of the way, and I reach for another...

But find nothing. I clap a hand against my thigh where my sheath should be, then look up at the still-bleeding boy where he stands, now a few yards away. His skin is ashen, one hand pressed against his neck, the other clutching my sheath with its remaining knives.

"Stealing isn't polite," I snap, but he is already rearing backward, launching my knives through the air. They land in the trees with the sound of rustling leaves and snapping twigs. "Hey!"

Alright, I've had enough of this. If Konstantin were going to show up, he'd be here by now, and this kid is doing nothing but getting on my nerves.

I reach for the stake on my right hip, and then my left, but they're both gone. Lost sometime in the fight...or while I was in the car with Tristan.

"Xander!" I cry, just as my nemesis turns back to face me, murder in his eyes. I reach an open hand toward my brother. "Stake!"

Xander's head snaps in my direction, his hand clenched around the throat of his attacker, and he nods once. His eyes are dark and furious, wreathed in black shadows that make him look more menacing than usual. He whips a stake from his belt and flings it in my direction. I catch it in midair, mere inches from my chest, and twist my body just as the boy leaps at me.

I plunge the stake upward, putting all my force behind the motion, and it sinks into the boy's chest with a squelching sound. His eyes widen in surprise and he clutches at his jacket, his mouth opening in a silent wail, his expression igniting with pain. He slumps to the ground.

I stare down at the dead body of Konstantin's minion. But no, not dead. *Suffering*. Stake deaths are usually quick and—from what we can tell—painless, but the boy is writhing, clawing at his chest as deep purple veins snake across his hands and up his neck. I watch in horror as his skin turns the color of rotting plums, an agonized howl tearing from his throat as he cries red tears. After a few long seconds of painful gasping, he stills, his lifeless, blood-stained eyes staring at the black sky.

My eyes snap to Xander, but he is alone, the girl nowhere to be found. Blood trickles from his brow, and the sleeve of his sweater is sliced open to reveal a deep gash on his shoulder. Otherwise, he seems unharmed.

"*Charlotte,*" he gasps, rushing toward me, his fangs out. "Are you hurt?"

"I had a little brush with my own knife, but it's nothing that won't heal." When Xander cocks an eyebrow, I wave him off. "I wasn't holding the knife, if that's what you're thinking. I'm not *that* incompetent." Blood from my ribs has completely soaked the front of my shirt, growing cold against my skin, and I'm secretly glad the black fabric prevents it from looking worse than it is. "Are there any other vamps?"

"Not that I can tell," Xander says. "Konstantin isn't here, which gives me a bad feeling about the others—"

Xander stills, his attention fixing on something over my shoulder. The skin around his eyes tightens, uncertainty plain on his face.

"What—" I begin, but then I hear a small, almost-whimper behind me. I will the fangs back into my gums and turn slowly to see Tristan standing, wide-eyed and gaping, behind the open door of the Maserati.

38

I AM SUDDENLY TOO AWARE of the blood dripping down my cheek, the heat under my eyes. Oh, and the body now lying dead at my feet. The boy's skin seems to hang from his bones, heavy with the blood that bruises every inch of him. The purple veins have darkened, carving lines of ink through his face and into his sunken eyes, staining them black. His neck is still flayed where I tore it open. Knowing it will never heal sends a surprising bolt of nausea through me.

Tristan watches us with an expression of mingled fear and intrigue, his fingers clamped around the top of the car door. Xander has gone completely still next to me, but he takes my arm gently.

"You better say something," he murmurs, low enough that Tristan can't hear. "I would tell you to Compel him, but—"

"But you know I'll rip your tongue out if you do?"

Xander's lips press into a tight line. "Something like that."

I swallow and wipe the back of my hand over my mouth, hoping it will remove some of the vampire's blood crusting around my lips.

"Tristan," I say carefully, taking a hesitant step toward him. He throws a hand into the air to stave me off, the other still white-knuckling the car door.

"Okay," Tristan says, his voice tight. "Okay. First of all, you two can stay right over there. I'm just—I'm processing. Give me a second."

Xander's hand tenses on my arm. He hates being ordered around, and hates it even more when someone other than him orders *me* around.

Tristan's expression is unreadable and eerily calm, considering the fact that he just saw four vampires battling it out in front of him, one of whom tore another's throat out then stabbed him with a medieval-looking wooden stake. Guilt and panic flicker through my chest as Tristan's eyes travel from me, to Xander, to the dead boy on the ground, and back to me. If I can read anything in his expression, it's an incredible amount of focus, like he's mentally trying to solve a difficult equation.

"So, Charlotte, I'm just going to take a stab in the dark here. No pun intended." His mouth quirks slightly at the corners, though the tremor in his voice betrays him. "The two of you are—I can't believe I'm saying this—*vampires*. Or something like vampires? God, I sound like a crazy person."

Tristan's eyes are wild, his free hand raking through his hair. I can't help but notice the muscles that ripple under his shirt, remembering how his skin felt beneath the palms of my hands. Beneath my lips.

This is a nightmare. I should never have listened to Tristan. I should have sent him home the moment I saw him. If I had, we wouldn't have kissed in the backseat. And he wouldn't be standing here now with that look on his face.

I hadn't considered what might happen if I told Tristan I was a vampire. In fact, the idea had barely crossed my mind. But if I could have chosen another way for him to find out, it would have been a long ways down the road. And I might have even been excited about it.

But now that the cat's out of the bag, I have an overwhelming desire to shove it back in, tail and all.

I glance at Xander, but he side-eyes me and hisses, "*I still think you should Compel him, but this is your problem now. Figure it out."

Xander is never any help.

I really *should* Compel him, but something tells me it will be for nothing. He was bound to find out sooner or later.

Besides, it's only Tristan. One human knowing about us is hardly going to threaten the future of vampire-kind.

"You might say we're *exactly* like vampires," I confess, and Xander exhales sharply through his nose. I wrap my arms around my waist, hoping Tristan can't see the growing stain on my clothes. Blood still pulses slowly from the hole between my ribs and I wince as my forearm presses against it, fire biting through my skin.

"That's...cool. Very cool." Tristan is trying hard not to freak out, but he's not fooling anyone. The tight set of his jaw, the tension in his shoulders, and the feverish terror in his eyes tell me he's about twelve seconds away from a full-on meltdown.

"Don't freak out," I urge, my feet carrying me forward with a single, bold step. This time he doesn't stop me. I take another.

"Yeah, sure," he says, his eyes narrowing minutely. "I won't freak out. No reason for that. I do have one very important question though." He pauses, his expression a mask of fear and anger, his honey gaze hardening to cold amber. "What—and I cannot stress this enough—the *hell?*"

Ah, there it is.

"She told you not to freak out," Xander says, his eyes wary.

"Nobody asked you, Xander," Tristan snaps.

My mouth falls open with a tiny pop, and Xander's wariness is replaced instantly by cold fury.

When I look back at Tristan, his expression has transformed from focused fear to pure terror. He stares at Xander like he has just activated an atomic bomb.

"I—I'm sorry," he stammers, backing slowly away from the Maserati. "I didn't mean—don't—don't hurt me."

My stomach twists into a painful knot. "Tristan, we're not going to hurt you—"

"Like you didn't hurt Jason at the Halloween party?" His voice is small, but strong.

The words crackle through me like lightning, slowing time, the seconds stretching into what feels like hours.

I hear Xander's teeth click together.

"What?" I manage.

"Yeah," Tristan says slowly, his vowels long, as though recalling a distant memory. "I'm suddenly remembering a lot about that night. Flashes of lost time that I chalked up to being drunk, though I couldn't remember taking a single drink." He hugs his chest, his hands clutching at his elbows. "I saw you there, Charlotte. With Pippa and Rose. And...and Nik. And Jason was hitting on you..." He shakes his head. "I tried to stop him, but he wouldn't listen. And then you—you *bit him.*"

Ice claws its way up my spine as I remember the look of horror on Tristan's face, the bounce of his long gait as he tore away from me and out the Majestic's doors.

There is no way Tristan could remember what happened at the party. Not unless I messed up the Compulsion. I think back to the street, the salty air, and the dark alleyways where shadows writhed, fighting for my attention. The thought of Kaleb's cold eyes on the back of my neck. The way my focus wavered.

"Tristan—"

"The real question is, why am I just remembering it now?" Tristan takes a few more steps backward. "Can you erase memories? Is that some kind of weird vampire superpower you have?" Emotions flash over his face at an alarming rate, and I get the distinct impression that the cogs in his brain are overheating. "I'll ask again. *What the hell?*"

"Tristan, please—"

"I don't need any more lies," he says, the false calm returning to his voice. "I told you about Alison—about all the weird shit surrounding her death—and then you looked me in the eye and said vampires weren't real. And I *believed you*. Why wouldn't I? It's not like I had any reason to think you were one of them. That you were the same type of monster that killed my sister."

His words find their mark, burrowing deep into my chest like shards of glass. I can do nothing but stare back at him, my heart heavy and my jaw tight.

"And to think, I let you—" He rubs a hand over his mouth, his cheeks flushing, and retreats into himself. His eyes meet mine for a few agonizing seconds and betrayal ignites in them. "You know what? I'm done."

Tristan turns and walks briskly back to his car. I start after him, but Xander catches me by the arm.

"Lottie, let him go," he says, concern edging his voice. "He's going to need more than a few minutes to process. Besides, I think we have a bigger problem."

Xander stares down at his phone and I pull my own from my pocket. There are four missed calls and a stream of text messages shining urgently on the screen.

Vamps on Pacific Avenue!

Ambushed at the Majestic. Come quickly.

Heading back. Pippa is injured.

Everyone get back to the house NOW. Do not go inside until I arrive.

I turn a frantic gaze on Xander and his expression mirrors my own. He yanks me toward the Maserati, but I pull away.

"Wait!" I dart into the trees, scouring the leaf-covered ground. It takes a few long minutes, but I finally find my knives. One is missing, but I don't have time to worry about that now.

I sprint to the car and leap inside as Xander throws Tristan's discarded coat into the backseat. He starts the car and tears into the night, the Maserati's engine snarling like a jaguar through the empty San Francisco streets.

39

Nik and Victoria are waiting outside the house.

They're leaning against Nik's Audi with their arms folded, talking in hushed, anxious tones. The moon has emerged from behind the clouds, trimming their faces in cold lines of white. When we climb out of the car, Victoria darts over to us and throws her arms around Xander's neck. He returns her embrace and kisses her fiercely.

I assess Nik's appearance—mussed hair, a few drops of blood on his face, and a cut that slices its way up his left forearm—and he takes a good look at me, his eyes widening when he sees my blood-soaked clothes.

"Lottie, you look terrible."

"Thanks for that," I mumble, curling into his chest. He wraps his arms around me. "What's going on?"

"I don't know," he sighs, pressing his lips to my hair. "We had only been waiting for a few minutes when two hooded vamps ambushed us. Neither of them said a word, but I can only assume they were working for Konstantin. They just...attacked. I managed to kill one of them, but the other got away. We got Kaleb's text to get back to the house and we came straight here—"

As if on cue, Kaleb's Mercedes flies around the corner, screeching to a halt in the middle of the road and stirring up the smell of burning rubber. Kaleb throws open the door and stalks over to us without closing it. Rose follows closely behind, her eyes wary. Xander catches her in a relieved hug.

"Is everyone here?" Kaleb demands, his voice tight. One of the sleeves is torn almost completely from his coat—a real tragedy—and his t-shirt has been slashed down the middle. Blood wells from a deep gash over his sternum.

I pull from Nik's grasp, reaching for Kaleb. "Are you alright?" I ask, but he waves an impatient hand in the air. Nik eyes me suspiciously.

"I'm fine," Kaleb snaps. "Where are Henry and Philippa?"

"We haven't seen them," Victoria responds, her cherub's mouth twisting into a deep frown. "I hope Pippa's okay."

"I'm sure she's fine," I assure her, though I can't help the worry that prickles in my chest.

"Very well," Kaleb says. "Alexander and Nikolas, with me." He stalks toward the house, leaving a trail of questions in his wake.

"Kaleb!" I yell, and he freezes. Everyone looks at me in confusion. "Will you *please* tell us what is going on?"

Kaleb spins to face me, his coat twirling around him elegantly. There is fury in his icy eyes, but underneath is a spark of panic. "Konstantin knew where we would be tonight, didn't he?"

I nod.

"If Konstantin knew where we would be," Kaleb says pointedly, "that means he also knew where we *wouldn't* be."

My heart sinks into my stomach as Kaleb runs toward the house, Xander immediately falling into step behind him. Nik hesitates for a few seconds before trailing after them with a troubled expression.

"Shouldn't we be going in with them?" I hiss at Victoria and Rose. "If Konstantin is in there, they'll need all the help they can get."

"Shh," Victoria says, putting an arm around my shoulders. Blood trickles from a gash on her forehead. "If the boys need us, they'll let us know. Besides, they're just doing what they do best."

"Showing off?"

Victoria rolls her eyes. "Protecting those they care about."

I frown. "What makes you say that?"

"Look at them, Lottie. You're blind if you can't see that Xander and Nik would rather die than see any one of us hurt." She glances up at the house. "And from what I've seen of Kaleb so far, I think he may share the same sentiment."

"For what it's worth," Rose adds, "I think Victoria is right. Kaleb was a good man once. Maybe he's trying to be that again."

Now I'm frowning at both of them. "Where is this coming from?" Kaleb may have told me his secret, but I doubt he would divulge that information to Rose, let alone Victoria.

Rose shrugs. "That gash on his chest? One of the vampires attacking us almost got me with a dagger, but Kaleb wrestled him away from me. Took the brunt of the attack himself. He's lucky it was only silver."

I'm starting to think that Kaleb may have hit his head. Or maybe Nik breaking his nose knocked some much-needed sense into him.

Xander curses loudly through the darkness, and it echoes eerily in the silent night. He emerges from around the row of hedges separating the house from the street.

"Well, Konstantin isn't here," he says through a grimace, "but he *was*. It'll take some work to scrub the blood from the porch steps."

Rose covers her mouth with one hand as Victoria slips past Xander with a sense of purpose; she's probably on her way to fill a bucket with bleach.

"How the *hell* did he know where we would be?" I ask. "And how does he know where we live? Do we have a mole?"

Rose and Xander silently contemplate my question.

"Maybe—" Rose starts, then hesitates. "It couldn't be Kaleb... could it?"

Xander and I both say a forceful, "No," and we look at each other in surprise. The thought occurs that I should tell Xander about Kaleb and Rayna, but this isn't the best time to violate Kaleb's trust. Especially when we want to keep him on our side.

I consider giving him a lame excuse for coming to Kaleb's defense, but I'm saved from embarrassment by the sound of squealing tires down the street. Pippa's red convertible speeds into view and a cool wave of relief washes over me.

Unfortunately, the feeling is short-lived: Henry is in the driver's seat, and Pippa *never* lets anyone drive her car.

Henry slams on the brakes just behind Kaleb's Mercedes and leaps from the open convertible, blood covering his exposed forearms and a deep frown marring his normally cheery face. He leans over the passenger's side door where Pippa is curled into the fetal position. Her pale hair is sticky with blood and her arms are clasped tightly over her chest.

"Pippa," Xander gasps.

"Come on, then," Henry says gently, lifting Pippa into his arms. She cries out as he cradles her against him. "Shh, darling. We're going to get you sorted out."

"What happened?" I demand as Henry approaches us. "What's wrong with her?"

"*Move*," Henry snarls, and we step back. His fangs stab into his lower lip. "Where is Kaleb?"

"He's—I think he's inside," I stammer.

Henry glides quickly past me, Pippa whimpering in his arms, and Xander follows closely, looking like he might be sick. Rose and I exchange worried looks before darting after them.

The night is quiet for only seconds before it's broken by Pippa's scream.

40

THERE IS SMOKE IN THE *air.*

It isn't uncommon in St. David's to catch the scent of a wood-burning stove in the late evening. The odor, however, is masked tonight by a chilly wind that blows salt air off the ocean.

Wales is a little bit damp all the time, one of the many reasons I haven't loved living here. The moisture creates frizz in my hair, clinging to my skin and the crisp, taffeta fabric lining my collar. I always feel like I just finished bathing and have yet to dry off.

The weather does not have the same effect on Alexander, who is currently bouncing down the street ahead of us with his hands in his pockets. The humidity seems to enhance the already beautiful curls in his feather-down hair, and I am once again jealous of the genetics he got from our mother. She always told me—with a wistfulness I never understood—that I had my father's hair, his big eyes and freckled olive skin. Maybe it would have meant more to me if I could remember him.

Xander spins to face us with a lopsided grin. "Is anyone hungry?" The wind whips through the narrow street, making his coat and the lamplights flutter.

Kaleb raises a bemused eyebrow, glancing down at a smirking Rayna on his arm. "You know Rayna is always hungry, Alexander," *he remarks, "and I will admit I'm feeling a bit peaky myself."*

Nikolas and Kaleb share a knowing glance before Nikolas saunters forward, a challenge in his eyes. "First to catch dinner gets the first taste?" Alexander opens his mouth, but Nikolas cuts him off. "No Compulsion. Innate charisma only. What do you say?"

It may just be the warm glow from the lamp lights, but Nikolas is looking especially handsome tonight, his tweed pants and matching waistcoat hugging him in all the right places. His eyes are the color of fresh maple syrup or cognac straight from the bottle, catching light that dances in their depths like fireflies. At times, when he isn't watching, I like to imagine how it would feel to have those eyes on me. To be at the receiving end of his warm gaze, to feel the touch of his cool fingers against my cheek.

"He is yours for the taking," Rayna murmurs. Her expression is dark and slightly naughty. "I would love for you to steal my brother's heart."

"I don't know what you mean," I retort, embarrassment bringing a flush to my cheeks.

"You have always been a dreadful liar, Charlotte," she grins. "Please. Do it for Nikolas. I think he likes you, though you didn't hear it from me."

I glance back at our brothers—one painted in shadows and the other in copper—and imagine for a moment that what Rayna says is true.

A mischievous glint enters Alexander's eyes. "After you, dear brother."

Nikolas winks at me before disappearing down the street, Alexander hot on his heels.

My heart does a slow somersault in my chest.

"I'll give them ten minutes before one of them returns with a broken ankle," Rayna murmurs, and Kaleb chuckles.

"I'll give them five."

There is smoke in the air. But somehow, it has grown thicker.

"Do you smell that?" I murmur, and Kaleb takes a few steps

away from us, opening his mouth to taste the air where it is not polluted by the rose-petal scent of Rayna's perfume.

"I believe there is a fire," he says and strides quickly away, leaving me and Rayna alone on the cobblestones.

We exchange an exasperated look before darting after him.

I grow more anxious as the smoke continues to thicken, choking out the light from the lamp posts. It is dark for only a moment; when we round a corner at the end of the lane, we are greeted by a wall blazing gold. My eyes burn in the sudden light.

A small home is engulfed by tongues of flame, the thatched roof crackling and sending sparks into the sky. Villagers have taken it upon themselves to fight the fire with buckets of water from a nearby well, but to no avail. The flames are too large, too hot for the water to do any good. We catch up to Kaleb where he is crouching in the shadow of a nearby house, and huddle together as we watch the humans do their best to quench the inferno.

A tall, slender girl in a simple blue dress stands in front of the burning house, her inky black hair hanging limply to her waist. There is a bundle of fabric at her feet—clothing, it seems—and a small basket spilling apples and a loaf of bread, as though it had been dropped. The girl seems close to my age, maybe a few years older. Her bright eyes are wide and unblinking, her soot-stained face streaked with tears.

Pity stabs at my chest. I nudge Kaleb with my elbow and point to the girl, who seems oblivious to the villagers rushing around her. Kaleb's eyes narrow and he takes a few curious steps in her direction, his blue eyes wide and flickering like will-o-the-wisps in the firelight.

The girl's mouth opens in a despairing wail and I see, just under her top lip, two white fangs glinting like pearls.

Kaleb springs into action, sprinting toward the girl without a second thought. Rayna attempts to catch the back of his coat, but he is already gone.

"Ne!" *she hisses loudly, but her voice is silenced by the crackling of the flames.*

I dash after Kaleb and hear Rayna curse behind me, followed by the sound of her heeled footsteps.

Kaleb has a gentle hand on the girl's arm, whispering urgently in her ear, but she doesn't seem to be listening. Her eyes are shining with horror.

"Fy merch," *she chokes.* "Fy *Gwen.* Roeddwn i'n rhy hwyr..." *She trails off, unable to form the words.*

I am still learning Welsh, but I know enough to understand: My daughter. My Gwen. I was too late.

Kaleb squeezes her arm but she jerks away. She straightens—matching Kaleb's height—and glares at him furiously. "I don't need your pity," *she manages in English, her sudden anger quelling her tears.* "In fact, I don't need anything. My daughter is gone. There is nothing left for me here."

Without another word, she leaps into the towering wall of flames.

Kaleb leaps in after her.

I gasp.

Rayna groans. "Good Lord."

Kaleb is only gone for a few moments before he emerges, covered in soot, with the girl in his arms. The sleeve of her nightgown is on fire, and she screams as it melts her skin. Kaleb carries her toward a protected alcove and sets her carefully on the ground, dousing the flames with the length of his wool coat.

"You should have let me die," *she sobs, pressing her face into Kaleb's chest.* "Why didn't you let me die?"

I join Kaleb where he kneels on the ground, Rayna standing a few feet away with her mouth turned down. She has never been one for sympathy.

I lift the girl's injured arm onto my lap and she winces. The skin is blistered and bleeding; I have no doubt that it will heal, but the damage is great enough that it is sure to leave a nasty scar.

"Because," Kaleb says quietly, smoothing her dark hair with a soothing hand, "your daughter would not have wanted you to die. And there are many things yet for you to live for."

The girl leans back from Kaleb to look up at him, her expression fading from one of rage to misery. She pauses for a long moment then nods once, cold determination hardening her gaze.

I pull the burned pieces of fabric from her arm and she cries out, her fangs flashing brightly through a grimace.

"It hurts," she whimpers, flinching at my touch.

"I know, darling," Kaleb says, brushing tears and soot from her cheek with his thumb. "But it won't last forever. We are the masters of our pain. It holds only the power we give it." There is a bite of sadness in his words, a shadow of memory clouding his eyes. "What is your name, child?"

"Philippa," she replies through gritted teeth, and for a moment the smoke clears, moonlight illuminating the royal blue of her eyes. "Philippa Rees."

Pippa screams again.

I try to ignore the blood on the front steps, undoubtedly from tonight's victim. The body is gone now, probably taken downstairs until we can figure out what to do with it. Victoria is already scrubbing the stone with a hard-bristled brush and bleach so strong that it stings my nose, but she abandons her chore and leaps to her feet the moment she sees Pippa shaking in Henry's arms.

"Kaleb!" Henry bellows.

Kaleb and a disgruntled Nik stand stoically in the foyer, facing away from one another. They both jump as Henry practically kicks the door down.

Nik's eyes widen in alarm. "Pippa?"

"What happened?" Kaleb demands.

"We were ambushed," Henry says breathlessly, "on the Pier. We never even made it to the island. Or on a boat, for that matter." Pippa whimpers and he looks down at her worriedly, all evidence of his usual brightness gone. "There were two vampires. I thought we had it handled, but one of them must have nicked a stake from Pippa. It all happened so fast. One moment I was tearing a girl's head off, and the next, Pippa was screaming. I thought she was dead. I pulled the stake out of her chest, but..." He falters, his gaze dropping to the ground. "She needs help."

I catch a glimpse of suspicion in Kaleb's gaze, but he hides it quickly.

"Henry, lay Philippa on the dining table," he instructs, his tone commanding. There is a focused competence in his voice that demands our attention, and for the first time, I truly see the Alpha in him. "Charlotte, I need a pair of scissors and a small knife. Preferably one that isn't silver." He shrugs off his coat and throws it on the floor by the door, the bloody gash on his chest glaring wickedly through the hole in Xander's t-shirt. "The rest of you, outside." When no one moves, he barks, *"Now!"*

There is a flurry of movement. Henry disappears into the dining room while everyone else hurries for the door. Xander lingers, unsure, but Nik snaps to attention, grabbing my brother by the arm and dragging him outside with the others. The door closes quietly behind them, and I frown at Nik's wordless obedience before darting into the kitchen.

I locate a pair of scissors and dig through the drawers for a few hectic minutes until I find a paring knife. I'm not even sure why we *have* a paring knife.

I run into the dining room and find Kaleb standing over Pippa where she lies, writhing, on the dining room table. The bitter scent of her blood is overwhelming, punctuated by something sweet and almost familiar. A memory tugs at my mind, but it slips away as Pippa screams again.

"Shh, darling," Kaleb whispers, brushing the wisps of bloodied hair from her forehead.

"Kaleb, *please*," she gasps, clawing at his arm. *"Help me."*

Pippa was always the closest to Kaleb—she loved him unconditionally, trusted his word above all else. I used to think that trust died with Rayna, but the way she clings to him now, her lips crying his name, is reason for doubt.

Kaleb ushers me over and he takes the knife, leaving me with the scissors. "I need you to cut her shirt off," he says.

I blink in surprise. "You need me to do *what?*"

"Did I stutter, Charlotte? Cut her shirt off. Right up the middle."

"Okay," I murmur, and take the scissors to Pippa's heather-gray t-shirt, now drenched with fresh blood. I carefully peel the fabric back over her black lace bra, exposing the pale, red-stained skin of her torso. There is a quarter-sized hole just above her left breast, its edges festering and feeding purplish, swollen veins that crawl menacingly toward her neck and down her stomach.

I suck in a breath.

I *knew* there was something wrong with the boy at the Labyrinth. That wound wasn't an ordinary one. And Pippa's looks no different.

"What is that?" I whisper.

Kaleb's eyes narrow and he rubs absently at his thigh. "If I had to venture a guess," he mutters, "I would say that a piece of the stake Philippa was stabbed with is still in her chest. It is causing her a lot of pain, which means...it may have grazed her heart." He enunciates each word in his last sentence slowly, as though choosing his words with extra care.

I know he is holding something back, but I don't have the time or brainpower to think about it. Pippa gasps loudly and clutches at her chest, sending a bolt of terror through me. I do my best to hide it but, based on the knowing look Kaleb gives me, I don't think I'm doing a very good job.

"Awesome," Pippa groans, her fevered, sapphire eyes flicking open. "That is...just...*marvelous.*" Her gaze is wild and unfocused, but she calms when she sees Kaleb leaning over her.

"Don't speak, Philippa," Kaleb chides. "You'll only make it worse."

Pippa nods, then winces. Kaleb presses two careful fingers near the wound, and his brows furrow as Pippa inhales sharply.

"I'll have to cut it out, darling," he says stiffly. "Your skin is already starting to heal, and we can't let the wood fester any longer." Unsaid words hover over him, as though he doesn't want to explain what will happen if it does. "It's going to hurt like hell."

"Okay," Pippa whispers, closing her eyes and taking a deep, shuddering breath.

"Charlotte," Kaleb says, his voice sincere, "I need you to steady her. If she moves too much, I won't be able to help her." I hesitate, and he frowns. "Now, please."

My heart pounds an uneven rhythm in my chest as I hesitantly reach over Pippa, bracing her arms against her sides. She doesn't resist—an unusual response for her—but simply whimpers, her hands clenching and unclenching sporadically.

"It's going to be alright, Pippa," I murmur, squeezing her wrists gently. "Kaleb is going to fix you up in no time."

Kaleb positions himself over her and, with a last, nervous glance at me, presses the knife into the wound in Pippa's chest.

A groan starts low in Pippa's throat, rising quickly to a sharp cry. Kaleb's jaw twitches, but he continues his work, Pippa growing more agitated with each passing second.

"It hurts," she whimpers, a touch of her Welsh accent surfacing, and flinches at his touch.

"I know, darling," Kaleb whispers. "I'm so sorry."

Pippa breaks into sobs, gasping with each movement of Kaleb's fingers. "*Lottie,*" she cries, her arms tensing under my grip.

"I'm here, baby girl," I answer, fighting to keep her still. Hot tears fill my eyes and slide down my cheeks. "I'm right here."

Without warning, Pippa's back arches off the table and a howl tears from her throat. Kaleb freezes, his eyes widening in panic as his fingers slip on the knife's handle.

"*Charlotte,*" he pleads, desperation written plainly on his face.

He doesn't need to ask twice. I leap onto the table and straddle Pippa, my knees digging into her arms while the heels of my hands press hard into her ribs, pinning her down.

"Hold still," I urge. "We're almost done."

Kaleb's hands work quickly as he makes a few more careful twists with the blade. He reaches two fingers into the wound then jerks his hand upward, producing a large splinter of wood broken from one of Henry's stakes, and fresh blood pulses from Pippa's chest. Kaleb exhales sharply and takes a relieved step backward, his arms sagging at his sides. He drops the knife and the wood shard to the floor where they clatter loudly in the new silence.

I release a shaking breath as Pippa goes slack beneath me, the tension draining from her all at once.

"*Diolch,*" Pippa says quietly, tears falling freely from her closed eyes, "*diolch,* Kaleb. *Diolch, diolch, diolch.*"

Pippa reaches for him and Kaleb pulls her hand to his lips, sinking into one of the chairs near the table. His expression is unreadable as he brushes fresh tears from her cheeks with bloodied, trembling fingers.

41

IT TAKES A FEW HOURS for Pippa to relax into sleep. Once she had calmed down, Kaleb carried her to my shadowed bathroom, leaving me to wash away the blood and help her into fresh clothes. She complained the whole time, insisting she take care of herself—typical Pippa—but I could sense her exhaustion. She fell asleep the moment she hit my pillow.

I wish I could say she is resting peacefully, but her dark brows are furrowed, her breath shallow. Every few minutes she tenses then relaxes again, clutching the blankets tightly against her chest like a child having a nightmare.

I am curled next to her on the bed, softly stroking her hair and wiping tears from her restless eyes. The dark veins on her neck have maintained their ripe-plum color, webbing up her left side to the base of her ear. I think of the vampire I killed at the Labyrinth—the black veins that covered his face in death, the way his skin hung, blood-filled, from his bones—and my stomach heaves upward.

That could have been Pippa.

And it would have been for nothing.

Konstantin was one step ahead of us tonight. Somehow he knew about our stakeout, and he was ready. What I don't understand is why he only sent two vamps to each of the locations—the fights were two-on-two, evenly matched. If he had wanted us dead, he could have sent three to each place, or four, or ten. We may have experience, but even Nik can't hold off more than a few attackers at a time.

Whatever Konstantin is planning, he intends to draw it out, to manipulate his pawns, to watch us dance like puppets on a string. He doesn't want us dead. He doesn't want *Kaleb* dead.

I think he wants Kaleb to suffer.

Jake's words resonate again in my head: *Konstantin is king. Konstantin will not stop until he recovers what was taken, and only Kaleb can return it.*

Whatever Kaleb took, it must have been valuable.

I wish Rayna were here. I would give anything to hear her voice, even if she were only telling me to, "Have a drink, Lottie! There's nothing that a bottle of whiskey can't fix." In reality, there was nothing *Rayna* couldn't fix. She was fierce and unyielding and sharp as a fox. Nothing escaped her notice. If there was a fight, Rayna ended it. Nothing mattered more to her than making sure we were all happy, together, and alive.

And look where that got her.

I squeeze Pippa's hand and kiss her knuckles, relieved to feel the pulse beating sluggishly in her palm. Relieved that this war has avoided another casualty.

"Kaleb?" Pippa murmurs behind closed eyes.

"No, Pippa," I say. "It's me. I'm right here."

"Rayna," she breathes, curling against me. *"Rwy'n colli chi."*
I miss you.

A sudden tightness in my throat prevents me from replying. Instead, I hug Pippa's scarred arm to my chest and press my forehead against hers. For a few long minutes, we lie huddled in the cool darkness in my bedroom as Pippa's fevered breathing slows to a comfortable rhythm.

"I miss you too, baby girl," I whisper, imagining, just for a moment, that the words actually belonged to Rayna.

◇   ◇   ◇

I'm not sure how long I've been asleep when I hear footsteps in the hallway. Pippa has managed to swaddle our arms in two layers of sheets, and it takes me a few seconds to disentangle myself before I cross to the door and press my ear against it. The footsteps—two or three sets if I'm hearing right—disappear into Xander's studio.

I glance back at Pippa, who has pulled the blankets over her face, then open the door and tiptoe down the hallway to peek around the studio's door frame.

Xander, Kaleb, and Henry are clustered in the far corner of the studio, as far away as they can get without actually being outside. An uncomfortable tension crackles between them. The moonlight filtering through the windows casts a pale glow over the boys, illuminating them in splashes of silver. With the varying amounts of blood on their clothes and skin, the light makes them look like a trio of attractive ghosts who all died particularly gruesome deaths.

Henry is closest to the window, his hair glowing a dull gray, and cowers under the icy glares of both Kaleb and Xander. They stand shoulder to shoulder, their arms crossed over their chests, creating a formidable wall of indignation.

"What aren't you telling us, Henry?" Kaleb growls, his voice deep and cutting. I flinch at his ferocity.

Henry stands tall, but the shame in his eyes reminds me of a scolded puppy with his tail between his legs. His shoulders sag under his bloodied waistcoat. "I don't—" he starts, then seems to think better of it. "Nothing. There's nothing."

"Don't bloody *lie* to me," Kaleb snarls, his posture rigid. "We both know Philippa's wound wasn't an ordinary one. *Tell me what you did.*"

A beat of silence stretches between them, and I'm struck by the confidence emanating from Xander, the familiarity that Kaleb seems to share with him. With each shift of Kaleb's feet, each tilt of his head, Xander mirrors it, an inky echo at Kaleb's side. They are an intimidating pair, to say the least. If I didn't know better, I'd say they had been together in similar situations before.

Henry's eyes flicker from Kaleb to Xander, and he swallows hard. "I—I dipped the stakes in hawthorn," he confesses.

Xander's breath hisses between his teeth and he leans forward, fangs glinting. "Come again?"

"*Dammit,* Henry." Kaleb's voice drips with acid.

Dammit is right.

It was one of the first lessons Kaleb taught us when he took us in: what we needed to avoid if we wanted to stay alive. He showed us how it felt to be touched by silver, the way holy water corroded a vampire's skin from bone. One afternoon, he offered me a tiny vial of thin, red liquid.

"Inhale, but do not touch," he said.

I obediently sampled the scent. It was sickly-sweet, burning through my nose with unexpected fire. I cried out, and Kaleb caught the vial as it slipped from my fingers.

"What is that?" I coughed, rubbing my nose with my forearm.

"Hawthorn," he said. "A wild berry that, for whatever reason, acts as a poison to vampires. A touch will not kill you, though I would advise against it. But when it comes in contact with the bloodstream, it can be deadly."

"How on earth would berries get in my bloodstream?"

Kaleb shrugged, his free hand brushing his thigh absently. "You could eat them."

"And why would I do that?"

"That" —Kaleb plugged the vial with a tiny cork, then slipped it into his pocket— "is beside the point. If you are lucky, you will never know the berry's sting. Just keep an eye on where you're walking. We can't have you stumbling into a hawthorn bush by accident."

Xander's voice jolts me back to the present. "Care to explain yourself?"

Henry's jaw twitches. "I thought that—that it would be helpful," he stammers, shrinking under twin gazes of ice and slate. "I figured that if we missed Konstantin's heart, we could at least slow him down—"

"That does nothing for us if we kill our own in the process!" Kaleb snaps. "The stake may have missed Philippa's heart, but the hawthorn almost killed her. There is still a chance that she may not survive this. And if she doesn't, you will have me to deal with."

On the one hand, I understand Henry's motives: a wooden stake anywhere but the heart is hardly a death sentence. With the added kick of a vampire-specific poison, it would be near debilitating.

On the other hand, it would have been nice to know that I was carrying two poisoned shivs on my hips all evening.

For Henry's sake, I hope Pippa is understanding. But I doubt it.

Henry frowns, furious confusion darkening his eyes. "Why do you care?" he sneers. "You haven't spoken to this sorry lot for decades and now here you are, practically groveling at their feet. As if they would ever take you back—"

But Henry doesn't finish his thought, because Kaleb rears back and punches him square on the mouth. I stifle a gasp, and even Xander looks surprised. It's not like Kaleb to resort to violence.

Henry staggers sideways, then fixes an appalled gaze on Kaleb, blood welling on his lip.

"If you *ever* keep something like that from me again," Kaleb snarls, jabbing a finger at Henry, "I will have your pretty little head on a spike. Understood?"

Henry nods stiffly, and I see my chance.

"You better hope Pippa lets you off so easily." Three heads swivel in my direction as I stalk into the studio, fuming.

"Charlotte," Kaleb says coolly, attempting to soften the fury grating in his voice. "We were unaware we had an audience."

"That's kind of the point of eavesdropping, Kaleb." I invite myself into their huddle, mirroring Kaleb and Xander's condescending stances, though the effect may be minimized by the fact that I'm shorter than everyone here. "Xander threw a stake to me tonight, Henry. One of *your* stakes. I killed one of Konstantin's pets with it, then watched his skin fill with blood as he died a slow and—from the looks of it—very painful death. What if I had missed the stake Xander threw? What if it hit me? I could be *dead.*"

Dull horror dawns in Xander's eyes. He shifts closer to me and presses his shoulder against mine.

Henry's eyes are luminous as he fights to maintain composure, the cut on his lip from Kaleb's fist dripping blood down his chin. He licks it away. "Charlotte—"

"Don't even try," I snap. It was only a few days ago that I watched Henry sever someone's neck in my basement. I was wary of him then, but not anymore. Now, I'm furious. "My best friend almost died because of you, you selfish, baby-faced bastard."

Henry regards me with shameful eyes. "I'm sorry—"

"I don't have the power to forgive you, Henry. You'll have to take that up with Pippa."

A charged silence follows, during which Henry awkwardly straightens his waistcoat. Xander and Kaleb remain motionless, offering no comment.

"I do have a question, while we're all here," I muse, abruptly switching gears. "Kaleb, for the love of all that is holy—or demonic, or whatever—would you *please* tell us what is so valuable that it warrants this type of psychological torture?"

Kaleb frowns, and there it is again: the sense of something strange about him, still present despite the absence of the sunlight on his skin. He is still in Xander's black clothes—which is unusual, at most—but the wrongness has nothing to do with his clothing. It feels almost like something is missing.

"What do you mean?" he asks.

"I mean *this.*" I gesture vaguely with my arms open wide. "The stalking, the stabbing, the cryptic notes, the ambushes." I remember the text messages on Tristan's phone and shudder. "Two of Konstantin's people have now said that you took something from him, and that you're the only one who can give it back."

Kaleb stills. Always thinking, always careful; never betraying anything that might give him away.

"Konstantin has always been a fan of torture," he starts, sharing a long look with Xander. "He has been perfecting his processes for centuries, starting back when we met Nikolas and Rayna. He will manipulate us as long as it takes for him to get what he wants. Nothing would bring him more pleasure." Kaleb's jaw tenses slightly at the last word, sending a shiver up my back. "However, I suspect he is waiting for something. And when that happens, he will reveal his hand."

"That's very poetic and all," I drawl, "but you didn't answer my question."

Kaleb inhales deeply, meeting Xander's gaze once more before responding. "I didn't *take* anything from Konstantin," he says, but his hand lifts, pausing in midair above his sternum before he raises it to his lips, frowning. Something about the motion stirs a thought in my mind, but it slips away as soon as I try to grasp it.

"Sure, you didn't."

"Believe me, Charlotte. I took nothing of his."

There is sincerity in his expression, a crack in that perfect, pretty-boy facade. My lips pucker. If Kaleb is holding something back, we should know about it. Maybe if I ask again, if I lean on him a little harder, that crack will break open.

"But," Kaleb says before I have a chance to dig deeper, "I may have an idea as to why he is behaving this way. It has been brought to my attention that Konstantin may have learned certain...*details*... about the circumstances surrounding Rayna's death."

"Her death?" I ask sharply. "You mean the details surrounding her *murder?* The murder *you* committed? I don't care if it was Rayna's—"

I cut off as Kaleb recoils slightly, his expression guarded. Xander and Henry eye me warily.

It wasn't his fault, it wasn't his fault, it wasn't his fault.

That's going to take a while to sink in.

"Well, whatever he found out," I snarl, "it almost killed Pippa." Henry winces. "I will not stand by while another one of our family dies at your hands. So, I suggest that you and Konstantin grow up and solve this like men, or you figure out how to catch him so I can rip his heart out myself."

I stomp out of the studio, leaving Kaleb, Xander, and Henry watching after me in shocked silence.

It isn't until I am halfway down the hallway that I realize what was off about Kaleb.

The emerald pendant at his throat—the one that hasn't left his neck since the moment I met him—was missing.

42

AFTER CHECKING ON PIPPA—SHE is now face down, her hair fanning around her like sun rays—I wander into the living room where Nik, Rose, and Victoria are whispering in a seated circle.

Nik jumps to his feet when I round the corner. "How is she?"

"Pippa? She's okay," I reply, combing my fingers through my tangled hair. The three of them relax visibly and Nik releases a shaky breath. "Sleeping, mostly. From what I can tell, she was really lucky."

"Good," Nik breathes, returning to his seat on the sofa. "That's good."

"What happened, Lottie?" Rose asks, rotating in her chair. "Kaleb refused to tell us anything, and we've been imagining scenarios for the last hour."

Victoria grins. "Our most recent theory involves Pippa operating on herself while you attempted to murder Kaleb in the corner."

"Wouldn't that be something?" Nik's eyes roll in a full circle. "Konstantin resurfaces after all these years, only to have Lottie kill Kaleb in the dining room before he can exact his revenge."

"I forget that you knew him," Rose says. "It's strange to know someone who used to be friends with one of the oldest vampires on the planet. It's like you were friends with a myth."

Discomfort and old fear war in Nik's eyes. "Not one of the oldest. *The* oldest. And as far as we know, the first. And we weren't *friends*," he scoffs, leaning into me as I sit down next to him. "We were barely enemies."

He falls silent, his expression haunted. When Victoria opens her mouth to ask what is sure to be a probing question, I decide it's best that we nip this conversation in the bud before it gets out of hand.

"Well," I say before she can get a word in, "you'll be happy to know that there were no murders attempted in that dining room." They sober as I recount my few minutes with Pippa and Kaleb, from her blood-soaked shirt to Kaleb's focused hands to the dark veins splaying over Pippa's chest. I leave out a few unnecessary details, including the way Kaleb brushed tears from her cheeks and the new information I learned about Henry and his little hawthorn experiment. Somehow, I don't think either will be well-received.

When I finish, the group remains quiet for a few minutes. Victoria and Rose seem intrigued, while Nik fixes his gaze on the ground. I can see the wheels turning in his head.

"That's two lives Kaleb has saved tonight," Rose whispers, a stray ringlet escaping from her bun. She smooths it back into place with a pensive expression.

"Two?" Pippa appears from around the corner, one hand clutching her chest. Her skin is paler than usual as she shuffles toward us, but there is a faint flush to her cheeks and her cobalt eyes are bright. The purple veins at her neck stand out conspicuously under my white t-shirt. "Did that bastard dig a knife into one of your chests, too? Damn. I thought I was special."

"Pippa," Nik scolds, though relief softens his shoulders. "You should be resting."

"Rest, shmest," she mumbles, brushing his comment away with a flick of her hand. "I don't plan on missing any of this riveting conversation." Pippa sits carefully next to me, her knees turned to rest on my lap. She winces faintly. "I assume you've already figured out how Konstantin knew our plan."

Nik frowns and reaches behind me to stroke Pippa's hair. "Pippa, really—"

"I'm *fine*, Nikolas," she interrupts. "If anyone here decides I need pity, I will burn all your clothes and you'll have to live the rest of your life as an undead nudist. Got it?"

The four of us eye each other before nodding reluctantly.

"Great," Pippa says. "Now, tell me what's going on." I open my mouth to respond, but she cuts me off. "Let me rephrase: I want to know what's going on as it pertains to anything but *this*." She gestures stiffly at herself.

I grimace. "You're impossible, you know that?"

"Why, thank you, Lottie."

"To answer your question," Rose interjects—she never seems to lose focus— "we have no idea how Konstantin knew our plan. Xander has been arguing with Kaleb and Henry about it for the last two hours. Their conversation didn't seem to be getting anywhere."

Victoria shrugs. "All we know is that there were two vamps ready to ambush us at each of our locations. Henry managed to kill one, as did Nik, but the others took off before we were able to learn anything useful."

"Hey, I offed one, too," I boast, and they all look at me in surprise. "I did *try* to get some information out of him, but he wasn't very talkative. Then he spat in my face and I thought, 'You know, this guy could really use a stake to the heart.' So, I gave him one."

Nik chokes on a laugh but I can only frown. We were supposed to *win* tonight. It was supposed to be the night that changed everything, but now we're left with more questions than we started with. The whole evening was just an absolute, bloody disaster.

"Once he was dead, the second one just...ran away. Then—" I break off. I had almost forgotten. "Then I had to explain the situation to a very distraught Tristan."

Four pairs of eyebrows shoot toward the ceiling.

"*Tristan* was there?" Pippa exclaims, hitting me on the leg. "Why didn't you lead with that?"

Needless to say, Pippa seems to be feeling better.

Victoria leans forward eagerly. "What was he doing there?"

I think back to my conversation with Tristan in the backseat of the Maserati—was it really only a few hours ago?—and my heart stutters uncomfortably. I did learn one thing about Konstantin tonight: there is nothing he won't do to get what he wants.

"Never mind why he was there," I reply, and am met by a chorus of annoyed sighs. "What matters is that he *was*. We weren't able to get him out before the ambush, so he kind of saw everything."

"*Everything,* everything?" Nik asks.

"Yep," I say with a resigned shrug. "The stabbing, the blood, the fangs...it wasn't pretty. And Tristan was not amused."

"You never know," Pippa shrugs. "Maybe he thought it was hot."

If Tristan thought anything was hot, it definitely wasn't the way I tore the skin from a boy's throat with my teeth, or the way I murdered him in cold blood.

But it might have been the way I threw myself on top of Tristan's lap, or the way my mouth explored his, or the drag of my tongue across his collarbone. Or the kiss I pressed to that scar near his belt...

I swallow the heat sliding up my throat.

Nik has been watching us with contemplative eyes, and they spark now with a touch of languorous mischief. "I'm sure Tristan's fine. It's nothing a little partying won't fix."

"Partying?" I ask. "What—" Then I remember the party I planned with Tristan. The one that is supposed to happen here in less than twenty-four hours. "Oh, the *party*. I totally forgot about—wait. How do you know about the party?"

"We all know about it, Lottie," Rose says easily. "Bree texted me, and Nik" —Nik glares at her sharply— "heard it from me. The humans are all pretty excited about it."

"Well, we obviously have to cancel it," I groan. "Konstantin is closer than ever, we just found a dead body on our porch, and Pippa—"

"Is *absolutely fine* and a very strong advocate for making this party happen," Pippa finishes. "All in favor?

Everyone raises their hands, including Nik, a smile pulling at his lips.

"Okay, fine," I concede. "But I'm not going to be the one to tell Xander."

"Oh, Alexander already knows," Victoria says with a sly smirk. "It took a bit of convincing, but I finally wore him down." I'm relieved when she doesn't elaborate on what exactly she did to convince him. "And it's a good thing, too. I happen to have the perfect dress for such an occasion."

"Dress?" I ask warily, realizing that this may have grown into something bigger than I had anticipated.

"Pippa?" Henry appears in the doorway. "May I speak to you in private for a moment?" He holds his chest high but his eyes betray his apprehension. Pippa's dried blood is dark on his forearms.

Pippa winks and rises carefully from the sofa. Henry glances at me and I fix him with my best death glare, forcing his gaze to the floor. The two of them disappear into the kitchen.

"I have a feeling," Rose grumbles, "that if those two start spending time together, they're going to spell trouble for the rest of us."

"Hey, as long as they don't make a mess," Victoria says.

"Or sneak into my house to 'borrow' my shower." Nik shrugs at our astonished expressions. "Pippa's done it before."

I strain my ears into the silence, trying to hear Henry and Pippa's conversation, but their voices are barely audible over the soft hum of the incandescent lights, the crackling of the fireplace.

There's a loud *slap* from the kitchen, after which Henry sprints through the foyer, a hand pressed to his cheek. He flies out the door without so much as a second glance. We stare after him, wide-eyed, until Pippa returns to our huddle.

The hollows under her eyes are dark and her fangs flash as she speaks. "Now that I've taken out the trash," she states, brushing her palms together, "let's plan a party."

◊　◊　◊

I'm in the loft sipping blood from a wine glass when the house begins to lighten with the first rays of dawn, bathing the bookshelves in cool morning light. Everyone left hours ago—including Pippa—to sleep and shower and do whatever it is they want to do before the party tonight.

Except for Kaleb and Henry. They're on Konstantin duty.

I watch as sunlight slowly creeps through the room, spilling molten gold on the rugs, the lounge chairs, the books, highlighting dust motes as they dance through the air.

It was a shock to see Kaleb yesterday, sleeping in a sunbeam like a lazy housecat, his hair and skin glowing with warmth. If he has ever shown such obvious tolerance before, I've never noticed. We spent so much time in the shadows. I cherish those memories of Belarus—before we were Turned—when Xander knelt in the garden, pulling carrots from the ground with gloved hands as the sun beat down on his neck. The light glinted in his eyes then, shimmering in the sweat at his brow.

The sun fully emerges over the horizon outside, turning the loft radiant. I yearn for it, even when bright daggers of light reflect off the glass coffee table and into my eyes.

I'm getting tired of the dark and the cold.

I may not *feel* cold anymore, but since last night, everything has a chilly edge, like my thoughts are carved from ice. It's the kind of cold you can feel down to your bones, that no number of blankets or hot showers can fix. The agonized look on the vampire boy's face as he died, made more horrible by the knowledge of the poison in Henry's stake; the terrified tremor of Tristan's voice; Kaleb's hands, slick with blood, as he fought to save Pippa's life...it's enough to freeze anyone's heart.

In what can only be described as pure insanity, I shove one arm into a patch of sunlight. The warmth immediately shoots needles through my skin but I fight the urge to retreat, focusing on the pain, letting it burn away all the ache and fear I've felt for the last week. I watch as the minutes tick by, my skin cracking and splitting over my wrist as the sun bakes it. Blood sizzles from cuts opening at my knuckles and I grit my teeth against the sting. And, for a few glorious moments, I forget.

We are the masters of our pain. It holds only the power we give it.

"Lottie." Xander appears from around the corner, his eyes widening when he sees my arm. He hasn't changed out of his bloody clothes— granted, I haven't either—and his hair is sticking up wildly like he just woke up from a restless nap. "What the hell are you doing?"

I yank my hand out of the sun and the flames in my skin are doused in cool shadows. I can't help my sigh of relief.

"Nothing important," I mumble, not meeting his eyes.

Xander purses his lips. "Come here. I want to talk to you."

I set my glass down on the coffee table and reluctantly follow him, rubbing my arm as the skin starts to knit back together. Blood drips down my fingers and I wipe them on my shirt; it's ruined anyway.

Xander's bedroom is a minimalist's paradise: a huge bed with a wooden headboard, simple nightstands, a single oak dresser, and a black, leather lounge chair. One wall is painted with the New York

City skyline, and the one window is lined with an impressive collection of potted plants. A huge fiddle leaf fig stands like a sentinel in one corner.

Xander sits on the edge of the bed and pats the comforter. I sink down next to him with a huff.

"What do you want, Alexander?" I growl. "I'm not in the mood for one of your lectures."

"I want to talk to you about what happened with Tristan."

"You see?" I groan, flopping onto my back. "That's exactly the sort of thing you would lecture me about. And, as I just mentioned, I'm not in the mood."

"It's not what you think." Xander shifts so he's lying next to me, propping himself up on one elbow. "I know you're going to hate what I'm about to say, but..." He fidgets uncomfortably and anxiety shivers through me. Xander *never* fidgets. "I'm worried that Tristan's affections are not exactly...genuine."

"Excuse me?" I ask, taken aback by the blunt statement. It's not at all what I was expecting. I picture Tristan's radiant smile when he met me on Embarcadero, Tristan standing on the front porch with coffee in hand, Tristan asking me to dance at Pier 39. His arms pulling me away from the ocean, his warm, calloused hands exploring my ribcage, his full lips on mine...I inhale deeply. "Why would you say that?"

"When Tristan saw you for what you truly are," Xander says carefully, "he remembered meeting you at Kaleb's party, which means you were distracted when you Compelled him. Am I right in assuming that much?"

Kaleb's party feels like it was decades ago. I think back to those first few moments outside the theater with Tristan, the marquis flickering above us. He had just run outside after seeing me attack Jason, leaving him in a bleeding heap on the floor. I chased after him, angry and afraid and more than a little intoxicated, and I remember the creeping feeling of eyes on the back of my neck, like someone was watching me.

I thought then that it was Kaleb. I wonder now if it was someone else.

Compulsion is supposed to be controlled and focused. But with those seething shadows and the threat of Kaleb on my conscience, my attempt that night was mediocre at best.

I nod reluctantly and Xander continues, his expression stony.

"Let me tell you a story," he begins. "When we lived in Prague, I lost control one evening in front of a human girl. Her name was Ivanka. I was newly-Turned—barely eight years at the time—and I panicked. My Compulsion was sloppy and rushed and desperate. Ivanka left, and that was that. Or so I thought.

"About a week later, I ran into her while hunting. She immediately became attached to me. I tried to discourage her, but she was annoyingly persistent. It's not that I didn't like her; in fact, she was kind and beautiful, almost painfully so. I started to look forward to our meetings, but I kept them a secret because I wasn't sure how Kaleb would react.

"One night, Ivanka followed me home. Nik and I were wrestling—you know how we were—and she saw us, fangs and all. I tried to explain myself but she wouldn't hear it. Then she brought up the incident I had Compelled from her mind weeks earlier. I was stunned. Until then, I didn't know humans had the potential to recall erased memories. It felt like the rug had been pulled out from under me.

"That's when I finally told Kaleb. As you can imagine, he wasn't happy. He explained that sometimes, when Compulsion is done poorly, a human can develop an obsession with the vampire who Compelled them and will do anything asked of them, similar to the vampiric Sire bond. It can often be mistaken for loyalty or—or romantic interest." He swallows. "But if, or when, the original memory is replicated in any way, the poor Compulsion can come undone, restoring that memory and its accompanying emotions. Kaleb Compelled Ivanka to forget me—correctly, this time—and I never saw her again."

Xander's words hover between us and my chest twists into a knot. If we switched out the names, his story would be almost identical to what happened between me and Tristan. He saw me bite Jason's neck on Halloween. The Compulsion must have shattered when he watched me tear out that fledgling's throat. I shake my head slowly, frowning down at the comforter.

Tristan asked me out for coffee the first time he saw me. *Me.* Of all the girls he could have noticed that day, he chose me. The day after I met him in a dark, hot theater filled with alcoholic angels and demons and centurions and vampires.

He invited me to hang out with his friends. He took me to the Land's End Labyrinth, a place that obviously holds special significance for him.

And he listened to me, even when he shouldn't have. He calmed down the other day when he saw Ty covered in blood. His heart rate slowed in the backseat of Xander's car when I told it to stop. He *trusted me.*

I spent the week running from him, but he welcomed me back again and again.

Stupid, stupid Charlotte.

How many times are you going to run away from that boy until he straight-up ditches you?

Apparently, as many times as I want, because he will always forgive me. At least, he has until this point.

Now that the Compulsion is broken, I may have reached my limit.

"Son of a *bitch,*" I moan, and my sun-soaked memories of Tristan fracture like a cracked mirror.

Xander's lips curl downward. "It's not your fault—"

"Stop. We both know that it is absolutely my fault." My brother's frown deepens, but he doesn't object. "I should never have gone to that *stupid* Halloween party. Then I would have never met Tristan and this whole thing wouldn't even be an issue." Frantic anger boils in my chest and I press the heels of my hands into my eyes. "I never would have hurt Jason. Kaleb wouldn't have shown up at our house, and he wouldn't have dragged us into this *feud* with Konstantin. Pippa almost *died* because of me!"

"Charlotte." I peek at Xander from under my palms. One of his hands lifts from the comforter toward me, but he lets it fall. "Calm down. This is not your fault, regardless of what you think. We've been part of this thing with Konstantin since the moment Kaleb found us in Belarus. Since the moment we became his family." He pauses and lifts his hand again, this time smoothing a strand of hair from my forehead. I swat his hand away. "We're not fighting Konstantin because you flipped Kaleb off at a party. We're fighting him because he's dangerous. We won't be safe until he's gone."

"How did you know I flipped him off?"

Xander raises an eyebrow. "Because you're *you*, Charlotte."

A cool numbness dampens the heat licking through me and I'm almost grateful. If I feel much more this week, I might shatter into a pile of debris labeled: *Here lies Charlotte, an emotional disaster.*

"Well," I say, staring up at the ceiling, "if Tristan doesn't work out, there's always Ty."

Xander watches me. Waiting.

"He texts me constantly. Very annoying. Won't leave me alone." After a beat, I add, "And I kind of made out with him in the walk-in the other night."

Xander's self-control is astounding. He says nothing, an impressive display of conflicted emotions flickering through his eyes like an old film reel.

Finally, he says, "Oh."

"Yeah. That pretty much sums up how I feel about it."

We sit for a few moments in silence, exasperation radiating from Xander in waves. At one time, he may have made fun of me for kissing two boys in one week, or maybe even congratulated me. But that was Xander *before*. Now he simply frowns disapprovingly and I avoid his eyes, still staring at the unremarkable plaster ceiling.

"I'm going to take a shower," Xander finally says, rising from the bed. "I've been covered in blood for far too long today, and I promised I would look presentable for our little soirée tonight."

"Sorry about that," I say, sitting up. "I wanted to cancel, but it kind of got away from me. It wasn't supposed to be a big thing—"

"I may not be a party person," Xander interrupts, "but I'll survive. We could all use a night off." He pauses, then flashes a rare, straight-toothed grin. "Besides, Victoria can be extremely persuasive." With a wink, he vanishes into the bathroom.

"Have I told you today that your love is beautiful and disgusting?" I call after him, but the shower is already running.

My phone buzzes and I open it to a text from Ty. I groan.

Is there a vampire speed record?

> That's a stupid question. How would we even test that?

Police radar? Foot race? I bet I could beat you.

> In your dreams, lover boy. I'm older than you, and therefore faster. And generally better at anything and everything vampire-related.

I'll take that bet. Want to test it? Tonight, maybe?

> Can't tonight, even if I wanted to.

An idea creeps its way into my mind and I try to squash it like the invasive worm that it is, but I fail. Miserably.

I'm going to invite this idiot to the party.

Ty and Xander might not be on good terms, but Ty is harmless— nothing more than an obnoxious college kid biting off more than he can chew. And if Tristan doesn't show, then at least I'll have someone to dance with.

> We're hosting a party, actually. You should come. Our place, 7 PM. The dress code is somewhere between I-have-a-date and I-have-a-date-to-the-Oscars.

> I'll be there ;)

Maybe tonight won't be completely terrible after all.

It will be even better if Tristan is there, though that seems about as likely as Pippa announcing a newfound life of celibacy. The absolute terror in his eyes last night is enough to convince me that he may never want to see me again.

But I still find myself hoping he will come, even if it is just to say goodbye.

I type out a quick message and hit send before I can talk myself out of it.

> Hey, Tristan. Just so you know, the party is still on tonight. We're using the ballroom and everything.

After a few seconds, I send one more.

> I promise I won't bite.

43

My hair is a disaster.

It's usually helpless at best—especially after a few hours of dead-to-the-world sleep—but tonight I actually care.

Leave it to Rose and Victoria to turn a casual hangout into a vampire prom.

Rose has already been here for an hour, decorating and moving furniture and baking cupcakes in our neglected kitchen. I think this might be the first time anyone has used our overpriced oven, and the alluring smell of sugar and chocolate fills the house. It's almost enough to make my mouth water.

In what I'm sure will be another fruitless attempt at a passable style, I run a brush through my hair and start pinning strands back into a chignon. Or at least what I hope will resemble one. Rayna used to do them for me back in London, her thief's fingers expertly weaving the strands into a tasteful knot. I was never very good at doing my hair. Even now, when I can actually use mirrors to see what's going on back there, it just looks like a family of birds has tried and failed to build a nest on my head.

Frustrated, I rip the pins out of my hair. I guess I'll be leaving it down. Again.

It's not like I have anyone to impress. I still haven't heard back from Tristan, and I'm starting to doubt that I ever will again. The thought is accompanied by a strong pang of disappointment. I can't believe I was stupid enough to think that Tristan actually liked me.

Though, in my defense, he could have fooled anyone with that performance in the backseat of Xander's car. The sounds I coaxed from his throat, the tension in his body under mine, the way his lips caressed my name...

Heats flares in my cheeks, pooling as shadows under my eyes. I shake my head roughly to dislodge the feeling, and take a long drink from my blood-filled wine glass that I rescued from the loft. Tristan might not be here tonight, but his friends will, and I am taking no chances with my hunger. Better to quell it now than regret it later.

"Ksusha," I chide, eyeing my freckled reflection in the mirror, "you are a certifiable disaster of a person."

There's a soft knock on my door. "Lottie?"

I blink a few times until the shadows under my eyes have disappeared, then call, "Come in!"

Victoria enters my room, her raven hair a study of vintage waves and unattainable volume. The dark liner on her eyelids extends to pointed tips, making her eyes look huge and cat-like. She hasn't changed into her dress yet, but even if she stayed in her leggings and blush t-shirt, she would still be the most beautiful person at the party. Sometimes I hate her.

"Hey, V," I say, then start to work on my own eyeliner. "What's up?"

"Well," —she flaunts the deep burgundy *something* hanging over her arm— "I figured you might need something to wear."

"Oh, no," I say, wiping off a failed wingtip. "No way, Victoria. Whatever ridiculous, over-the-top dress you have for me, I'm not interested. I have something black and strappy in the back of my closet that I've been saving for a special occasion."

"Nonsense. Black is safe, and if you're going to win Tristan over after last night, you need something positively dangerous. You need *this.*" Victoria tosses the dress onto my bed.

"If Tristan actually shows up," I grumble, doing my best to strangle the stubborn hope still alive in my chest.

"He will," Victoria says matter-of-factly. "Now put the dress on. I paid good money for it, but it never quite fit. My chest is too big."

"Gee, thanks."

"Your thanks will be genuine once you try it on. Trust me."

Ten minutes later I'm standing in front of my floor-length mirror, admiring the hourglass figure that has somehow materialized under a shroud of burgundy fabric. It may be velvet—the fabric of *Kaleb*—but the cut is modern enough that it doesn't feel lavish: a floor-length skirt with a side slit up to my mid-thigh and a deep V-neck accentuated by thin straps that loop gracefully over my shoulders. Its best feature is the fact that it is entirely, unapologetically backless.

Victoria wasn't wrong. I look *incredible* in this dress.

"Fine. I look hot. This is me thanking you."

"I told you." Victoria leans against the doorframe with the cupid's bow of her mouth stretched into a grin. "One more thing. I thought about finding a necklace to match the dress but, seeing as you haven't taken it off for the past few days, Alexander thought you might want to wear this instead." She opens her hand to reveal Rayna's coin on a dainty silver chain, polished to a bright sheen.

"Wow," I breathe, taking the necklace and wincing slightly as it burns my fingers. "It looks brand new."

"He polished it while you were in the shower. The chain is from my personal collection. It's stainless steel, not silver." She rubs her hand, frowning at the angry red circle in the middle of her palm.

"This is—" The words catch in my throat. "This is amazing."

"Even though I never met Rayna, I feel like I know her," Victoria says quietly. "Everyone knows how special she was. She was lucky to have you as a friend, Lottie. And a brother like Nik. Rayna may be gone, but she lives on in your stories. In here." Victoria reaches to press a gentle palm to my heart, a touch of wistfulness in her voice. "I know how much she meant to you, but as long as you remember her, she will never truly be gone."

Emotion burns at the corners of my eyes and I dab at the tears with careful fingers. "Shut up, Victoria. You'll make me ruin my makeup."

Victoria smiles fondly. "I've got to go get dressed and check on your brother. You know how he is; I'll be lucky if I can get him in something nicer than black jeans and a sweater." She moves toward the door.

"Wait," I say, throwing my arms around her. "Thank you."

She smiles and brushes her cool, delicate fingers across my jaw, then glides out of the room.

I manage to dry the tears in my eyes without ruining my eyeliner, then fasten Rayna's newly-shined coin around my neck; the skin underneath it immediately starts to redden. The bright silver is striking against the burgundy velvet of Victoria's dress. I finish off the look with a pair of diamond studs and a deep shade of red lipstick. The color makes me feel powerful. Strong.

Fearless.

My phone buzzes.

> I know I'm early. Sorry about that. Can you talk?

> Outside, I mean. I'm outside.

I stare at Tristan's messages, sure I must be imagining them. But they stare back at me, circled in blue, waiting for a response.

> Yeah, I can talk. I'll meet you in the garden
> on the side of the house.

K

It takes a few minutes for me to muster enough courage to go outside. I fluff my hair, adjust the straps of my dress, center the coin over my sternum. The fact that Tristan is here means he must not be *completely* out of his mind with fear.

He might just be out of his mind.

I slip into the empty foyer and pause, listening to the tiny indicators of life in the house: the clicking of the hot oven, Rose's soft humming as she whisks something in a metal bowl, Victoria and Xander murmuring overhead.

"Hey," I call to no one in particular. "Tristan's here. I'm going outside to talk to him."

"Does he want a cupcake?" Rose asks, her head peeking out from the kitchen, the bowl clutched to her chest as she whisks. "They're almost done."

"If everything goes well, he'll eat lots of cupcakes at the party."

Rose shrugs then disappears again.

"Be careful, Lottie," Xander says quietly from what I assume is his bedroom. "I don't want—" He hesitates. "Just remember what we talked about."

I nod, then, realizing he can't see me, respond with a simple, "I will."

The sun is just kissing the horizon when I open the front door, the golden light warm and glorious and biting. I scurry through the yard in bare feet, lifting my dress so it doesn't drag against the cool grass. It's a relief when I dive into the thick shadows of the garden, and my nose fills with the scent of frozen earth and sharp evergreen.

This side of the house reminds me a bit of the manicured gardens of Versailles in France, though on a much smaller scale. There are neatly-trimmed hedges, stone benches, and a collection of flowers that bloom yellow and red in the summer months. Now, however, most of the green has turned to gray, but at least the thick wall of towering Cypress trees is enough to protect me from the evening sun.

Tristan is sitting on a bench tucked next to a small oak tree, wringing his hands with his arms resting on his knees. The sleeves of his white dress shirt are rolled to the elbows, the black guitar pick ever-present on his wrist, and he wears a pair of slim-cut burgundy slacks and tan suede shoes. I can see the pulse throbbing at his neck where his top buttons are undone. My mouth waters.

I'm suddenly grateful for my rare moment of foresight to eat before the party.

Warmth seeps through me at the sight of him: the bronze skin of his forearms, the gold threaded through his sandy hair, the honey glow of his eyes as they lift to meet mine. A sunflower searching for the light.

Damn, he looks good.

Tristan stands abruptly and takes a sharp step backward, colliding with a large potted plant that nearly knocks him over.

"Hi," I offer with a half-hearted wave.

He hurries to right himself, then his eyes flicker back to me. "Hi." Tristan's tone is not unfriendly, but there is an unfamiliar edge to it, like he's talking to someone he doesn't know. His eyes sweep from my face to my feet and back again, lingering on Rayna's coin where it rests over my sternum. Heat blooms over my cheekbones and he regards me with a strange, wide-eyed expression. Finally, he says, "We, um…we match."

"What?" I look down at my dress then at Tristan's burgundy pants. "Yeah, I guess we do." I smile encouragingly, but he doesn't return the favor.

There is a beat before Tristan speaks again. "I'm just going to start with the obvious question here. There's no chance I imagined everything last night, right? I didn't have some wild fever dream brought on by stress or lack of sleep or something?"

I wish it had all been a dream: that Tristan hadn't seen me covered in blood, tearing open someone's throat with my teeth. That he hadn't seen me murder someone.

And I wish that had been the only one of my murders he'd witnessed.

Alison? Alison, are you there? Alison!

"Unfortunately, no." Better to rip the Band-Aid off, I suppose. I fold my arms tightly over my chest, bracing myself for what is sure to be a miserable conversation. Tristan frowns at me, then recoils when I say, "I'm a vampire. It sounds kind of ridiculous, I know, but I'm not sure how else to say it. I've never actually had this conversation before." I chuckle dryly. "It's weird for me, too."

"I think 'weird' is putting it lightly."

"That's fair."

Tristan shakes his head in disbelief and stares at me, his expression a mixture of intrigue and wariness. "So, you and Xander just live here, as *vampires,* in this giant house in San Francisco, and no one knows? I'm having a hard time wrapping my head around it." He checks himself, and his frown deepens. "Your friends were at the Halloween party with you. They're vampires, too, aren't they? Pippa, Rose…Nik."

His voice hovers on Nik's name and his eyebrows pinch together, as if the idea of Nik's vampirism is somehow worse than the others. I decide not to press the matter. I'm not in any place to ask questions.

"And Victoria." I nod, confirming his assumption. "All of us."

Tristan exhales slowly through his nose. "Right. That makes sense."

I take a deep breath to steady myself then sit gingerly on one end of the bench. "You can ask me anything," I tell him. "Within reason, anyway. We don't have time for my entire life story."

Tristan eyes me carefully as he perches on the other end of the bench, as far from me as possible. "Okay," he says, twisting a silver ring on his middle finger. "First thing's first. You asked me to trust you, Charlotte, and, against my better judgement, I'm still trying. But tell me honestly: should I be afraid of you?"

The words land in my chest like an anvil, dragging my heart into my stomach.

My mouth starts to form the word *no,* but I hesitate, swallowing it before the lie can escape. Of course he should be afraid of me. I'm a monster. A disaster. A cold-blooded killer.

"I don't want you to be afraid," I say, worrying at a stray thread fraying from the slit in my dress. "But maybe."

A visible chill shivers through him, and my heart clenches in my chest.

"I wish I could say no," I continue. "I wish I could tell you that you're safe with me, that you can trust me completely, but I can't. If there's anything I've learned over the last two centuries" —Tristan's eyebrows shoot toward the sky— "it's that relationships are built on honesty. So, I'm telling you the truth: you should absolutely be afraid of me. I'm a supernatural, undead creature that, until last night, you thought only existed in fairytales. There is so much that you don't know about me. There are things I've done that would horrify you." Alison's face surfaces in my thoughts. I squeeze my eyes shut, smothering it, before opening them again. "The fact is, I can't deny what I am, and you've already seen what I'm capable of."

Tristan stills, his jaw tensing. His eyes bore into mine for a few seconds before he moves to stand, but I catch him by the wrist, my heart clenching even tighter when he flinches.

"Wait," I plead, even as his eyes widen in fear. He yanks his arm away, rubbing his skin as though my touch burned him. "Don't go."

I hate the sound of my voice—the desperation in it.

Tristan exhales, long and slow. I can see the fight-or-flight battle raging within him, brightening his eyes with indecision. If it were me, I'd be ten blocks away by now. But he's still here, watching me the same way he eyed Xander last night: like I'm a bomb ready to explode. After another deep breath, he gives me a tiny nod. *Go on.*

"Um," I stammer, searching for the words. "Look. I'm not known for my self-control, if you couldn't tell by what happened with Jason. But I made myself a promise—albeit, a subconscious one—the moment I saw you that afternoon on the Embarcadero. I swore I would never do that to you—that my fangs would never pierce your skin—and I've kept that promise. All I want is the chance to prove that I can be Char, the girl you thought I was. The girl you kissed last night." He pales, but his jaw softens, just a bit. "Please. Give me a chance."

Tristan nods, considering me. He wrings his hands a few times, and the light catches the surface of the guitar pick on his wrist. I finally make out the words:

> *Make your*
> *own luck,*
> *Lemongrass.*
> *- A*

"Lemongrass?" I ask, the word passing my lips before I can stop it.

"What?" Tristan glances sideways, confusion in his eyes. "Oh." He holds up his wrist, flashing the guitar pick. "Lemongrass, like the tea. 'T' as in 'Tristan.' Alison used to call me a different tea name every time she wanted to get under my skin. I hated it. So, naturally, she never stopped. 'Lemongrass' is the one that actually stuck."

I try not to smile. I *really* try. "I still think 'turnip' is worse."

He laughs once through his nose, then draws a hand over his mouth. "Yeah? Try being a fourteen-year-old boy with the nickname 'Lemongrass.'"

"Touché."

Tristan stands, and this time I let him. My eyes follow him back and forth as he paces in front of me, and I feel like I'm watching the world's most stressful tennis match. My heart pounds in my ears, drowning out the sound of Tristan's anxious footfalls.

"I appreciate that you're telling the truth, Charlotte," —*not Char*— "so I'll be honest with you, too. What I saw last night... that's the stuff of nightmares. I don't think I've ever been so scared in my life."

My heart feels like a black hole about to collapse in on itself. "Tristan—"

"Let me finish. Please," he adds when I open my mouth again, and I snap it shut. "I wasn't planning on coming here tonight. Until a few hours ago, no amount of money in the world could have convinced me. But then you texted me and I—I reread my list. You know, the list of things that make you not normal?" I nod. "And I realized that part of why I was so freaked out last night—a small part, but enough—was because I was enjoying our time together. And I didn't want it to end, despite, well, everything."

Something inside me tightens and loosens all at once. Emotion prickles in the corners of my eyes, but I force it back. I spent too much time perfecting my eyeliner to ruin it now.

"I will try to trust you," Tristan says with another deep breath, stopping mid-pace to face me. "But Charlotte, I need to be clear. If I think, even for a second, that I am in danger—that my *friends* are in danger; *especially* Noah—then I'm gone. I can't take that risk. Not after what happened to Alison."

His eyes meet mine and I gasp a little at the accusation in them. He can't know about Alison, can he? But after last night, I'm not sure about anything anymore.

"I know she was killed by a vampire," he says in a rush, and the panic in my chest simmers, even though he's closer to the truth than he's ever been. "It's the only thing that makes sense, and it terrifies me. I can't let that happen to anyone else."

The sun finally sinks below the horizon, dousing the world in gray twilight. I rise slowly, holding my hands outward in a gesture of submission. Tristan watches me with those honey-gold eyes and stands his ground, his jaw working.

"I promise that I will use every ounce of self-control that I have with you," I say softly. "You don't have to worry about anything tonight, or any other night. You'll be safe whenever you're with us. I'll make sure of it." I frown, then amend my statement. "*Xander* will make sure of it."

Tristan scoffs. "Xander hates me."

"It isn't personal," I say, shrugging. "Xander hates everyone."

Tristan's mouth twitches and a tiny bit of the usual light returns to his eyes.

"Okay, then. I have another question." He pauses, considering me carefully. "Do you sparkle?"

"*Hell,* no," I respond immediately, and am rewarded with the faintest hint of a smile. The tension ebbs from my shoulders like a wave retreating from the shore.

"Then how does it actually work? The whole" —he gestures vaguely at me with both hands— "vampire thing?"

"It's about what you'd expect. There's the blood-drinking. Pretty standard." He nods, wariness still coloring his expression. At least he's trying. "We're immortal, which is cool. But the sun doesn't agree with us. Think of vampires in the sun like pieces of fruit in a dehydrator. More than thirty minutes and" —I snap my fingers— "we're dead."

Tristan's eyes widen. "Yikes. I'm starting to think that the sparkling might have been better."

I shrug. "It is what it is. We can build up a tolerance to sunlight, but few of us bother with it. The process takes years. Maybe decades."

It's silent for a few seconds. Tristan shoves his hands in his pockets. "Anything else?"

"Well, we can't say the name of" —I pause as the name chokes me, and instead gesture heavenward— "the big guy upstairs, but wooden crosses don't do a thing to us. And neither does garlic, unless it's on someone's breath."

"Huh," he says when I'm finished. "Hollywood was pretty close. Though I was really betting on the garlic thing. I threw a few cloves in my pocket before I left just in case anyone tried to eat me." His lip quirks. "Guess I'll just go to Olive Garden next time."

"Like I said, garlic isn't going to *hurt* us—wait. Did you just make a vampire joke?"

Tristan chews on his bottom lip for a moment before saying, "I guess I did."

I have a sudden urge to move closer to him, to touch the freckles on his cheeks, the hollow where his jaw meets his neck. But I resist, digging my heels in, not knowing how he will react. Not knowing if any of this is real. I gather fistfuls of my dress to keep my hands occupied.

A car door slams on the street, and a chorus of excited voices echoes through the fading dusk. We can't see them from where we're standing, but I recognize the deep rumble of Jason's voice, followed by a bright response from Noah. Olivia and Bree chirp over one another, marveling at the ivy growing up the front of the house.

"Your friends are here," I say as Jason lets out a low whistle. Apparently, the house is impressing him, too.

"What?" Tristan frowns. "How do you know?"

I point at one ear, smirking. "Supersonic hearing. One of the many perks of being a vampire."

Rose answers the door when one of the humans knocks, ushering them inside with a few words of welcome. Noah hangs back, saying he wants to take a picture of the house. I hear the click of his heels as he walks back down the concrete path that leads to the street.

"Perks, huh? What about...*you know*," Tristan says, his expression turning serious, "the memory-wiping thing?"

The question catches me off guard, and I focus my attention back on Tristan. "Right. That. It's called Compulsion. I can use it to erase memories, but it's more than that. I could tell you that your real name is Albert, and that you've spent the last five years living underground, and you would believe me."

"You can make anyone believe anything?"

"It doesn't work on other vampires, but yeah. Anything."

"That hardly seems ethical."

I raise an eyebrow. "When you're a vampire, ethics don't really apply. Basic survival, and all that. If we couldn't Compel, we couldn't feed without the world knowing about us. And we can't have that, for obvious reasons."

Tristan grimaces at the word *feed*. "So, with Jason—"

"Jason was a mistake," I say. "A stupid, impulsive mistake. I would take it back if I could, but I can't. And the guy who threw the party...let's just say I know him. He would have murdered me if I had let you run off without Compelling you."

"You wanted me to forget."

"I *really* wanted you to forget."

Tristan sombers, and he looks at me with a wary expression. "Was that the only time? Or were there others? How much have I forgotten?"

A sudden gust of wind stirs Tristan's hair, bringing with it the damp scent of impending rain. I glance upward, but see no clouds, only the deep blue of twilight.

"I've only Compelled you once, after the party," I say, and Tristan relaxes slightly. I decide not to tell him about Rose's Compulsion after Ty's visit the other night; he doesn't need that memory, anyway. "And I won't do it again."

Tristan has started pacing again, one hand raking through his hair. Somehow it looks even better than before. "Why do I remember? Why now?"

I pull distractedly on Rayna's coin. "That one is on me. Compulsion requires a certain amount of conviction. If it isn't done correctly, there can be...unexpected consequences." Like accidentally making a human boy fall in love with you, then finding out later that he never really cared about you at all. "I was distracted that night outside the theater. And when you saw me last night in all my monstrous glory, it snapped you out of the Compulsion."

"I'm going to be honest again." Tristan pauses, kicking at a few rocks that have strayed from the dirt and onto the concrete path. "After the Halloween party, I felt odd. Like I was in a haze. When I saw you the next day, it was like the sun burning through fog. I'd never seen anyone so beautiful—" He fixes his gaze on the ground. "Then last night..."

He trails off, and any lingering hope I had about his feelings for me vanish with the last glow of evening light.

"When I saw you...*you know*...the fog disappeared completely, and my mind was clear for the first time in days. Looking at you was like looking at a stranger. And everything I felt—what I *thought* I felt—was gone."

I bite my lip, staring into a nearby bush to avoid revealing how much his words hurt. Xander was right: I screwed up my Compulsion. Tristan never cared about me. Not really. But, like the absolute idiot that I am, I still fell for it.

"I'm sorry," I say quietly, balling more of my dress into my fists. "Compulsion isn't supposed to do that. When you saw me the next day, you should have felt nothing. Remembered *nothing*. It wasn't supposed to make you—" My throat catches on the words I wish I could say: *It wasn't supposed to make you fall in love with me.* "It sounds kind of terrible."

"It *was* kind of terrible," he says, his tone surprisingly casual. "But, to be fair, you didn't mean to do it. How can I hold that against you?"

At least one thing hasn't changed about Tristan: he's too quick to forgive. If only he knew just how much I still need to be forgiven for.

"I think most people would hold it against me," I say. "And they definitely wouldn't be at my house a few days later, dressed for a party."

"Well, *I* am not most people. Everyone deserves a second chance."

"I don't."

Tristan's brows pinch together. "Of course you do," he says, as though the idea were as undeniable as the time of day.

I don't deserve a second chance, or even a third one—and I *know* that—but the sincerity in Tristan's voice shatters whatever conviction I had. I can't remember the last time someone actually believed in me. Emotion burns in my eyes again and this time it escapes, a single traitorous tear snaking down my cheek.

Tristan lifts a hand, then drops it again. "When I read through the list I'd been making, a few things surprised me, to say the least. It made me realize that, despite what I saw last night, you can't be *all* bad." He hesitates, choosing his next words carefully. "And I think—I would really like to get to know you, Charlotte. The *real* you. The one who exists outside the fog."

I wipe the tear away with the back of my wrist. "I can't guarantee you'll like the real me."

"I won't know until I meet her, will I?"

Tristan considers me for a few seconds before smiling softly, his eyes crinkling at the corners—a smile that brightens the space between us like the first golden rays of dawn.

44

The shadow can hear them, Charlotte and the golden boy.

Their hushed, miserable voices whisper over the grass that spans from the mansion to the street, making their way to where he hides in the fading light on the other side of the house.

He crouches on the peaty earth beneath the arched ballroom windows, still and cold as carved marble, his eyes trained on the front walkway. Waiting. Listening. But not to the pathetic conversation Charlotte is trying desperately to salvage.

Listening for the arrival of his mark.

He inclines his ear upward and closes his eyes, pressing his fingertips against the cool stucco wall as he focuses on the sounds echoing from inside the house. The pretender is upstairs, whispering with his mistress as he zips her into a gown of soft fabric, while the help toils in the kitchen, metal scraping metal as she whisks something that sloshes against the edges of the bowl. He catches the telltale scent of chocolate baking through an open window and grimaces.

Unnatural, *he thinks*, for a vampire to prepare human food.

As he predicted, he has seen nothing yet of the whore, nor of dear Nikolas. But they will be here, he knows.

The woman told him as much.

The sun descends through the sky at an agonizing pace, painting the lawn in dull gold before it finally dips below the horizon. He has been waiting here for hours, but his patience is unmatched.

He waits.

So much of this game is waiting.

Charlotte is still talking, still trying, and the boy actually seems to be warming. Pitiful.

Slam.

He snaps to attention as a loud cacophony of voices fills the air and a human comes into view: the brawny one with a brain made of meal. The shadow watches him as he saunters up the front walkway, followed by the two giggling girls. The pretty one brings up the rear, his gait bouncing, his eyes widening when he lays eyes on the house.

Finally.

He knows that speaking aloud is a risk. Any one of the creatures in the house—or outside it—may hear him, but he is sure they won't. Their guard has been lowered, lulled into a false sense of security by Kaleb and his futile promise of protection.

This risk is one he is prepared to take. One he has to take if his plan is to succeed.

"Noah," the shadow hisses loudly enough for the human boy to hear, stilling as he waits for any indication of his discovery. But the pretender continues his whispers, Charlotte continues her worthless pleas.

The shadow grins.

Noah stops at the base of the front steps, just as the others knock and are ushered inside by the help.

"Uh, hang on guys," he says, making his way back down the walkway. "I'm going to take a picture of the house. For posterity."

When the door closes after the others, Noah side-steps onto the grass, following the sound of his name. He squints into the darkness as the shadow rises to his feet, smoothing his lapel.

Noah sees him and his brows pinch together. "What—"

"Noah, listen."

The human boy's eyes soften, staring straight forward as he relaxes into the Compulsion.

The shadow grins again.

"Now, pretty boy, there is something I need you to do for me."

45

WHEN TRISTAN AND I WALK through the front door, we're met by the elegant sight of Xander and Victoria descending the curving staircase arm-in-arm. Victoria looks like a goddess in a flowing halter dress of pale gold satin, while Xander cuts a handsome silhouette in all black, from his button-up shirt to his skinny tie to his polished, cap-toe shoes. His sleeves are rolled up to reveal the geometric tattoo on his inner forearm: two interlocking triangles, one for Victoria and one for me.

"Honestly," Tristan groans quietly, leaning toward me. His sleeve brushes my shoulder and my skin prickles with heat. "It has to be impossible for anyone to look that good all the time."

"Clearly, you've never met anyone like Xander and Victoria."

"I guess they've probably had a lot of time to practice, being immortal and all." Tristan starts, then eyes me suspiciously. "You mentioned centuries. That was an exaggeration, right? How—how old are you?"

"Two hundred and thirteen," I say, cringing slightly as Tristan's eyes widen.

He exhales again through his nose, his lips pursed. I have a feeling he'll be doing that a lot tonight. "And that makes Xander—"

"Two hundred and eighteen. I wasn't kidding when I said he's older than he looks."

"No, you weren't. But I thought he looked maybe twenty-nine, thirty *tops.*"

"Are you saying I look old, Tristan?" Xander asks as he and Victoria step into the foyer. "You do know I can hear everything you're saying with that supersonic hearing Charlotte mentioned."

Tristan stares at Xander for a few seconds as a week's worth of realization sinks in.

"You can hear...everything? Even..." Tristan swallows a tremor. "Even last night...in the car..."

"Oh, yes." Xander actually grins. *"Everything."*

Tristan's cheeks flush bright red and Victoria stifles a giggle.

I punch Xander hard on the shoulder.

Xander glowers at me, then at Tristan, whose eyes flicker between us, the air around him warming as embarrassment burns under his skin. He draws a hand over his face to smooth his expression and closes his eyes for a few seconds. When he opens them again, they are fixed on my brother.

"Speaking of last night," Tristan says, rocking back on his heels. "I'm sorry I snapped at you. I don't want—"

"I'm not going to murder you, Tristan, if that's what you're getting at," Xander says, and I'm taken aback by the kindness in his voice. "Just promise you'll never do it again and we won't have a problem."

Tristan nods once. "Deal."

Xander's eyes spark with mischief as he says, "On the other hand, there is the matter of the comments you made about my ego in the ballroom the other night."

Tristan's face goes white, and I punch Xander again.

Victoria rolls her eyes. "No one in this house is going to murder you, no matter how many times you snap at them or insult them. Isn't that right, Alexander?"

Xander glares daggers at her, though the effect is diminished by the obscene amount of affection in his eyes. He pecks her quickly on the forehead.

"Ugh," I groan. "I apologize for my cringe-worthy brother and his shameless fiancée. I'm sure they'll keep the PDA dialed down to zero tonight, for all our sakes."

Victoria eyes us impishly before the two of them head toward the kitchen.

"It's good to see you, Tristan," Victoria trills, flashing Tristan a fanged grin as they disappear around the corner.

Tristan blinks. "That's going to take some getting used to."

◊   ◊   ◊

Rose has outdone herself.

The ballroom, which usually stands depressingly cold and empty, has somehow been transformed into a cozy, intimate party space. Lounge furniture from the living room has been brought in and arranged so the room is split in half: one side lit by dimmed overhead lights, the other steeped in shadows. The disco ball—which, after its original installation, I had completely forgotten about—spins lazily on the ceiling, casting dancing pinpoints of light on the damask walls. One pair of doors leading to the rear balcony is open, the breeze making the white curtains flutter like a pair of ghostly ballerinas.

Considering the meager number of humans in attendance, the amount of food on the two tables flanking the double doors is staggering. There are chocolate cupcakes with bright red frosting, a carefully-arranged pyramid of cream puffs, a chocolate fountain, strawberries and powdered donuts and crackers with cheese and even a veggie tray with two kinds of dip. The second table is arranged with glistening bottles of a dozen different kinds of alcohol.

I stare at Rose, my mouth agape. "How did you manage all this?

I wouldn't know what food to bring to a party, let alone how to bake cupcakes."

"Magic," Rose smirks. She has changed into a strapless pink cocktail dress with a huge bow over her abdomen, a pearl necklace gleaming over the warm brown of her throat.

Tristan, who has been following me around the house like a displaced shadow, eyes the table dubiously. "You *made* those cupcakes, Rose? I'm not sure I can trust the baking of someone who doesn't eat real food. You don't eat real food, do you?" he asks, glancing at me.

"Technically, we can," I reply, "but it tastes like dirt, and comes right back up in about a minute and a half. Alcohol, on the other hand..." I motion to the drink table. "It's the nectar of the g—" I choke. "You know what I mean."

Upbeat music blares to life from the overhead speakers, making the three of us jump. Victoria stands near the piano, selecting the appropriate playlist on her phone before setting it down on the glossy wood. She grabs Xander from where he has been standing by the window, yanking him into the middle of the dance floor.

"Hey, T!"

A familiar, booming voice sounds over the music. Jason bursts into our little circle, followed closely by Noah, Bree, and Olivia. Rose flits toward the two girls—Bree in an iridescent mermaid-cut gown that accentuates her hips, Olivia in glittering turquoise—giving them quick hugs, while Noah scans the room carefully, as though he's looking for something. His shoulders are tense under the royal blue of his suit coat.

Jason grabs Tristan by the arm. "Dude, have you seen this house? It's freaking insane!"

Tristan rolls his eyes and relaxes into an easy smile. "Yeah, Jason. I've obviously seen this house. I'm standing in it."

They greet with a half-handshake, half-hug in the stupid way boys do. I distantly wonder if Tristan will ever feel that comfortable around me again. Or if he'll even want to touch me at all.

◊ ◊ ◊

Pippa arrives fifteen minutes late, in typical Pippa fashion. I'm surprised she brought her motorcycle, since what she's wearing can only be considered a dress in technical terms. The metallic, bright purple getup is long-sleeved and low-necked, and the hemline barely brushes the tops of her thighs. Her pale legs look upsettingly long when punctuated by a pair of strappy, silver stilettos.

Much to my dismay, none of the dark veins have faded from her skin, though Pippa doesn't seem to mind. They peek out from under her neckline and spread like a spiderweb across her chest and up her neck. A wide grin splits her face when she enters the ballroom, and her eyes turn naughty when she notices Tristan hovering behind me at the food table.

"Hey, golden boy," she croons. "I'm surprised to see you here after the glimpse you got of Lottie's alter ego."

"I'm surprised to be here, too, so you're not alone." Tristan is staring conspicuously at the veins on her chest.

Pippa smirks, elongating her neck to expose more of her skin. "If you take a picture, it will last longer."

Tristan's eyes widen before his gaze snaps to the ground, his cheeks flushing. I glare at Pippa reproachfully.

"What?" she asks.

"Don't torment him."

Pippa claps a hand to her chest in mock offense. "I am doing nothing of the sort. Tristan is simply admiring my devilish good looks. I can't blame him, since this purple bolt of lightning on my chest makes me at least twenty percent hotter."

Nik appears behind her then, looking dapper in slate-colored

428

slacks, leather suspenders, and a pair of wingtip, cognac shoes.

"What's this about tormenting Tristan?" he chides, eyeing Pippa while adjusting his deep red bowtie. "Give the guy a break. It's not every day you meet an undead girl and her group of devilishly-handsome, undead friends."

Tristan shoots Nik a grateful look and something familiar flickers between them. Pippa sticks her tongue out.

Nik smiles and turns to me. "Thanks for this, Lottie."

"For what?"

"For planning a party right in the middle of all this craziness with...well, you know."

"It was Tristan's idea, really. I just provided the house."

Nik grins that heartbreaking grin of his, wrapping me in a quick hug and pressing his lips to my hair. He pulls away—Tristan watches him intently—and raises an eyebrow.

"If we're being honest, *Xander* provided the house."

I roll my eyes.

"Are you going to behave tonight, Nikolas?" Rose appears at his side, hugging one of his arms. She looks like a child next to him—the top of her onyx ringlets barely reaching his shoulders, even while wearing heels—and she stares up at him with dark, reproachful eyes. "We both know what happened last time."

"Last time?" I narrow my eyes at Rose, but she ignores me.

Nik shrugs. "Ask me after I've had a few drinks."

The smile Nik flashes Rose is bright, mischievous, and achingly familiar. It's the same devil's grin that would appear on Rayna's face when she was about to do something exciting or morally ambiguous. She always loved parties; I can see her now, twirling in that gold jacquard ballgown of hers, Kaleb holding her tightly with a cigarette between his teeth, his matching waistcoat shimmering in the ballroom lights.

"Rose actually brought *food*, Nik," Pippa says loudly, snapping me from my reverie. "Can you believe it?"

"It smells heavenly," Nik says. "Too bad it tastes like dirt."

We all snicker at the shared joke.

"That's too bad." Tristan plucks a cupcake from the table. "More for me I guess." He takes a bite, crumbs falling to the floor, and his eyes widen. "Oh my *god*. This is *amazing!*"

Pippa and Nik turn baffled gazes his way, and Rose smiles appreciatively.

"Thank you," she says, just as Pippa's attention snaps away.

Jason eyes her from across the room and the corners of her mouth curl upward, but her excitement seems muted somehow. She touches the veins on her chest surreptitiously as Jason approaches with a nauseating amount of swagger, but she manages a bright smile in greeting.

"May I have this dance?" Jason asks, offering his hand and a little bow.

"Don't mind if I do," Pippa says, and she allows Jason to lead her into the middle of the floor.

"When I said I didn't know if Jason could handle Pippa," Tristan says, swallowing the last bite of his cupcake, "I was giving him too much credit. I'm pretty sure she could eat him alive."

"Literally," I mumble, and he flinches. "Not that she will," I add hastily. "Pippa may act like a thirsty little demon, but she's really just a big teddy bear."

"I heard that," Pippa hisses under her breath, and I hide a smile.

"That goes for all of you, right?" Tristan asks, watching as Nik and Rose join the other humans across the room. "You're sure we can trust you not to, you know, eat us?"

Tristan is pulling no punches tonight, and I find myself appreciating his bluntness.

"Not all vampires are murderous psychopaths," I tease, reaching a reassuring hand toward him, then drop it as he shies away. My chest falls. "We really try to be as human as we can. And humans usually don't murder their friends."

Or their friend's sisters.

Something in Tristan's eyes sparkles as he looks down at me, and I wonder if it's the ever-changing reflection of the disco ball or something else. He opens his mouth to say something, but is interrupted by Rose as she bounces back over to us.

"Lottie, come dance with us!" she grins, grabbing my hand and motioning toward a circle of girls forming a few yards away.

Uncomfortable regret passes over Tristan's face as Rose drags me away, and I wonder if I'll ever find out what he wanted to say.

◊　◊　◊

By some miracle, everyone at the party is getting along better than I expected. Even Xander, who has spent most of the night dancing effortlessly with a starry-eyed Victoria, has managed to have a normal conversation with every human, only rolling his eyes once when Jason made a single eye-roll-inducing joke.

Nik, on the other hand, has only spoken to one other human besides Tristan, and it's becoming increasingly clear who he has been sneaking off to meet. The way Nik has been hovering around him—pouring him drinks, grinning at him slyly, straightening his tie for him—has me convinced. My theory is seconded when Pippa sidles up to me holding two glasses of champagne, one of which she hands to me.

"So...Nik is hooking up with Noah, right?"

"Absolutely," I agree, leaning close to her and taking a sip of champagne. I feel like a meddlesome, rich housewife gossiping about the latest neighborhood scandal. "Though I'm not sure Noah is ready for anyone to know about his *preferences* just yet."

"Ah," Pippa mutters, sipping from her glass. "That would explain Nik's awkward hovering."

"Mhmm." I take another drink, enjoying the tickle of bubbles as they slide down my throat. "Speaking of Nik, where is he?"

Pippa glances around the ballroom, then shrugs. "No idea. Last I saw, he was refilling Noah's drink."

I set down my champagne on one of the tables and make for the door, but Pippa catches me by the arm. "Hey. Kaleb wasn't invited to this thing, was he?" she asks softly. "Or—or Henry?"

"No," I say reassuringly, frowning at the hesitant note in her voice. "They're on Konstantin duty."

Pippa nods, her brows furrowing. "That's good."

She stalks across the room and snatches Jason from where he sits on one of the big lounge chairs, dragging him to his feet. They rejoin the others on the dance floor as I slip out the door.

"Nik?"

The house is dark outside the ballroom, the music muffled, and I creep quietly through the empty hallway and into the foyer.

It's not that I care about what Nik is doing—he seems to be in a good enough mood tonight—but I *am* worried about Konstantin. Xander mentioned that Kaleb would be sending scouts to guard the house, but that does little to calm my nerves. None of us should be alone, especially now that Konstantin knows where we live.

As soon as the thought enters my mind, my scalp prickles with the familiar feeling of being watched. I spin around, peering into the darkness of the dining room, twisting around the corner into the kitchen, but see no one. Still, I feel my hackles rise.

I glance out the kitchen window where the colored lights from the pool cast flickering reflections on the surrounding trees. There's something…something there, in the shadows…

My thoughts are interrupted by a soft *thump* in the living room. I dart from the kitchen, pressing myself against the cool wall as I peek around the corner.

Two figures are entangled in the shadows near the bookshelves, and I recognize Nik's broad, strong shoulders. I know I shouldn't intrude, but I feel a jolt of excitement at the prospect of proving my theory true. As I creep closer, I see the narrow frame and swath of ebony hair that is unmistakably Noah.

The two of them are devouring each other, their lips parting around gasps, Noah's hands yanking on Nik's once-perfect hair. I exhale loudly in surprise, then clap a hand over my mouth, not wanting to disturb such a *moment.* But the moment remains undisturbed, each boy groaning desperately as the other touches his waist, his neck, his chest.

Nik shoves the human boy back against the bookcase and braces himself over Noah with one arm. He grips the back of Noah's neck with his other hand, drawing a soft moan from him, and coaxes his head sideways, exposing the soft hollow of his throat.

Realization dawns slowly, and I watch with mounting horror as Nik leans down and buries his fangs deep in Noah's neck.

"Nikolas!" I gasp, exploding from my hiding place. "What are you *doing?*"

Nik leaps backward, wide-eyed and crouching like a deer in the headlights. Noah remains against the bookshelf, one hand reaching to press his fingers to the holes in his neck. His gaze drops to the floor while Nik stares at me worriedly.

"It's not what you think," he urges. There's a small drop of blood at the corner of his mouth and he wipes it away hastily.

Hunger buzzes through me as the salty-warm scent of Noah's blood wafts through the room, and I hold my breath to smother it.

Noah removes his hand from the wound at his neck—which is unusually clean—and clasps his arms uncomfortably around his body, careful not to let his bloodied fingers touch his coat. He seems remarkably calm. Maybe *too* calm.

"Good hell, Nik," I growl, smacking his arm. "Tell me he isn't Compelled. We didn't invite the humans here to take advantage

433

of them."

Disgust colors Nik's expression. "Of course not—"

"Because if Xander knew what you were doing—or heaven forbid, *Tristan*—we would have a serious problem on our hands."

Tristan's warning echoes in my mind: *If I think, even for a second, that I am in danger—that my* friends *are in danger; especially Noah—then I'm gone.*

And here Nik is, barely an hour later, slamming Noah into bookshelves.

I bristle. "Come on, Nikolas. You, of all people, should know better—"

"Charlotte," Noah says quietly, and I tear my attention from Nik to look at him. He meets my gaze with a surprising amount of defiance. "Nik didn't Compel me."

He leans forward slightly, waiting. There is a glimmer of embarrassment in his eyes, but they are clear and bright, not clouded. I frown, glancing back at Nik, who watches me with the same sense of nervous anticipation. For a few uncomfortable seconds, I get the feeling that I'm missing a crucial piece of the puzzle.

"I needed to get him away from the party for a few minutes," Noah continues slowly, raising an eyebrow, "so we could be alone. If you know what I mean."

The pieces snap together with a near-audible *click.*

"Oh," I breathe, taking in the warm flush over Nik's cheekbones, the way Noah's foot taps anxiously on the floor. *"Oh."*

Some humans have been known to find vampirism, for lack of a better word, *alluring.* Noah had definitely seemed intrigued by the idea at Olivia's party. I guess I didn't realize just how deep that intrigue ran.

"Oh," I say again, and Nik runs a hand through his hair.

"Lottie—"

"No, Nik. It's—it's fine." I stare at them both as my anger melts

434

into pleasant surprise. I force back a grin. "I mean, it's not my cup of tea, but you know, if that's what you're into—"

Nik's eyes squeeze shut. "Please stop."

"As long as no humans are permanently harmed in the making of your" —I gesture in their general direction— "whatever this is."

Noah chokes back a laugh and Nik's head snaps sideways. Their eyes meet and a soft, knowing smile passes between them.

The same soft smile that Nik and I once shared in Paris.

I whirl around, practically bursting at the seams with new gossip for Pippa, when Noah's voice stops me.

"Wait," he says, and I pause to look over my shoulder. "Please don't tell anyone. About me and Nik, I mean. I'm not..." He hesitates, then releases his breath in a huff. "Just don't tell Tristan, okay?"

Sympathy stabs in my chest at his uneasy expression.

"I won't tell anyone, Noah," I say. "I promise."

When Noah looks unconvinced, Nik takes his hand and pulls him close. "You can trust Charlotte," he says reassuringly. "She always keeps her promises."

Noah narrows his eyes in my direction, then gives a single nod.

With one more bewildered glance at the two boys, I leave, but not before I see the grin Noah flashes as Nik leans in to lick the blood from his neck.

46

KALEB IS IN HIS OFFICE when he gets the message.

It has been a long day of planning and worrying. Henry, Yara, and James have been fully briefed, each leading a group of scouts through the city in search of Konstantin. Kaleb did not join them, opting instead for dinner alone, followed by a lovely evening with a cigar and a very old bottle of scotch as his companions.

When the message lights up his phone, it takes him a few moments to interpret its meaning. But when he understands, wild terror rips through his chest.

He calls the scout leader he posted at the Novik house. When there is no answer, he calls the only other number he can.

"Dammit, Alexander!" he snarls when the call goes to voicemail.

He calls again. And a third time. But there is still no answer.

There is only one thing he can do.

He runs.

47

I WALK BACK INTO THE ballroom—feeling different—and am surprised to see Ty chatting animatedly with Xander and Victoria. Xander seems ready to strangle him. Ty looks disproportionately formal in full black-tie attire, a gold watch gleaming at his wrist. My heart dances in my chest: not quite a flutter, but it's definitely excited about *something.*

Ty's eyes lock onto me as I approach, and his mouth splits into an effortless grin.

"Hey, hot stuff!" he exclaims over the music, his eyes raking me from head to toe, pausing at the slit over my thigh. "I was just telling Xander about my vampire speed theory. He thinks the Golden Gate Bridge would be a perfect place to test it."

"I said no such thing," Xander says dryly.

"Theory?" I ask.

Ty smirks. "The theory that I can outrun you."

"You *wish.*"

Tristan appears in the corner of my vision, holding a plate that suggests he made a recent trip to the chocolate fountain. I suddenly feel guilty for talking to Ty, even though our conversation is about nothing more than the hypothetical testing of vampire speed records.

Even though Tristan all but admitted he doesn't care about me anymore.

Not that he legitimately cared about me in the first place.

Still, my heartbeat accelerates as Tristan strides over.

"You again," Tristan says to Ty, a slight edge to his voice. "I didn't know Jason invited you."

"Actually, I invited him," I say casually, ignoring the look of triumph on Ty's face. "The more the merrier, right?"

"Yeah, *Tristan*," Ty sneers. "The more the merrier."

Tristan's eyes flash but his responding grin lights up his face. A dull ache throbs in my chest. "You're right. Now that you're here, we can *really* get this party started."

Victoria's playlist morphs from an upbeat dance song to a slow ballad, and Ty doesn't miss a beat.

"Dance with me." His mouth quirks into a crooked smile that draws me in.

I glance sideways at Tristan, whose jaw clenches noticeably, and I almost ask permission. As if he cares.

"I'm all yours," I say to Ty, and he leads me across the dance floor. I feel golden eyes on me as Ty wraps a cool hand around my waist.

"Enjoying the party?" Ty asks. His palm presses against the skin of my lower back and I flinch, though I suppose it's my fault for wearing a backless dress. The last hand to touch me there was Tristan, his skin warm and soft against me in the backseat of the Maserati...

I clear my throat. "Considering the circumstances, yes." Ty's cologne has a sharp and slightly acrid scent, mingling with the sweetness of the chocolate fountain and the faint, hovering scent of human blood. The combination is surprisingly intoxicating. "It's been an interesting few days, so it's nice to let loose a bit. Get dressed up, put on makeup. All that good stuff."

"I have to admit, you look *sexy* in that dress."

I feel it again—that tiny thread pulling at my ribcage. Something about Ty is magnetic, despite his obnoxious attitude and nauseating compliments. I can't deny the fact that he also looks, well, hot. I won't allow myself to go as far as *sexy*.

"You look pretty good yourself."

Ty leans into me, pressing his cheek to my temple, and I stiffen. His hand—bonier than Tristan's, but stronger—slides to the base of my spine, his fingers brushing the skin just below the fabric of my dress. I reach around myself and coax his hand a few inches north.

"I'm just glad you invited me tonight," he says, breathing against my hair. "It's nice to be at a normal party with normal humans. It almost makes me feel normal, too."

I raise a skeptical eyebrow, drawing back so I can look up at him. "You've been a vampire for what, a few months? Just wait until you're old and gray like me. You'll learn to change your definition of 'normal.'"

"It feels like it's been centuries," he says. "I don't know how you do it." He spins me away then pulls me back in, his arm wrapping more tightly around my waist. I gasp quietly. "But if you're an example of what it means to be abnormal, I think I could get used to it."

Ty might be growing on me.

We twirl in silence for a minute or so—the music morphs from one ballad to another, and we slow our steps to match the new rhythm—and I take advantage of the lull in conversation to glance around the dance floor. It isn't until I see him that I realize I'm looking for Tristan; he is near the shadowed half of the ballroom with Olivia, grinning as they spin together in unpracticed circles. She throws her head back with a bright laugh, and Tristan joins her.

My chest constricts with jealousy and I unwittingly catch Tristan's eye. His grin falters and he abruptly drops Olivia's hands, moving toward us and leaving her alone at the edge of the shadows. She pouts after him.

"Mind if I cut in?" Tristan asks, offering a tentative hand.

Ty's shoulder twitches. "Actually," he says without breaking stride, fixing Tristan with an icy stare that rivals Kaleb's, "I do mind. Charlotte is *my* partner. Why don't you run back to Olivia? I'm sure she would love for you to break her heart again."

Tristan recoils as though slapped, and fury boils behind my ribs.

"Excuse me?" I force us to a halt, shoving away from Ty's grip. "I didn't invite you here to be rude. I did it because I thought we might have some fun. Obviously, it was a mistake."

Ty stares at me, his jaw working, but I turn away before he has a chance to speak.

"Come on, Tristan," I grumble, grabbing him by the wrist and pulling him to the other side of the dance floor. Ty watches us for a few seconds before melting away, heading for the table of alcohol.

Tristan doesn't meet my eyes as he wraps one arm around my waist, careful not to rest his hand too low, and takes my right hand in the other. His skin is warm against mine, his pulse beating rapidly where I can see it through the opening of his unbuttoned collar. I close my eyes as he begins moving us in slow circles, breathing in the scent of him: vanilla and dryer sheets and that salty-sweet skin.

The memory of last night surfaces behind my eyelids and warmth pools low in my abdomen. For a moment, I let myself remember. Tristan's emotions may not have been genuine, but the urgency of his lips on mine, the way he shivered under my touch... that was real.

"Olivia was my neighbor in San Diego growing up," Tristan says, and my eyes snap open. The familiar sights of the ballroom swim into focus, forcing away the memory of Tristan's eyes and the way they glowed with desire in the darkness.

I swallow hard. "What?"

"She and I dated a few times in high school. Or, rather, we tried." There is a note of wistfulness in his voice. "*She* tried. But it never felt right to me, you know? Like we were holding onto an idea too desperately, even though we knew it was destined to fail."

I think of Nik and I after Rayna died, and frown at the old heartache. "Yeah. I know the feeling."

Tristan shakes his head. "Jason must have told Ty about it. Sometimes I wish he would keep his stupid mouth shut."

"Ty was out of line," I say, and Tristan finally looks down at me, his hand flexing on my waist. "I'm sorry. I shouldn't have invited him."

"It's not your fault Ty's a dick." I allow myself a laugh, and Tristan's eyes brighten. "But I *have* to ask, even though I know I'm going to hate the answer: is Ty, you know...a vampire, too?"

"He's...new—" I start, but am interrupted by Kaleb bursting through the double doors, his expression wild.

"Alexander?!"

Kaleb is wearing dark pants and a burgundy, single-breasted blazer—that color seems to be all the rage tonight—his buttons slightly askew, like he fastened them in a hurry. There is a slight tremor in his hands, though his posture is perfect as always.

Panic prickles its way up my spine and I tense against Tristan, pinpointing Xander where he perches casually on the arm of a lounge chair.

"Who is that?" Tristan whispers, eyeing the disheveled Kaleb. The other humans stare at our new party guest in confusion for a few seconds before resuming their conversations. Pippa, Rose, and Victoria, however, are watching him carefully. "Another vampire?"

"Yes," I murmur, "and he's not supposed to be here. Excuse me for a minute."

Tristan's hands linger on my skin as I pull away and walk briskly toward Xander, grabbing him by the arm.

"What is Kaleb doing here?" I hiss. "I thought he was keeping an eye out for Konstantin."

"He was," Xander says, his eyebrows pinching together. He stands from his perch and I follow as he makes his way across the floor.

Kaleb's eyes flicker around the room a few times before he sees me, and his rigid posture relaxes significantly. Something at his throat catches the light: his emerald, sparkling dimly, hanging just behind his open collar.

I'm not sure if the sight makes me feel better or worse.

"What's going on?" I demand, keeping my voice low so the humans don't overhear. "Was there another murder? Did you find Konstantin?"

"Charlotte," Kaleb breathes, ignoring my question. He cups my cheek with one hand. "I was so worried. Are you alright?"

My heart skips. I look up at Xander, but he only shrugs, confusion darkening his gaze. I place a reassuring hand on top of Kaleb's, but it does nothing to stop the pounding of my heart. "Of course I'm alright. Why wouldn't I be alright?"

"I received a concerning message a few minutes ago," Kaleb says. "Alexander wasn't answering his phone."

Kaleb slips his hand from mine and produces his own phone, a single text message glaring on the screen.

Our Charlotte looks positively mouth-watering tonight. It would be a pity if something unfortunate were to happen to her.

"What—" I say, every nerve tingling, the back of my neck burning again with the feeling of being watched. Xander shifts closer to me. "What does that mean?"

"I don't know," Kaleb confesses, pocketing his phone and mechanically smoothing the front of his blazer. "But if Konstantin is nearby, then we need to get these humans out of here, and quickly—"

Something behind me catches Kaleb's eye. He blanches, his

expression transforming in an instant from confusion to recognition to cold, unadulterated horror. I whirl around only to see Ty chatting with Jason in the middle of the dance floor.

"Oh, that's just—"

But the words die on my tongue. Ty turns deliberately toward us and locks eyes with Kaleb, his easy expression twisting into a dark perversion of his usual bright smile.

"You got my message," he says with a devious grin, his voice deep and accented and jarringly unfamiliar.

With a quick flash of his arms, Ty reaches forward and snaps Jason's neck.

48

SOMEONE SCREAMS.

I can't be sure who, but I'm almost positive it wasn't me.

Jason slumps to the floor with an unceremonious *thud,* his once-bright eyes now pale and lifeless.

Time slows. I stare, dumbstruck, at Jason's body, his neck resting at a grotesque angle, and clench my fists at my sides.

No one moves.

No one breathes.

We can only gape at the shadow in our midst, an arrogant smirk twisting the corners of his mouth.

Ty is unruffled, smoothing his hands down the front of his sharp black suit, adjusting the cuffs of his dress shirt with an air of nonchalance. As though he didn't just murder someone in the middle of the ballroom. The same spot where, moments ago, he had his hand wrapped possessively around my waist. His gaze drags over Jason's body with no trace of remorse—just a cool, calculating indifference—and he carefully adjusts the gold watch at his wrist.

When his eyes rise to meet Kaleb's, I stifle a gasp. This man—this *monster*—is not Ty. He still looks like him, sure. But all the distinguishing features of Ty—the glint of mischief in his eyes, the languid grin, the ease of his posture—are gone, replaced by something powerful. Something almost regal.

Ty's silver eyes burn with the centuries-old confidence of someone who knows how to play the game. And who knows he has already won.

Horror heaves in my abdomen, filling me until it is almost blinding.

I was right. Inviting Ty here tonight was a horrible, *horrible* mistake.

"*Konstantin,*" Kaleb hisses.

The room wakes from its stupor. Xander moves to stand in front of me, Rose shoves Olivia and Bree from the room with a few hushed commands, and Victoria yanks Tristan behind her. She snatches her phone from the piano and taps it once, the music cutting off and leaving a shocked silence in its wake.

Pippa freezes mid-pour near the table of drinks before carefully setting down her bottle of pinot noir, exhaling a curse that perfectly echoes my own thoughts.

"Well, *shit.*"

Ty—*Konstantin*—leers at Kaleb, and his eyes alight with triumph.

This must be a nightmare. Or a hallucination. Or maybe I have died and gone to Hell, forced to live out my worst fear for the rest of eternity.

Anything is more appealing than the idea of Konstantin standing mere feet from me, in our ballroom, at the party *I* invited him to.

A dull roar starts in my ears, silencing everything but my own breathing and the frantic pounding of my heart. I press the heels of my palms into my eyes until it hurts, until I see stars, leaning my forehead against Xander's shoulder blade.

It's a dream, all a dream. It has to be.

But when I open my eyes again, I see Jason's body, and the reality of it makes my stomach heave.

"Hello, brother," Konstantin says to Kaleb, his voice deep and silky smooth, punctuated by an accent I can't quite place. "I am

445

so glad you could make it. It's about damn time we had a family reunion."

When Rayna spoke of Konstantin, she had painted him as a monster: incomparable strength, teeth sharp as razors, eyes and words devoid of kindness. A man who had lived so many years and fought so many battles that his humanity had burned away, leaving nothing but an emotionless corpse behind.

Never in my wildest imagination had he looked like *this:* handsome and perfectly-tailored with a white-toothed grin that might as well belong to Lucifer himself.

I clutch at Xander's shirt with both hands, not trusting my legs to hold me up. He presses back into me and I can feel the rigidity of his back muscles, each pulled tight as a wire.

I want to fight or run or do *something,* but my feet are cemented to the floor.

Kaleb takes a single step forward, and Konstantin lifts a commanding hand into the air.

"Now, now, Kaleb," he muses with a sharp flick of his wrist, "you wouldn't want us to make a mess, would you?"

The rooms wavers. Shadows melt from the darkened half of the ballroom, but they aren't shadows at all. They're *vampires.* A few dozen, at least. Fanged smiles flash wickedly under matching black hoods. There is a fluid connectedness to their movements, made strobe-like by the continuous spinning of the disco ball. A chill shivers through Xander, and I press closer to him.

The fledgling army outnumbers us at least three to one; more if we consider the fact that one person in the room isn't a vampire at all.

Tristan's eyes are glued to Jason's body, his hands clasped tightly behind his head. Anxiety pulses from him, his muscles poised to flee, though whether he wants to run toward Jason or jump out the window, it's hard to say. I only hope he has enough sense to keep his head down.

Kaleb and Konstantin stare at one another with their hackles raised, energy crackling between them like cold lightning. Rayna told me once that Konstantin often took over as Alpha whenever they moved to a new city, and it doesn't surprise me. Looking at him now, I see nothing of Ty and his cocky smile or blasé demeanor. The man I see radiates power—in his elegant posture, the slight incline of his chin—and he seems bigger somehow—*stronger*—as he considers Kaleb with a sneer of superiority.

Kaleb, in contrast, is coiled tight like a metal spring. He may be an Alpha in his own right, but there is something submissive in his gaze as Konstantin stares him down.

The submissiveness is a little concerning.

Nik bursts into the room. "Is everything okay? I heard a scream—" He locks eyes with Konstantin and staggers backward, his eyes dropping immediately to the ground as they fill with a dull, abject terror. *"Kostya,"* he chokes as his shoulder slams into the doorframe.

Konstantin grimaces. "Nikolas. I knew you would return at some point. Noah was such a clever little distraction, wasn't he? I couldn't have you here to spoil the big reveal. It would have ruined all my fun."

I dare a quick glance at Tristan, whose face has gone white as a sheet. Thankfully, Noah doesn't seem to have followed Nik back to the party.

"We were just discussing our need for a family reunion," Konstantin continues. "I suppose it wouldn't be complete without the Vesely twins."

Nik's jaw tenses, but his eyes remain on the wood floor. "Rayna is dead, Konstantin. You must know that."

"Is that right?" Konstantin's tone drips with condescension. "I had no idea. Killed by her own lover, wasn't she?" He spits the word *lover* like it's acid. "What a pity."

Kaleb glares at Konstantin and a vein throbs in his forehead. "At least she is free from you."

Adrenaline pulses through me as a cloud of unsaid words hovers above the Alphas, two pairs of pale eyes glinting dangerously.

Konstantin frowns for a few moments before his expression shifts, his eyebrows pinching together in mock sadness. "It is unfortunate, really. I had so wanted her to be here to witness the moment when I finally ripped that adulterous head from your neck." His mouth quirks wickedly. "I might have done the same to her, but it appears you have taken care of that yourself."

A dam inside me finally bursts, and I snarl, "You *bastard.*"

Konstantin's head swivels slowly toward me and his gaze fills with disgust. The expression transforms the usually soft planes of his face into hardened carvings of chiseled stone.

"Shut up, Charlotte," he says, his lip curling. "The adults are talking."

My mouth falls open, but the thread in my chest pulls taut. I fight the growing pressure, straining against the strength of it, but it holds fast, muting my words before they form.

A slow smile splits Konstantin's face and he takes a calculated step toward me, his head tilting sideways. Xander pushes me more fully behind him, and I peek around his shoulder.

"I do apologize for the grief I've caused you, *Char,*" Konstantin sneers through Tristan's nickname. I flinch at the way his voice disfigures it. "But you were such an easy target, weren't you? I had been devising a plan for *months* in order to draw Kaleb from his hiding place, but one misstep from you and the imbecile ran straight to your door." He kisses the air. "Perfection. I couldn't have planned it better myself. All I had to do was push your buttons for a few days and Kaleb became putty in my hands. He must care for you deeply to so carelessly risk his own safety."

I turn to Kaleb, whose eyes are trained on Konstantin's feet.

"And," Konstantin continues, "you must admit I played my part exceptionally well. Didn't I, *hot stuff?*"

I glare at him with every ounce of ferocity that I have, but the words still won't come.

"Oh, come now," Konstantin says. "Don't be shy. Let's hear what thoughts are rattling around in that empty head of yours."

The thread goes slack.

"You mean to tell me," I growl, shaking with fury and fear and a healthy dose of confusion, "that this had nothing to do with me at all? That you've been torturing me—*us*—because I just happened to be the first one Kaleb decided to threaten?"

"Among other things," Konstantin says, and his eyes flick sideways before steadying. "It's not your fault you have such loathsome self-control, my dear. If Kaleb would have disciplined you more strictly from the beginning, it may have prevented you from becoming such an appalling disappointment."

I grimace. Nik tenses. Xander growls. Pippa moves carefully toward Nik, opening her mouth to speak, but is interrupted by a loud snarl as Kaleb launches himself into the air.

"Kaleb, *no!*" Nik cries, but it's too late.

Kaleb, usually the picture of poise and propriety, slams into Konstantin with the force of a runaway freight train, and the room explodes into chaos.

Konstantin's hooded army descends on us like wraiths, leaping at the nearest body they see. Three of them head straight for Kaleb where he and Konstantin have collapsed into a snarling, writhing heap on the floor, two sets of fangs glinting viciously.

And Konstantin is laughing.

The bastard is actually *laughing.* Even as Kaleb rakes sharp fingernails down his neck and bright red blood splatters the pressed collar of his white shirt.

Rage—and, admittedly, a wild fear for Kaleb's life—propels me forward, and I shove past Xander to leap on one of Kaleb's would-be attackers. The girl howls as I tackle her to the floor, driving a fist into her temple. She swings a clumsy arm at me and I block it easily. Her form is sloppy and unpracticed, but her ferocity more than makes up for it as she slashes a clawed hand across my face.

I shriek as she tears open my skin, blood oozing down my cheek. A silver dagger appears in her hand—again with the daggers—and she shoves me off of her, lunging upward with the weapon.

I catch her hand and change its trajectory, plunging the dagger into her heart. The reek of her stale blood fills my nose as she gasps loudly then collapses, paralyzed, to the floor.

There is a loud cry to my left and I turn to see Victoria being overpowered by a team of hooded vamps. Tristan is pressed against the wall, his eyes wide with terror.

"Tristan, get out of here!" I shout, dashing toward Victoria. The smaller of her attackers sneers in my direction, catching me with strong hands as I crash into him. I grab him by his curled, brunette locks and throw him to the ground, stepping down hard with my stiletto heel. It breaks off, lodging into his chest, and I kick my shoes off. They were old anyway.

I look for Tristan, but he has disappeared.

Victoria snarls next to me, her angel's face twisted into a wicked grimace. She tears at her assailant's throat with her teeth and he howls in agony before she swipes his dagger and buries it in his heart.

"Nice one, V!" I yell, and we both charge back into the fray.

I search for another target. Xander is grappling with a blond boy about Henry's age while Nik and Pippa stand back-to-back, blocking incoming attacks with practiced expertise. Rose is fending off two men twice her size, flitting around them like a deadly hummingbird.

Though Konstantin's numbers are greater than ours, the hooded vampires are dropping quickly. Their attacks are wild and amateur, easily staved off by our combined centuries of experience. There is no way they will win this fight. Which can mean only one thing.

These vampires aren't here to kill us. They're here as a *distraction.*

"Charlotte!" Xander rushes toward me, his voice bright with panic. There's a large gash on his forehead that drips blood into his eyebrow and one of his legs hangs at an awkward angle.

"Xander, your leg!"

He blinks in confusion. "What?" he asks, then, "Never mind that. Where's Victoria?"

I look around wildly and notice with distant horror that Konstantin is also missing. Kaleb is struggling with a girl in the middle of the floor, but dispatches her quickly with a well-placed dagger.

"Kaleb!" I shout, and he turns a fierce gaze on me. "Where's Konstantin?"

"I'm right here, Charlotte."

Konstantin stands in the doorway of the ballroom, his eyes alight with manic excitement. His jacket is missing and there's a large gash running down his arm, soaking his shirt in bright red.

What makes the scene so upsetting isn't his glittering mercury eyes or the blood or the fact that he doesn't seem to care that his fangs are stabbing into his own lip.

It's the fact that Konstantin has Victoria propped in front of him like a shield, her eyes shining as he holds a wooden stake to her chest. Splatters of blood decorate her silk dress. Konstantin's height diminishes her, and she looks like a lost child in the embrace of his thin arms.

"That's enough," he commands quietly, and the chaos in the room comes to an abrupt halt. Only five of his soldiers remain standing and they melt quickly into the shadows, leaving Nik, Pippa, and Rose alone and bewildered, their once-pristine party clothes now tattered and bloodstained.

Xander is frozen beside me, his eyes locked on Victoria.

"Well, this *has* been a delight," Konstantin announces, "but I've had my fun." He turns his fevered gaze on Kaleb, his eyes narrowing murderously. "Kaleb, my friend. I think it's time you told me the truth."

Kaleb stares back at him narrow-eyed, his ruined blazer hanging limply from his shoulders, his expression guarded. "I don't know what you mean."

"Don't lie to me!" Konstantin roars, his left shoulder ticking upward, and the room flinches. Fear licks through my chest. "Tell me what you did."

Kaleb regards him stonily. "I did *nothing.*"

Konstantin's expression darkens and he presses the tip of the stake against Victoria's chest. She whimpers as the wood catches, blood dripping down her porcelain skin and blooming in a bright spot of red on her dress. Xander inhales sharply and my mind screams in panic.

"Just give it to him!" I cry, and both Alphas turn hard eyes on me. Kaleb tenses. "Charlotte?"

"The emerald," I say. "That's what you took from him, isn't it? That's what he wants. *Just give it back.*"

The silence that follows is deafening, the dull roar returning to my ears. I push against it, desperate to hear Kaleb's reply, but he says nothing. Pity creeps into his expression, twisting one corner of his mouth downward.

Always pity.

I turn to Konstantin. "What is so important about a stupid rock, anyway? Why won't you just *leave us alone?*"

Konstantin throws his head back, a cruel laugh tearing from him and echoing eerily through the room.

"Oh, Charlotte. You think you're such a clever little bird." The endearment alights something in the back of my mind, but it vanishes as quickly as it appeared. "But, I'm sad to say, you couldn't be further from the truth. You should stick to being hot and leave the big ideas to the men."

Humiliation burns through me and I clench my jaw against the fire growing under my skin.

Xander extends a protective arm in front of me. "Don't you *dare* speak to her that way."

"Or what?" Konstantin drawls. "You'll kill me?" He twists the stake in his hand, burrowing it deeper into Victoria's skin. She winces. "She will be dead before you've taken a single step."

Xander stills, raw terror in his eyes, and I squeeze his hand tightly.

Konstantin leers at Xander for a few more seconds before turning back to Kaleb with a superior smile. "So?"

Kaleb looks more afraid than I have ever seen him, his shoulders hunched, his eyes wild and shadowed with purple. Blood drips from his nose, staining his fangs where they peek out from behind a curled lip, and both of his hands rhythmically clench and unclench at his sides.

Despite the tension radiating from him, his eyes are fierce when he spits, "So *what?*"

Konstantin's false humor vanishes, his expression sinking into one of dangerous fury. "That's how it's going to be, is it? Well, then, I have a proposition for you, Kaleb. I won't let this little bird go until you tell me the truth about Rayna."

Xander stiffens next to me, standing awkwardly on one leg. "Please," he begs, his voice trembling. "Please, just let her go. She has nothing to do with this."

Konstantin's head snaps sideways. "Don't think I'm not aware of your involvement, Xander."

He is met by a tense silence. My breath catches. *What is that supposed to mean?*

Kaleb reclaims Konstantin's attention. "There is nothing to tell, Kostya. Just" —he steps forward, his hands held outward in a motion of surrender— "let Victoria go."

There is a beat, then Konstantin shrugs. "No, I don't think I will."

He presses the tip of the stake deeper into Victoria's chest and she cries out. Her eyes meet Xander's reassuringly. *It will be okay,* they seem to say, and Xander's eyes shimmer as he mouths, *I love you.*

Konstantin grimaces at Xander, then at Kaleb. "You have one week to tell me the truth, dear brother. Or I kill the girl."

I blink once and Konstantin is gone, Victoria with him.

49

"VICTORIA!" XANDER HOWLS AND LUNGES forward, collapsing immediately as his broken leg gives out.

"Xander." I sink down next to him, my ragged dress bunching at my thighs, and gather him into my arms. He clings to me, his hands clawing at my dress, his eyes trained on the door.

Pippa and Rose look at Xander then at each other, and Pippa kicks off her shoes. They sprint out the door, though I don't know what they expect to do. If Konstantin has avoided discovery so far, I doubt they'll be able to find him now.

"Lottie," Xander whimpers, "we have to find her. If she—"

"My jaho znojdziem, Alexander." I stroke his soft curls in a vain attempt at comfort, rocking him gently. "She will be okay."

If the words are meant to be reassuring, why do they make me feel worse?

"Alexander." Kaleb approaches us, his expression distraught, and wipes the blood from his lips. "Are you alright?"

"Get away from him," I snarl, glaring up at Kaleb. He flinches. "This is *your fault*. If you wouldn't have taken Rayna from Konstantin in the first place, none of this would be happening."

He looks down at me dejectedly. Pleadingly. "Charlotte—"

"To Hell with you, Kaleb. Unless you can give Konstantin what he wants and get our Victoria back, I'm done with you. Your sob stories aren't going to work on me anymore."

Kaleb takes a step backward, stunned, as I return my attention to Xander. He presses his face into my neck.

"*Mnie choladna,* Ksusha."

I'm cold.

I hug his head to my chest and close my eyes, inhaling the cool, inky scent of him. An old memory surfaces of Xander in our Chicago loft, sitting cross-legged on the floor as he sketched a sleeping Victoria. Her hand was resting on her forehead, her lips parted slightly, and Xander's pencil captured her so perfectly that I thought the drawing might leap off the page. I remember thinking I had never seen my brother so happy.

Now, as his shoulders begin to shake, I wonder if he will ever be happy again.

"I know, Alexander," I whisper, burying my nose in his hair. "I know."

◊ ◊ ◊

We find the still-living human boys in Xander's studio.

Bree and Olivia are gone, sent home by Rose before the melee began, for which I am grateful.

When Noah sees Nik, he runs into his arms, Nik catching him tightly against his chest. It's a stark contrast to Tristan, who has retreated into one corner of the room next to a table of unfinished sketches. His unseeing eyes rest on the floor, and his hair carries the distinct air of having been mussed a few too many times.

I approach him slowly, wishing I hadn't invited him. Wishing he hadn't come.

Wishing I never would have met him in the first place.

"Tristan, are you—"

"I've known Jason since I was five years old," Tristan murmurs, his gaze hard. "We've been through hell and back together. I never thought—"

His voice catches, and the pain in it fills me with a sympathetic agony. There is no evidence of the sunshine I saw in Tristan's smile at the Embarcadero, or the warmth in his topaz eyes I first noticed at Pier 39. Everything golden about him seems to have faded to a dull bronze, tarnished and forgotten and left to rust.

I take one of Tristan's hands in mine. He cringes, staring down at my blood-spattered knuckles, and pulls away. "I'm so sorry, Tristan. I didn't—" I pause, unsure of what to say. "I didn't know about Ty."

"But you *should have*," Tristan snaps, ferocity shimmering in his eyes. "You should have warned me. You *knew* he was a vampire and you did nothing, even when you found out we knew each other. Ty was in my *apartment*. He went drinking with Jason. He played video games with Noah..." He glances sideways, where Noah is sobbing into Nik's shoulder, and presses his trembling palms over his eyes before dragging them down his face. "I said what I said, Charlotte. We're in danger here. Jason is *dead*. And I'm—I'm gone."

He steps to the side but I catch him by the arm. "Tristan—"

"This never should have happened," Tristan says firmly. "I should have called this off the *moment* I learned about...about *you*. You're a *monster*. All of you are. Why couldn't I see that?"

"*Please*—"

"No, you know what, Char?" He winces at his casual use of the nickname, then yanks his arm from my grip. "I thought it might be okay. I thought we could still be friends. But I don't know if there's any coming back after this."

Tristan brushes past me and out the door of the studio, leaving me to stare after him with my fractured heart bleeding out on the floor.

◊   ◊   ◊

After Noah leaves with Tristan, Nik takes care of the bodies.

There are, after all, quite a few of them in the ballroom.

We find more scattered around the perimeter of the house; it seems Kaleb's scouts didn't make it.

Nik dutifully gathers the fallen vampires in his arms and carries them, one by one, downstairs to the incinerator. I suspect it's more to keep himself busy than anything—he hasn't spoken to anyone but Noah since Konstantin left, and I get the feeling he won't for a while—but I'm glad someone is doing it. I sure as hell didn't want to.

Jason's body isn't burned. He is placed in the driver's seat of his car before Nik rolls it down one of San Francisco's short but sloping streets. It crashes hard into a telephone pole and by the time an ambulance arrives, Nik is gone.

◊   ◊   ◊

There is blood on the floor.

I've scoured the house twice looking for Victoria's cleaning supplies, but to no avail. So the dark spots stay, drying to conspicuous patches of sticky rust on the parqueted wood.

Xander has been sitting on the floor in silence, leaning against the side of a lounge chair while he waits impatiently for his leg to heal. When I finally give up on my search for ammonia and scrub brushes, I join him, pressing as close to him as possible without upsetting his injury. Nik is in a nearby chair, staring worriedly at the door.

Pippa and Rose still haven't returned.

Kaleb sits alone in a windowsill at the far side of the room, elbows on his knees, both hands tangled in his hair. He hasn't moved in ages, his shoulders hunched in what I hope is overwhelming shame. Though I've asked him multiple times, he still refuses to give me any details about what Konstantin wants. About the secret he is supposedly keeping.

I wish he would leave.

"He was right in front of me," I whisper numbly. "How did I not see him?"

"*Darahi,*" Nik says quietly, and I startle. It's the first thing he's said in over an hour. "It's not your fault. If Konstantin wanted to fool you, there was nothing you could have done. He is a mastermind, and always has been." I look up at him and his copper eyes are distant. He glances at the windowsill. "He even fooled Kaleb a time or two."

Kaleb exhales slowly but doesn't look up.

"Yes, but—" I think of Ty at the Pier party, Ty sending obnoxious texts about vampire superpowers, Ty kissing me wildly in the basement. Ty's fingers tickling my lower back, his breath at my ear.

But that wasn't Ty. In fact, Ty never existed. He was a role devised by Konstantin, a pretense of innocence meant to break through my defenses.

And it worked.

"He got to me. He *really* got to me."

Nik sighs. "It could have been any of us, Lottie."

Somehow, I doubt it.

Xander stirs next to me, grunting quietly as he manually shifts his still-healing leg. His head rests on my shoulder while I stroke his hair, the physical closeness both uncomfortable and more familiar than my own heartbeat. I hold his hand in mine, relishing in the fact that here, in this moment, the distance between us is closed.

A footstep echoes in the black hallway.

I stiffen, searching around me for a weapon, when a girl's deep voice echoes through the ballroom.

"It looks like I missed one hell of a party."

Recognition shudders through me. It claws its way through a fog of old memories, fighting against the week's worth of exhaustion clouding my mind.

I know that voice. *Why do I know that voice?*

My head snaps toward the darkened doorway where a figure has appeared, looming like a confident, foreboding shadow. The girl is strong, dressed in slim jeans and a russet leather jacket that hugs her curves tightly. Both arms are folded across her chest, a crop of shocking amber hair hanging straight to her shoulders, and there is mischief in her luminous eyes as she regards our battered group. After a few seconds, her mouth twists into an impossibly-familiar devil's grin.

Xander lifts his head from my shoulder.

Kaleb looks up with wide eyes.

I catch a startling whiff of rose petal perfume.

No. It can't be.

My jaw sags open, but before I can say anything, Nik is on his feet.

He walks slowly toward the girl, his shoulders curled forward, and approaches her with the cautious desperation of a man stranded in the desert. One who has spotted an oasis—who is afraid that if he moves closer, he will find it is nothing but a mirage.

The girl takes a few careful steps toward him and her expression softens, her boots echoing loudly in the speechless room.

Nik stops a few feet from her, his hand shaking as he lifts it to her face. He exhales excruciatingly as his fingers brush her skin.

"*Nikolas,*" the girl says, catching his hand in hers. Tears glitter in the corners of her eyes. "Oh, *můj bratr.*"

The look of pure, incredulous joy that fills Nik's expression nearly breaks me. He pulls the girl into his arms, clutching fistfuls of her leather jacket as she buries her face in his chest.

"*Rayna,*" he sighs, and the name sends a shockwave through me, as if the universe has been holding its breath and finally, *finally* lets it go.

EPILOGUE

LIGHTNING FLASHES IN THE BLACK sky.

And Konstantin laughs.

There are many normal ways to laugh—a soft chuckle, a bright guffaw, a breathy giggle behind a raised hand—but Konstantin is anything but normal.

His laugh starts deep, roiling, the energy collecting in his chest like thunder in a stormy sky. And just when lightning is about to strike, the sound tears from him, crackling into the night air with an unbridled thrill.

"It was too easy, wasn't it?" Konstantin crows to the girl thrown over his shoulder. She screams, wriggling wildly in his grip, but cannot break free. She is nothing. She is weak. "Oh, the *look* on that bastard Kaleb's face. I do wish I had been ready with a camera. Such a lovely invention, and yet I find myself missing so many of those Kodak moments."

The girl claws at Konstantin's back. "Let me *go!*" she shrieks, the sound coming out as a broken sob. *"Please.* I have done nothing to you!"

Konstantin stops dead and flings the girl to her feet, wrapping long fingers around both her wrists like manacles. Wind whips dark strands of hair over her tearstained face, and she looks up at him wildly. He resists the urge to grimace.

She is, after all, extremely beautiful in her own way. In another life, he may have even considered her.

But this girl is simple, plain. Pale skin and wide eyes and dark hair. Common.

Nothing like his love, with her wild amber hair, sharp cheekbones, and skilled hands.

She is not Rayna.

"Victoria, isn't it?" he croons, pulling her close. He takes her silence as confirmation. "Tell me, sweetheart. How long have you belonged to that Xander of yours?"

"I don't *belong* to him." She bristles, and Konstantin smiles. Maybe she does have a little fight in her, after all. He stares at her, waiting, letting the silence stretch. Finally, she says, "We've been together since 1926."

"Ah. Nearly a century," he says, drawing her closer. She squirms against him, but his grip is relentless. "Now tell me: if someone took him from you, how far would you go to retrieve him?"

"I would die for him," she says without hesitation. "I would *kill* for him."

Konstantin grins at her, then. Bright and wide and wicked.

Thunder rumbles.

"Then you understand," he whispers, leaning down to touch his lips to her ear, "just how far I will go to get what I want. To get Rayna back."

Victoria jerks her head backward and stares up at Konstantin, confusion and fear dancing in her eyes.

"But Rayna is *dead*," she says defiantly, though her confidence wavers, just a little. "You can't get her back." Something seems to click in her mind, and she starts struggling again. *"They can't get her back.* What are you going to do to me? They can't get her back!"

Konstantin fights against her escape attempt, growing more weary with each twist, each punch, each kick.

"*Enough!*" he bellows, throwing Victoria over his shoulder once again, where she collapses into terrified sobs.

The storm breaks.

Lightning illuminates the night, followed by an earth-shattering peal of thunder. Fat droplets of water crash to the ground at Konstantin's feet, pelting in the trees overhead, dripping into his eyes. He raises his face to the sky, grinning as it celebrates his victory.

He emerges onto a darkened street where a black SUV is waiting, its driver—a tall man with a scarred, chiseled jaw—leaning casually against the hood. He doesn't seem to notice the rain. When he sees Konstantin, he immediately opens the back door, offering him a little bow.

"The party went well, I take it?" he asks, motioning inside.

"Oh, not at all," Konstantin says, tossing Victoria into the back-seat where she lands with a startled squeak. "But it went exactly as I planned."

The driver bows again, opening the passenger door for Konstantin and closing it after him. Konstantin glimpses Victoria in the rearview mirror, where she has curled herself into a frightened ball.

"A pretty little bird," he says, slicking back his rain-soaked hair with one hand. "It is a shame I have to keep you locked in this cage. But some pieces must be sacrificed in order to win the game."

Victoria glares at him from behind wet lashes, mascara staining her cheeks. The blood on her chest glows against her pale skin. "Xander will come for me. The game isn't over yet."

And Konstantin, the first of his kind, the betrayed, the abandoned, laughs again. Loud and boisterous and bright, like lightning striking a tumultuous sea.

"Oh, darling. The game has only just begun."

APPENDIX

BELARUSIAN

Darahi: Dear

Hetaha dastatkova: That is enough.

Ja ciabie kachaju: I love you

Ja nie razumieju ciabie: I do not understand you.

Jaki čort: What the hell?

Маŭčy: Be still.

My jaho znojdziem: We will find her.

Nie: Don't

Nie chvaliujciesia: Don't worry.

Repa: Turnip

Sistra: Sister

Što vy dumajecie pra?: What are you thinking about?

Što zdarylasia: What happened?

Ustavać: Get up.

Niama: No

Vy huscie jak alkahoĺ i škadavannie: You taste like alcohol and regret.

CZECH

Můj bratr: My brother.
Ne: No

FRENCH

Tu pourrais dire à Jason que ses chaussures sont déliées: You could
tell Jason his shoes are untied.

SPANISH

Un poco: A little.
¿Qué pasa con el español?: What about Spanish?

WELSH

Collwr: Loser
Diolch: Thank you.
Uffer dda: Good hell.

ACKNOWLEDGEMENTS

I knew it would be hard to put this into words. There are so many things that have happened in the last three years to make this book possible. Some were good, some were not. But without this perfect storm of people and events and downright insanity, Charlotte would still be nothing but a little voice in my brain.

I have a lot of thank yous to hand out, so I might as well get started.

To Rachel, who has given as much heart to this story as I have. She has done so much, from fixing plot holes to coming up with witty dialogue, and she has helped breathe life into these characters. We spent hours discussing character backstories, eating knock-off Girl Scout cookies, staying up late to edit pages, and discussing chess strategies. Her fingerprints are scattered on every page. She has been a confidant, a writer, an editor, a proofreader, a shoulder to cry on. Without her, this would be a very different (and worse) novel. I will never be able to thank her enough.

To my husband, Garrett, who works so hard to provide us with a good life. He has always been one to shoot for the stars, and reminds me every day that I can do the same.

To my parents, who have always encouraged me to follow my

passions, and who have never questioned them.

To my alpha readers, Erin and Kelsey, who read a messy manuscript and helped me hone and refine it through Zoom calls and lots of proofreading. They supported this story before they read it, and I'll forever be grateful for their willingness to help a little no-name author like me.

To my beta readers—Clara, Esmerelda, Eunice, Kacie, Karina, Katie, Katlyn, Lauren, Megan, Michele, and Natalie—who had to read *very fast* but did so without complaint. Their feedback and enthusiasm was what I needed through the final push.

To Fran, who designed my beautiful cover. She was so patient with all my crazy ideas, and her talent is absolutely incredible.

To Dezeray, who read an early copy of my book so she could create character art that makes me cry to this day.

To Holly, who answered every question I brought to her about self-publishing, and then some.

To Cassandra Clare, who has inspired me since 2009. Her writing brought me into the YA fantasy world and it brought me one of my best friends. Words cannot express my gratitude.

And to the online book community, who welcomed me with open arms at the beginning of 2021 and hasn't let go. Thank you, *thank you* to everyone who has been a friend, a cheerleader, a supporter, a listening ear. Thank you for being here and for reading my book. Thank you for loving these characters like I do. I have and will continue to appreciate you forever.

Wait! I forgot one.

To Covid-19. First of all, you're the worst. Second of all, without you and your lockdowns, this story would still be 25 pages of nothing in a Google doc. So, thanks. I guess.

ABOUT THE AUTHOR

LINDSAY CLEMENT is a huge nerd who loves reading books almost as much as she loves talking about them. She writes paranormal and fantasy stories with memorable characters, witty banter, plot twists, and a healthy dose of romance. She currently lives in Utah with her husband, her craft room, and her growing book collection.

CPSIA information can be obtained
at www.ICGtesting.com
Printed in the USA
LVHW032223210921
698373LV00001B/3

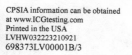

9 781737 359319